Taming the Storm

Never Give Up : Book One

by

Suzie Peters

GWL
PUBLISHING

First Published in 2021
by GWL Publishing
an imprint of Great War Literature Publishing LLP

Produced in United Kingdom

ISBN 978-1-910603-88-8 Paperback Edition

GWL Publishing
2 Little Breach
Chichester
PO19 5TX

www.gwlpublishing.co.uk

Dedication

For S.

Chapter One

Bree

"This green… you weren't thinking of using it in the dining room, were you? Because I'm not sure it's going to work. Not with the color scheme we've got in mind."

I smile, looking at Eva, who's sitting opposite me, holding up a small square of material, in a pale, subtle, olive green. "I couldn't agree more. We could use it in the lobby though."

She nods her head in agreement and flips over the fabric swatches she's holding, pulling a face when she sees huge, bright vermillion flowers, on a dull, beige background. "Please tell me you don't want to use this." She shows it to me and I grimace, and then we both laugh.

"I'm not even sure why the suppliers sent it."

"I am," she says. "They're desperate to get rid of it."

We laugh again, and I let out a sigh as I settle back in my chair. Eva's been working for me for about a month now. Although, when I say 'me', I naturally mean my family, or rather our company, which owns one of the largest chains of hotels in the USA… well, and the Caribbean, now that we've branched out a little. It just feels like she works for me, because even though I'm in charge of the whole interior design department here at Crawford Hotels, and have been for the last five years, this is the first time I've had an assistant of my own. And I'm thoroughly enjoying it. Which is why my desk is currently covered in fabric swatches and paint samples, and we've been sitting here for the last forty-five minutes, going over concepts for our newest hotel… the one that's about to break ground, down in the Caribbean.

I love working like this, bouncing ideas around and actually discussing designs and suggestions, rather than sitting by myself, fretting over whether my ideas are going to fly, or fail.

I discovered Eva through a charitable foundation I'm associated with. They'd asked me to judge a design contest they were organizing, which was being held in London last fall, and I was delighted to help them out. I'm always keen to bring on new talent, but in this instance, I was also desperate to get away for a while. I'd left my husband, Grady, about six months beforehand, and although I'd filed for a divorce straight away, he was being really difficult about the whole thing. It wasn't just that he was refusing to sign the papers, or even acknowledge our separation, he also kept turning up at my apartment in the middle of the night, either drunk or just plain loud – and often both at the same time – shouting his mouth off about how unfair life was, and how I'd regret leaving him. As a result, my brother, Chase, had encouraged me to be somewhere else, and this offer to travel to London came at the perfect time. Not only did I enjoy my time over there, taking in the sights and getting some well-earned rest, but I also escaped from Grady, and I discovered Eva, who was studying at university, and who was – well, *is* – an absolute genius. She's twenty-one, beautiful, and very talented, and I knew straight away she'd be a valuable asset to the company. So I hired her on the spot, without bothering to refer to either Chase, or our older brother Max. I wasn't sure how they'd feel about my decision, but at the end of the day, Eva works for me and not for them, so I decided they could suck it up. The only problem lay in the fact that Eva hadn't actually finished her degree at that stage… and she really wanted to. So I've had to wait eight months for her to get here.

But now she has, she's proving to be indispensable.

"What do you think of this blue brocade… for the bedrooms?" she asks, sounding nervous, although I'm not sure why. So far, she hasn't made a bad call about anything.

"I think it'll be perfect."

She smiles across at me and then picks up her coffee cup, raising it to her lips before she notices it's empty.

"Shall I get us some more?" she offers and I nod, as she stands and takes both our cups over to the small kitchen area in the corner of my office, where she pours us both a fresh cup, bringing them back to my desk.

"Thanks," I murmur, studying the pictures on my computer screen, of the place in the Caribbean, where we're about to build our newest hotel. It's called The Mermaid's Chair and is on the island of St. Thomas, and judging by these photographs… it looks like paradise.

"When are they actually going to start building?" Eva asks, as though she's read my mind.

"Everything's planned in for the end of this week. But that all depends on Chase." She looks at me, frowning slightly, so I explain, "He's currently in Seattle, working on another of our hotels, so the start of the new one is all going to depend on whether he gets finished there, and down to the Caribbean in time."

She smiles. "He sounds very busy."

"He is."

She shrugs slightly and sighs. "It seems odd that I've never met him."

"Yeah, I suppose it does."

"Is he like Max at all?"

"No." I chuckle, thinking about that prospect. My brothers couldn't be any more different if they tried. "Max is much more serious and sensible… although I suppose that's only to be expected."

"Because he's the oldest?" she asks.

"And because of some of the things he's been through."

She nods her head, but doesn't pry… which is another thing I really like about Eva. "My brother's quite sensible too," she says.

"I didn't realize you had a brother." I'm surprised. She's never mentioned him before, and I sit forward slightly, holding my coffee cup between both hands, cradling it. "Is he back in England still?"

"No, not at the moment. He's an archeology lecturer, so he spends most of his spare time digging things up… somewhere. He's currently in Greece for the summer."

I sense a sadness in her voice, despite the obvious affection she has for her brother. "Do you miss him?" I ask, and she nods her head, her eyes sparkling slightly.

"Yes, I do." She manages a slight smile. "I'm sure you must miss Chase too… when he's not here."

I think about her question for a moment. Do I miss Chase? We've never been on those kind of terms, although we sometimes played together as children, being as there are only two years between us. But that was when we were very young, before our father intervened and our lives became about doing well, working hard, success… competing.

"I guess. Although my brothers and I aren't really that close," I murmur, putting down my cup and looking back at my computer screen, just as it pings to let me know I've got an email, and the door to my office opens at exactly the same time.

"Sorry…" Max hesitates on the threshold, his enormous six foot five body filling the frame. "I didn't realize you were busy."

"It's okay." I wave him in, while opening my email app, just in case the message is important, my blood turning to ice as I see the name of the sender… grady92@uwhomail.com. "No…" I mutter, my voice a choked whisper. "Why now?"

"Bree?"

"What's wrong?" Max and Eva speak at the same time, but it's Max who makes it around my desk first, striding over and placing his hand on my shoulder. "Sis?" He looks down at me as I raise my face up to his, his deep brown eyes giving away nothing, except maybe concern for me, which takes me by surprise.

"Look…" I point to the screen and he turns his head, his eyes darkening.

"What does that son-of-a-bitch want now?" he says through gritted teeth.

"I don't know." I move my mouse to click on the message, but Max places his hand over mine, halting me.

"Leave it," he says, and then releases my hand and turns my computer screen around, pulling my keyboard toward him, before he starts typing.

"What are you doing?" I ask him.

"Forwarding his message."

"To whom?"

"To me." He replaces my keyboard and screen and then pushes his fingers back through his dark hair. "I'll deal with it."

I'm struggling to stop myself from shaking. "You don't have to do that, Max."

"Yeah, I do. I still feel guilty that I wasn't here for you when Grady was messing you around before. I should never have left Chase to deal with all of that."

"Why not? He did okay." Neither of us mentions the fact that Grady messing me around cost Chase two hundred and fifty thousand dollars, which Grady had insisted on, before he'd agree to sign the divorce papers, claiming he needed it to 'tide him over'.

"I know he did. But I still feel guilty."

I turn my chair, looking up at him, and rest my hand on his arm, or at least on the arm of his hand-made suit. "Then don't. You weren't yourself at the time… and we all understood that."

He gazes at me, his eyes misting over, and I know we're both thinking back to last spring… to that horrific day, when Eden – Max's wife and high school sweetheart – was killed, in a moment of madness that changed all of our lives. But no-one's more than Max's.

"Maybe, maybe not," he says, refusing to cut himself any slack, as usual. "But either way, this time, I'll deal with it."

He gives me a smile and turns, and I do the same, only now remembering that Eva is still in the room, although she's standing over by the window, presumably having moved there to give us some privacy. I imagine she'll have heard most of what we've just said though.

"Did you come in here for anything in particular?" I ask Max, trying to sound businesslike, although my head is spinning and my stomach is churning.

"Yes. But it was only to let you know Chase has been in touch. He asked me to tell you he's just about finished what he needs to do for now in Seattle and everything should get started on time in St. Thomas. He thought you'd want to be kept updated, being as you're working on the designs."

"Yeah… thanks." I nod my head.

He goes to the door, but turns at the last moment and looks back at me. "Are you okay now?" he asks.

"I'll be fine."

"Sure?"

"Yeah. I'm sure… and Max?"

"Yeah?"

"Thanks."

He grins at me, and without another word, he leaves.

There's a momentary awkward silence before Eva comes and sits down again, opposite me, picking up a swatch of materials and attempting to look busy… or at least preoccupied.

"I'm sorry about all of that," I say, being as there's no point in trying to pretend the last few minutes didn't happen.

"Don't be." She looks up. "Are you sure you're okay?"

"No, not really," I reply honestly. "In case you didn't guess, the email I just got was from my ex-husband."

"Oh." She looks surprised, which I'm assuming means she didn't guess at all.

"Yeah… the biggest mistake of my life. So far." I try to smile and almost get there. "I haven't heard from him since our divorce… and I hadn't realized it would affect me so much."

"Was it a bad divorce?" she asks, tilting her head to one side, and because she's so kind and is clearly not looking for office gossip, I don't mind telling her.

"It was… but it was a worse marriage."

She nods her head now and whispers, "I'm sorry."

"It was no-one's fault but my own. Well, and Grady's, I suppose. We were young and stupid and should never have married in the first place. But when you're young and stupid, you think you're right… about everything. Only it turned out I was wrong about him. What I thought was love, was actually jealousy. When I assumed he was being attentive, he was actually being possessive. And the two things are very different… believe me."

"So you left him?" she asks.

"Yes. Eventually. Chase had to talk me into it in the end, and then, when Grady kicked up rough about the divorce, Chase also had to pay him off."

"Oh?" She seems intrigued, but then I suppose she's never met Chase, so that's hardly surprising.

"Grady was contesting everything about the divorce," I explain. "He was refusing to agree to anything, even though I was offering him a very generous settlement. He wouldn't even acknowledge that I wanted a divorce, and refused to look at the papers, let alone sign them. And he was coming to my apartment at all hours of the day and night, creeping me out. To be honest, I was starting to think I was gonna end up being married to him for the rest of my life. It was affecting my health, both mentally and physically, and I was at my wit's end. Then, out of the blue, the foundation asked me to fly over to London to judge the contest you were in, and Chase convinced me I should go. I had a great time and felt so much better for being away. When I got back, expecting more of the same from Grady, my lawyer told me he'd signed all the documents and agreed to everything. I was stunned… relieved, but stunned. Of course, it was only later on that I found out Chase had paid him a quarter of a million dollars to do the right thing."

Eva tilts her head again and lets out a breath, like she wants to say something, and then she hesitates again, before she says, "Are you sure you're not that close to your brothers?"

"We're closer than we used to be," I admit, recalling that look of concern in Max's eyes just now. But I don't say anything else, or qualify my statement. I'm not sure I feel like going into my childhood right now… it's complicated to even think about all the issues I used to have with my dad, let alone explain them to someone else. "I guess Eden's death might have had something to do with that," I say instead.

"Who's Eden?" Eva asks.

"She was Max's wife. His high school sweetheart."

"And she died?"

"Yes. Well, she was killed, to be more precise."

"Killed?" Eva sucks in a breath, her eyes widening in shock.

"Yeah. In the spring of last year… she was kidnapped, and although Max was willing to pay the ransom, the police had other ideas about trying to catch the kidnappers at the handover. It didn't end well… there was a shoot-out. Eden was killed…" I let my voice fade, recalling that dreadful time, and how it felt to watch my big, strong brother fall apart… even if he kept his distance at the time, shutting out almost everyone, except his baby daughter, Tia and his best friend Colt Nelson. In the brief glimpses he let the rest of us have, when we called round and he gave us a few minutes of his time, we still saw the change in him. And we mourned it.

"I—Is it always like that around here?" Eva asks, her voice a frightened whisper, and I do my best to smile.

"No. Normally, life is really quiet. Boringly so." I'm not lying. Life is boring. It's been that way since I left Grady, and although I don't regret that decision for a moment, I wish there was more to my life than work. I wish I could get out more, live a little, do something. Except I can't see how that's ever going to happen… especially as Max now insists that everyone in the family has a bodyguard with them whenever we go out… which just about kills any chance I might have had of ever having fun again.

Because first, I'd have to lose my shadow.

Dana comes with me up to my apartment, just like she does every other night, after she's driven me home from work. I'm not sure why she does this; there really is no need. The block I now live in, since Eden's death, has more security than the average bank. There's a guard downstairs, who sits behind a desk… and then you need a passcode to operate the elevators, which in my case is only known by me, my brothers, Dana, and Colt Nelson… because, as well as being Max's best friend, he's the guy who owns the security company Max called on when he needed help. Even my mom doesn't know the code and has to be buzzed up.

Although that's not a bad thing. Not where Mom's concerned.

As I take out my key and open the door, Dana moves back toward the elevator, her task complete. She's probably around five foot eleven tall, always wears a business suit, even when it's boiling hot, like it is today, and has long brown hair, which she wears tied up in an immaculate bun.

"I see you tomorrow," she says. "Seven-thirty, as usual?"

"Yeah…"

"Goodnight, Bree."

"Goodnight, Dana."

She presses the elevator button and the doors open immediately. For a second, I think about calling her back, asking if she wants to stay for a drink, just to take the edge off of the loneliness. But she's got a life of her own… unlike me. So instead, I enter my apartment and close the door behind me, letting out a long sigh, before allowing my purse to fall from my shoulder to the floor and kicking off my shoes. I'm still clutching the mail I picked up from the lobby, and I rifle through it, as I by-pass the kitchen area, before dumping it on the dining table, padding through to my L-shaped couch, and staring down at it. I could sit and stare out at the skyline, or watch a movie, but I'm not in the mood for being reminded that I'm here all by myself, with nothing to do. Again. So I head for my bedroom instead, strip off and go through to my bathroom, where I take my time having a shower. I wrap myself in a fluffy white towel and come back out to the bedroom to dry my hair before putting on some pajamas and sauntering into the living area again.

I can see the clock on the microwave, and I sigh, realizing I've only killed a little over forty-five minutes, and flop down into my couch, trying to decide whether to cook or order in. Cooking takes more time, but it's not much fun when you're always cooking for one, and I decide to get a Thai takeout, rather than be reminded of my loneliness.

I put on the TV for some background noise, and am just getting up to grab my phone, when it rings, making me jump, and I go back to the front door and pick my purse up off the floor, pulling out my phone, but leaving my purse on the table this time, as I come back through to the living area, checking the display, to see that it's Max.

"Hi." I answer just before my voicemail kicks in.

"Hello." He sounds kinda tired.

"Is everything okay?"

"Yeah. I just wanted to let you know I've dealt with Grady."

I suck in a breath and flop down onto my couch once more, staring out the window at the city skyline. "Did he want more money?" I ask, like I don't already know the answer to that question.

"He did. But you don't need to worry about it."

I shake my head. "Thanks, Max."

"You don't need to thank me. Just get some rest and forget all about him."

I thank him again, even though I know I don't need to and we end our call, leaving me to wonder about what he said… 'get some rest'… That's all I ever do with my evenings. I don't even remember the last time I escaped my prison cell and had some fun. As for forgetting about Grady, I have done. Or I had, until today… but I guess hearing from him has just reminded me of all my past mistakes, and how much I regret them.

My marriage to Grady happened in such a whirlwind, I sometimes look back – when I can be bothered – and wonder whether things might have turned out differently, if I'd just slowed them down a little, if I'd just waited a while, taken stock and thought things through. But I didn't… and that's the point.

With a controlling millionaire for a father, as well as two older brothers, I'd lived a very dull and secluded life, until I went away to college and found myself with more freedom than I'd ever known, surrounded by people of my own age. And it all kinda went to my head.

Those first few weeks seemed to be filled with parties and supposedly intellectual gatherings, where people sat around and talked in loud voices about things they probably didn't understand. There didn't seem to be very much studying involved, so I took full advantage of my newfound liberty, letting down my slightly untamable hair, to my heart's content. I avoided the intellectual gatherings and headed for the parties instead, and it was at one of them that I met Grady for the first time… and was simply blown away by him. He seemed utterly perfect to me… tall, with reddish-brown hair and an athletic build that sat well in his tight jeans and t-shirt, his blue eyes followed me around the room. And I knew it. I liked it too. And when he sauntered over and put his arm around me, without even bothering to introduce himself, like he was claiming me, I didn't mind in the slightest. I kinda liked the idea of being claimed by him… even owned by him, if he wanted. And it seemed he wanted… because within minutes, he was kissing me. The kissing led to touching… and the touching led to whispered entreaties to join him at his place. I was in such a breathless, mindless whirl, I think I'd forgotten how to say 'no'… or even 'let me think about it'. So I didn't think about it. I went home with him, and in the privacy of his bedroom, he took my virginity.

A few of my friends in high school had told me tales of their 'first time', filling me with a certain amount of fear. They'd said it hurt, which it did – although only briefly. But they'd also told me how disappointing it was, how it didn't live up to their expectations… and there I had to disagree with them. I loved every moment with Grady, and no sooner had we finished groaning in ecstasy after my first time than I wanted to go again… and again. Two hours later, he rolled onto his back, puffing hard, and looked across at me.

"I'm gonna have to tie you down, sweetheart," he said, struggling for breath.

My stomach lurched with excitement and anticipation. Because although I didn't really know what he had in mind, the idea of being restrained was utterly thrilling. I sat up and then straddled him, resting my hands on his chest. "Really?" I breathed, unable to hide my enthusiasm, and he laughed out loud, sitting up and pushing me down onto my back.

"Not like that," he replied, leaning over me and shaking his head, even though he was smiling. "I meant I'm gonna have to strap you down, so you'll leave me alone long enough to get an hour's sleep."

I pouted up at him, running my hands down his chest. "Don't you want me then?"

"Yeah… just give me a little while to get my breath back, and I'll prove it."

He did too.

And that was how we spent the entire weekend.

And the whole of the next week, when lectures permitted.

And that went on for the next two months.

It was breathless. It was exhausting. And it was completely perfect.

Until one evening, when I was lying on his bed, on my back, with my legs about as wide apart as they could go. He was licking me intimately, my hand on the back of his head, and he halted, looking up into my eyes.

"You have the sweetest pussy I've ever tasted," he murmured. And while I knew I should be flattered by that, I wasn't. I didn't mind so much that he'd tasted other women, but I hated the idea that he was comparing me with them.

I sat up, pulling my legs together, and he kneeled, looking confused.

"What's wrong?" he asked, crawling up to me.

"Nothing."

"Yeah… right." He sighed with just a hint of impatience. "Tell me what's wrong."

I looked him in the eye. "I don't like you making comparisons," I said, figuring I might as well tell him the truth.

He smiled and then smirked. "Are you jealous?"

I wasn't completely sure if I was, but I felt I had a right to object. "So what if I am?"

He shrugged and then shifted down the bed again, grabbing my ankles and pulling me down too, so I was lying on my back once more, exposed to him. "I can't help the past, Bree," he whispered, moving into position again and blowing across my sensitized skin. "But there is one way to ensure I never taste anyone else again…" He left his sentence hanging, while his fingers parted my lips and circled over that tightened bundle of nerves, making my back arch as I sucked in a breath.

"What's that?" I ground out the words through gritted teeth.

"Marry me," he said.

So I did.

Exactly one month later.

We didn't bother to tell anyone either. Grady convinced me it was more romantic that way, and our first few days as husband and wife were nothing short of incandescent. We burned for each other and barely came up for air.

But our return to reality – or more precisely, to my family – soon put out our flames.

My parents were speechless, especially as our honeymoon meant I hadn't made it home for Christmas as I'd planned. When I called to explain why, after we got back from our week in ecstasy, Mum and Dad were disappointed by my absence, and then disbelieving about my reasons, and then dismissive of the whole situation. They simply refused to believe what I'd done. I was their precious little girl, and they didn't understand that I was in love with Grady. After I'd repeated that fact to them three or four times, though, they told me they thought I was insane. My father accused Grady of only marrying me for my money, which hurt. Later, Dad even looked into ways of getting our marriage annulled, until the family lawyer told him it was hopeless. Max and Chase weren't much more supportive. I think they suspected Grady of some kind of ulterior motive too… but Grady held me and caressed me, as they all continued to reject us and our relationship over the coming months. He told me I didn't need them. I had him… and that was enough. And it was. Which was just as well, because a little further down the line, there was a huge bust-up.

I remember, it happened the following Christmas, which is always a firm favorite for a family argument. We arrived a little late because Grady didn't really want to go, and had done everything he could to hold us up, and when my dad answered the door, he made it very clear that Grady wasn't welcome. And that made me angry, because they were happy to have Eden there. She and Max were married too, by that time. We'd been invited to their wedding, which had surprised me, but I took it to be an olive branch from my brother and was looking forward to going, until Grady came home from work two days after the invitations arrived, with tickets to Aruba, which just happened to coincide with the date of Max's wedding. I was stunned, and grateful, but upset at the same time, and although I asked if he could change the dates, he said no.

So we went to Aruba.

And that meant we didn't see my family again until that fateful Christmas.

It was beyond awkward, standing in the den, making conversation, when I knew they didn't want Grady there. Even Colt Nelson was a welcome guest, and yet my husband was treated like an outcast. A pariah. I thought about leaving straight away… just walking right back out the door. But I didn't. I felt like I had a point to prove… that Grady and I were part of the family, too.

Except we weren't…

My dad had always tried to control my life and I remember him asking me if I was still studying hard enough, now that I was married. I told him, of course I was… it was important to me to do well. He'd instilled that work ethic into all of us, since we were tiny children. He then went into one of his customary lectures about how my future was already set… and I shouldn't do anything to mess it up. Grady stepped in at that point and asked what this future entailed, saying that, as my husband, he had a right to know. My dad told him, with a patronizing tone to his voice, that I had a job already lined up with one of the company's suppliers, because back then, my dad outsourced everything, except the management of the business itself. Chase was due to finish college the following summer and was all set to start working for the architects who designed and built all of our new hotels. I was destined to go and work for the company who handled all the interior design. I knew Max had always thought my dad's way of running the business was restrictive, and they'd fought about it a lot. And being a bit of a rebel back then, that was at least a part of the reason Max had gone against Dad's wishes and, rather than joining the company straight out of high school, as Dad had always intended, Max had gone into the military, shocking the hell out of everyone. Grady obviously wasn't convinced by Dad's methods either and told him, in no uncertain terms, that he didn't get to call the shots in my life anymore. The look on my dad's face at that moment is something I'll never forget. And while Max and Chase may not always have seen eye to eye with him, they took his side. Grady and I left before we'd even had lunch. It seemed better that way.

As much as I felt the pain of being rejected by my family, I also felt kind of proud that my husband had stood up for me… until a while later, when I realized that what he'd meant was, while my dad didn't get to call the shots, he did. Looking back, I suppose Grady had always been a little controlling. Even his proposal had come with the caveat that I really ought to marry him if I wanted to stop him from being with other women. Naturally, at the time, I hadn't seen it that way. I'd been swept off my feet and into his arms, and I suppose things weren't too bad, all the while we were together at college. It was when I started work that the real problems began.

For the first year or so of my career, I was an executive at Taylor & Sutton, my instant arrival at board level due entirely to my father's influence. He may not have been talking to me, but Dad still insisted on maintaining the appearance of family cohesion. So, I worked exclusively for Crawford Hotels, and although I sometimes felt out of my depth, I soon got the hang of things and I loved my job. Maybe that was the problem; maybe it was my enthusiasm that annoyed Grady. I'm not sure. He certainly wasn't as happy in his job, which was in marketing. And either way, I'll never know now. I just know that the point at which I started work was the point at which my marriage really changed. And not for the better.

Suddenly, he wanted to know everything, from who I'd been in meetings with, to where I'd gone for lunch – and even what I'd eaten. I found myself explaining my every movement and action, every phone call, every conversation. And if I didn't have an explanation, or he wasn't satisfied with my answers, he'd ramp up the questions, higher and higher, until I felt so intimidated, I could barely think straight.

He never actually threatened me, and he certainly never hit me, but I felt so stifled I was struggling to exist in my own skin anymore.

Slowly but surely, piece by piece, Grady started to dismantle me. He dictated everything, from where we ate, to how long I could spend on the phone and who I could talk to. From how I dressed, to how often we had sex, which wasn't as often as it had been… once upon a time.

I thought about talking to Max or Chase, because I was starting to feel like I was drowning in my own marriage. But my family were cut off from me… partly because my father hadn't forgiven me, either for marrying Grady in the first place, or for letting him be so outspoken in the family home, and partly because Grady wouldn't let me near them. I was isolated and desperate… and then I got the phone call that changed everything… well, and nothing.

The call came from Max, one evening, to tell me our father had suffered a serious heart attack. Chase was flying back from LA, where he'd been working on a project, and Mom was at Dad's bedside. Max thought I'd want to know.

"Would I be allowed to come?" I asked him, feeling scared of the reply.

"You're still his daughter, Bree," he replied. "If you wanna come to the hospital, I'll drive by and pick you up."

"Would you?" The sense of relief was overwhelming.

"Of course. I can be there in twenty minutes."

I paused, because I was feeling so tearful. "Thanks, Max."

"Anytime, Sis."

Grady wanted to know who'd been on the phone. Naturally. And when I told him it was Max and that our father was sick in the hospital, he told me to call Max back and tell him not to come.

I turned on him then.

"This is my father we're talking about. He might be dying."

"So? What do you owe him?"

"It's not about owing him, Grady."

I moved away from him, putting my phone into my purse.

I heard him let out a long breath then. "Okay… if you really wanna go. I'll take you."

I shook my head and turned around again. "No. I don't think having you there is gonna help, do you?" His eyes widened, but he said nothing. "And besides, I want to go with Max." I really felt the need for my big brother at that point. Maybe for the first time in my life, I wanted Max.

Grady stared and then turned away and slammed out of the room.

My dad died early the next morning.

Chase made it back just in time, and although Dad never regained consciousness, I felt grateful and relieved that we were all there together, as a family, at the very end.

Grady calmed down for a while after that, perhaps out of respect for my grief, which was genuine enough, despite my differences with my father. But Max informed us that, under the terms of our father's will, not only had he left us a small fortune each, but we also had an equal share in the business. I hadn't expected any of that, having barely spoken to my family for so long… any more than I expected the second phone call I got from Max a short while later, when he informed me he'd decided to bring all the services in-house.

He'd asked Chase to form the design and construction side of the business and he wanted me to set up an interior design department. I jumped at the chance. The hours were crazy, but I relished the prospect of being my own boss, and working so closely with my brothers… being back in the family fold.

Grady wasn't so happy, and his possessive jealousy knew no bounds, as I worked longer and longer hours and had to travel more. He questioned everything in much more detail, flew off in jealous rages if I was five minutes late getting home, checked my text messages, went through my luggage whenever I returned from visiting any of our hotels, even scoured the wastepaper basket. It didn't matter how many times I told him there was nothing to find, he still kept looking.

Months became years, and they all passed like that, and although I occasionally contemplated going to one or other of my brothers, I never quite plucked up the courage to admit I'd been wrong.

Everything came to a head anyway, all of its own accord, when I had to go on a business trip with Chase, to Charleston, where we were working on a major refit to our hotel down there. I'd told Grady where I was going, and why – because he'd insisted on knowing – but he evidently hadn't believed me, even though I'd shown him my airline ticket as 'evidence'. He followed me down there, presumably hoping to catch me out in some indiscretion or other – arguing with his boss and walking out on his job in the process – and he barged in on a meeting Chase and I were having with some contractors we were planning on using. Although Grady must have been able to see that everything was very businesslike and professional, he still stood there, just inside the door and yelled at me, accusing me of cheating on him – as though he'd actually caught me in the act. It was the most humiliating experience of my life. Chase intervened in the end and persuaded Grady to leave. And then later on, my brother sat me down and we talked, and I revealed how awful my marriage really was. He was shocked, but supportive, and over the coming months, he helped me to see the light, to understand that Grady was dragging me down, and that if I left him, I'd be able to live again.

So I did.

The problem was, it wasn't that easy.

Not only did Grady make the divorce itself very tough, pushing me into a whirl of anxiety, depression, and dejection, but living again wasn't as straightforward as I thought it would be. I'd thought I'd feel free, that I'd be able to spread my wings and fly again. Except it wasn't like that, because I hadn't expected the gut-wrenching loneliness that comes with finding yourself single after so many years of marriage.

Any more than I'd expected to still be sitting here, months and months later, like a caged bird, desperate for freedom.

Colt

I lean across and undo the rope that's binding her to the bedstead, freeing her and checking her wrists for marks. She's clear. But then she would be, because I know what I'm doing, and I stand up straight again, coiling the rope neatly in my hands.

"That was better than ever," she purrs, stretching out her long, lithe body, with a satisfied grin on her face, before she shifts onto all fours, crawling across the wide bed to kneel before me, and rest her hands flat on my chest. *What the hell is she doing? She knows better than that.* I drop the rope and grab her wrists, pushing her away as I step back.

"Don't touch," I growl, angry that I'm having to remind her of one of my golden rules.

She looks up, with an excellent imitation of a sorrowful expression on her face. "Sorry, Jack," she simpers. "But I've missed you. Please don't make me wait so long before you call again…" I stiffen and move a little further away. I hate that pleading, needy tone to her voice.

I don't do needy.

"I'll make you wait as long as I feel like making you wait," I bark, reminding her who's in charge here. Not that she should need reminding. About any of it. She knows how this works. I've been fucking her for months now… on and off. When it suits me. And it's never been any different.

"Sorry," she says again, more genuinely this time, instantly lowering her eyes, the image of contrition… and submission.

She knows she's crossed a line.

I glance down at Carrie's slim, naked body, her long brown hair falling over her shoulders, but I don't react to the sight of her. I'm finished with her now. The need is quenched… until the next time, anyway. If there's going to be a next time for her, that is. Because, while I'll admit I don't particularly want to give her up, I will if I have to. It's not like we're exclusive. I don't do exclusive. Just like I don't do needy. I don't relationships either. That's not who I am.

That's why I make use of this very nice, very classy, and very anonymous hotel room, rather than my own apartment. It's why none of the women I fuck ever know my phone number… or even my real name. Or anything about me. I won't give them anything personal. Even fucking them is remote. There's no emotion involved. It's distant… passionless. It's just a means to an end.

Anything else wouldn't be my style.

Without another word, I head for the shower, in the sure and certain knowledge that, if Carrie knows what's good for her and wants to redeem herself for that slip up, she'll be gone by the time I come out.

Standing under the cascading water, letting it fall over my body, I brace my arms against the tiled wall, giving myself a moment to think… to feel. I rarely allow myself the luxury of feelings, but when I do, I often find myself wondering about what might have been, and how my life could have been different. Don't get me wrong, I'm not unhappy with the way things are. And in any case, I'm not sure I know any other way. Not now. I've been doing this for so long, I can't remember any other way of life. And I don't really want to. I like not having to answer to anyone, and I have no ties, other than the ones I use to bind the women I fuck… and they know exactly what they're letting themselves in for with me. I make no bones about that. No-one gets hurt, because the moment they show any signs of attachment, or they become demanding, or emotional, I cut them loose. I can't handle emotions…

Emotions make you weak.

They expose you.

I learned that lesson when my mom died, and I perfected it in the military. Having served seven years, and made it through three tours in Afghanistan, I know exactly how to detach myself from my emotions, and how to hide my feelings… I've made a goddamn art form out of it.

And even though it's been over a decade since I left the army, lessons like that aren't easily forgotten.

I enlisted straight out of high school, alongside my best friend, Max Crawford. I guess you could say Max is the closest thing to family I've got… and probably the only person in the world who really knows me. But that's because we've been through so much together. We've been through too much together. The military saw to that… and then life finished us off…

We'd just graduated from high school. It was a few months after 9/11, and joining the army in the fight against terror seemed like the right thing to do. For me, I guess it was partly because I couldn't think what else to do with my life. I had no family – apart from Max, that is. My dad had left when I was a baby and my mom had been sick for most of my high school years. I'd spent that time caring for her and trying to ignore the fact that I didn't have a life of my own. Max was having fun, falling in love with the prettiest girl in school – the cutest little brunette, who answered to the name of Eden, and had him wrapped around her little finger – while I was at home, looking after my mom.

And then, just two months before I graduated, she passed. I didn't know whether to be relieved or heartbroken, so I decided not to feel anything and surprised myself by being quite good at it. I found it easy to be detached… and it was something that got even easier when Max and I enlisted.

It was Max's suggestion, but I didn't argue. In fact, I jumped at the chance to belong somewhere. At last.

Max was doing it as an act of outright rebellion. I knew that much. Although I also knew there was more to it than that. Not that we ever talked about it. His defiance of his father was more than enough reason for both of us. He'd always been expected to join his family's business… Crawford Hotels. They own dozens and dozens of hotels all over the country, and Max's dad was always domineering and had set out Max's future from an early age. He'd done the same with Max's brother, Chase, and his sister, Bree, as well. But I think Max felt it harder than they did, being the oldest… and being expected to step into his father's shoes and run the whole thing, while having no say in the matter. Or so his dad thought.

Max was never great at taking orders, though… not even in the army. And I can still remember the fall-out when he informed his parents what he'd done. Because he enlisted before he told them about it and presented it to them as a done-deal. His dad was furious. But as Max put it to me afterwards… what could his old man do? He couldn't do a damn thing.

Neither could Eden, although she wasn't anywhere near as upset about it as Max's dad. She was proud of him for taking a stand and doing the right thing… and the fact that he looked pretty good in uniform probably didn't hurt. Of course, she only stayed calm about the whole thing while we were in the States, while we were training, and Max was safe. As soon as we got our orders to ship out, everything changed. She got scared. She didn't want him to go, and she and Max fought then, real hard, for a couple of days, until it all came to a head. I'd driven him over to her place and had assumed I'd be sitting in my car, waiting for him to argue it out with her one last time, before we left… but it didn't work out quite like that. Eden was clearly hurting and their disagreement spilled out onto the porch. I could hear every word they said… and so could most of their neighbors, I imagine. She yelled at him for being selfish. She hadn't asked for this, she said, and he took that, because I guess she was right. But he countered, telling her he needed to do it, anyway. She asked him why… why he felt he had to defy his dad. And that was when he explained it. He said it wasn't just about his dad. He said he felt like he had something to prove. She cried then, collapsing to the floor, telling him he had nothing to prove to her, and he dropped to his knees in front of her and said he knew… he was proving something to himself.

They stared at each other for what felt like ages, and then they whispered a few words, and Max grabbed her, his hand behind her neck, and he kissed her. I looked away then, with a mixture of embarrassment and jealousy, until I heard Eden calling out my name, and I looked back. They were still kneeling, still holding each other.

"Colt?" she said a second time, to make sure she had my attention, I guess.

"Yeah?" I called out.

"Don't you dare let him die, you hear?"

I nodded my head, gave her a kind of waved salute and just said, "No, ma'am," and then I watched them go into the house together.

It was another hour and a half before Max came out again. And it didn't take a genius to work out what they'd been doing.

I suppose I envied the relationship Max had with Eden. I'd never been in love, but seeing how they were together… seeing that connection between them, it made me want the same thing myself. The problem was, where to find it.

Especially as we were shipping out the next day.

And so we left, and much to our surprise, we made it through our first two tours unscathed. It seems strange, looking back, to think that I was known as the sensible one back then… and I wasn't that sensible. Not really. I was just more sensible than Max. We looked kinda similar in uniform too… especially as we both had to wear our hair short. I've kept that military buzz-cut ever since, but Max has grown out his dark mop to a more civilian length. He's only an inch shorter than me though, coming in at around six-five, and we're both fairly powerfully built, so we were hard to tell apart… and we had some fun with that, to the extent that we were both hauled in before our commanding officer on more than one occasion and ordered to stop fooling around. And for a while, we'd behave. But that would never last for long because, as I say, Max wasn't great at taking orders.

We had a few dark moments too, not that we ever told anyone back home about what went on over there. We had each other to talk to, if we needed it, and it always felt like the people back home wouldn't really understand. They watched the news reports and listened to the politicians' bullshit, and they thought they knew it all… so what was the point in us telling them what was really going on? They'd never have believed us, anyway.

As we came to the end of our third tour, Max and I started to talk about leaving the army. We felt like we'd had our run of good luck, and neither of us wanted to push it any further. And besides, I knew he was getting impatient to settle down with Eden. He'd talked about proposing, and while I wasn't in any hurry to get married myself, I wasn't averse to the idea of a relationship… or at least something a little more permanent than I'd managed in the past. In the meantime, however, Max continued to retain that unique ability of his to ignore orders, even though I kept telling him that, one day, his rebellious streak would land us in trouble, and I didn't relish having to tell Eden the bad news. He'd laugh, with the crazy reassurance of someone who thinks they're invincible… which, of course, he wasn't. And he found that out. Eventually. Not that what happened had anything to do with his rebellious nature. Not in the end.

We'd been involved in a routine patrol that afternoon, in the Sherzad district in Nangarhar province. We'd been there for a while, and this was something we did all the time, thinking nothing of it. Even working alongside the Afghan forces didn't worry us by that stage, although there wasn't a great deal of trust between them and us. We did our best to get along with each other, and until that day, it had been going okay.

I'm still not entirely sure exactly what happened. I was walking about three paces behind Max, thinking to myself that I couldn't wait to get back home to Boston… away from the heat… back to something resembling 'normal' – especially if 'normal' involved a deep bubble bath, a decent bottle of red wine, a juicy steak, and a bed wide enough to spread myself out in, while I slept for twelve hours solid – when I saw a sudden movement up ahead out of the corner of my eye, and then I heard the gunshots…

I hit the deck, not really knowing what was going on, my heart racing, adrenaline pumping, and then I realized it was one of the Afghan soldiers at the front of the patrol, who'd turned his weapon on our guys. I got a shot off, hitting him in the head, and it was only then that I noticed Max was lying beside me, clasping his thigh. Crawling over to him, I saw the blood pouring from the gunshot wound that had ripped through his thigh, exposing flesh and bone. And that was when Eden's words rang out in my head… 'Don't you dare let him die.' I knew it was bad. The wound itself was gaping and ugly, and he was losing a lot of blood, so I yelled for a medic and did my best to staunch the flow, and keep him talking, even though he was dipping in and out of consciousness all the time. I felt fear like I've never felt before that afternoon, but eventually the choppers arrived and Max was airlifted out of there to safety, and the rest of us made it back to base. We lost two guys that day, with three others wounded, including Max, who was shipped back to the States a couple of days later.

I felt like I'd done my duty after that, both to Eden and my country, so I came out of the army not long afterwards. Max had already been discharged, because of his injury, although he recovered eventually, after several surgeries and lots of very painful rehab, and married Eden, going into the family business, just like Mr. Crawford Senior always planned. Max's dad died about five years ago and he, Chase and Bree inherited the whole corporation... as well as becoming multi-millionaires overnight. Not that it changed him. He was still the same slightly rebellious guy he always had been, still bucking the trend and doing the polar opposite of what his dad would have done.

As for me, I drifted around for a while, feeling kinda lost, and then I decided to set up a security business. I wasn't really qualified to do anything else, and to start off with, I wasn't sure I was even qualified to do that. But I got lucky. A few of my old army buddies were looking for work, and I'd obviously stayed in touch with Max, who put some initial contracts our way, helping out in his hotels. I'm not sure his dad approved at the time, either of me, or Max's idea, and it wasn't what I really wanted to do. But it was a start and it enabled me to build the business into something better... namely what it is now: a fairly exclusive personal protection service.

It's the kind of work that doesn't involve you putting down roots. And you get to be anonymous. Because, let's face it, no-one ever looks at the bodyguard; they're too busy looking at the person he's guarding... and I kinda like it that way.

I've now got about twenty men and women working for me, and an extremely healthy bank balance. And I can't say I'm unhappy with my lot.

Of course, I never expected to get that phone call... the call that Max made to me just over a year ago, early last spring. I never expected to hear my oldest friend crying down the phone at me, inconsolable. And to start off with, I couldn't even work out what he was saying. I caught, "Eden," and "killed," and told him I'd be with him in fifteen minutes, which took some doing, considering he lives thirty minutes outside of Boston, and I was at my apartment in the center of town.

I made it though, and he invited me in, and managed to stay calm enough to explain to me that Eden had been kidnapped that morning... and that he'd received a call demanding a million dollars in ransom money. I asked him why he hadn't called me there and then, and he shrugged and said he thought the cops could handle it... and besides, he was gonna pay to get her back. He didn't care about the money. But, it had all gone wrong at the handover, someone had gotten trigger happy, and Eden had been gunned down in the crossfire. He'd seen the whole thing unfold in front of him, and although he'd run to her, defying the orders of the cops – in fairly typical Max style – he'd gotten there too late. She was already dead, and there was nothing he could do to save the woman he loved.

He broke down again then, and I waited for him to recover, watching the most solid man I'd ever known literally sobbing his heart out, before I asked him what he wanted. I knew the answer to that. He wanted his wife back. They'd had a daughter – a beautiful baby girl called Tia – not that long before, and I couldn't even begin to imagine what he was going through. Oddly enough, though, he didn't say he wanted Eden back, or that he wanted his baby daughter to remember her mommy. He knew none of that was possible. So instead, he asked me for something practical; something I could actually do. He looked at me and said, "Protect my family, Colt. I want them to be safe."

I nodded my head, remembering Eden's words to me and replied, "Consider it done."

I could see in his eyes that Max had already changed. He'd lost that rebellious streak to his character, closed down in a sea of grief. And in a way I felt relieved by that. It was gonna make my job a lot easier, after all.

And yet, I knew I'd always miss that renegade who had walked by my side… who'd had my back when I'd had his.

I step out of the shower and wrap a white towel low around my hips, moving through into the bedroom again.

Carrie's gone, which is a merciful relief, and I sit down on the edge of the bed and resolve that I'll probably leave it a good long while before I call her again… if I do at all. Not that it'll be a problem. I belong to an agency, specially created for people like me… for Dominants… where I can easily find someone who fits my needs, whenever I want. The membership is stupidly expensive, but they guarantee anonymity and I like how the process works. Basically, you choose your submissive from a list, which shows their profile, including photographs, and tells you what they will and won't do, and then the agency gives the sub your details, and they're allowed to see the Dom's profile at that stage. If they're interested, they respond, and if not, they don't. After that, it's up to the Dom. You can meet up, do whatever you've agreed to, and you can carry on seeing that particular sub for as long as you want. Doms, of both sexes, have to state whether they expect exclusivity, and subs have to state whether they're amenable to that. For myself, I don't. I'm not exclusive and I don't expect it in a sub. Exclusivity makes a sub more emotionally dependent, which is the last thing I need. And I don't care who else they're fucking as long as they're safe about it. But then the agency takes care of that too, being as everyone has to submit to a six-monthly health check and, if you don't use condoms, you can be reported and your membership canceled. What I like best, especially in situations like the one I've just found myself in with Carrie, is that, when you're done with a sub, you simply get in touch with the agency, and tell them you're through, and they handle it from there, informing the sub, and making the Dom's profile invisible again. It's the ideal arrangement. It's impersonal, it saves any awkwardness and any recriminations, and my membership saves me the time and effort of finding what I'm looking for the next time around. I'm also saved the trouble of explaining my rules, over and over, every time I start off with someone new. A lot of subs have certain expectations of this lifestyle, and you have no idea how boring it gets having to tell them I don't like to be called 'Sir', or 'Master', or any of that bullshit. Actually, I prefer it if they don't call me anything at all, and most of the time I use a ball-gag to ensure they keep quiet. But I have to have a name, for the purposes of my profile… so I'm known as 'Jack'. And that's it.

I reach over and grab the rope from the floor, coiling it up again and putting it into my bag, along with the nipple clamps and leather collar, before picking up the butt plug and the wand, carrying them through to the bathroom to clean them up. It's all part of the process, and I go through the motions like I'm on auto-pilot. It's mechanical.

Like me.

*

I input the code into Max's security gates, on yet another bright and sunny morning, waiting as they swing open, and then I continue down the long tree-lined drive that leads to his house, which remains cleverly concealed, until you turn a corner and it suddenly comes into view, set in its own beautiful grounds.

Max had the house built not long after he married Eden, and while it's a little too modern for my tastes, he likes it. Even now… even though she's not here anymore.

As usual, I park my Range Rover in front of the garages, which are off to the right of the main house, and walk up the wide steps to the front door, letting myself in with my own key. Max doesn't mind me doing this, as long as he's expecting me. And I wouldn't dream of doing it at any other time.

"Hi, boss," Sadie calls out from the security office, which is just inside the entrance, off to the left. She'll have seen me coming on the cameras, which she's paid to watch, in her role as Tia's bodyguard. It's a role she's fulfilled for a few months now, and she's doing a fabulous job, from everything I've heard.

"Morning," I reply, not bothering to disturb her, before I wander through Max's dining room and into the enormous kitchen where I find him, sitting at the breakfast bar, with his back to me.

"Hi," he says, without turning around, and I notice his broad shoulders are hunched over as I walk across the room, standing beside him. "Do you want one?" he offers, holding up his half empty coffee cup.

"No, thanks."

"We should probably get going anyway," he muses, sounding kinda low. "I'll just go upstairs and say goodbye to Tia, and I'll meet you out by the car."

"Okay." I pause for a moment. "Is everything okay, Max?"

"Sure," he says, in a tone that tells me everything is very far from okay.

"Is it your nanny again?" I ask, because that's a fairly common problem with Max these days. He's employed several since Eden's death, none of whom have proved successful, for various reasons, which seem to involve them either being too strict with his daughter, or too flirty with him.

"No… well, yes. The nanny's being a pain in the ass, actually. But that's not the problem. Not today."

He gets to his feet, but I don't move away, which means he can't either. "So you're admitting there is a problem?"

"Yeah, okay. But I'll tell you about it on the drive into work," he says, and accepting that's the best answer I'm gonna get right now, I step back, giving him the space to get past me, before he makes his way out of the room.

I stand for a moment and then stroll back to the front of the house, letting myself out again, without bothering to say goodbye to Sadie. She'll be able to see me go, if she's interested.

Once outside, I open the garage and get into Max's car, which is another Range Rover – like mine, but a top-of-the-range model – reversing it out and leaving it running while I wait for him, wondering what can have happened. It seems to have ground Max down, whatever it is. And I just hope I can help.

He comes out a few minutes later, wearing a dark gray jacket now, that matches his pants, and carrying a black briefcase. I hop out of the car and open the rear door for him, waiting until he's sat down on the seat before I close it again and climb back behind the wheel.

He doesn't say a word, so I select 'drive' and slowly pull away from the house, wondering if I should prompt him, or wait for him to tell me what's wrong. The situation resolves itself as the gates swing inwards, and I pull out onto the street, hearing him let out a sigh behind me.

"You're never gonna believe who I ended up talking to last night," he says and I look in the rear-view mirror to see him shaking his head.

"Who?"

"Grady fucking Sharp, that's who."

My fingers tighten around the steering wheel at the mention of his sister Bree's loser ex-husband, but I make a conscious effort not to let

Max see my reaction and to relax my muscles, even though they're fighting against me.

"What did he want?" I ask, because I know he'll have wanted something.

"Money," Max replies, like it's a foregone conclusion, which I guess it is with Grady. "He sent Bree an email yesterday afternoon, which scared the hell out of her…"

"Is she okay?" I interrupt, unable to help myself.

"Yeah. I think she was shocked to hear from him, though, after all this time."

"And he asked her for money?"

"He did. Although she never actually saw the message herself. I was with her when it came in, and I forwarded it to myself and deleted it from her inbox, so she couldn't read it." He sighs again. "I read it when I got back to my office and sent him an email, asking for more information about why he needed the money, and he insisted on talking last night."

"And you didn't tell me about this on the way home yesterday because…?"

"It was a phone call," he reasons. "If he'd wanted a face-to-face meeting, I'd have told you."

I can't argue with that. "Why did he need the money?" I ask, intrigued, because I've got a fairly good idea that it won't have been anything good… or necessarily legal.

"He said it was for medical bills."

I'm surprised, although I don't let it show, and from where he's sitting, Max can't see me, anyway.

"Did you believe him?"

"Yeah, I did. He sounded kinda desperate. Although I did have to ask him what he'd done with the settlement that Bree had given him when they divorced… and the money Chase paid him before that."

"And what was his answer to that?"

"He wasn't exactly forthcoming…" He lets his voice tail off.

"Did you give him the money?" I ask.

"Yeah. But not as much as he was asking for, and only on the basis that he leaves Bree alone from here on in… and that it's the last time he's gonna get anything out of us."

"You think he'll pay any attention to that?"

"I told him I'd give you a free hand if he didn't, so I imagine he might do."

I can't help smiling. The idea of getting even on Bree's behalf is very satisfying, but I can't say anything about that. And besides, I can tell from his tone that Max has said all he's going to say on the subject, so I continue the drive into the city in silence, wishing he and his family would stop paying this guy off, and just let me do my job and take care of them all, like he asked me to. I know dealing with Grady Sharp wasn't part of our arrangement, but I'd do it in a heartbeat, if he'd only ask me to. And my way of dealing with that low-life would be a lot more permanent than Max's. I think he probably knows that, though… which is why he doesn't ask. Instead, he just lets me be his bodyguard, because that's what he *did* ask me to do, and right from the word go on this assignment, there was no way I was trusting Max's safety to anyone else. Not when I'd seen, first-hand, how devastated he'd been over losing Eden. I couldn't let that happen to him again. I'd seen his pain… I'd felt it. And I knew he'd regretted not acting sooner when she was kidnapped. Because we both knew that, if I'd been there, Eden would never have died. She'd never even have been kidnapped, because I'd have put my life on the line to keep her safe… just like I'd do for him.

When it came down to it, it wasn't just Max that needed guarding, though. He'd said he wanted his entire family protected, and that meant finding someone suitable to assign to Chase. And, for me, that was always gonna be hard, because Chase and I don't get along. He's six years younger than Max and makes him look like the most sober, upstanding man you're ever gonna meet. Chase is a really good looking guy… not that Max is any slouch. But Chase is one of those guys that women just fall for… or at least they fall into bed with, anyway. He's not as tall as Max and me, but he's charming, where we're more aloof, I guess. And he has what I always think of as movie star looks… you know, the square jaw, dark hair, startling blue eyes kind of vibe… as a result of which, to put it mildly, Chase has a really complicated social life… by which I mean he sleeps around. Like it's a profession. And I knew we were going to have to accommodate that. So, I chose Eli to be his shadow. He's another army buddy, with a fairly high sex drive himself, and he's good at turning a blind eye to pretty much everything, which is just as well with Chase. I decided they'd be a good fit for each other, and from what I've seen over the last year or so, they're doing just fine.

Max's mom was much easier. I assigned Alexis to look out for her. She has the patience of a saint… and I knew she was going to need it. Kathleen Crawford is a wonderful woman… on the outside. She's tiny, softly spoken, and everyone's idea of the perfect grandmother figure. But on the inside, she's fiery. I think she spent a lot of her married life trying to please her husband, or at least ensuring he wasn't displeased. And now he's gone, she's pretty damned determined to please herself. She's more strong-willed than any of her children – and that's saying something. And she knows what she wants and doesn't hold back in telling you. Not only that, but she loves to shop, like it's an Olympic sport, and she's going for the gold medal… and she also takes herself off to Florida a couple of times a year to visit her sister. And I didn't figure any of the guys working for me were gonna go along with that kinda gig. But Alexis has coped with everything Kathleen has thrown at her… so far.

For Tia, Max was much more involved in the selection process, and we originally chose one of my female operatives called Hailey. I think he wanted a woman there, because he wanted Tia to have female influences in her life, and also because he was worried that some of his younger nannies seem to be quite flirtatious and he was concerned they might end up distracting the bodyguard, if he was male. I reassured him I only employ the best, but in the end, he couldn't be convinced, and Hailey was superb at her job… so good that her talents were wasted, because looking after Tia doesn't really involve much more than sitting in the security office at Max's house and keeping an eye on things. Unfortunately for us, Hailey announced she was pregnant just a few months later, and while she could work on for quite a long time, she left to have her baby boy, and Max agreed to her being replaced by Sadie, who seems to be fitting in well.

As for Bree, I guess, in an ideal world, I'd have taken her on myself. Except I couldn't. Not only did Max need me, but it's impossible for me to be that close to her. Simply because she's the reason I don't do emotions or relationships. She's the reason I sometimes wonder about what might have been. She's the reason I am who I am.

Because I've been in love with her for nearly a third of my life.

And she doesn't even know it.

I've known Bree since I first met Max, back in high school. But she was tiny then… probably about five years old, I guess, and my earliest memories of her are of a cute, but kind of annoying brat. She grew up – obviously – but then so did we, and we spent less and less time at Max's house, and more and more time with Eden, and our other friends, so I barely noticed Bree… that is, until we came home from that last tour; the one when Max was injured. I was twenty-five by then, which I guess means Bree would have been around seventeen, and when I called at the house to announce my return, it was Bree who answered the door… and simply took my breath away. There she was… suddenly all grown up. She was still really cute, and not even remotely annoying. She'd filled out in all the right places, and with that dark, long curly hair of hers, and those deep brown eyes, she really was the complete package. And it was all I could do to keep my hands to myself. As for my heart… I'd already lost that. It was hers. There and then.

I didn't say anything, or do anything either. I still had a couple of months before I was due to leave the army, and I decided I'd bide my time and wait for her until I was completely free. By then, I reasoned, she'd be eighteen, and I thought it best to use my time wisely, working out how to tell Max that I wanted to date his sister, while plucking up the courage to ask her out. And dreaming about her. I did that a lot.

In the end, dreams were all I got, and I never had to pluck up the courage, or work out how to tell Max, because when I came back the next time, discharged from the army and a supposedly free man – except for the fact that, in my head, I belonged to Bree – I discovered she'd gone away to college. I was devastated, but hid it well, and just made a kind of routine enquiry about whether she'd be coming back anytime soon. Kathleen assured me she'd be home for Christmas, and I decided that, while it was frustrating, she was worth waiting for. And I did wait. I stayed in most nights, and didn't even look at another woman, because there wasn't another woman who could compare to Bree Crawford... so why bother?

She didn't come home for Christmas in the end, though. She called and announced she'd met someone... a guy called Grady. And that she'd married him.

The whole family was in an uproar over it – even Max, who was home from the hospital by then, and going through his therapy. He mumbled something, under his breath, about it being 'typical' of Bree. And I guess she had always been kinda headstrong. But I liked that about her. At least I did until she upped and married another guy.

And broke my heart.

The next time I saw her was a year later, at another family Christmas. Max and Eden had married in between times, although Bree hadn't come to their wedding, which I wasn't sorry about. I was Max's best man, and I didn't need the distraction of having her there. I know Max was kinda disappointed, though. He still didn't particularly like the idea of Bree's marriage, but he wanted to make things right with her, so he'd sent out an invitation, even though his dad told him it was pointless. Bree proved her father right when she called Max and told him Grady was taking her away to the Caribbean on the same weekend as his wedding, which meant they couldn't come. Max thought that was probably a lie... or at least an excuse not to attend, and his dad found it hard not to crow that he'd been right all along. For myself, I didn't care. Well, I did. But I found it easier not to think about it.

After that episode, everyone was stunned when they both turned up that Christmas at the Crawford family home. I was there too, because Max had asked me... and it wasn't like I had anywhere else to be, although seeing Bree again was harder than I'd thought it would be.

Much harder.

They arrived late, and her husband had 'loser' written all over him. I wasn't sure what Bree had ever seen in the guy, and that wasn't jealousy talking. It was common sense. Sure, he was good looking enough, but he was selfish and possessive and had a mean streak as wide as an eight-lane highway running right through him. He was controlling, too… telling Bree's dad that he couldn't call the shots around her anymore, which clearly meant he thought he could. I wanted to pull her aside, to make sure she was okay, to ask if she needed my help. But how could I do that? And anyway, he and Bree left again not long after his brief exchange of views with her dad, the opportunity leaving with her. Once they'd gone, Mr. Crawford poured himself a large whiskey and reiterated his view that Bree had made a huge mistake in marrying Grady, which no-one disputed, and then he remarked how domineering Grady was, which I thought was kinda rich coming from him. I could hardly talk, though. Because in the year or so that had gone by since I'd last seen Bree, I'd become kind of domineering myself.

Just not in quite the same way.

Because my need for dominance was – and still is – limited entirely to the bedroom.

I'd had a few sexual encounters during my time in the army, which I always put down to the uniform. Some women just loved it. Don't ask me why though, but every time I'd slept with a woman, I'd always felt there was something missing. And then, when I saw Bree again, all sweet and sexy and seventeen, I worked out what the 'something' was. It was her.

Finding out that she'd married some guy she barely knew, and that I was never gonna have her, was devastating… and it changed me completely. I made some decisions about my life. For one thing, no-one was ever gonna hurt me again. I wasn't going to let them get close enough. And for another thing, I was going to take control.

So I did.

The next woman I slept with, I held her down, and I fucked her so hard I thought she was going to pass out. Hell, I thought I was going to pass out. She loved it. She wanted more. I didn't. And even though she begged me to stay, I walked away. I didn't want to get involved. I didn't want the responsibility.

But I'd discovered one thing; I liked to dominate. No… it was more than that. I needed it.

Since then, I've ramped things up, quite significantly, and I couldn't go back to the way I was before. Even if I wanted to.

And I don't.

I know Bree is free of her loser ex-husband now, but that doesn't change a damn thing. She's still off limits. At least, she is to me.

Because even though I'll always love her, I'm not the same man I was back then.

And that means it's better this way.

For both of us.

Chapter Two

Bree

"How's it going?" I switch the phone onto speaker and swivel my chair, turning it away from my desk, as I lean back, staring out of my eighth-floor window at all the other office blocks, letting out a long sigh and wishing I could have a change of scene… or a change of life, perhaps.

"Okay… I guess." I sense a note of doubt in my brother's voice, which is unusual for Chase. While both of my brothers are confident, I'd have to say that Chase is the more… well, arrogant. Apart from his job, I've never known him to take anything seriously in his life. Max and I have both been married, and although we're now single again – for very different reasons – Chase has never even been in a relationship. In fact, as far as I know, he's never even slept with the same woman twice.

And right now, I'm kinda jealous of him… or at least of the carefree, fun life he seems to have. I could do with some of that for myself.

"What do you mean by that? You only broke ground four weeks ago. Surely you can't be that far behind schedule already," I reply, focusing on the conversation, rather than the train wreck that is my life.

He sighs. "We're not. I don't think. We've never built a hotel from the ground up down here," he says, referring to our new hotel, which he's currently overseeing in St. Thomas. We've built hotels before, and we already have a complex on the island which Max bought a few years ago, but because this is our first full construction in the Caribbean, it feels like there's a lot hanging on this project.

"What do you mean, 'you don't think'?" I latch onto his original, worrying comment. "Don't you know?"

"Not really. Supplies aren't always easy to get hold of, not exactly when you need them, anyway. And if there are any problems, they seem to take forever to fix."

"Chase, I'm not feeling altogether confident about this. You know I've had Eva working on the interior designs for the last month, don't you? She's done a fantastic job of them too, and we're due to present the first illustrations to Max in thirty minutes… I'm thinking of asking Eva to handle the project by herself, and be down there at the beginning of October, as we'd planned, to oversee everything… but if you're now saying you're not going to be ready…"

"Stop panicking, Sis. October is still three months away yet."

"Yeah… and if there's no hotel for her to decorate, there's not much point in me sending her all the way down to St. Thomas to oversee it, is there?"

He sighs again. "What's wrong, Bree?"

"Nothing's wrong."

"Then why are you being so uptight? You're not normally like this."

"I'm not being uptight, Chase. I just wanna give Eva a chance at running an extensive project by herself… and I can hardly do that if the project is incomplete."

"I get that," he says, sounding impatient now. "But like I just said, October is a long way off yet. And even if we are having a few teething problems, I'm sure I can iron them out by the time your assistant gets here." He lets out a breath. "Now, tell me what's really wrong with you. Because I don't think it's got anything to do with your assistant, or this project."

"I'm bored," I blurt out, before my brain has time to stop my mouth from working.

"Bored?"

"Yes… and lonely." There. I've said it. Not that I know what Chase is going to make of it.

There's a significant silence before he replies, "That's not surprising. You were with Grady for a long time."

"Don't remind me." I let my head rock back and stare at the ceiling.

"And being single again is gonna take some getting used to." He continues speaking, as though he didn't hear me.

"I'm not sure I like being single." I keep my voice low, working on the theory that he didn't hear my last comment, so he won't hear this one either.

"You mean you wanna dive straight back into a full-on relationship again?" Okay, so I got that wrong. He heard me that time.

"No. That's not what I mean at all. And I certainly don't wish I was back with Grady, before you ask. What I mean is, I'd like to at least get out of my apartment every once in a while, so I can remember what it's like to have a life. I've been cooped up there for so long, I'm talking to myself, just so I can make believe there's someone else there with me."

He chuckles. "Well, I guess it can't help having Dana on your back the whole time."

I shake my head, even though he can't see me. "Oh… she's nice enough, but all I ever do is come to work and go home again."

"You could go out, you know. It is allowed." He's talking about the rules that Max laid down when we were first allocated our bodyguards, which at the time didn't seem too bad. But I'd only just left Grady then… and Eden's death was very fresh in our minds.

"I know," I say. "But taking a bodyguard on a date is hardly spontaneous." And it's not like I'm falling over men asking me out, either. Although I don't tell Chase that.

"They're very good a blending into the background. I don't even notice Eli anymore."

"I'm sure you don't. But then I'm also sure you're otherwise occupied most of the time."

"I'll have you know, I've been very well behaved of late," he says, and I can hear the smile in his voice now.

"Somehow, I find that hard to believe."

"Well, believe it. I've gotta be back in Seattle in two weeks, so I need to be focused on getting this place to a point where I can feel confident about leaving it in Trent's hands and walk away for a while, knowing I'm not gonna come back to a disaster."

Trent is the site manager on this hotel and he's worked for us for quite a few years now, so I'm not sure what Chase is worrying about, unless things are going a lot worse down there than he's telling me… but I'm not going to ask, in case he accuses me of panicking, or being 'uptight' again.

There's a knocking at my door and I turn to see Eva walk in, clutching her laptop. She looks stunning, as usual, in a navy blue sheath dress with a belt at the waist, her blonde hair tied up in a loose bun, and I nod my head to her in acknowledgement, knowing she's here to prepare for our meeting with Max.

"I'd better go," I say to Chase, sitting forward at my desk. "Eva's just arrived and we've got a few things to check over before our meeting."

"Okay," he replies. "Make sure you tell Max how well things are going down here, won't you?"

"You mean you want me to lie to him for you?"

"Yeah. That's why I called you. He'll believe whatever you tell him… so big it up, will you?" I hear him laughing as he hangs up the call, and I shake my head.

"That was Chase." I say, looking up at Eva.

She sits opposite me, crossing her legs. "I suppose I'll get around to meeting him one day," she replies, and we both smile.

"Don't hold your breath. I don't think things are going too well down in St. Thomas, and he's going back to Seattle when he's finished there, so God knows when he'll be home… and speaking of St. Thomas, I wanted to ask how you might feel about supervising the design work down there."

Her eyes widen, the blue irises darkening just a little. "Me? Y—You want me to supervise… the… the… entire project?"

I smile across at her. "Yes. I know you've only been here for a couple of months, but I think you're ready, or at least you will be by October. And besides, these designs are yours, not mine. You'll have a support team to help you out, and we'll hire local artisans and laborers… so you'll only be supervising. It's not that hard. I promise."

She swallows, seemingly with some difficulty, and bites her bottom lip, and then a slow smile forms on her face as she nods her head. "I—I think I'd like that. And thank you… for the opportunity."

"You don't have to thank me. I've seen your designs. You've earned it."

"You're here to see Mr. Crawford?"

Valerie, Max's secretary, looks up at me over the top of her glasses before turning her gaze on Eva, somewhat disapprovingly, although I'm not sure why. Valerie's probably in her mid-forties, has mousey brown hair, and looks rather unassuming... and yet she runs Max's office like a boot camp. She's worked for him since before Dad died – before Chase and I even joined the company – and to be honest, I think Max is just too damn scared of her to fire her now.

"Yes, Valerie." I can't keep the annoyance out of my voice. She knows perfectly well that's why Eva and I are here, so I don't know why she can't just let us go in.

"I'll see if he's available," she says, getting up from her desk and darting into his office. I turn to Eva and roll my eyes, but she's too nervous to respond.

"Don't look so worried." I have to whisper, because Valerie has left the door ajar. "You've met Max before. He doesn't bite."

"No... but his secretary looks like she might." She nods towards Valerie's vacant seat.

I smile, but can't reply, being as Valerie has reappeared in Max's doorway.

"You can come in," she says, standing aside to give us access.

"Why, thank you." I lace my voice with sarcasm this time, although she doesn't seem to notice, and closes the door behind us. I wait until I hear the click of the lock and then turn to Max, who's sitting at his desk, his dark head turned towards us. "Jesus..." I say to him through gritted teeth. "Why don't you just employ a Doberman?"

"It would cost too much to feed," he replies, and I hear a deep male chuckle from behind me and spin around to see Max's bodyguard, Colt Nelson, sitting on the gray leather couch at the other end of the room. I narrow my eyes at him, but he doesn't respond. In fact, he seems to look right through me, which is always the way with Colt... at least in my experience.

I've known him since I was a tiny child. He met Max when the two of them were in high school, and they became inseparable, going into the military together when they were eighteen, each leading the other on, no doubt. Although I was only ten at the time, I remember how angry Dad was, and that while I was surprised, I was also very proud of my big brother and his best friend. Not that Colt ever noticed me… even years later, when he finally came home for good, and I was old enough to be noticed. But then, by that stage, I was on the verge of leaving home myself. I was excited about going to college and finding my freedom… so I wasn't really in a noticing kind of mood either. But I remember Colt coming to the house, after Max had been injured, looking utterly gorgeous… and being very quiet, as ever. I can't deny that he's still absolutely gorgeous, because he is. He's even taller than Max, which I guess puts him at about six foot six, and he still wears his dark hair very close cropped and has a chiseled, clean-shaven jaw, the broadest shoulders I've ever seen, and muscles where most men only ever dream of having them. He's still really quiet too… to the extent that he acts like I don't exist. But then that's fine by me… because Colt is way too repressed to feature on my radar. Gorgeous or not, I doubt he'd know how to have fun, even if you gave him an instruction manual.

I turn back to Max, and then take a seat opposite him, indicating that Eva should do the same. "We've brought Eva's designs to show you."

"Okay." He sits forward and Eva tentatively opens her laptop, passing it over to him, and he sits in silence, perusing her work, while she wrings her hands anxiously in her lap. I want to tell her to chill because her designs are fantastic. But I can't. It would only draw my brother's attention to her nervousness, and that would be cruel.

"What do you think?" I ask eventually, when I consider he's had more than long enough to form an opinion.

"I like them." He looks up, focusing on Eva, because he knows as well as I do that this is her work, and not mine. "I like them a lot."

She smiles and smoothes her skirt, whispering, "Thank you."

"I've asked Eva to supervise the work down in St. Thomas… when we get around to it." I wonder if I should have added that last comment; whether he'll pick up on my doubts about the schedule for this build.

"Great idea," Max says, clearly not noticing my skepticism, his eyes still fixed on Eva. "Do you think you can handle it?"

"Bree thinks I can, so…"

He smiles at her. "That's not what I asked."

She sucks in a breath. "I'm sure I can manage," she says, with more confidence than I've ever heard her express before – especially about herself – and he nods his head.

"That's good." He turns his gaze on me. "Because Bree is gonna have her work cut out for her…"

"I am?" I've got no idea what he's talking about.

"Yeah." His lips twitch upwards. "As you know, once he's finished in Seattle, as well as overseeing things in St. Thomas, Chase is gonna be working on extending five of the existing hotels, and we've got four new builds coming up in the next twelve to twenty-four months, on top of the one in the Caribbean."

"I know. I am aware of the itinerary. The interior work is scheduled in already." Max is the CEO of the business, but we all own it equally… except sometimes he seems to forget that. It's the problem with him being so much older, I think. Not that I mind most of the time. I've never wanted that much responsibility, and neither has Chase. Max is welcome to most of it.

"Sorry," he says, giving me a smile. "I didn't mean to talk down to you."

"You weren't. But what's your point?"

"That we're adding some additional work into the mix."

"We are?"

"Yeah. Unfortunately, we've had some negative feedback on three of the hotels…" He picks up a piece of paper from his desk, glancing down at it for reference. "In Chicago, Minneapolis and Houston."

"Saying what?" I'm intrigued.

"That the decor is…" He looks down at the page in front of him again. "Dated… tired… oh… and straight out of the 1980s." He almost flinches at that last comment.

"I'm not that surprised. Those are three of the hotels we've never really done anything with, since we took over from Dad," I reply.

"I know… and that's gonna change. Right now. That negative feedback got me thinking, and I've made a list of all the sites we've never touched, the ones that need a revamp – or a facelift, if you prefer – and I've sent it to you on an email. I need you to start working on them straight away."

"Are you kidding me? How many hotels are we talking about?"

"Thirteen in total. They're the worst of them."

I glare at him. "We're already completely slammed with the ongoing projects, Max. Do you have any idea how much time is involved in these kind of 'facelifts'?" I use his word, but add a hint of sarcasm to my tone, because he seems to be acting like he's just asking me to touch up a few specks of cracked paintwork, rather than redesign and redecorate entire interiors.

"Yeah. I do," he replies, trying to sound soothing. "But Eva won't be going to St. Thomas for another few months, so you can work on this together. And it's not like you're gonna have to visit any of them to see what they're like now… you've already seen them."

"Haven't I just." I roll my eyes at him, temporarily forgetting my workload and remembering the crazy round-trip I made of the hotels right back at the beginning, when I set up this department, and how Grady responded to my lengthy absences from home, when I only returned for weekends, here and there. Needless to say, he didn't like it one little bit.

"You've got the original blueprints for each of the hotels," Max continues, as though I didn't speak – just like Chase did earlier. "And there are photographs of all of them on the website… and you took some when you went to see them, didn't you?"

"Yes. I thought they might come in useful." I glare at him. "Although I never expected you'd throw this much work at me in one go."

"Well, it'll give you something to do," he replies, and I struggle not to scream.

"Something to do? Wow… thanks, Max." It's only Eva's presence that prevents me from losing my temper with him, but he smiles at me again, like he thinks he's doing me a favor, and I wonder to myself how he can't see how unhappy I am… that working long hours may be a distraction, but it's not going to fill the empty hole in my life. It's not going to make me less lonely, or less miserable… and it's certainly not going to make me less inclined to want to break free. If anything, it'll have the opposite effect of making me feel even more chained in… and I can already feel the need to escape rising within me.

"Okay?" he asks, because I haven't said anything for a while.

"Sure." What else can I say? I can hardly spill my guts to him in front of Eva… or Colt, who's still sitting in silence behind us. "I'll get right on it."

Colt

I hadn't realized Max was meeting with Bree today. If I'd known, I'd have made myself scarce, like I usually do when she's around. I find it safer that way.

I sit in his office most of the time; not because he needs that level of protection, but because we enjoy each other's company, and we work well together. And we are both working. I still have a business to run, even if guarding Max is my primary focus, and right now, I'm negotiating several new contracts. At times like this, it's good having Max around… it helps to have someone to talk things through with, and he's got a better business head than me.

But when Valerie came in and announced that Bree and her assistant were outside – in that really annoying way she does with everyone, even if they're related to Max, for crying out loud – I wondered if it would be too obvious if I left the room. Because the very last place I wanted to be was in the same space as the woman I love. For a second, as I heard her footsteps approach and saw Valerie move back to let her in, I even contemplated jumping out the window. And if we hadn't been on the eighth floor, I probably would have done.

As it was, I had to sit in silence and watch the most beautiful woman in the world walk into the room and completely ignore me. It cuts so deep when she does that, but I have to suck it up. Every. Damned. Time.

I sat and watched, my eyes raking over her, while trying to control my own reactions... and while control isn't normally an issue for me, this is Bree we're talking about. She's around five foot eight, or maybe nine, with a perfect hourglass figure... generous breasts, a narrow waist and slightly flared hips, and the most breathtaking ass, that today was hugged by a tight-fitting pale pink dress, her dark ringlets falling in cascades down her back. I sat, staring at her, admiring her shapely calves and I longed to wander over and turn her around, take her in my arms and kiss her. Not that I'm usually into kissing, but for her I'd make an exception.

She made a joke about Valerie being like a Doberman, and Max's reply made me chuckle... and at that point, Bree obviously realized I was there, being as she turned around to face me, and I had to focus on something other than her divine face, and those dark and deeply sensual eyes, because I was genuinely scared about what I might do. So, I fixed my gaze on the back of Max's laptop, which was just slightly to Bree's right, and I fought hard not to react to the fact that, to Bree, I'm just part of the furniture. It's always been that way, I guess. I've always been either Max's high school friend, or Max's army buddy, or Max's bodyguard. However she sees me – if she sees me at all – Max is the connection. He's the only connection.

She had her associate with her today – a pretty, kind of delicate blonde, originally from Oxford in England, called Eva Schofield. She started with the company about two months ago now, and as I took her in, noticing that she was maybe an inch or two shorter than Bree, with a similar figure, but in my opinion, nowhere near as beautiful, I couldn't help smiling to myself as I remembered how pleased Bree was when she returned from that trip to London last fall, having found Eva and recruited her on the spot, without referring to either of her brothers. They'd both smiled and praised her to her face. And as far as I'm aware, Chase didn't have a problem with Bree's decision. Max, on the other hand, was a whole different ball game. Once Bree had left the room, positively bouncing with enthusiasm, which I've got to say was kind of cute, he'd spent the next forty-five minutes bending my ear about how irresponsible she'd been. In reality, he was just bristling because he likes to do all the hiring and firing himself, but he wanted me to check the girl out anyway.

I did as he asked, just to set his mind at rest, and discovered that her parents had both been killed in a car accident when she was small, and that she and her brother had been raised by their maternal grandmother, who was now also deceased. She'd gone to university in London, which we already knew, since that was where Bree had discovered her. I couldn't find any history of boyfriends… or at least none that were significant enough to show up. The brother – named Ronan – was an archaeology lecturer, and was aged twenty-nine, which made him eight years older than Eva, and was well respected in his field. In other words, as far as I could see, there was nothing to report, and Max concluded that, providing she was good at her job, he had nothing to worry about.

I could've told him that anyway, because Bree isn't an idiot and was never gonna employ someone who couldn't do their job. I couldn't really blame him for being paranoid, not after what happened to Eden. It's just that sometimes I wish he'd cut Bree some slack… like today, when he gave her a mountain of work, and acted like she should be pleased about it. She clearly wasn't, but Max didn't even seem to notice.

It was very tempting to follow her out into the corridor, to find a quiet space to talk, so I could ask her what's really wrong… because something clearly is. I saw it – unlike Max – when she turned away from his desk. I caught just a momentary glimpse of a deep-seated misery in her eyes and I desperately wanted to find out more… to see if I could help her. Not that she'd talk to me anyway.

We're just about on nodding terms, so why would she bare her soul to me?

She wouldn't.

So I'll have to just leave it.

For now.

"Is everything okay?" Max is sitting behind me while I drive him home.

"Yeah. Why?" I reply, making eye contact with him in the rear-view mirror.

"You're distracted, that's all."

He sounds concerned and, as I focus back on the road ahead, it strikes me as odd that he notices my moods, but not those of his own sister.

"I probably just need to get laid." That's not really the best way of phrasing that, considering my lifestyle, but it's the only excuse I can think of on the spur of the moment. There's no point in me trying to deny that I am distracted, because he knows me too well. At the same time, though, I can hardly tell him the truth… not when the truth would involve me confessing to having been in love with his sister for over a decade.

He chuckles. "Has it been that long?"

I work it out in my head, which means it's been long enough. "About a month, I guess."

I glance in the rear-view mirror again and notice him shake his head. "Man… that's a long time… for you."

"Yeah, well… my last time was with Carrie…" I let my voice fade, remembering that afternoon and evening at the hotel. It feels like a distant memory now. But that's because I don't think about my subs very often.

"What's she like?" he asks, reminding me that he knows a little of how I choose to live my life. It came up in conversation a couple of weeks after Eden died. I'd kept it from him – from everyone – until then. But he was really struggling to cope, and I'd offered to stay with him. I didn't stay all the time… not every night. Just when I could see he needed me to. Anyway, on that night, we both got very drunk… and somehow we ended up talking about sex. I can't remember how. He told me how surprised he was that he didn't miss it. It hadn't been that long since Eden's death, but he still seemed bemused by his own reactions, and slightly fearful, I think, that he might feel that way forever… that he might never want to have sex again. I tried to explain that I didn't think it worked that way. Yeah, it might take time, but he was in shock still, he was grieving, and his body's responses were being overwhelmed by everything that was going on around him… and because I wanted him to feel better about himself, and I was drunk, I let my guard down and told him I was perfectly capable of going for weeks, or even months, without sex. Out of choice, not necessity. He marveled at that, questioning why anyone would choose to abstain if they didn't have to, until I revealed the truth about my lifestyle, about how controlling I can really be, not only of other people but also of myself… how sometimes a forced delay can make things more intense. I didn't tell him that my feelings for Bree had been the catalyst for the way I lived my life. I blamed my time in the army instead. And, to be honest, I kind of hoped he was so drunk that he wouldn't remember the conversation. But he did. And the next morning, while we drank strong coffee in his kitchen, he asked how I 'found' the women I had sex with, and I explained about the agency, which he found highly amusing. Max didn't judge me, though. He never has. He just accepts that's who I am. In the same way that I've always accepted everything about him. We're like that, Max and I.

"The last time I saw her, she was annoying," I reply, somewhat evasively, in answer to his question about Carrie. I skirt around the fact that, before she became annoying, she was actually quite good, as subs go. She was obedient, and very compliant, and we shared a lot of similar tastes, right from the beginning, so I never felt like I was having to train her, or – worse still – accommodate her.

"Oh… why's that?"

"She started talking about the next time… asking when I was gonna call her again."

"Oh, dear." I look in the mirror again, and see he's smirking, because even he understands enough to know that a sub asking about the 'next time' isn't allowed. "What did you do?"

"Nothing."

"What are you going to do?"

"Cut her loose."

"Permanently?" he asks, sounding intrigued.

"Probably. I'm not sure yet. I haven't decided."

I can't tell him it's not something I've devoted any thought to, because I haven't needed to contact a sub in the last four weeks, being as all I've been able to think about is his sister. I might do my best to avoid seeing her, or even talking about her most of the time, but ever since he told me about the message she got from Grady, she's been on my mind. And that means I can't be with anyone else. It messes with my head too much.

"Why does that stop you from contacting the agency?" he asks, interrupting my train of thought. "Surely you can just see someone else and keep Carrie on the back-burner for a while, can't you?"

Yeah, I could. If I wasn't spending all my time thinking about your sister, to the point of distraction. "Yeah. I'm just a bit busy… a bit preoccupied." *With Bree, and how I wish things could be different between us. How I wish I didn't have to avoid her, but could tell her how I feel, and take her to my bed, to the exclusion of every other woman I know, or am ever gonna know. Because she's the only woman I'd want to have a relationship with. She's the only woman I'd want to be exclusive for… if she even knew I existed.*

"Hey… if I'm taking up too much of your time…" he says, and although I'm at a crossing and can't look in the mirror, I can hear the smile on his face.

"You're not."

He coughs, clearing his throat. "Did you think Bree was okay today?" he asks, and I almost choke.

"How do you mean?"

"She seemed a bit… I don't know… grouchy."

I'm not sure if 'grouchy' is the word I'd use. And although I could either agree with him, or stay silent and plead ignorance, I realize that, if I really want to help her, I could tell him what I saw, so maybe he can help her instead.

"I don't know about grouchy," I say, speaking my thoughts aloud. "But I thought she looked kinda sad."

"Sad?" I'm aware of him leaning forward, his voice suddenly much closer to my right ear.

"She had a look in her eyes."

"Like she was sad?"

"Yeah."

He sighs and falls silent for a moment, before he says, "Bree can be like a closed book sometimes. It's almost impossible to know what's going on inside her head. Let's face it, she stayed married to that dick of a husband of hers for nearly a decade, without telling any of us what he was doing to her. I swear to God, if the guy hadn't barged in on that meeting, in front of Chase, and accused her of sleeping with every other man in the room, I don't think we'd ever have found out what was going on between them."

"Maybe she didn't feel she could talk to you." I find myself defending Bree, which doesn't surprise me at all, although I think Max is a little shocked.

"Why the fuck not?" he says, proving my point.

"Oh, come off it, Max. You guys are hardly close."

There's a brief silence before he says, "No, I guess not."

"It's not your fault," I tell him, picking up on the hint of guilt in his voice. "Your dad made you too competitive with each other. And you've done what you can for her… as much as she'll let you." Bree can be just as stubborn as Max, and Chase. And she hasn't lost that hot-headed streak she used to have when she was growing up, either. There's no point in denying it, or dressing it up. But that's the whole point of loving someone. It's not just about how great they look, or how sexy they are, or how much they turn you on, or how good your name sounds on their lips. It's about knowing their faults – all of them – and loving them, just the same.

"She had that message from Grady last month," he says, bringing it up for the first time in ages. "Do you think that got to her?"

How would I know? I'm only in love with her. "I've got no idea… although I wish you'd left him to me, instead of paying him off."

"I threatened him with you," he says.

"It's not quite the same thing."

"I know… but if I actually let you loose on him, you'd end up in jail, and I'd have no bodyguard."

"They'd have to find the body first, and besides, it'd be worth it." It genuinely would.

He chuckles, and then falls silent again, before he says, "We're sitting here trying to work this out, but knowing Bree, it's probably nothing at all. She was probably just pissed with me for giving her so much work."

That seems really dismissive to me, but then he didn't see the look in her eyes. I'm not sure I can describe it either, without giving myself away. So instead, I continue the drive to his home, letting us in through the security gates and continuing up the drive.

I park outside his double garage, alongside my own car, and Max hops out, grabbing his briefcase from the back seat.

"Do you need me any more tonight?" I ask him. His property is completely secure. Everything was upgraded after Eden was killed, and we found out, courtesy of the detective in charge of the case, that the kidnappers had actually followed her from the house, despite Max's assumption that they'd just picked her up randomly at her gym. Not surprisingly, after hearing that, Max installed new gates that require a six-digit entry code, and a state-of-the-art alarm system, so once he's here, I know he's safe. That said, if he needs me to stay, I will.

"No. I'm just gonna spend some time with Tia. And you'd better go and get laid, before you become any more distracted."

I smile at him, even though I've got no intention of doing any such thing. Like I said, I can't have Bree in my head when I'm with one of my subs. And based on how worried I am about her right now, I think that means I'm gonna be abstaining for quite a while…

Chapter Three

Bree

It's been one helluva week.

Still, I guess I should congratulate myself that I made it to Friday. Because when I got back to my desk after that meeting with Max on Tuesday morning, and saw the reality of the list of hotels he wants to 'revamp', as he put it, I thought there was every chance I would never see my apartment again.

Eva was incredibly helpful at that point, because I didn't honestly see how we were going to get everything done, not with all the work we already had on our schedule. But she got all methodical on me, and looked at the photographs I'd taken when I'd visited the hotels, as well as the ones on the website, and then came up with a plan of action. She reasoned that, with our drawings for Seattle already in the bag, and the ones for St. Thomas virtually complete too, we could focus on these 'facelift' ones for Max for the time being, starting with the hotel in Chicago, being as that had received the worst of the complaints… and she suggested that for now, we might work together, to speed things up. So, she's been busy with redesigning the decor for the bedrooms, while I've been working on the public areas, and we've actually achieved quite a lot in just three short days.

We're both exhausted, of course, and I've never been quite so relieved to get to the weekend. Of course, that means two days at home by myself… with just my own voice and the television for company, and that's not exactly a thrilling prospect, because no matter how tired I am, I could do with a little more excitement than that in my life.

Dana's been gone for over thirty minutes, although I'll be honest and admit, I thought about asking her to stay. I also thought about asking Eva if she wanted to come out with me over the weekend… but in both cases, I knew I'd end up sounding desperate. And even if I am desperate, I don't want the people I work with to realize that.

And besides, they probably both have a life already.

Well, I suppose Eva might not. She's only lived here for a couple of months, after all…

But Dana? I'm not sure.

She's been my bodyguard for well over a year, and – while I hate to admit it – I know absolutely nothing about her. And that's really rather awful of me, isn't it?

Admittedly, at the time she first became my shadow, I was so wrapped up in what Grady was doing to me, I didn't pay that much attention to anything or anyone around me. He might have agreed to the divorce by then – courtesy of Chase's bribe – but he still seemed hell-bent on making my life a misery… in his own inimitable way. I know Colt gave Dana instructions not to let Grady anywhere near me, and I was grateful for that, although I have no doubt the instruction actually came from Max. That didn't stop my charming ex from sending me numerous texts and leaving messages on my phone… at three in the morning. And while he may not have been drunk, or abusive any longer, he took to standing outside my apartment building… just watching me leave, or come home. I never knew when he'd be there and when he wouldn't. And I think that was what made it so damn scary.

Still, that all stopped when Max decided I needed to move into a more secure building and helped me find the apartment I'm living in now. Grady has no idea of my address, and it's not listed, so it's been blissfully quiet without him… at least until that email he sent last month. Although hopefully I won't hear anything again, now Max has paid him off. He didn't actually say that was what he'd done, but I know he did. And again, I'm grateful.

Looking around at my apartment, I know I'm better off than many. I've got two brothers who care about me; I'm safe, I've got more money than I could ever hope to spend, and I have a job I really enjoy. But I've forgotten what it feels like to have a man look at me like he wants me. And I'm so damn lonely, I could cry…

"Oh, to hell with it," I mutter out loud, getting up off the couch and heading into my bedroom, unzipping my skirt as I go and letting it fall to the floor, before I make my way through to my dressing room.

I don't care anymore. If I spend another hour in this apartment, I'm going to go insane… completely batshit crazy insane. And yeah, I know I'm supposed to call Dana, if I want to go out; Max and Colt both made that very clear to me when she was assigned to me, laying down the law in no uncertain terms. But how on earth am I supposed to have fun if Dana is watching me, making me feel self-conscious about my every move?

I rake through my drawers, finding some sexy underwear to make me feel better about myself, and then grab my little black dress from the closet and carry everything through to the bedroom, throwing it on the bed.

I hesitate for a second, wondering if I'm doing the right thing. I could call Dana and get her to come over. And I could dress a little less provocatively… I guess…

But why should I?

I'm an independent woman, and I'll wear whatever I damn well want. I'll go wherever I damn well please, too. And as for calling Dana… I don't need to. It's not like I'm going to do anything stupid, is it? I'm just going out to have some fun.

For once in my life.

"Are you gonna get out, lady?" The taxi driver turns to me, frowning.

I don't blame him. We've been here for a couple of minutes now, and this is the exact bar I asked him to bring me to, so it probably makes little sense that I'm just sitting in the back of his cab, refusing to move. But then, I didn't expect my nerves to get the better of me. I got kind of jittery back at my apartment, when I had to sneak past Hank, who was the security guard on duty tonight. But in the end, I just told him Dana was meeting me outside, and he gave me a smile... distracted by the shortness of my dress, I think.

The cab driver huffs.

Come on, Bree... you can do this.

"Sorry," I say out loud, reaching into my purse for a twenty-dollar bill and handing it over to him. He gives me a nod of his head as I climb out onto the sidewalk and look up at the bar. I checked it out on the Internet, once I'd got dressed and applied my makeup, wanting to be sure I wasn't being taken to some sleazy dive, and to be honest, from the outside, it looks really anonymous. But I guess that's probably a good thing.

The cab pulls away behind me, and taking my courage in both hands, because I can hardly stand on the sidewalk for the entire night, I step forward, opening the wide, smoked glass door in front of me.

I'm hit by a wall of heat, and sound – mainly laughter, with a backdrop of jazz – and I feel myself relax almost instantly, as I wander over to the bar and put my purse down on top of the shining wooden surface. It's very nice in here – even nicer than the photographs on their website. The decor is modern and sophisticated, but not all glass and chrome, and anonymity. Instead, there's a lot of wood, with the occasional exotic plant, and soft lighting, and as I order myself a gin and tonic, I glance to my left to see two suited men, who I'd say are in their late twenties or early thirties, who seem to have stopped their conversation and are staring directly at me. In fact, one of them has his glass, which appears to contain red wine, poised halfway to his lips. They look almost comedic, but I manage not to laugh, and the other one – the one who doesn't seem to be catatonic – raises his shot glass in my direction, and I nod my head in acknowledgement. Wow... that felt good... just to be noticed.

I pay for my drink and take a sip, swallowing down the iced liquid, as I notice that the two men have disappeared. I'm just wondering where they might have gone so suddenly, when I feel a hand on my shoulder and turn around to find they're standing right beside me.

"Hello," says the man who was drinking the red wine, now clearly not so paralyzed just by the sight of me. He's got blond hair and is quite tall, with a thin, handsome face.

"Hi." I smile at him.

"I'm Shawn, and this is Cory." The other man, who's a little shorter, with brown hair, offers his hand, having left his glass behind, and I take it, giving him a firm handshake.

"I'm Bree."

"Wow… that's a lovely name."

"Thank you."

"Do you mind if we join you?" It's Shawn doing all the talking, but I don't think that's because Cory is especially shy. I think it's just because Shawn isn't giving Cory a chance to get a word in.

"Not at all… why don't we get a table?" I can't believe I just said that… but I did. I heard my own voice uttering the words.

"Yeah… sure." Shawn looks around and spots somewhere we can sit before he grabs my drink. "Follow me," he says, so I do, and we step further into the room, where it gets a little darker, until we come to a booth that's almost at the back of the bar.

"After you," Cory says, finally speaking, with a slightly deeper voice than his friend's, as he nods toward the bench seat and I slide in, watching as he takes his place beside me. Shawn glares at him, and then sits opposite, his eyes fixed directly on mine, and I struggle not to smile at the way they're competing for my attention, which feels sublime.

"We've never seen you in here before," Shawn says, using about the lamest chat-up line in history.

"No… but that would be because I've never been in here before," I reply, and they both laugh.

"So, are you not from around here, then?" Cory asks, and I turn to face him.

"Yes. I just don't go out very much." I'm not sure why I told them that, but it's too late to take it back.

"Oh? Why's that?"

I can hardly say it's because I'm kept a prisoner in my apartment by my brother's fear – and the bodyguard that goes with it – so instead I give them the other version of the truth. "I—I got divorced recently," I say, lowering my voice. "It's just taken me a while to get used to being single again."

"You're divorced?" Shawn asks, sounding surprised.

"Yes. Why?"

He shakes his head. "Oh… no reason. Except you don't look old enough to have been married."

I laugh out loud at his corny line and take a long sip of my drink, settling back into my seat and getting comfortable… very comfortable indeed.

I've almost finished my second gin and tonic, which Cory went and bought for me, and we've spent the last hour or so discussing what we all do for a living, which in their case turns out to be that they work in sales, while I've played down my own role, and just told them I'm an interior designer, not that I own a chain of hotels. They seemed genuinely interested in knowing what I do and how I do it, and I've found that quite refreshing, considering that Grady was either dismissive or suspicious about everything I did, and I've enjoyed talking about my job and myself for the first time in ages. I'm feeling more than comfortable now and I'm really quite relaxed in their company, as Shawn moves the conversation around, telling us about a new restaurant he tried out last night, which leads me to wonder if they're going to invite me to dinner… and reminds me I haven't eaten yet tonight, even though I've drunk quite a lot. I'm just wondering whether I'll accept when I become aware of Cory's hand on my leg. My dress is fairly short, so I can feel his skin against my own, quite high up on my thigh, and for a second, I suck in a breath at the contact.

"When you've finished that," he says, leaning toward me and nodding at my drink at the same time, "why don't we call it a night?"

"Call it a night?" I can't disguise my surprise. I was just starting to enjoy myself and was looking forward to that dinner I'd invented in my head.

"Yeah… my place isn't far away. We could go back there, if you like."

His place? *Oh…* Cory seems very sure of himself, and I can't say I'm not attracted to him… but when I glance up at Shawn, expecting to see a look of disappointment on his face, or even that he might be angry with his friend, I'm surprised to find him smiling at me.

"What do you say?" he asks.

"What about?" I'm feeling confused now.

"About coming back to Cory's place with us?"

"Us?"

Shawn smiles and Cory moves his hand a little further up my leg, so his fingertips are skimming the lace edging of my panties. "Yeah," he says in my ear, lowering his voice to a mere whisper. "All three of us."

All three of us? Is he saying what I think he's saying?

"Do you mean…?" I can't finish my sentence, but judging from the smile on Cory's face, he understands my meaning.

"Yeah," he says, keeping his voice low. "If you're trying to get used to being single again, what better way than to let the two of us show you a good time? You won't be disappointed. I promise." They're both gazing at me with longing, heated expressions.

"I… um… I've never done anything like that." I don't think I've ever felt more self-conscious in my life, and I think it probably shows.

"Well, there's a first time for everything."

Maybe there is. And I have to admit, I'm tempted… I'm so tempted, my whole body's throbbing with anticipation… because it's been that long. But at the same time, it doesn't feel right. And don't ask me why, because I don't know. I just know that something is holding me back.

"I'm sure there is," I reply. "But this isn't it."

They both look a little crestfallen, although I notice Cory hasn't moved his hand away.

"You sure about that?" he asks, and as he speaks, I feel his fingers rubbing me through my panties, and I instinctively spread my legs and even shift forward slightly. I let my head rock back, my fingers clutching at the edge of the seat as I flex my hips, soft moans escaping my lips, relishing Cory's intimate attentions… until I come to my senses, realizing what I'm doing, and I sit upright, shocked by my own behavior. *What's wrong with me?* Cory removes his hand, although he's still staring at me.

"Yes, I'm sure," I breathe, struggling for control. "Look, I'm sorry if I gave you the wrong idea, but I'm really not into that kind of thing." *At least, I don't think I am.*

Cory sucks in a breath and then moves his hand back. But this time, he places it on top of my clothes and uses it to straighten my skirt, surprising me with his gentlemanly action.

"Would you like another drink?" he asks, leaving me to wonder whether I just imagined those few moments of madness. Except I know I didn't because my panties are soaked and I can still feel his fingers on my pussy… even though they're not there anymore.

"N—No, thanks," I stutter. "I think I'd better go home."

He frowns. "Hey… don't go on our account. We can take 'no' for an answer, you know."

His remark makes me wonder if they do this kind of thing all the time, but even so, I smile. "I know." At least, I do now.

"We haven't offended you, have we?" Shawn asks, from the other side of the table.

"No." I'm actually kinda flattered, but I'm not about to admit that.

"And you don't blame us for trying?" he asks.

"No, of course not."

We all sit back at that point, and finish our drinks… and, despite their words, I know the evening is over.

Later, as I lie in bed, I can't help thinking about Shawn and Cory, reliving that moment when they made their suggestion, and when Cory touched me the way he did. I still can't quite believe I let him do that, but the frisson of excitement that passed through my body in that moment was like nothing I've ever felt before. The thing is, I know – and I knew even then – that my reaction wasn't because I actually wanted to be with both of them at the same time. I didn't. It was just that it felt so damn good to be wanted again…

I turn over and snuggle down into my pillows, smiling to myself, and deciding that when I next get the urge to go out, I'm not gonna fight it. I'm gonna have fun.

Colt

"I'm not gonna make it." I don't bother to say 'sorry'… I don't have to.

"Oh… Jack." I can hear the disappointment in Tamsin's voice, but that's not my problem. "I've been looking forward to meeting you," she adds, and for a moment, I'm reminded of Carrie's needy pleading, and I feel a shiver run through me. It's been over two months now since I fucked Carrie… or anyone else, for that matter. It's taken me the last four weeks or so to get that image of Bree's sad eyes out of my head. Although I have been helped by the fact that the last couple of times I've seen her, she has seemed to be a little more cheerful.

I guess maybe Max was right. Maybe she was just pissed with him for giving her so much work. I wondered, to start off with, when I first saw her sitting at her desk with a dreamy smile on her face, whether she was seeing someone, but I checked with Dana and she assured me that Bree has never – not even once – asked her to accompany her anywhere in the evening. Dana brings her to work and takes her home again. Period. She told me it's been the easiest gig she's ever had, and gave me a smile because she's getting paid very well, for doing damn all, basically.

Anyway, I guess the thought of Bree being with someone else – even if it wasn't true – coupled with the fact that I'm not so worried about her as I was, and a growing and increasingly desperate need for my own release, was enough to inspire me to contact the agency. I'd gone through the list already and had chosen Tamsin. Her photograph showed her to be blonde, with quite small breasts and narrow hips… which made her the polar opposite of Bree. Because I never fuck anyone who looks even remotely like her. For obvious reasons. And once we'd gone through the preliminaries and she'd agreed to my rules, I arranged with Tamsin that we'd meet up tonight. Except that's not gonna happen now… and I really don't need her whining about it. Even though we've never met, she knows my terms. She's read my rules. And she knows complaining at me won't get her anywhere.

"I'll call you," I say to her, and hang up, knowing I won't. I never give explanations, and I never give excuses. Just like I never apologize. That's not who I am.

Putting my phone back in my jacket pocket, I glance up at Max's office door. He told me this meeting should be over by five, and it's gone six-thirty, which is why I've just canceled my evening with Tamsin, because even if Max finishes his meeting now, it'll be seven o'clock before I get him home, and seven-thirty before I can get back to my place, change, and pick up everything I need to take to the hotel. And I know that means I could have put Tamsin off until eight or eight-thirty, but I'm tired. If it was a Friday, I might take a chance, because I could sleep in tomorrow morning. Not with Tamsin, obviously, because no-one gets to sleep with me. But as it is, it's Wednesday, and I can't afford a late night, which I know it will be if I go over to the hotel and get all tangled up in knots… quite literally.

So, it's best to forget about it. I can wait.

And that probably says more about my state of mind than I'm prepared to admit.

I sit back, trying to get comfortable, relieved that Valerie has already gone for the night. She doesn't scare me, or intimidate me, like she does pretty much everyone else. She just annoys me.

I stare at the wall clock, watching the time tick by and try not to think about Bree. It's hard, because she's the only thing I do think about most of the time, even when I'm fairly sure she's okay, and happy, which I am at the moment. I wish sometimes we were friends, at least… that she felt able to talk to me. But then at other times, I know how hard that would be for me. To have to listen to her pouring her heart out and not be able to show my own feelings would be torture. So, I guess maybe it's better this way. And, in any case, I'm not sure she's the type to pour her heart out. I don't think she's ever done so with Max. I think he'd have told me if she had. Although I guess she might feel more at ease with Chase. They're closer in age, after all… and just because I don't particularly like him, doesn't mean she can't see his redeeming features. Assuming he has any, that is.

Over the years, I've sometimes wondered whether the reason I don't like Chase is because we're too similar… at least sexually. But whenever I try to work it out – which isn't very often, I'll admit – I end up concluding that we're not similar at all. Chase uses women and then discards them. And I don't. I know it might seem like I do. But I don't. The women I go with know exactly what they're getting into. They belong to the agency, just like I do. All of them understand the lifestyle and what it's about. They've read my profile and signed up to my terms. So, they know I won't commit to anything other than sex, and that any attempt on their part to coerce me into something more will result in the termination of our arrangement. They know I have to have complete control of their body, for the entire time they're with me, and that they must submit to anything I require of them. They know they're not allowed to touch me unless I give them permission, and that I guarantee, absolutely, not to hurt them physically in any way. I know their limits… each and every one of them… and I make a point of sticking to them.

In return for their obedience, they know I will pleasure them beyond their wildest imaginings, and that they won't regret one moment spent with me. Ever.

Unless, of course, they ask for more.

And then, I'll cut them loose.

Does that make me like Chase… discarding women who've become inconvenient? No. I don't think so. With me, it's a mutual arrangement, all out in the open, right from the beginning. They know the rules, and if they choose to break them, they know the consequences.

With Chase, there are no rules.

And that's the difference.

Max's door opens and I spring to my feet, checking the clock to see that it's now seven-thirty, and watching while he shakes the hand of the balding man in front of him.

Neither of them says a word, but I can see the tiredness in Max's eyes and can tell he's desperate to get out of here. He'll have missed Tia's bedtime by now, and I know that will annoy him. He gets to spend little enough time with his daughter as it is, and while his business matters a lot to him, his daughter matters so much more.

The guy walks away, and Max rolls his eyes at me, while we both wait for his visitor to pass through the frosted glass double doors and make his way down the corridor, toward the elevators.

"Jeez, I thought he was never gonna leave." Max turns back into his office and goes straight over to his desk, shutting the lid of his laptop and gathering up his things, before putting on his jacket, which he left over the back of his chair. "Ready?" he says, looking up at me.

"Sure, boss."

He gives me a frown, because he hates it when I call him that, but he doesn't remark on it, which tells me how tired he is.

"I sent Christina a text message about an hour and a half ago, warning her I was gonna be late. She said Tia had already gone to bed, so there's no point in rushing…" He lets his voice fade and I hold the door open, to allow him to pass through. He dotes on Tia, and I don't blame him. I dote on her too, and she's not even mine. She's gorgeous, though… just like her mom.

Christina is the latest in a long line of nannies, who take care of Tia when Max isn't home. She's a twenty-something red-head, and I give her no more than a month before she drives Max completely insane with her flirting. If she doesn't, she'll drive me insane and I'll get rid of her… only his method will be more humane than mine.

"I'm really sorry about the meeting," he says as we make our way down in the elevator. "It wasn't meant to go on for so long."

"Was it worthwhile?"

"Yeah." He smiles. I know this is a guy from whom Max has been looking to buy a small chain of hotels, and he was hoping to seal the deal tonight, so I guess it must have all gone through. "It took me about an hour to find out that he was hiding something," he adds, surprising me.

"He was?"

"Yeah. He suddenly came over a bit too keen to get the deal done."

"I thought you were keen too." The doors open and we exit into the parking garage, walking over to Max's car.

"I was… but there was something not quite right about him."

"So what took up the other two-and-a-half hours, then?"

"Finding the great big black hole in his accounts."

"Holy shit."

"Yeah."

"So, you're not gonna be buying his hotels?" I guess.

"No. I'm not a complete fucking idiot. I have, however, given him some advice on how to get out of his current predicament… so hopefully he'll avoid going bankrupt. Not that it's really my problem."

"No, it's not." But that's Max for you. Considering the guy was basically trying to swindle him into buying what seems to have been a failing business, Max is the only person I know who would have offered to help him, rather than bury him.

He gets into the car and I close the door, going around to the driver's side and climbing in myself, starting the engine and setting off. Max doesn't seem in the mood for conversation now, and I don't blame him. It's late. He knows Tia is already in bed and he's probably got nothing much to look forward to tonight. I think about suggesting we maybe get a takeout and have a few beers. It's something we do every so often, when I think he seems low… because I can be considerate too. Well, I can with Max anyway. But, glancing at him in the rear-view mirror,

I think I'll let him be for now, and maybe put the idea to him when we get nearer to his place.

We've been on the road about fifteen minutes, which puts us roughly half-way to Max's house, when my phone rings, and I check the display on the dashboard and see Dana's name come up. That's weird. It's nearly eight o'clock now, and I know she left the office with Bree at six… so what on earth can she want?

"Hi." I connect the call, knowing Max will be able to hear everything we say. "What's wrong?" Something must be, or she wouldn't be contacting me.

"It's Bree."

My skin tingles, my blood freezing, and at the same time, I'm aware of Max sitting forward.

"What's happened to Bree?" he says in my ear, loud enough for Dana to hear.

"Oh… hello, Mr. Crawford. I didn't realize you were there."

"We're just driving back to Max's house," I explain. "Now, what's happened to Bree?"

"I don't know that anything's happened. It… It's just that I can't find her."

I don't even hesitate. I check my mirrors, and seeing that there's nothing I'm actually gonna hit, I spin the car, turning it one hundred and eighty degrees, so we're facing the way we've just come… and then I floor the gas.

"Jesus Christ!" Max shouts from the other side of the back seat, where he's just landed. "Give a guy some warning, will you?"

"Sorry, boss." I don't take my eyes off the road. "Where are you, Dana?" I raise my voice.

"I'm at Bree's place."

"And she's definitely not there?" I know it's a stupid question, but I have to ask.

"No. I've gone through the whole apartment."

"Okay. We'll be there in ten minutes. Go downstairs and check with the security guard whether he's seen her, or anything suspicious… and then wait for us to arrive."

"Do you want me to call the police?"

"No. Not yet. Just wait for us to get there."

We don't know what we're looking at yet, and the last thing Max needs is to alert the cops, if all Bree's done is gone down to the store for some milk. He'll kill her if she has, because she's not meant to leave the apartment without Dana, but we'll worry about that later. For now, we just need to get there… and find her.

"What do you think's happened?" Max is leaning right forward now, so I can feel his breath on the side of my head. "Do you think she's okay?"

I don't have a clue. I know I'm more scared than I've ever been in my life… and that's saying something, considering some of the things both Max and I went through during our service.

"I've got no idea," I tell him truthfully, trying to control my voice, although it's a struggle.

"You… you don't think this might be like Eden…" His voice fades, and I know he's having difficulty talking.

For myself, I'm having difficulty breathing, but I manage it – just about – and mutter, "I don't know, Max. But if it is, I imagine you'll be the first to know."

I grip the steering wheel and dodge through the traffic, pulling into the entrance to Bree's apartment complex and parking up in one of the very few visitor spaces with a screech of tires.

I'm out of the car in moments, holding the door open for Max, who's paled noticeably in the last ten minutes.

"She'll be okay," I whisper, for my benefit as much as his, and he glances at me before taking the steps up to the main entrance, two at a time.

I follow him inside, where Dana's waiting for us by the elevators and I notice straight away that she's not wearing her usual business suit, but has on a pair of tight jeans and a pale gray t-shirt, and that her brown hair, which she normally wears in a fairly stark bun, is loose around her shoulders.

"Tell me." I bark at her and she steps forward, her hands by her sides, and then she lowers her eyes and lets out a sigh.

"It looks like Bree might have gone out for the evening," she says, shaking her head.

"How do you know that?"

"Because Billy, the guy on the desk, saw her leave, wearing a very short red dress, at about seven-thirty. She told him I was waiting in the car outside." *She did what?*

"But she didn't call you?" I demand, my blood boiling.

"Of course not, or I'd be with her."

"Sorry. I know that was a dumb question."

I usher Dana and Max towards the elevators, input the code, which I know by heart, and we step inside, before I press the button for the penthouse.

"Tell me exactly what happened this evening." I turn to Dana and she sucks in a breath.

"I brought Bree home, as usual," she begins, glancing at Max, who's standing beside me.

"What time?" I ask, and she returns her attention to me.

"Six-fifteen?"

"Are you asking, or telling?"

"Telling."

"Okay. Then what happened?"

"Bree said she didn't need me anymore, so I went back to my place and had a shower, and I was just getting dressed, when I realized we hadn't finalized what time I was supposed to be collecting her tomorrow morning. I'd remembered her saying she had a breakfast meeting, but we hadn't set a time for me to drop by and pick her up. I called the landline here." She rolls her eyes upwards, indicating Bree's apartment. "I got no reply," she continues. "So I tried Bree's cell, which went straight to voicemail. I got worried then, so I came over here. She didn't answer when I knocked on the door, so I let myself in... and found the apartment empty. And that's when I called you."

"I see." I glance at Max. His lips are pursed, like he's struggling with his temper. I know how he feels, but right now, I'm more concerned with getting Bree back safe and sound. "Has she done anything like this before?"

"No." Dana looks me in the eye, her answer prompt, before she adds, "Not to my knowledge, anyway. She always sends me home straight away… obviously I've got no idea what she does after that… or at the weekends."

I close my eyes and shake my head, wondering to myself how long this has been going on… how long we've all been living in ignorance of Bree's stupidity.

The elevator doors open and we step out; Dana first, then Max and finally me, and Dana lets us into Bree's apartment, her door being the only one on this floor, lying straight ahead of us. In reality, we all have a key, although I don't think Bree is aware of that. I also have keys to Max's house, and his mom's, and to Chase's apartment, just in case I ever need to get into any of the properties for any reason.

Inside, I look around at the familiar surroundings. They're familiar because I checked this place out right before she moved in here, which was not long after I first took on the contract to guard Max's family. I remember feeling guilty for being in Bree's space, when she didn't know about it, but I had a job to do, and reasoned with myself that her safety was more important than my feelings.

But that's nothing new…

Walking, past the kitchen area on my left, which is all white and pale gray, and looks so damn tidy, it's hard to believe anyone even lives here, I move further into the apartment, checking out the enormous living space, the shiny wooden dining table, with eight leather chairs surrounding it, and the large L-shaped soft gray couch, the cushions and throws so neatly arranged that it looks like it's never even been sat on. Beyond that is the roof terrace, reached via sliding doors, which overlooks the city. I know that down the hallway to the right is the guest bedroom and main bathroom, as well as her home office, and that the door to my left leads into the master suite… because I've seen them all before.

I don't need to see them now though, because Dana's already worked out that Bree's not here.

"What are we gonna do?" Max asks, standing beside the dining table and looking straight at me. "We have to go find her."

"How?" I shake my head at him. "Where would we look? There are thousands of bars, clubs and restaurants in Boston. She could be in any one of them. That's assuming she's even at a bar, club or restaurant. She could be anywhere... at someone's apartment..." I let my voice fade as I contemplate the idea of Bree being with a man... a man who isn't me, and my blood freezes in my veins.

I start to pace, but then stop myself, because I know Max will wonder what the hell I'm doing... and why. Even so, I can't stop my heart from pounding in my chest. Because, as much as it hurts to think of her being with another man, what worries me even more is that she's in danger... that she's somewhere she doesn't want to be, with someone who might hurt her. I can't stop the fear from building. I can't stop the thoughts from racing through my head that I'm not there to protect her... and I damn well should be.

"Shall I try her cell again?" Dana suggests.

"Let me do it." I pull my phone from my back pocket and go to my contacts, connecting a call to her, which goes straight to voicemail. I don't bother leaving her a message, but disconnect the call straight away.

"You're not gonna leave a message?" Max queries.

"No." What would be the point? And besides, what would I say? *I'm scared... I love you... I don't care what you've done, just please come home?* Yeah... right. That might all be completely true, but there's no way I'm saying any of it out loud.

"Then I damn well will." Max glares at me and pulls out his own phone, wandering over to the doors that lead out onto the terrace. He puts it to his ear, waits a moment, and then says, "I don't know where the fuck you are, Bree... but wherever it is, when you pick this up, I suggest you call me. Or get your ass back home. Fast."

He hangs up and drops his phone onto the couch before falling onto it himself.

"You think that's gonna help?" I ask, gazing down at him, kinda stunned.

"Can't hurt." He shrugs.

"Oh… you think?" He looks up at me, raising his eyebrows. "What if she picks that up and feels too scared to come home?" My argument seems blindingly obvious to me; I don't understand why he doesn't get it. "What if she stays out, rather than come back here to face your anger?" I shake my head at him and then turn away, because I'm getting angry myself now, and I don't want him and Dana to witness that.

I'm staring at one of the few pictures adorning the walls of Bree's apartment – a kind of abstract seascape which is basically made up of horizontal lines in different shades of blue – when I hear Max talking behind me.

"It's me," he says and I turn to see he's on the phone again. "I'm sorry about that last message. I'm just scared, that's all. When Dana said you weren't here, I thought I'd lost you… and I can't let that happen. I can't lose anyone else. Please… just come home, Bree. Okay?"

He pauses for a moment and then ends the call and looks up at me.

"Better?" he says, and I can see the emotion in his eyes.

"Yeah. Better."

He nods his head, pushing his fingers through his hair as he leans back into the couch.

"Does anyone want coffee?" Dana offers and, although I'm not sure I can swallow anything, Max and I both accept. We're gonna be in for a long night, by the looks of things…

It's quite a surprise that it's only just gone ten o'clock, when we hear the key turning in the lock and we all stand up from our seats on the couch, just as Bree walks through the door and stops dead, her face turning a polite shade of crimson, as she stares at us. I stare right back, before lowering my eyes and letting them rake up her body, taking in her long, long legs, and the short, sexy red dress she's wearing, which barely covers her panties, and hugs her perfect figure like a glove. I pause for a moment, struggling to breathe, and then focus on her face again, which is made up a little too heavily for my liking, but which is still the most beautiful sight in the world, her hair cascading over her shoulders, in wild ringlets.

"What the…?" Her eyes flick from Dana, to Max and then to me, where they settle for a moment, before moving back to her brother. "What's going on?" she asks, coming further into the room, and putting her purse down on the island unit that separates the kitchen from the living area.

I'm about to step forward when Max beats me to it, and although that's probably fair, considering he's her brother and I'm… well, I'm nobody… I'm not sure it's a good thing. Because Max is mad. He's madder than hell.

"What's going on?" he echoes, in a voice that's so still and quiet, I know there's trouble brewing, because I know Max far too well.

"Yes." I can sense the bluster in Bree's eyes. She knows she's in the wrong here, but she's determined to ride it out.

"What's going on, is that we've all been sitting here for the last couple of hours, worried sick and waiting for you to get home… because you decided, for some stupid, selfish reason, to go out by yourself." Bree opens her mouth to speak, but Max holds up his hand, silencing her. "How could you, Bree?" he asks.

"I didn't…"

I can hear the emotion cracking her voice, and even from here, the tears in her eyes are easy to discern, but regardless of that, Max goes on, "Don't you care about anyone, other than yourself?" Wow… that seems harsh.

"I didn't think," she says, finally completing her sentence, although I struggle to hear her voice.

"No, you didn't," he snaps, moving closer, so he's towering over her now. I'm kinda tempted to get between them, because I can only imagine how intimidating that's gotta be for Bree. But I can't show my hand… I daren't. "Where have you been?"

"I went to a bar," she mutters. "I just needed to get out."

Max shakes his head. "And what if something had happened to you? Did you stop for ten seconds to think how the rest of us would feel? Haven't we been through enough already?"

That was a low blow coming from him. Bree obviously felt it, because she stares up at him, her bottom lip trembling, and then she lets out a sob, clamping her hand over her mouth, as she starts to cry.

I want to go to her. I want to hold her and tell her that, yeah, she was stupid, but at least she's safe… and in the grand scheme of things, that's all that matters. Because it is. Except Max has other ideas.

"Wasn't it bad enough that I lost Eden?" he continues, like he's immune to her feelings, like she's not falling apart in front of him. Bree shakes her head and reaches out to him, but he steps back and mutters, "For Christ's sake, Bree," and that's enough for me. I may not be able to comfort her, but I can at least stop him from making things worse. I move forward and put my hand firmly on his shoulder.

"I think you've made your point, Max," I say quietly. "I'll take you home now."

I don't remove my hand, but steer him toward the door, refusing to give him any choice in the matter. I feel terrible leaving Bree when she's sobbing so hard it seems like her heart is breaking, but I imagine she'd rather be alone right now than have us here, witnessing her misery.

I can feel the anger pouring off of Max still and neither of us says a word as we make our way down in the elevator, remaining completely silent until we're in the car. But then, as I'm about to start the engine, I can't hold back any longer, and I turn in my seat to face Max, who's glowering out the side window.

"I know it's not my place," I say, and he turns to face me, "but you were way out of line back there."

"Excuse me?" I can hear the rage building in his voice again already, but I'm in the right frame of mind to match him.

"You didn't need to lay into Bree like that."

He leans forward. "I'm not sure what it's got to do with you," he snarls, "but I'm not ready to lose my little sister yet, if it's all the same to you."

"I'm not ready for you to lose your sister, either. But couldn't you see how upset she was? We talked about the fact that Bree seemed unhappy a while ago, but you wrote her off as being grouchy and pissed with you for giving her too much work. Has it occurred to you that, maybe if you'd paid a bit more attention to her, none of this would've happened?"

I don't bother waiting for an answer. I start the car, slam it into gear, and floor the accelerator.

I may have overstepped the mark, but this is Bree we're talking about, so I don't care.

Chapter Four

Bree

God… what a terrible night.

After Max and Colt had left, Dana offered to stay and make me a coffee, but I declined and she left as well, and I sat on my couch and cried for an hour or two, before I finally made my way through to my bedroom, and collapsed into bed. Not that I slept very well, because all I could think about was the look on Max's face.

This morning, I don't feel much better. Except that my sadness and misery have been replaced by anger.

How dare Max have said all those things to me? And in front of Dana and Colt.

If Colt hadn't stepped in and dragged Max away, I dread to think how long my brother would have ranted on, sending me on the guilt-trip of a lifetime. It was like he didn't care about me at all… except he did. But only that I was safe; not that I'm happy.

Because what does happiness matter?

Dana picks me up at seven, as we arranged, before she left last night, and we ride into work in silence, neither of us mentioning last night's embarrassing interlude.

I make it through my breakfast meeting, although I wish I could have canceled, because concentrating on anything is virtually impossible. But once the supplier has gone, and I'm alone again, all I can think about is last night…

I didn't even enjoy myself that much, which is probably what makes all of this so unfair. I decided not to go back to the bar, which I've been to a few times now since meeting up with Shawn and Cory. They haven't been there on any of the nights I've been back, and I've never been sure whether to feel relieved or disappointed about that. I still don't think I'd say 'yes' to their offer if they made it again, but they made me feel wanted, and I liked it. I've had a good time in their absence and have met some very attractive men. But none of them have appealed... and I was getting a little tired of seeing the same old faces. I guess that was why I decided last night that I would go to a club instead. It felt like a good idea at the time until I got there and realized that twenty-eight-year-olds don't hang out at clubs. I felt about ten years too old to be there... and not only that, it was so loud that, even when one or two men came over to talk to me, I couldn't hear a word they were saying. So, after a couple of hours, I gave up and came home... to find my brother, Colt and Dana all waiting for me in my apartment.

I look up at the sound of knocking on my door to find Max standing there on the threshold.

"What?" I glare at him.

He holds up his hands in surrender. "I just came to see if you're okay."

"Like you care," I mutter under my breath, although I know he'll be able to hear me.

He steps further into the room, approaching my desk. "That's the whole point," he says. "I do care. That's why I was so goddamn scared last night."

I stare up at him. "Yeah... because it's all about you, isn't it?"

I know that's unfair, but I'm too angry to be polite. He frowns and I can see the hurt in his eyes, and a part of me wants to retract my words. Except I'm still smarting from his lecture, and from the way he let me cry, and didn't even try to comfort me.

"No," he says, attempting to sound reasonable. "Look, I'm here, if you wanna talk."

"Well, I don't..."

"Bree, I get that you're lonely. Colt and I have..."

I can't believe what I'm hearing. "Wait a second," I interrupt him. "Are you telling me you and Colt have been talking about me behind my back?"

"No. It wasn't like that."

"Sure it wasn't." I get to my feet now, even though I'm still looking up at him, because he's so damn tall. "I can just picture the two of you, sharing a couple of beers and a few jokes about poor, sad little Bree… and how she can't even get laid these days." The blush creeps up my cheeks, and I wish I'd thought to engage my brain before my mouth ran away with itself.

"We haven't done any such thing," he says, keeping completely calm. "Colt told me he thought you looked unhappy, that's all."

"And what the hell has my happiness got to do with Colt?"

"Nothing. I guess…"

"Precisely. It's nothing to do with him. Or you. And now, if you don't mind… I'm busy."

He stares at me for a moment, and then turns around and walks slowly out of my office, closing the door behind him.

I stand, looking at the space he's just vacated, wondering if I should go after him. But what would be the point? I'm still too angry. So, I sit back down again and reach for my phone, remembering that I haven't checked my messages since I left work yesterday afternoon. And it seems I've got a few…

There's one from my gynecologist's office, reminding me I'm due for my contraceptive shot in the next four weeks, and that I need to make an appointment. I shake my head, letting out a long sigh as I wonder if it's worth bothering. It's not like I need to worry about contraception right now, is it?

I delete the message, but make a note in my diary anyway, just in case… and then move on to the next message, which is from a fabric supplier, telling me they've got some new samples for me to see and asking if I'm free to take a look at them sometime next week. I should have time, and I make a mental note to get back to them.

The next message is from Max, from last night, timed at just after eight, and he sounds roughly as mad with me as he did when I got home.

I clutch my phone tightly as I delete his message, erasing his angry words, thinking to myself that I wish I'd bothered to turn my phone back on last night. If I had, I could have saved myself the trouble of going home.

I get to the last message, which is timed just ten minutes after Max's one... and am surprised to hear his voice for a second time.

"It's me again." His voice is much softer this time around. He's clearly calmed down in that ten-minute interval. "I'm sorry about that last message," he continues. "I'm just scared, that's all. When Dana said you weren't here, I thought I'd lost you... and I can't let that happen. I can't lose anyone else. Please... just come home, Bree. Okay?"

I feel a tear hit my cheek. Why couldn't he have said that to me last night, rather than yelling at me? I can understand why he'd feel that way after what happened with Eden, but I'm not sure that gives him the right to keep me prisoner in my own home... to dictate my life to me in the way that he does. And what's worse is, he says he knows I'm lonely, but he doesn't seem to want to help me do anything about it...

I sit down at my desk and sob... and sob.

Because it feels like no-one understands. Or even wants to.

"I wasn't sure what to say this morning," Dana says as she pulls out into the traffic on the way back to my apartment.

"I think it's best if we don't say anything," I murmur in reply.

"Are you mad at me?" she asks.

I glance up at the rear-view mirror, seeing her eyes looking back at mine. "What for?"

"For calling Colt. You know I had no choice, don't you?"

I exhale. "Yeah... and I'm not mad at you. That wasn't what I meant. I just meant that last night was embarrassing, and I'd rather not talk about it. If it's okay with you."

She nods her head, and because she's as good as her word, doesn't utter another syllable, all the way home.

Once inside, though, I'm just faced with the magnitude of my isolation again, and rather than bothering to eat, I go straight to bed. It might only be six-thirty, but what does it matter?

I don't have a life, so what is there worth staying up for?

The weekends are the worst. They have been for ages, but I suppose today was always going to be bad, after what happened on Wednesday. I've spent the day sitting by myself in my apartment, because even though I knew I could call Dana and go out somewhere, I couldn't think what I wanted to do… not by myself, anyway.

It's eight o'clock now, and I've already eaten, had a shower, and am watching a truly awful movie… and while I suppose I could go to bed and read a book, I know what I'd rather be doing on a Saturday night.

I sit up slightly and try to work things out in my head. Dana has no reason to contact me tonight… none whatsoever. So the chances of me being caught out are almost non-existent. And while I know Max would be livid with me if he ever found out, he's gotta find out first… and where's the harm in going back to the bar? I've been there lots of times now, and nothing bad has ever happened. The barman, Jimmy, and I are even on first-name terms, and I'm fairly sure he'd watch out for me if anything went wrong…

"To hell with it."

I jump up, that familiar tingle of excitement buzzing through my body as I rush into my bedroom, feeling more alive than I have in days.

The bar is busy tonight, but then I don't normally come here on Saturdays. Still, I find a seat, attracting Jimmy's attention, and he gives me a smile.

"Gin and tonic?" he asks, used to my regular order now.

"Please." I nod my head. "It's busy tonight."

He looks around. "Just the usual Saturday night crowd."

I notice that almost no-one is wearing a suit, which I guess makes a difference from a weekday evening, when people come in here straight from the office. Instead, the men are wearing casual pants and button-down shirts, and most of the women are in short cocktail dresses, like mine.

Jimmy hands me my drink and I pay him, and twist around in my seat, noting that just about everyone here seems to be part of a couple, either holding hands, or leaning in to each other, smiling and flirting. It makes me feel even more lonely than usual and for a second I wonder whether this was such a good idea. I feel self-conscious by myself, and I'm thinking that I might just finish my drink and leave when I notice a man on the other side of the room, who's sitting by himself too. He catches my eye and smiles, and I smile back. And then he gets up and walks over, a glass of red wine in his hand, which for a moment reminds me of Shawn, although this man is nothing like him. He's taller and more muscular… and very handsome. And I can't help the way my body responds to him.

I've met and talked to quite a few men in the last few weeks, and they've all been pleasant enough, but none of them have made my body pulse like Shawn and Cory did, with their illicit suggestion, and Cory's brief but intimate fondling. Until now, that is. And the thought crosses my mind that maybe this is someone I could spend some time with…

He's standing in front of me now, his intense eyes gazing down at me, and his dark blond hair looking a little tousled, like he's just got out of bed.

"Hi," he says. "I'm Evan."

"I'm Bree."

He nods his head, but unusually, doesn't comment on my name. "May I join you?" he asks, nodding to the seat beside me, which seems to have miraculously become vacant.

"Sure."

He sits and we both turn to face the bar. Jimmy smiles at me, and then moves away, right to the other end, to serve a new customer.

"Have I seen you in here before?" Evan asks, and I smile to myself at the number of times I've heard that line now.

"You might have done. I come in here quite often."

He nods his head. "It's a nice place, isn't it?"

"Yes. Although I rarely come at weekends."

He raises his eyebrows and smirks. "Really?" And then he leans a little closer. "We'll have to see what we can do about that, won't we? You seem to me like someone who should come as often as possible."

For a moment, I feel confused by his response, until I think about what I just said, and then I feel myself blush. Considering we've only been sitting here for two minutes, that seems like a very bold statement. Shawn and Cory may have suggested I have sex with both of them... together... Cory might even have touched me for the briefest of moments. But at least they had the decency to talk to me for an hour or so first.

I'm not sure how to respond to Evan, so I don't, and instead, I take a sip of my drink.

"What do you usually do with your weekends?" he asks eventually, when the silence has stretched just a little too far.

I turn to him, to find him studying my face. "Not very much," I reply, trying to keep my answer simple. "I'm a fairly quiet person, really."

He nods his head and then leans in even closer. "Come home with me," he whispers. "Give me twenty minutes, and you'll be anything but quiet. In fact, I'll make you scream..."

As he speaks, he rests his hand on my leg. But this is nothing like Cory's flirtatious touch. There's something possessive in Evan's movements, and I don't feel that frisson of excitement I got before, with Shawn and Cory. Instead, I feel a claw of fear creeping up my spine. This man is different. And something about him feels all wrong.

I glance up, in search of Jimmy, to find that he's still busy at the other end of the bar, completely engrossed and not even glancing back this way at all.

"I—I think I'd better be going," I say, squeezing the words out through my fear.

"Going?" Evan says, clamping his hand down tight on my leg so it almost hurts. "You've only just got here... and we're nowhere near finished yet."

I look up at his face, and all of a sudden, I know coming here tonight was a big mistake. These are not my kind of people, or at least Evan isn't. I'm completely out of my depth with him… and I'm more scared than I've ever been in my life…

Colt

I don't think I've ever been this tired.

Okay… so 'ever' might be an exaggeration. I may have been this tired once or twice, especially when we were on our second tour in Afghanistan, and things got a little crazy. We kinda forgot what it was like to sleep properly for a while back then… but I was younger in those days. I could handle it better.

Max has been keeping me busy. He's had a lot of early meetings this week, so I've been getting up at five-thirty, to be at his place within the hour.

The day after his fight with Bree, he got into the car and I half expected him to fire me… or at least ask me to put someone else on his detail. But he didn't. He apologized. And I have to say, I was quite shocked by that. I apologized too, because I felt bad for speaking to him the way I had, and we cleared the air. He told me he was going to speak to Bree as well… and he did. Although it didn't go as well as he hoped it would, and he came back to his office looking a little dejected, and told me she'd thrown his apology back in his face.

"Give her time," I suggested, pouring him a cup of coffee.

"I will… but I'm so damn scared. What if she pulls a stunt like that again, and we don't know about it? What if some asshole decides to…" He stopped talking, and I turned around to face him. He had his head in his hands, and I knew he was thinking about Eden.

I wandered over to his desk and put down his coffee cup in front of him, letting my hand rest on his shoulder. "She'll be okay," I said, reassuringly. "I seriously doubt she's gonna do anything like that again. Not after last night."

"I hope to God you're right," he replied with feeling… and I strolled back to the couch in the corner and sat down… smiling to myself, because I knew it didn't matter whether or not Bree decided to be dumb again. I had every intention of making sure that, if she did, she was gonna be safe.

And that's why I'm so damn tired.

Because, every night, after I've dropped Max off at his place, I've been driving over to Bree's apartment, and sitting outside, across the street, watching… just in case.

I know I could've arranged with the security guards – whichever one of them is on duty – that they'd keep a lookout for her and call me if she went out without Dana again. But what would be the point in that? I wouldn't know where she was going, or what danger she was in. I'd just know she'd gone out. And in any case, I don't want Max to find out, and he'd be bound to, if I alerted them, so it's better if I just handle this myself.

For the last couple of nights, she's stayed home and gone to bed at around nine-thirty. I know this because her bedroom faces onto the street, and I can see when she turns off her light. On both nights, I stayed on for an extra hour, just to be on the safe side, and then I drove home, grabbed something to eat and finally fell into bed.

Today is Saturday though, which means I've been here since seven this morning. Not that I'm paranoid. I'm just in love. Desperately in love.

She's been home all day, and it's now nearly eight-thirty. The light is on in her bedroom and has been for the last half hour. But that could mean anything… most of which I'm trying really hard not to think about.

I glance down at the motoring magazine I'm pretending to read, and flip a page or two, before looking up at the apartment block again, just in time to see Bree coming out of the front door. She's wearing the shortest black dress I've ever seen in my life, with sequins all over it, and fuck-me heels that make her legs look too long to be believed, and just at the sight of her, my dick hardens to epic proportions, even as my blood boils with anger. What the hell is she doing?

Well, she's making her way out onto the street and hailing a cab… and climbing inside.

I throw my magazine over my shoulder onto the rear seats and start the engine of my car, following the taxi as it sets off into town.

The journey is short – roughly seven minutes – before the cab pulls up outside a fairly well-known bar, and Bree climbs out, closing the door behind her. She must've already paid the driver, because he takes off, leaving her standing there… not that she stays that way for long. With a slight smile on her face, she steps forward and opens the door, disappearing inside.

I park up around the corner, in a side street, and jog back to the bar, taking a breath, before entering. Inside, it's heaving with people, which is a good thing, because Bree won't notice me… not that she notices me anyway… even in an empty room. I quickly size up the place and take a long and circuitous route to the bar, watching Bree the whole time and noting that she seems kinda friendly with the bartender, which tells me this isn't the first time she's been here. By the time I find myself a seat at the furthest end of the bar from Bree, she's been joined by a fairly tall, quite muscular looking guy, and they seem to be talking. I order a mineral water and keep my eye on what's happening, observing that the guy keeps leaning in closer to Bree, and that she looks a little uncomfortable. Before long, she glances down toward this end of the bar and I have to sit back so she won't see me. I'm not sure what she's looking for, but her eyes are screaming 'help', and even if I wasn't in love with her, there's no way I could ever ignore that. So, abandoning my drink, I get up and make my way to her, placing a hand on her shoulder and leaning right over, getting between her and Romeo.

"Hey, baby…" I purr, trying to sound as sexy as I can. "I'm so sorry I'm late. I had no idea of the time. Can you forgive me?"

I do my best to look contrite, even though this is bullshit, and she turns and looks up at me.

"Colt?" she says, confusion written all over her face as she completely gives the game away.

"Yeah…" I try to rescue the situation. "I know I was meant to be here like… an hour ago, or something, but I got tied up." *Oh, the irony of that phrase…*

The guy who's been sitting beside her makes his presence felt, nudging into me.

"I don't know who the fuck you are," he says, "but Bree and I were just leaving."

I let her go and turn to face him. "Well, you're half right. Bree is just leaving… but she's leaving with me."

He stands. So I pull myself up to my full height, which at six foot six, is a good four inches above him. Even so, he's not fazed and glares up at me.

"I don't think so," he snarls, reaching out for her.

She pulls away. And that's all the incentive I need to place a restraining hand on his chest, holding him firmly in place.

"Make one more move toward her," I whisper, just loud enough for him to hear me, "and I'll break every fucking bone in your body… and then I'll take your sad, limp carcass out, and I'll bury you so deep, no-one will ever find you."

His face pales and he swallows hard, sitting back down on his seat, and I turn to Bree, a fake smile still etched on my lips.

"Shall we go?" I say, and she looks up at my face, assessing her predicament. I guess she knows it's not gonna end well if she comes with me, but the guy obviously scared her. And now she has to decide which is the lesser of the two evils. I'm relieved to say, she chooses to take my hand, when I offer it, because otherwise I was gonna have to throw her over my shoulder and really humiliate her.

I lead her out of the bar and onto the sidewalk before she wrenches her hand free of mine, turning to face me.

"What are you doing here?" she snaps, glaring up into my eyes.

"Rescuing you, by the looks of things." I try to ignore how hot she looks when she's mad and focus on doing my job.

"I don't need rescuing, thank you very much."

"Yeah. It really seemed that way."

She swallows hard. "Well, I don't need rescuing anymore. I can make my own way home."

"You think?"

I grab her hand, but she pulls away again, and I turn on her.

"Stop fucking with me, Bree." She almost cowers at my anger, and I bite it back. "Sorry. I didn't mean to scare you. I'll take you home."

"And what if I don't wanna go home?"

"For fuck's sake." I struggle not to raise my voice again, because no matter how much I love her, she's pushing all my buttons. And I'm tired. "I'm gonna give you two choices… you can walk to my car, like an adult. Or you can keep on behaving like a child, and I'll pick you up and carry you there. You decide. Only decide now, because you're really trying my patience."

She narrows her eyes for a moment and then lets out a sigh and stomps off, muttering, "Fine," under her breath.

"It's around the corner," I call after her, following a pace or two behind, and opening the doors with the remote as we approach. She climbs in, refusing any help, and I walk around to the driver's side, unable to stop myself from shaking my head, even though I know she'll be able to see me.

Our journey back to her apartment is silent, which is just as well, because she's too full of rage to speak, and I'm too scared of giving myself away. Once we get there and I park up in one of the visitor bays, she opens the door and jumps out before I've even unfastened my safety belt.

I'm not leaving it there though. I'm gonna see her to her door, whether she likes it or not. So, I follow her in, giving the security guard a nod as we pass, and I stand with her, waiting for the elevator. She's breathing hard, her anger almost overflowing, even though I'm a little calmer now.

We ride up in the elevator together, both staring straight ahead and, as the doors open, I let her go first. I even let her open the door, although I've got my key and could do it for her.

It's only when she's on the threshold, about to slam the door in my face, that I stop her, holding up my hand against the wooden surface.

"Why do you do this?" I ask her, keeping my voice quiet, to show I'm not mad. Not anymore.

"Do what?" She stares up at me.

"Put yourself in harm's way."

"I'm not. I know what I'm doing." She's got that childish, petulant tone to her voice again, and I can't help laughing.

"It really looked like you knew what you were doing back in that bar."

"What were you doing there?" she asks, changing the subject. "It's not your sort of place, is it?"

I'm not sure she knows me well enough to be the judge of that, but she's not wrong. "No, it's not. I've never been there before. But I've been watching you since Wednesday night… since you pulled your last stunt."

She folds her arms across her chest, which has the unfortunate effect of pushing her breasts upwards, distracting my eye… and my brain. And I'm not even gonna describe what it does to the rest of me.

"You've been following me?" She's clearly outraged. "Did Max put you up to this?"

"No. Max doesn't even know I'm here. But you need to stop this, Bree. You're teasing grown men… and one day, if you're not careful, you'll go too far."

"Dear God… why does everyone have to treat me like I'm a child?" She's getting even madder now, the tension between us almost crackling.

"Because you keep acting like one. To be honest, I think the best thing I could do with you would be to put you across my knee and spank some sense into you… and if I thought it would work, I'd damn well do it."

I stop talking, because the thought of her naked ass, pinking under my hand has just drifted across my mind, and my hard-on is aching now… and she's standing right in front of me, so close I can see the blush on her cheeks, as her eyes sparkle and widen… so close I can hear her gasp, the breath catching in her throat. *Oh, fuck…*

She likes the idea. I know she does. And she's turned on by it, too. The signs are so familiar to me… I'd know them anywhere.

I've never fucked a woman I've been in love with. Obviously. Because the only woman I've ever been in love with is standing right in front of me. But now I've contemplated it for real… now I've put the thought out there, I know I'm gonna struggle to think straight. Ever again. As it is, all I can see right now, is Bree's naked, restrained body, the sting of my touch on her soft skin making her cry out with need, until she's begging me to allow her to come… and me prolonging her pleasure, until she can't take it anymore.

Her eyes fix on mine and she bites her bottom lip. *Well… that helped.* "I'm not a child," she whimpers. "But I'm so bored… and so lonely."

My heart shatters in my chest, taking all my daydreams with it and crushing them to dust, and I step forward. "I know," I whisper, reaching out to hold her.

She slaps my arms away, stepping back into the room. "Then don't judge me," she yells at the top of her voice. "You can go out pursuing women and no-one says a word. But the moment I do the same thing, everyone comes down on me. It's so unfair."

"I'm not judging you." I keep my cool, despite the temptation to lose it with her in a far more spectacular fashion than she's just managed. "And I'm not coming down on you. I know you feel trapped by the situation, and I do understand that. But whatever your problems are, you don't have the right to judge me either. I don't pursue women. I'm not like that. Why do you think Chase and I don't get along? It's because I hate the way he uses women… like they're disposable."

She glares at me. "And what if I want to use men like they're disposable?"

Her words pierce my skin like arrows, her rejection stabbing at my heart. I thought she might soften toward me if I opened up a little. I hoped we might talk… hell, I hoped she might even want me, like I want her. But it seems not.

"I guess that's up to you." The harshness of my voice is obvious, even to me, and she blinks rapidly, making me wonder if she's gonna cry. I'm not hanging around here to find out, though, and I turn away and head for the elevator.

Riding down to the street level, I can't help feeling hurt by her attitude. It's an unusual sensation for me, and it doesn't sit well. I thought she knew me better than that… except, of course, she doesn't know me at all. Not the real me. And even though I've just given her a hint of what I'm really like, and she seemed to like it, it seems I'm not what she's looking for.

And that's a good thing, because the reality of what I do would probably break her… and although I love her more than life, now I've seen a glimpse of what she really wants, I know that if I ever let her in, she'd almost certainly break me too.

Chapter Five

Bree

Colt's words keep echoing around my head.

They have done all weekend, and I can't seem to stop them. I'm not talking about the things we said about men or women being disposable, or the things he said about my behavior… not that my behavior has anything to do with him. I'm talking about that moment when he said he wanted to put me over his knee and spank me.

His voice was unusually deep when he said that. I mean, really deep and intense, and it felt like he wasn't talking about it as a punishment, but as a deeply sexual act… one we'd both enjoy. But was that what he was saying? I could hardly ask him, could I? And yet, while no-one has ever made a suggestion like that to me before, I have to admit, the thought of it was really exciting. It reminded me of the time when Grady suggested tying me down, and even though he meant that as a joke, I can still remember the thrill that rushed through my body at the thought of being restrained. Of course, nothing ever came of that. And Grady found other ways to control me. But when Colt made his suggestion, my whole body felt like it was on fire, and my insides seemed to melt under that fierce heat. I think part of my reaction, part of my confusion, was because it was Colt who was standing in front of me. He's so incredibly aloof normally, so detached from everything around him. And that was why that intensity came as such a surprise. He's also a man who just exudes power and masculinity from every fiber of his being. I know, just from looking at him, that if he'd really meant what I thought he meant, then he wouldn't hold back. Ever. And maybe that's just what I need... not someone who's going to hurt me, or try to control my life. Like Grady. I don't need that again. What I need is someone who'll keep me safe, like Colt always does, but who'll look at me the way he did on Saturday night... like he wants to consume me.

Except he doesn't, of course, because he didn't mean it. He can't have done. I know that. Because, rather than staying and answering my question, working out our argument, helping me resolve my difficulties, and then seeing where that took us... he left. And that hurt. It hurt more than I would have expected it to, and I can only assume that was because my emotions had been heightened by the closeness of his body, the fact that he was towering over me, all domineering and masterful, and typically protective at the same time... with a strange, arousing and deeply sensual look in his eyes... right before he turned and walked out of my apartment, leaving me alone. Yet again. For a moment, I'd thought he actually cared. But I was wrong.

Even so, I've spent the rest of the weekend reflecting on that brief interlude between us... and while I'm still in a turmoil of mixed feelings, I'm also very grateful to him. That's not to say I'm not still angry that he's been spying on me, or that I'm not still upset that he dismissed me so readily and spoke to me the way he did... or that I'm not intrigued about his words, and what lies behind them and that dark, intense glare in his eyes, and disappointed that I didn't get to find out. But I am grateful. He may have been spying on me, and he may have turned up, unannounced and looking hotter than even I remember, in a dark gray suit, his tie undone and hanging loose around his neck, and he may have dragged me from the bar very unceremoniously, but I know that, if he hadn't intervened, I could well be lying in an alleyway right now... or something far worse.

So, as much as he's got me confused – not least because I'm still not really sure what he was doing at the bar in the first place, or why he's been following me – I am thankful.

*

This morning, as I arrive at the office, I'm still in a state of confusion, wondering how I'm going to react to seeing Colt… assuming I do see him, of course. Because I can often go for days, or even weeks, without setting eyes on him. I know, if I do see him, I'm going to find it very hard not to think about his words, or how they made me feel. But, I wonder if I should apologize, and maybe thank him for being there. I'm just contemplating that, as I switch on my computer, to find a message awaiting me from Max, asking me to go to his office as soon as I get in.

I put down my purse, noticing that my hand is shaking. Surely Colt wouldn't have told Max about Saturday night, would he? I guess he might… they're old friends, after all. And while he said Max didn't know he was there, that doesn't mean he won't have felt obliged to inform my brother that I'd broken the rules… again. *Dammit.*

Squaring my shoulders, I head down the corridor, pushing open the frosted glass double doors to be faced with Valerie's desk and her chair… but no Valerie. I smile to myself and knock on Max's door. I can hear his voice coming from inside and open the door just a fraction. He's got his phone to his ear, but waves his hand, motioning for me to enter. So I do, closing the door again behind me.

I take a moment to glance to my left, to see whether Colt's sitting there. The couch is empty though, and I heave out a sigh of relief, although I'm not sure why. It seems odd to me that I've thought of no-one but him for the last thirty-six hours, and yet now I'm not sure I want to see him. Not yet. Not until I've worked out what it all means. If I ever can…

"Of course it isn't acceptable." The sharp sound of Max's voice brings me back to reality, and I turn to face him. He's leaning back in his chair, shaking his head, looking exasperated, although as he focuses on me, he smiles and I smile back, assuming that, whatever's wrong, it's got nothing to do with me. For once.

I wander over and sit down on one of the two chairs in front of his desk.

"No… I'm not willing to give her a second chance." He pauses and then adds, "Because I don't appreciate having my nanny creep up on me and my friend, when we're using my private pool… and making lewd suggestions."

I sit back myself, stunned by what I'm hearing, and Max rolls his eyes, leaning forward now and letting his elbows rest on the edge of his desk.

"Well, I think her standing at the edge of my pool, suggesting she'd like my friend and I to fuck her constitutes a lewd suggestion, don't you?" He raises his voice, then adds, "Find me someone else… and this time, make sure they've got their mind on doing the damn job, will you?"

He ends the call, throwing the handset onto his desk.

"Can I take it things didn't work out with Christina?" I ask, trying hard not to smile. After all, this is fairly standard practice for Max… he's constantly changing nannies for one reason or another.

"That would be one way of putting it." He sounds tired.

"What happened?" I ask, and he sits back, looking across his desk at me and shaking his head.

"I still can't believe it now, actually… it was all so surreal." He pauses. "Colt came over yesterday…"

I feel like my throat is closing over. "Oh?" I say, even though I'm not sure he's expecting a response.

"Yeah. I'd called him in the morning, because I was feeling kinda low, I guess, and I invited him to come over."

"Why were you feeling low?" I ask, wondering why he didn't call me instead, except of course I did virtually throw him out of my office the last time we spoke. And I feel guilty about that now. Even more so than I did before…

"It happens sometimes," he says.

"Is this about Eden?"

He shakes his head. "Not this time. I'd had an awful nightmare… about the time I was injured, and I needed to talk to Colt." He looks at me with a contrite expression on his face, like he's silently apologizing for calling Colt instead of his own family, even though he doesn't need to. I understand, and so does Chase. He never talks to either of us about what happened to him in Afghanistan. But I guess that's because we weren't there… and Colt was. It's a bond we can never share.

"Anyway," he says, like he's coming out of a trance, "Colt stayed for the afternoon, and then when Tia had gone to bed, we decided to go for a swim. We'd only been in the pool for a few minutes when Christina suddenly appeared, wearing a very skimpy robe, which she promptly dropped to the floor, revealing that she had absolutely nothing on underneath."

"Oh, my God. What did you do?"

"Nothing, to start with. I was in shock, I think."

"What did she do then?" I ask, because someone must have done something. Surely.

"She made it very clear that she wanted to have both of us… together." He blushes. "At the same time."

"I get the picture, Max. You don't have to draw me a diagram." I've got a fairly recent one of my own, in my imagination, created by Shawn and Cory.

He looks relieved. "Thank God for that."

"So what happened?"

"I was about to yell at her, when Colt just moved… like lightning. He was out of the pool before I could even get the first word out of my mouth, and he had her up against the wall before…"

"What? You mean he took her, right there… up against a wall… in front of you?"

He smiles. "No, Bree. What I mean is, he pushed her up against the wall, like she wasn't even naked… hell, she could have been wearing a suit of armor for all the attention he paid her… and then he told her in no uncertain terms, to get her ass out of my private part of the house."

I can't hide my surprise. I wouldn't have thought, from the look in Colt's eyes on Saturday night, that he'd be the kind of man to hold back in those circumstances.

"I take it she left?"

"Oh yeah. She grabbed her robe and ran out of there, and then Colt and I got dressed and went and found her… and I fired her on the spot and told her she had twenty minutes to get out of the house."

"So who's looking after Tia now?" Christina clearly isn't, and I doubt that's where Colt is. Babysitting isn't his forte, I don't think… unless you count looking out for me, of course.

"Mom…" Max mutters the word, with an edge of despair to his voice, and I feel for him.

"Oh… oh dear."

Our mom is well-intentioned, but she dotes on Tia, to the point of idolatry. I think that's because she's pretty damn sure that Tia is likely to be her one and only grandchild… at least that's what she's always telling us. Having kids with Grady would have been insane, and I'd need to have a man in my life before I could consider having them now… and as for Chase, I know how careful he is. He doesn't want any mistakes to come back and bite him. It's not a given that Max won't meet someone else at some stage and maybe have more kids in the future… but I can't see it happening yet. And in the meantime, whenever Mom gets to spend time with Tia, she spoils her… something awful.

"I dread to think what they're getting up to. She's got Alexis with her, but it's not her job to look after my daughter," Max replies, referring to Mom's bodyguard, who Mom treats like a fourth child most of the time… poor Alexis. "And not only that," he continues, "Mom reminded me this morning that she's due to go visit Aunt Celia in Florida at the beginning of September, so I've only got a couple of weeks to find a replacement."

"I'm sure you'll manage it."

"I hope so. Mom offered to postpone her trip… but I'd really rather she didn't." He grins at me, and I smile back, because I know exactly what he means.

We love our mom, but she can be quite hard to take sometimes. In Max's case, she dwells on his sadness too much, which doesn't help him get over it… and in my case, she reminds me constantly of my mistakes… especially in marrying Grady.

"Anyway…" He sits up a little. "I didn't get you in here to discuss my staffing problems."

"No… but speaking of which… where's Valerie."

He tilts his head. "I don't know. Wasn't she outside?"

"No."

"Oh… I guess she must've gone to the ladies' room, or something."

I let out a sigh, my shoulders dropping. "You mean it's not my lucky day, and you haven't fired her?"

"Hell, no. I've got enough problems as it is."

We both chuckle, and he stares across the table at me. "I actually got you here for two reasons… the first one being that I wanted to apologize to you. Again."

"What for?"

"For the way I spoke to you the other night, at your apartment. I—"

"Max, please don't," I interrupt him. "You're not the one who needs to apologize… I am. I shouldn't have talked to you the way I did, when you came to see me in my office. I should have been more… gracious."

He smiles. "Gracious?"

I smile back. "Okay, I know it's not my strong point, but you came to apologize to me then, and I behaved like a brat. And I'm sorry. After you'd gone, I listened to your messages, on my phone…"

"Oh dear. Both of them?"

"Yeah. And I'll admit the first one made me kinda mad." He nods his head, but doesn't say a word. "The second one," I continue, letting out a sigh, "was different. I just… I just wished you'd been able to say all of that to my face, when we were at my apartment, instead of yelling at me."

He shakes his head, looking contrite. "I know. I shouldn't have done that. It was wrong of me to take my fear out on you, and I'm sorry."

I look across at him and reach out my hand, which he takes, giving it a squeeze. "I think we're both kinda sorry."

"Yeah," he says with a slight smile. "Am I forgiven though?"

"Only if I am." He nods his head and I do likewise before he releases my hand and I sit back in my seat. "What was the second thing you wanted to see me about?"

He doesn't say anything for a moment, but reaches into the top drawer of his desk, pulling out a card. "I need you to do me a favor, by agreeing to attend this charity function for me." He glances down at the card in his hand.

I feel my heart sink to my shoes. I can't think of anything I want to do less. But then, I know how much of a pain I've been to him lately, and how tired he is… and I also know now that he's having nightmares again.

"When is it?" I ask.

"Thursday evening."

"This Thursday? Thanks for the warning, Max." I shake my head at him.

"Yeah. Sorry about that. I was gonna go myself, but I doubt I'll have a nanny by then, and I can hardly ask Mom to stay on at my place for an entire evening. Tia will have worn her out during the day."

"Why don't I babysit Tia for you? That way Mom can go home… and you can go to the charity function?"

He smiles. "I thought you wanted to get out more, Sis?"

I can't argue with that one, and while it's not exactly my idea of 'getting out', I can hardly say 'no' to him.

"Okay. I'll go."

"I'll get Colt to make the arrangements with Dana," he says. "He's done so many of these things with me, he'll be able to tell her what's expected."

I feel myself blush at the mention of Colt's name, but console myself that at least it will be Dana accompanying me and not Colt himself. And I guess that might make the evening more bearable.

Who knows… I might even have some fun…

Colt

I take the walk back to the office fairly slowly, Max's dry cleaning slung over my arm, enjoying a bit of fresh air... if the air around the Boston streets can be called 'fresh', at nine-thirty on a Monday morning.

Still, I'm in no hurry to get back. Max is perfectly safe, and I know he wanted to have a word with Bree this morning about something. He wasn't very forthcoming about what, although I imagine he might want to clear the air with her, being as I don't think they've spoken since last week, and I know how much he hates difficult atmospheres. Either way, I didn't enquire. I didn't want him to think I was interested... even though I am. Because I've thought of nothing but Bree since Saturday night, when I walked away from her apartment, torn between anger and a deep-seated need. Well, to be truthful, I've thought about nothing but Bree for the last eleven years... which means the last thirty-six hours haven't really been that different to normal. Except I can usually control my thoughts, and there was no way I was gonna be able to do that this weekend... not after I saw the glint in her eyes when I told her I wanted to spank her. I saw the way her lips parted in a silent gasp, the flush on her cheeks, and the way her pupils dilated... and no matter how hard I've tried, I can't get that image out of my head.

I have to try, though, simply because I can't forget her rejection. I can't forget that she said she wanted to treat men like they're disposable... and that thought is kinda ugly. It is to me. Because she's better than that. Even if she's so down on herself at the moment that she's forgotten it.

I shift Max's dry cleaning to the other arm and push open the main door to the office building, giving the briefest of nods to the receptionists and walking to the elevators. Chores like this are the kind of things that Max's nannies normally take care of for him... but after what happened last night, he's without a nanny again. Not surprisingly.

Luckily, I was still at the house, just getting into a leisurely swim, having spent most of the day with him and Tia. He'd called me earlier in the morning, and I could tell just from the tone of his voice that something was wrong… and then he told me he'd been having nightmares about our time in Afghanistan, and before I could offer to go over, he invited me… so I knew it had to be bad. We spent the day together, although he didn't wanna talk that much, but then, he didn't need to. I have those same nightmares myself from time to time… or very similar ones. And sometimes, when that happens, you just need to be with someone who gets it. Anyway, we were just starting to relax, when Christina came wandering into Max's pool complex at the back of his house and dropped her robe, revealing her naked body. Although she was aware of my presence, her eyes were fixed on Max, and she put her right foot onto the step leading down into the water, and said that she'd like us both to fuck her. Actually, she was a lot more graphic in her language, and her descriptions, but that was the point at which I started across the pool, reaching her before her left foot hit the next step, and lifting her off the ground. I slammed her up against the wall, making sure not to hurt her, but wanting to shock her into realizing that her behavior was a long way from being acceptable. I kept my hands where they should be, one on her shoulder and the other on her upper arm, and told her to get the fuck out of Max's private space. The look in her eyes spoke of fear. And nothing else. This wasn't like looking into Bree's eyes the night before, and seeing that slightly questioning lust… the burning need to be devoured, accompanied by that internal debate… was I really serious…? *If only she knew…*

Christina bolted, not surprisingly. And Max and I quickly got dressed and followed her up to her apartment, where he fired her. He should have done that ages ago, to be honest, when she first started playing up to him. And if he hadn't been so busy at work, and worrying about Bree, then he probably would have done.

He has been worrying about Bree. I know that. Part of me even wanted to tell him I've been watching her at night, to set his mind at rest. But then I'd have to tell him she went out on Saturday night… and how close that guy got to her. And then Max would only worry more.

And besides, Bree is my problem.

Even though she doesn't want to be… because she wants to treat men like they're disposable. Evidently.

I went over there last night, after I'd finished at Max's, just to check she hadn't gone AWOL again. I'd have been surprised if she had, given what had happened at the bar. But when I drove past her place, the lights were on, and I parked up, waiting until nearly eleven, when she finally went to bed, and I knew I could go home and get some rest at last.

I exit the elevator and walk along the corridor to Max's office, entering through the double doors. Valerie's sitting at her desk and glances up at me.

"Is he alone?" I ask, nodding towards Max's door.

"Yes. I'll just…" She goes to get up.

"Don't bother." I put just the right amount of emphasis in my voice to stop her, and she sits back down again. We have this battle every time I come in here, and I really don't know why she bothers anymore. She's never going to win.

Now I know Max isn't busy, I open the door and enter, closing it behind me, and hang up his dry cleaning on the coat rack.

"Thanks," he says, looking up from his laptop, hesitating, tilting his head at me, and then taking a breath. "Can I ask you a favor?"

"You mean you want me to do something else, as well as collecting your dry cleaning?" I joke, because he knows damn well I'm not about to say 'no' to him.

"Yeah. In light of the fact that I don't have a nanny right now, I've just asked Bree to go to a charity function for me… on Thursday night."

"Oh… okay. You want me to talk to Dana about accompanying her?" I'm guessing that's what this is about. Charity functions are normally Max's responsibility, so he and I are old hands, and I imagine he'll want me to brief Dana on the protocols.

"I was going to suggest that, yes. But then I had a thought…" His voice fades and I wonder why I'm suddenly feeling nervous… why I've got a churning sensation in my gut, and a prickling up my spine.

"Which is?" I ask.

"Well, I know Dana would take care of Bree, and she'd do her job… but thinking about it, being as it's a formal function – you know, black tie and everything – it might be better if you went instead. You're more experienced at these things, and I think it would look better if her companion for the evening was a man."

I sit down, because my legs suddenly feel a little weak. "Companion?" I query. "If I went, I'd be doing my job, Max… not taking her as my date." I can't remember the last time I went out on a date, but that thought is kinda captivating, as far as Bree is concerned. And for a few moments, I let myself dream…

"I know that," he says, bringing me back to the nightmare my life has just become. "I know perfectly well you don't do dating. But I'd feel more comfortable, knowing you were there."

What the hell am I supposed to say to that?

"Okay. But how do you think Bree's gonna feel about this?" It's the only weapon I've got in my arsenal, so I use it.

He frowns. "Why would it matter to her? Like you say, it's not a date, so she won't care who's with her." That doesn't hurt… much, even though it's the truth. "And anyway, you guys are excellent at blending into the background…"

Don't I know it. I'm so far in the background, Bree doesn't even seem to know I exist… not as a man, anyway.

I nod my head because I can't say anything.

And, taking that as my acceptance, Max starts typing again, while I let my shoulders drop, wishing I was back in Afghanistan… because I think I'd rather be under fire right now, than have to face an evening alone with Bree.

Chapter Six

Bree

I perch on the edge of the bed to put my shoes on, wishing I'd gone for something with perhaps a little less heel now. God knows how I'm gonna survive an entire evening with these things on. But I've made my choice, and I don't have anything else I can wear… because the shoes are gold… and they match the embellishments that wrap around the bodice of my dress.

I stand and check myself out in the mirror, and for a second, I wonder if I've gone too far. Again. The dress itself looks transparent, although it's not. It's flesh colored with a gold, linear pattern that emphasizes every curve of my body, enhancing my natural shape. It cost a fortune, but I decided after I'd finished in Max's office on Monday morning that if I was going to go to this function, then I might as well get a new dress out of it. So I dragged Dana around a few boutiques on Tuesday afternoon, and eventually found what I was looking for… namely a jaw dropping, statement-making outfit.

My doorbell rings, which I guess means Dana's here. Not that we made any arrangements about timings, because I've been here all afternoon, having awarded myself a few hours off to get ready, in return for giving up my evening. And besides, Max said Colt would explain what was required of Dana, and I wasn't about to interfere. He's the expert, not me. So, checking that my hair is in place, and my makeup absolutely perfect, I grab my purse and rush through the living room to answer it. I say 'rush', but these heels won't let me do any such thing, so it rings a second time before I get there.

"Sorry," I say, as I pull open the door, and then my breath catches in my throat, because it's not Dana standing before me, but Colt. And he looks divine. He's wearing a tux, and while I'm used to seeing him in a suit, there's something about a man in a tux that's… wait a second… "What's going on?"

He doesn't reply, although I am aware of his dark, intense eyes staring at me, like he's never seen me before.

"Colt?" I say, raising my voice a little, and he jumps and focuses on my eyes.

"Yes?"

"What's going on? Why are you here? And why are you dressed like that?"

"Max asked me to accompany you to this function tonight."

"But I thought Dana…" I let my voice fade, silently cursing my brother.

He shakes his head. "Max thought it would be more appropriate if I went with you."

I narrow my eyes at him. "Oh, did he now?"

"Yeah… so, are you ready?"

"I guess."

I'm not sure I want to go anymore, especially as that momentary heat I saw in his eyes when I first opened the door has vanished. He's back to being cool, hard, and anonymous again… and I realize that, whatever he might have said about spanking me the other night, he clearly didn't mean it. Not in the way I want him to have meant it. Or, if he did, he's gone off the idea. Because I don't think anyone has ever looked at me with less interest.

He doesn't hold out his hand to me, or even say anything else, but just steps aside, letting me exit my apartment… and as he follows me to the elevator, I know that tonight is just about business for him. And nothing else.

After a silent, but thankfully short drive, we arrive at the venue, which is one of Boston's most prestigious hotels, and once he's helped me from the car, keeping his eyes fixed on something over my right shoulder, Colt hands his car keys to the parking valet. He drives a similar car to Max's, I believe, although Max's is dark gray, while Colt's is black, and I think Max's has a few extra features… but then it would. He's Max.

The valet hops into the car and we turn away, Colt walking a pace or two behind me, which makes me think he couldn't look any less like my date if he tried. But then he's not trying, is he? I imagine the idea of posing as my date is abhorrent to him, so why would he be trying?

Inside the foyer, we're directed to a function room on the same level, toward the rear of the hotel, and we walk down the corridor, my heels sinking into the plush red carpet, making it even harder to walk. Part of me wants to ask Colt for his arm, for support, but I'm not about to give him the satisfaction. Knowing him, he'd just tell me I should've worn more sensible shoes.

When we reach the function room, I hand over the invitation Max gave me, once he'd talked me into this farce, and the attendant opens the door, directing us inside, while pointing out where the bar is. The room is dimly lit and already thronging with people. I don't recognize anyone, though, and I'm damned if I'm just going to stand around looking like a loser, so I make my way over to the bar, knowing there's only one way I'm going to make it through tonight…

Halfway across the room, my heels are still giving me trouble, when I feel a hand on my shoulder and spin around, coming face-to-face with Colt's chest, and I tilt my head up and look into his dark eyes.

"You're here with me," he says with a calm, controlled tone to his voice.

"Am I?" You could have fooled me.

"Yeah. So behave yourself."

I shake my head. "For your information. I'm not here with you. You're here with me… and I'll do whatever I damn well please." Who the hell does he think he is?

I don't bother waiting for his reply, but turn around again and, as fast as my stupid heels will allow, continue my journey to the bar, where I order a dirty martini… because it looks like it's gonna be one of those nights.

I'm most of the way through my second drink, when I become aware of a tall presence beside me, standing closer than feels necessary, and I put down my glass, turning to tell Colt to back off, when I realize, just in time, that it's not him. This man is older, although not by much, and he's smiling down at me, his blue eyes twinkling in the dim lights. Which means he can't be Colt. Because Colt doesn't smile.

"Hello," the man says, with a very soft voice… and perhaps a hint of an Irish accent.

"Hi."

"Are you as bored as you look?"

I grin. "Probably."

"Well, why don't I join you, and we can look bored together? Because other than donating vast amounts of money to this very worthy cause, I've got no idea why I'm here… except to meet a gorgeous woman like yourself, of course."

I turn in my seat. "Have you had much luck with that line in the past?" I ask, still smiling.

"No, but then I've never used it before… still, I thought it was worth a try."

We both chuckle and I pick up my almost empty glass, clinking it against his tumbler, which looks like it contains whiskey or something similar.

"My name's Bree," I tell him.

"That's an unusual name."

"I know… and believe it or not, you're not the first person to tell me that."

"I'm sure I'm not… and I'm equally sure I'm not the first man to tell you how beautiful you are."

"You're the first man in quite a long time," I say, without thinking, and he leans closer.

"Then I can only assume there's something wrong with the men around here."

"There is with some of them, yes."

He nods his head, like he understands how I feel – which he can't possibly, because I'm not sure I do at the moment – and then he says, "My name's Randall, by the way."

"It's a pleasure to meet you, Randall."

He switches his glass to his left hand and places his right one over mine, on top of the bar. "I think the pleasure is all mine," he says, and then lifts my hand to his lips, kissing my fingers, before lowering it again. He keeps a hold of me and says, "Shall I get you another drink?"

"Why not?"

He raises his hand, attracting the barman, and orders my third dirty martini of the night, and when it arrives, we clink glasses again, even though the first two drinks are already making things spin a little.

The hair on the back of my neck suddenly tingles and I turn my head to my right, spotting Colt, who's standing over by the wall, glaring at me. I raise my glass in his direction before gulping down half of my cocktail, knowing I might regret that in a short while… but not giving a damn.

Because clearly he doesn't.

Colt

I knew this was a bad idea when Max first asked me… I just didn't know how bad.

I suppose I should've guessed, though, when Bree opened the door and I saw her in that dress. I thought I'd seen pretty much everything when it came to women… but I'd never seen anything quiet like that. It fitted her body like a glove… and the color of it was the same tone as her skin, so at first glance, she looked naked. That got me hard, in an instant. Then I noticed those golden lines, which seemed to flow around the dress, following the contours of her body, like they knew exactly where to fit and where to bend.

Like I say, that was bad enough, but it's gotten so much worse. Max clearly hadn't warned Bree that I was gonna be accompanying her, and she wasn't best pleased to see me standing at her door… and as a result, she's been acting up ever since.

She's on her fifth dirty martini now and I'm gonna have to step in soon. I know that much. Bree's far too drunk to know what's good for her and the guy she's with has a look in his eye that says he knows it too… only he's not gonna be a gentleman about it. He's been edging closer and closer since the moment he sat down, and at one point in their conversation, he took advantage of Bree adjusting her position on her seat to move his hand onto her thigh. She didn't seem to notice, and they carried on talking, like nothing had happened… like she wasn't even aware of what he was doing. But then I'm not sure she was. She's too far gone.

I'm just wondering how I can bring about a seamless exit without making a fuss, when Bree laughs and slips forward, demonstrating that she really has lost control. The guy catches her, and then, as she rights herself, rather than putting his hand back on her thigh – which was bad enough – he leaves it on her ass. And she lets him.

Jesus Christ!

I see red in an instant, and stride across the room in their direction, trying not to focus on my jealousy, or my anger. Instead, I keep my mind on the fact that I'm here representing Max, and his company, even though Bree seems to have forgotten that, and is doing a reasonably good job of making an exhibition of herself.

I can't afford for there to be a scene, though. There are photographers here, which means I need to handle this carefully, otherwise Max will be livid… with both of us. So, as I get closer, I pull my phone from my pocket and hold it to my ear.

"Yes, boss," I say to absolutely no-one, and then step up close to Bree, putting my hand on her elbow and being every inch her bodyguard. "I'm sorry, Miss Crawford. We've gotta leave." I still have my phone to my ear and she glances up at me, frowning. "I've just had word from your brother," I add, before she can say anything. "We have to go… now." I add just a hint of urgency into my voice and Bree pales.

"Oh… okay…" She looks around for her purse, and I drop my phone into my pocket, grabbing it for her from the bar, as she goes to stand, slipping yet again. *Dammit.* It's me who catches her this time, putting my arm around her, and I smile at the guy who's been feeling her up for the last hour.

"I'm sorry," I say. "I'm afraid I've got my orders."

He holds up his hands, seemingly bewildered, and probably a little drunk himself, judging from the amount of whiskey he's been putting away, and without looking back, I turn Bree around and steer her across the room. She's unsteady on her feet, but then she has been all evening. I can only guess that, underneath that sexy dress, she's wearing equally sexy shoes, and now the martinis have taken their toll, so I keep my arm around her, holding her up, as we make our way through the crowd toward the front entrance.

Once we're outside, though, the fresh air seems to hit her like a wall, her legs giving way beneath her, and feeling her slump against me and slide toward the ground, I bend and lift her into my arms.

"The ticket's in my left jacket pocket." I tell the parking valet, and with a knowing smile, he reaches in and finds it, giving me a nod.

"Won't be a minute," he says, and disappears.

I look down at Bree, who seems to be barely conscious now.

"Why do you do this?" I whisper, narrowly avoiding the temptation to kiss her forehead… or her lips.

She mumbles and moans softly and I shake my head, letting out a long sigh, just as she snuggles down into my chest and I struggle not to hold her just a little tighter.

The guy re-appears with my car, and helpfully opens the passenger door for me, so I can place Bree on the seat, leaning across to pull the safety belt around her and fasten it, before I give the valet a hefty tip and walk around to the driver's side, settling myself in, and glancing over at Bree. She's got her eyes closed, and I know I could take her back to her place… I've got a key, after all. But I can't leave her like this. She needs sobering up, and my place is closer. If I'm gonna be pouring coffee down her for the next couple of hours, I'd rather do so in the comfort of my own home… and I'll take her back to her place once I know she's capable of looking after herself.

I turn left out of the hotel and take the short drive back to my apartment, parking in the private garage below, before coming around to her side of the car and lifting her into my arms again. I purposely don't look down at the way her dress gapes slightly now, revealing a hint of bare breast, and I try hard not to think about how good she feels in my arms, and instead I carry her over to the elevators, and ride up to the second floor, letting us into my apartment.

I put her down on the couch, letting her head rest on the cushions and bend down to straighten her dress, making sure she's decent. As I stand up again, she opens her eyes for a moment.

"Where am I?" she asks, shaking her head and then frowning, regretting the move, I guess.

"You're at my place."

"Why?"

"Because you're drunk… and I need to get you vaguely sober."

She doesn't reply, so leaving her where she is, I go over to the kitchen and put on a pot of coffee, grabbing a bottle of iced water from the refrigerator at the same time. I take a glass from the cabinet and carry both of them through to Bree.

"I'll bring your coffee in a minute, but drink this for now." I pour the water into the glass and put it on the table in front of her, only realizing then that she's still lying down. "Do you want me to help you sit up?" I offer. She's too awake now for me to just move her without her consent, and she looks up at me.

"I'll manage," she says and raises herself up, with a little difficulty, until she's sitting, her back in the corner of my couch. She reaches out for the water and takes a long sip. "Didn't you say you had a message from Max… or that he was on the phone, or something?" she says, looking up at me.

"Yeah… I lied."

She frowns. "Why?"

"Because I had to get you out of there."

"Excuse me?"

"Bree, you were putting yourself in danger. Again. I was doing my job."

She tilts her head, looking confused, and for a moment, she bites her bottom lip, before she says, "So, bringing me back to your place is part of your job, is it?"

"For tonight, yes."

She smiles unexpectedly. "Just for tonight?"

Fuck… is she teasing me?

I decide against replying, because I'm not sure how. And anyway, she's drunk, so I can't be sure she means what she's saying, or that she's even aware of it. Instead, I go back over to the kitchen, pouring her a large cup of coffee, which I carry back into the living room, where she's still sitting, with the glass in her hand.

"You need to drink this too," I tell her, and she looks up at me, putting her glass down on the table beside the cup, and slowly licking her lips.

"Can I ask you something?" she says.

"Sure." I'm not certain I should have agreed to that, but I feel like it would have been rude to say 'no'.

She rolls off of the couch onto her knees and I step back, giving her space, except she doesn't stand up, like I expect her to. Instead she shifts closer, looking up at me through her eyelashes, her face roughly level with my groin, and my dick hardens in an instant as I watch her. She's about six inches from me when she says, "Do you still want to spank me?"

I almost choke. Hell, I almost come, as her words sink into my fuddled brain, the reply, 'Hell, yes,' poised on the tip of my tongue, because right now, I can't think of anything I want more than to take her to my bedroom and restrain her. Properly. To teach her, maybe, not to mess with things she doesn't understand. But, looking down into her upturned face, I also want to kneel in front of her and hold her in my arms, and ask her – yet again – why the hell she does this to herself… why she keeps selling herself short, when she's so much better than this.

In the end, I don't do either.

Instead, I put my arms beneath her elbows and raise her to her feet.

"I'm gonna take a shower," I say, between gritted teeth. "And then I'll drive you home. I suggest you sit and drink your coffee."

She blinks a few times, but doesn't reply, and I turn around, making my way through to my bedroom, where I close the door, stripping off my clothes and leaving them on the floor as I walk straight into my shower, which I turn on, cooling off the water and standing beneath it, my arms braced against the tiled wall. I'm so turned on, I think I could drive nails with my dick, and I could certainly drill Bree… from here to next week. But I'm not the man for her. I'm not sure what's going on in that head of hers, but she obviously thinks this is all a game. And it's not. Not for me. Especially not where she's concerned.

And in any case, I'm still too damn mad at her for behaving like she did tonight… for thinking so little of herself that she could have let that guy touch her so intimately. And that's not jealousy talking; it's common sense. Does she have no idea…

I feel a prickling sensation all over my body, and tense against it, knowing something's not quite right… and then I flip around and grab Bree's arm, just as she reaches out to touch me. In the split second I have to take in the sight of her naked body, I notice her full, firm breasts, her elongated, erect nipples, toned flat stomach and slightly rounded hips… and… Jesus… that smooth, shaved pussy, which is enough to take my breath away. And then I push her hard up against the wall, spinning her around at the same time, holding one hand behind her back, while the other is trapped in front of her, between her perfect body and the tiles. It's taking all of my willpower to fight the urge to kick her legs apart with my own and just take her, being as I've got her exactly where I want her. Except I'm fairly sure she's still drunk. And this isn't where I want her at all. Not like this.

I lean into her, regardless of the fact that my cock is being crushed painfully between us, and I press my lips up against her ear. "Don't ever sneak up on me like that again. Do you hear me? You don't know me. You have no idea what I'm capable of, Bree."

She turns her head, just enough to look at me and says, "Then show me…" and I pull back, releasing her.

"You don't know what you're saying… what you're asking," I mutter, dragging my hand down my face as I struggle to breathe. "You need to stop teasing, or one day you're gonna find yourself in the middle of a storm you can't get out of."

I step away, putting more space between us, and she turns around, letting her eyes roam down my body, her mouth dropping open when they reach my hardened dick. "Oh. My. God…" she whispers.

I turn and shut off the water, grabbing a towel from the shelf beside the shower and covering myself, wrapping it around my waist, handing her a second, larger one at the same time. She takes it, holding it against her body, but then moves closer to me, looks up into my eyes, and says, "There isn't a storm in the world that can hurt me, not when I'm with you…"

She doesn't mean that. I know she doesn't. She's just teasing. Again.

I shake my head, then grab the back of her neck, pulling her into me, quite roughly, holding her body hard against my own, and then I growl, "That's where you're wrong… I am the fucking storm," and I let her go, staring down at her wide eyes. "Go and put your clothes back on," I say, more softly, knowing I've probably scared her. "And I'll take you home."

She sucks in a stuttered breath and then runs from the room, and I let out the longest sigh of my life… wondering why the hell I didn't just take her back to her place straight from the hotel, and leave her there to sober up by herself. It would have been so much easier.

I dry myself off, taking my time, because I need to calm down. But as I'm finishing up, I realize it's gone really quiet in the rest of my apartment, and I re-wrap the towel around my hips, going back out, through my bedroom, and into the living room again.

Bree is still there – thank God – standing with her back to me, trying to fasten her dress. But from her demeanor it's clear she's hurrying, like she wants to get out of here as fast as she can.

"What are you doing?"

She jumps at the sound of my voice and turns around.

"I—I'm trying to get dressed," she says. "Like you told me to."

"Yeah… like you've ever done anything I tell you. And what were you gonna do once you were dressed?" I ask, moving a little further into the room.

"Go home," she replies, glaring at me. And although her eyes drift southward, she quickly raises them again, as though that deviation was a mistake, which I have no doubt it was… in her mind.

"By yourself?"

"Yes. I don't need you to…" I take the few steps required to stand right in front of her and grab her arm, just above the elbow.

"I said I'd take you home."

"I don't care what you said. I can get a cab."

I tighten my grip, and she winces, but I don't release her. "You're pushing me to my limits, Bree."

"Does it make you wanna spank me again?" God… she's a smart-ass.

"Yeah, it does… but trust me, you don't wanna go there." She opens her mouth, but I don't let her speak. "Wait here," I bark at her. "I'm gonna get dressed, and then I'm gonna take you home. And don't even think about leaving here before I come out again. If you do, I'll come find you… and believe me, you do not want that to happen. Are we clear?"

She stares at me for a second, and then nods her head, and I release her arm and turn around, going back into my bedroom and slamming the door.

I grab some jeans and a t-shirt from the drawer and, discarding the towel, put them on, wondering to myself at the same time, why I don't just take her. Not only did she come into my shower naked, but she basically asked me to spank her… twice. And I didn't do anything. I know why not, of course. I don't want to be disposable. And now more than ever, I get the feeling that's exactly what she's looking for. She wants a guy for now… and I want to be her forever. Nothing less will do. And anyway, it's all well and good for her to tease me about spanking her, but if I actually let her see the real me… I wouldn't see her for dust.

Chapter Seven

Bree

It's nearly six in the morning and I haven't had a wink of sleep… which isn't surprising, considering how much I drank last night.

Except I know that's not the problem.

The problem is, I can't stop thinking about Colt.

Because now, I'm not just haunted by his words, but also by the fact that he pushed me away… more than once. And that I've seen him naked… and that he's magnificent. Actually, he's better than magnificent. I'd expected muscular. Just seeing him in a suit has always been enough to give that away… but literally every part of his body is toned to perfection, from his broad shoulders and powerful arms, to his perfect chest, and rippling abs… and as for his cock. Dear God… it's glorious. It's long, and thick, and so beautiful. Just like the rest of him. I don't think I've ever seen anything as beautiful as Colt Nelson, standing naked in a shower, and I wanted him. Which was the whole reason I'd taken off my clothes and followed him into his bathroom in the first place. Because I wanted him more than I'd ever wanted anything.

Even if he didn't want me.

And he clearly didn't.

He may have been hard when I walked into the bathroom – hard as nails, actually – but that obviously had nothing to do with me. Let's face it, I flirted with him. Hell, I practically threw myself at him, and all he did was to warn me off. I don't know why he did that. I've certainly never thought of him as someone I need to be wary of. But he even called himself a storm, and while I can't deny that there's something wild about him, he also makes me feel safe. He's always been there when I need him… like he was tonight, when that man – Randall, was it? – was getting a little too familiar.

Still, it doesn't matter how Colt makes me feel. He doesn't want me. That much is obvious.

Because, as if him rejecting me at his apartment wasn't bad enough, he then drove me home in absolute silence and took me up to my apartment. And when the elevator doors opened, rather than seeing me to my door, he waited, letting me go ahead, and just watched me until I put the key in the lock, and then I heard him sigh and turned around in time to see the elevator doors closing, with him on the inside, his head bent.

He could've come to the door with me. He could've given me the chance to invite him in… to apologize, if nothing else. But he made it really clear he wanted nothing to do with me.

My alarm goes off and I let out a groan, turning over to switch it off, and for a moment, I contemplate calling in sick. Except I've got a lot of work to do today… and I doubt Max would let me get away with not coming in… especially if Colt were to tell him how many cocktails I had last night. Not that I can remember exactly how many it was myself. I lost count. And that's not something I'm proud of…

I clamber out of bed, my head spinning still, and make it to the shower, turning it on and trying not to recall what it felt like to stand under Colt's shower, with him, even if only for a few moments… to feel his body up against mine and wish he'd at least pretended to find me attractive… just for once.

It's a struggle not to cry, but deep down, I know it's just the hangover and exhaustion. And I'm not going to let a man like Colt Nelson get me down. So, once I'm washed, I get out and dry off, putting on a short, floral skater dress. This isn't the kind of thing I'd normally wear to the office, but I don't have any meetings today, and it's Friday, and I'm not really in the mood for getting dressed up.

I put on the slightest amount of makeup, and leave my hair loose, going out into the kitchen to make myself a quick, but very necessary coffee, with which I swallow down a couple of Tylenol, before Dana arrives to take me to the office.

"Are you okay?" she asks.

"No. Not really." There's no point in lying. I know I look a mess… or at least, I don't look my usual self. "I went to a charity function last night," I explain, because it seems rude not to. "And I had a little too much to drink."

She smiles at me as I climb into her car.

"Oh dear."

"Yeah… something like that."

Perhaps out of sensitivity for my fragile state, Dana doesn't get into conversation with me on the way to work, and once we're parked up, she accompanies me to my office, and fetches me another coffee, before disappearing, like she usually does.

Eva arrives for our nine a.m. meeting, and I get through it somehow. We've completed the designs for the Chicago hotel, and one of us has to go and oversee the remodeling. Frankly, I'm not in the mood right now, and aside from the fact that she's proved herself to be incredibly organized and diligent, I think it'll be good experience for Eva, considering that she's gonna have to handle the work down in St. Thomas all by herself, in just a couple of months' time.

"Me?" she says, looking startled, once I've explained my reasoning to her.

"Yeah."

"But they're mainly your designs."

"I know. But, like say, it'll be good practice for you ahead of what's coming in St. Thomas. A re-fit is always easier than starting from scratch. And you can meet the team."

"Okay. If you think I can handle it."

"I'm sure you can handle it. You'll need to be there on Monday, so use the company account and book yourself a flight over the weekend…"

"I need to leave so soon?" She's surprised.

"I'm afraid so. We've got so many damn hotels to fix up, we don't have time to sit back and relax. While you're away, I'll make a start on the ones in Minneapolis and Houston… using the same ideas for the bedrooms, and adjusting them where necessary for the public rooms."

She nods her head in agreement and we spend another hour going over the details for the Chicago hotel, before I remind her she can call me if she needs to, and that she's good enough to do this… and she leaves.

Once I'm alone, I open my laptop, but my headache has returned and all the words seem to jumble in front of my eyes. I can't concentrate. I can't even focus. So, I lean back in my seat and close my eyes, trying to get my head to settle, feeling grateful that at least my stomach seems to be behaving… so far.

I startle, aware of someone entering my room without knocking, and sit up, feeling myself blush as I look up at Colt, who's closed the door behind him and is standing two feet inside my office, gazing at me.

"I—I wanted to come and check you're okay," he says, stuttering for probably the first time in his life. "And…" He pauses, stepping closer still, so he's just the other side of my desk now. "And… I wanted to say I've been thinking about what happened last night… between us… and I owe you an apology. I know I was a bit rough with you. I—I hope I didn't hurt you."

God… could this get any more embarrassing? Not only did he reject me on numerous occasions, but now he's apologizing?

I stare up at him, and although it's hard to erase the memory of how good he looked in the shower, I suddenly see red. How dare he come in here and do this to me? Isn't it bad enough that he turned me down? He needs to humiliate me, too?

I reach out and slam shut the lid of my laptop.

"I'm fine, thank you… Mr. Nelson." I grind out his name between my gritted teeth. "You don't need to worry about me. But I'm sure my brother must have something he needs you to do. Perhaps you'll close the door on your way out?"

Almost immediately, I know I've screwed up. It's not just that Colt's eyes darken, almost to black, or that his face hardens, or that he stands taller than ever, towering over me, it's the tension that crackles between us. And the eruption, which, when it comes, is no less terrifying, for its quiet stillness.

"Don't you ever call me that again," he says, in a whisper that's so harsh it frightens me more than any shout ever could.

"Call you what?"

"Mr. Nelson." What's he talking about? Okay, so I've never called him that before, but it is his name. I'm about to point that out when he starts talking again. "You were flirting with me last night," he says. "You were teasing me. And today you wanna treat me like I'm the hired help? Well, you can't have it both ways… so from now on, you're on your own. You can do what you like, Bree. Go out and get drunk. Let other guys feel you up. Hell, let them fuck you, if that's what you want. Only the next time that *isn't* what you want, and you're out of your depth, don't look for me. Because I won't be there."

He turns and leaves the room without a sound. And I think it's the silence that scares me the most… that and the thought that I'm on my own.

I'm truly on my own.

And it's not a good place to be.

I haven't been able to get any work done all afternoon.

I haven't been able to get Colt or his words out of my head.

I know I've treated him badly, and I regret those final few words I said to him, more than anything. Could I have been any more condescending? I may have been hurt, but that's no excuse. There aren't any excuses for my behavior… none that I can think of. And that's half the problem. I don't even know why I'm doing this…

I make it home at the end of the day, courtesy of Dana, and she leaves, telling me to get some rest over the weekend. It's a nice idea, except I've never felt more restless in my life.

I could go out… it's not like Colt is going to be watching me, is he? He told me he won't be there anymore. But then, what if I end up in trouble? What will happen then?

I feel a tear hit my cheek.

"What am I gonna do?"

I flop down onto the couch and cry, knowing I need to talk to someone. Because I can't keep doing this. The loneliness is killing me. But I can't keep going out and behaving the way I do. Not only is it out of character, but I'm putting myself in danger… and I know it.

Maybe I could talk to Max… except he'd only get mad with me… again. He'd probably get mad with Colt, too, if he found out what happened last night. I shake my head and try to stop crying, although it's hard.

Chase? Could I try talking to him? No… he's still away. And even if he's not working, he'll be otherwise occupied. I know Chase too well to think any different.

I could try my mom… but I know she'll only say, "I told you so," or words to that effect, because she still likes to remind me I was crazy to marry Grady in the first place, and I really don't need reminding of my own shortcomings at the moment.

There's no way I can discuss this with Dana… not when she works for Colt. And Eva sent me a message earlier, telling me she was catching a flight out to Chicago this evening. I don't have any friends. Not any more. That's the penalty I'm still paying, for Grady having alienated me from everyone, all those years ago.

And it means there's really only one person I can talk to.

But I'm not even sure he'll listen.

And I wouldn't blame him if he didn't.

Except, if I don't, I'm gonna break… and when that happens, I don't think they'll be able to find all the pieces to put me back together again.

I get up and, without even bothering to check my makeup, or my hair, which I'm fairly sure are a mess, I grab my purse and head out the door, going down in the elevator, ignoring the security guard at the desk and walking out onto the street to hail a cab.

I give the guy directions to Colt's apartment, because I'm not entirely sure of the address, but I remember the journey back here last night, sitting in his car in silence, so it's easy to do it in reverse, and in less than fifteen minutes, we pull up outside.

I'm nervous now, as I go in and make my way up to his apartment, wondering if I've made a big mistake… another one.

He was furious with me this morning. He told me I was on my own. It's highly unlikely he's going to want to see me… but I only want to talk. I'm not going to humiliate myself, or embarrass him by throwing myself at him again. I not going to ask him for anything, other than a few minutes of his time, and maybe some understanding. And if that's too much, then I really am lost.

I reach out and ring the doorbell, standing back slightly as I try to blink away my tears.

The door opens and he's standing there, still wearing his shirt and tie – the same ones he was wearing earlier, when we argued in my office – which I guess means he's only just come home from work. His face becomes dark and angry the moment he sets eyes on me and I immediately regret my decision…

"What the hell are you doing here?" he barks.

"I'm sorry… I shouldn't have…" It dawns on me he might have plans, or company, for that matter. "If you're busy… or you've got someone here…"

He shakes his head. "I never have people here. Not like that, anyway." He stops talking abruptly and then starts again. "That wasn't what I meant… what I meant was, how did you get here? Where's Dana? Haven't you learned anything, for fuck's sake?"

I look up into his face. "I—I didn't tell Dana I was coming. When I got home, I just… I needed to talk to someone. And when it came down to it, you were the only person I wanted to talk to. I—I thought you might under… stand…"

Without warning, a sob leaves my mouth, and I burst into tears.

Colt

I don't bother to think. I'm done thinking.

I reach out and pull her into my arms, holding onto her and backing us into my apartment, kicking the door closed as I go. It's like there's some instinct deep inside me, telling me this is where she belongs, and she comes willingly, her head buried in my chest, her tears seeping through my shirt.

I'm still madder than hell with her for the way she spoke to me earlier today in her office. I still can't forget the fact that she made me feel like the hired help, when all I'd wanted to do was to make things right between us, because I'd been awake most of the night, beating myself up, worrying that I'd been too rough with her... that I should have tried harder to help her, even if it had meant revealing my hand and telling her – or maybe showing her – how I feel about her. So, I figured I'd go to see her this morning. I thought I could apologize for what I'd done, and maybe we could talk... and I could try to get her to explain why she keeps doing these crazy things. And maybe, just maybe, she'd let me help her. What I hadn't expected was for her to talk down to me, like I was something she just wiped off of her shoe. God, I was mad... I was actually too mad... I was too mad to do anything about it, because if I'd have made one move toward her, I'd have lost control. And I never lose control. Ever. And that's why I told her I was done with her... because she'd come too close to making me lose it. All of it.

But, no matter how angry I am – and I am – I still can't stand by and watch her crying.

She's sobbing so hard, it feels like she's breaking, so I bend and lift her into my arms, carrying her across the huge expanse of my open-plan loft apartment, to the couch, where I sit down, with her on my lap. She doesn't even seem to have noticed the change of position, or scenery, and just nestles into me, weeping. I keep my arms around her, hoping it gives her some comfort, because I don't know what else to do for her… and then I wait. And I wait. And eventually, her breathing starts to regulate, and slowly returns to normal, and although she doesn't lean back, or make any move away from me, I sense the time has come for one of us to say something.

"What did you wanna talk about?" I ask, keeping my voice as quiet as I can.

"Everything," she murmurs, although her own voice is muffled, because she's still got her head buried against me.

"Care to try and narrow it down, just a little bit?"

She leans back now; her face streaked with tears, her eyes puffy and her nose red and swollen… and I want to kiss her more than ever, especially when she looks up at me through her tears and smiles the sweetest of smiles. She aims it right at me, and like sunshine after a storm, all my anger just melts away, swallowed up in my love for her.

"Why do I keep doing this?" she asks, echoing the question I've been asking her myself, for quite a while now. "Why do I keep putting myself in these situations?"

"I don't know."

She sighs, lowering her head again, and in a subconscious action, she starts to play with the button on my shirt… the third one down. She doesn't undo it, she just rolls it between her fingers, absent-mindedly.

"Can I tell you something?" she whispers.

"Sure."

"Promise you won't get mad at me again?"

That's a hard promise to make when I don't know what she's gonna say, but I know if I don't tell her what she wants to hear, she's gonna clam up on me, so I mutter, "I promise," and hope I'll be able to keep my word.

She twists the button around, first one way, and then the other, like she's nervous. "You know the bar… the one you found me at?" she says, sounding a little fearful.

"Yeah."

"Well, that night… it wasn't the first time I'd been there."

"I kinda guessed that."

"How?" She leans her head back again and looks up at me.

"I watched the way you were with the bartender. You seemed to know each other."

She nods, just once, and then stares at the button again. "Oh, I see."

"Is that what you wanted to tell me? That you'd been sneaking out before that night... because I already knew that, Bree."

She hesitates for a moment. "No, that's not what I was going to say. I was just letting you know I'd been there before. My first visit was a few weeks before the night you found me there, and that time – that first time – I met a couple of guys."

"A couple?" I feel my muscles tighten, but try not to let it show.

"Yeah. We got talking, and they seemed really nice." She pauses and I want to ask her how she'd know. She seems like a really poor judge of character from what I've seen. But I don't comment. Instead I wait, and eventually, she continues, in a really low voice, "One of them said he lived nearby, and they invited me to go back there."

"They? You mean, both of them?"

She nods her head, still focused on my shirt button, clearly embarrassed. "I've never done anything like that before, and I wasn't sure about it... but one of them was touching me at the time, and I'll admit, I was tempted..." Her voice fades.

"Excuse me? Did you just say one of these guys was touching you... while you were in the bar?" I can't help myself, the words just spill out of my mouth.

"Yes. But it was through my panties, not..."

"Did he force you, Bree?" I ignore her remark, needing to know the truth.

"No," she says quickly. "It wasn't like that." She finally looks up at me, her eyes clouded with confusion, like she doesn't understand what happened, even though she was there. "He had his hand on my leg, and he kept moving it up, and up, until eventually he was touching me. And for that brief moment, it felt so good to be wanted," she says, with an element of desperation to her voice. "But at the same time, I couldn't believe I was letting him do that. It's not who I am."

"I know," I murmur.

"I stopped him after just a few seconds," she says, taking a breath. "It was like I'd been in a trance and I suddenly came to my senses."

"And he didn't try anything else?" I ask, fearing the worst.

"No. Not at all. They were both really nice about the whole thing." *Yeah, I'm sure they were.*

"Why are you telling me this?" I ask her.

"Because I want you to know the worst," she whispers, which doesn't really make sense to me. But then she adds, "And because I don't understand why I keep going back for more."

"It's happened again?" I'm stunned.

"No." She shakes her head. "But why do I keep going back to the same place? Why do I keep letting men get too close for comfort? Why do I keep doing this?" She repeats her question and then lowers her gaze, looking at my button again, her fingers still fiddling with it.

"Why do you think you keep doing it?" I ask, because while I've got my own theories, I can't believe she doesn't have any ideas herself.

She shrugs and tilts her head to one side. "Do you think it might have something to do with Grady?" she says, like she's still trying to work it out, while her eyes are fixed on her fingers and what they're doing. "With the way he treated me, I mean? Because I never used to be like this, when I was younger."

I let out a half laugh and she startles, and looks up at me again. "Are you kidding, Bree? You married the guy after just a couple of months."

She laughs herself, and I can't help smiling, because it's such an incredible sound – especially now, when she's sitting here, on my lap, in my apartment, baring her soul to me at last. "Okay… so I was headstrong."

"That's one way of putting it."

She narrows her eyes, but she's being playful, not angry. "I was headstrong," she repeats. "But I wasn't stupid. I've never been stupid. Not like this…"

"Yeah, you have. Marrying Grady was about the stupidest thing you could have done. It was about the stupidest thing any woman could have done, from what I've heard."

She leans back, just slightly, her hand falling into her lap, and I regret the action, because I'd gotten used to her touching me over the last few minutes... even if it was through my shirt.

"Do you know how bad he was?" she asks, frowning slightly.

"I know what Max has told me."

She nods her head. "Then you don't know. Because Max only knows what I've told him, and what Chase witnessed when Grady stormed into that meeting we had down in Charleston."

"I heard about that, yeah."

She sighs deeply and surprises me by leaning back into my chest again, letting her head rest on my shoulder. "Chase and I talked after that happened, but even then, I didn't tell him everything."

"Why not?"

"I suppose I was scared of what he might do. And I think, back then, I hoped I could still work things out." *Was she crazy?*

"Even after Grady had humiliated you like that?"

"Yeah. It took Chase quite a long time to convince me to leave Grady."

"Why?"

"Because it's hard."

"What is?"

"Realizing you're wrong... about everything. I thought... I thought we were perfect for each other, Grady and I. I thought he loved me as much as I loved him. And maybe at the beginning he did. Either way, I was so wrapped up in him, I didn't notice that, even while we were at college, he was busy alienating me from my friends... and my family. I thought we were so in love, we didn't need anyone else. I guess I was blinded to all of it really... until I started work and got a life of my own... or tried to. And then he started to question everything I did." She twists and looks up at me. "I'm not exaggerating, Colt. He literally used to question my every move. I couldn't take a phone call, without him asking who I'd been talking to. He used to check my text messages and my emails... even my work ones. If I wore a different perfume, or changed my hairstyle, he wanted to know who I was doing it for."

"Wasn't it allowed to just be for you? Because you liked the perfume, or felt like changing your hair?"

She shakes her head. "No. In the world according to Grady, there always had to be something going on. There always had to be another man, even though there never was. It got so much worse when Max brought everything in-house, after Dad died. I had to travel around the country quite a lot to start off with… and Grady naturally assumed I was sleeping with someone different at every hotel." She leans back slightly, tipping her head. "I realize my behavior of late hasn't been exactly innocent, but I didn't cheat on Grady."

"You don't have to explain yourself to me, Bree. Not about then, and not about now." She really doesn't. Sure, I don't particularly like hearing about her relationship with Grady, and I'm not gonna say I'm thrilled that she was letting a stranger touch her so intimately… especially in a public place. But I don't have the right to object. We're not together. She has no idea how I feel about her, and we've made no promises to each other. She's a free agent and she can do what she wants.

"I often wonder why I didn't cheat on him," she says, like she hasn't heard me. "He assumed I was, so I might as well have been."

"I imagine you didn't cheat, because you loved him." It pains me to say it, but she did love him… once upon a time.

"At the beginning, yeah, I did. But not by the time he started accusing me. By then, being with him was so damn miserable. He'd suffocated the life out of our relationship, and out of me. He'd stifled every ambition in me, to the point where my life was no longer my own. And he'd taken control of everything… until I felt I had nothing left that I could call my own. Not even my spirit. I don't think I had the energy to cheat on him… or to leave him. Not until the very end, when Chase made me realize that, if I didn't, he would crush me completely."

I've often wanted to hurt Grady for what he did to Bree… but never more so than now.

"Do you think that maybe you're trying to get back some control?" I ask her, trying to stick to her original question. "Let's face it, having a bodyguard on your back for most of the day isn't that different to living with a guy who wouldn't let you breathe your own air, without asking his permission, is it?"

She shakes her head. "No. That had occurred to me, too. But do you think that's what it is?"

I love that she's asking my opinion, even though I'm not sure why. "It wouldn't surprise me. I know a thing or two about control, and it's a very definite state of mind for some people." *Like me.* I've revealed a little of my hand there, but I don't think she'll pick up on it. And I'm not sure I want her to. Having heard her story in more detail, especially her need for freedom in her life, I'm more afraid than ever of her finding out the truth about me. There's no way she'd wanna be with someone like me. And that's quite understandable.

"But why do I put myself in danger?" she says, looking up at me again and confirming that my point about control went way over her head. *Thank God.*

I smile down at her. "You always were a bit of a rebel. In fact, all three of you spent most of your time kicking back against something or other. And that's down to your dad and the way he brought you up. I know I didn't have a father to speak of, so I can hardly comment, but I always thought yours was way too strict for his own good. He pushed you away, from both himself and each other. All of you. That's why Max joined the military… which was all his idea, not mine, in case you didn't know."

"Really?" She's surprised by that. "I assumed you'd kinda led each other into it."

"No. It was all down to Max. I didn't know what I was gonna do with my life, and when he suggested it, I agreed. He was doing it to prove a point to your dad… that he wanted to be his own man, for once." I don't mention the fact that Max had another reason for enlisting. It's not relevant… and besides, he's never told me what that reason was.

And I've never asked.

"It was a little extreme isn't it?" she says.

"What?"

"Enlisting in the army, to prove a point."

"And marrying a loser like Grady wasn't? We only served seven years… but yours could have been a life sentence."

She sucks in a breath and lets it out slowly. "Yeah… I see what you mean."

"You swapped one controlling person for another. Grady was a lot worse than your dad, obviously, but they both wanted to stamp their authority on you, and clip your wings. And then, when you got divorced, you were hoping to be able to fly, to find some freedom and learn to live again… and within a few short months, before you'd even had a chance to get used to being single again, Max slapped a bodyguard on you."

She smiles, although she's shaking her head. "That's *exactly* how it felt," she says, quietly. "But does that make sense of what I'm doing now?"

"Yes. Think about it. What are you doing?"

"Behaving like an idiot?"

I chuckle. "Yeah… sometimes. But in reality, you're proving a point too."

"To whom?"

"Yourself mainly. And maybe Max."

"And what would the point be?" she asks, looking up into my eyes.

"That you're finally free. That you want to be your own woman, for the first time in your life. And you won't be dictated to by anyone either… not even someone who loves you, like Max does." She lets her eyes fall, and frowns, like she's thinking. "There's nothing wrong with that, Bree," I add, before she can beat herself up for what she's done. "Honestly, there isn't. No-one wants to be caged against their will. But you need to be more careful. You've gotta stop taking risks."

She looks up again, and now there are fresh tears welling in her eyes, and as she blinks, they fall onto her cheeks, and she starts to cry again. I pull her close to me and she rests her head on my chest, sobbing. Through the sounds of her sniffling and crying, I can hear her mumbling something, but I can't make it out.

"What's that?" I ask.

She looks up, her tears still falling. "I—I said, I'm sorry."

"What for?"

"For the way I've treated you… for what I said to you earlier today…" Her voice fades into tears again and she goes to lower her head, but I put my finger beneath her chin, raising her face to mine and looking into her eyes.

"You don't have to be sorry."

"But you were so angry with me."

"Yeah. I was."

"Are you still angry?"

"No." I shake my head. "No, I'm not angry anymore, Bree."

She leans back into me, and I cling to her, because I get the feeling there's still a chance she could fall apart. And there's no way I'm gonna let that happen. I reach up with one hand, and tentatively stroke her hair, knowing there's an intimacy in that action; an intimacy she might not want. She doesn't flinch, though. Instead, she nestles further into me, like I'm her safe place, or something… and there's nothing more I wanna be right now, than somewhere safe for Bree to rest her head.

Settling back into the couch, with her on my lap, our breathing synchronized, slow and steady, I think about how different this feels to last night, when I got back from taking her home. I sat here then, in this very spot, contemplating everything that had gone on between us, feeling cross and confused and turned on, all at the same time. I was cross still about the way she'd behaved at the function, and later, when we'd got back here, which was equally confusing, because it was hard to tell with Bree, when she was teasing, and when she was being serious… and at the same time she had me so turned on, I didn't really know which way was up. That's unheard of for me, considering how controlled I normally am. But deep down, in the cold light of my lonely apartment, I knew I shouldn't have manhandled her in the way I did. I should have seen through her behavior and noticed there was something else going on behind it. And then I should have tried talking to her, like we did tonight. Because that's what you do when you love someone. You don't judge them, or get angry with them, or treat them like they don't belong. You love them. Regardless.

I don't know how long we've been sitting before I become aware that her breathing has changed and I know, without even having to check, that she's fallen asleep. And that feels kinda weird. It's like she's here with me, and yet she's not, which is odd. But I like it. I've never let anyone sleep on me before, but this feels right. I guess that's because it's Bree… and this is where she belongs. At least, as far as I'm concerned, anyway.

I let the time drift past. An hour… maybe two. And then, when it becomes clear she's not going to wake up anytime soon, I get to my feet, bringing her with me, and carry her through to my bedroom, laying her on one side of the bed. It's only when I stand and look down at her that I realize the dress she's wearing is as short as it is. It's ridden up a little and I can see the very tops of her thighs, and I can't help the slight groan that escapes my lips as I pull it back down and then reach over and drag the quilt from the other side, covering her over. I'm tempted to lean down and kiss her, even if it's just on the forehead. But I don't. For some reason, it doesn't feel right. So I go across to the far side of the room and pull the drapes closed, blocking out the street lights and shutting the room in darkness, and then I leave her there and return to the living room, closing the door behind me and gazing across at the couch, which is where I guess I'm gonna be sleeping tonight.

I'm okay with that. It's a comfortable enough couch, although I'm not ready for sleep yet. I'm feeling kinda wired still, after tonight.

It was good having Bree here. I feel gratified and maybe a little humbled that, out of all the people she could have gone to when she needed to talk, she came to me. She said she thought I'd understand. And I did. Or at least, I tried to. I did my best, anyway.

It was hard listening to parts of her story. I hated hearing about the way Grady treated her, and knowing that, if I'd taken my chances earlier, when I'd first come back home and fallen for her, all those years ago, she might never have ended up in that situation. Her revelations about the men in the bar shocked me. But I felt kinda pleased that she'd was okay with telling me about it, and that she'd admitted her behavior was out of character. I'd already worked that out for myself, but I'm glad she knows that what she was doing was wrong… at least, it was for her. And that means she's unlikely to do something that dumb again. Thank God.

I meant it when I told her there's nothing wrong with her finding her own feet and learning to be herself again. There isn't. The only problem with that is, while she's her own person, and she's free to do what she wants, that thought is terrifying me. Because I'm scared she's gonna learn to fly again... and that she'll fly away from me.

And now I've spent an evening with her... talking and listening, and learning about her... and holding her in my arms while she slept... I know I can't lose her.

I know something else too... I can't go on as I was before. It's a big step for me, but I know I can't be with anyone else. I'm not with Bree. I get that. And I get that I may never be with her... especially not if she ever she finds out who I really am. But the thought of being with another woman now is just wrong. It's abhorrent actually.

I grab my laptop and log on to the agency website, taking a few minutes to find the page where you can unsubscribe yourself... because, needless to say, they've made a point of burying it. It seems I'm going to have to pay a penalty for terminating my membership in the middle of the year, and that's a little steeper than I'd expected. But I don't care. What's a few thousand dollars, compared to doing the right thing?

I complete the form, hit up my credit card, and press the 'submit' button, and then, closing my laptop, I lie back with a smile on my face, feeling strangely relieved and liberated.

I wake early, disorientated, and unsure, until I remember I'm not in my own bed. I'm in the living room, on the couch... and Bree is in the bedroom. At least I think she is. Unless she crept out in the middle of the night. *God, I hope not.*

I push back the blanket I used to cover myself during the night, and although I'm only wearing trunks, and nothing else, I pad over to my bedroom, and quietly open the door, letting out a silent sigh of relief, when I see Bree is still lying in my bed, fast asleep. It's impossible to see her clearly from here, because the drapes are closed, and it's kind of dim in here, even though it's a bright sunny morning outside. I don't need to see her, though. She's still here, and that's all that matters.

Leaving the door ajar, I go back to the couch, folding up the blanket and leaving it over the back of the chair. Then I pick up my clothes, taking them through to the laundry room, which is around the corner, beyond the kitchen area, where I dump everything in the washing machine, and grab a pair of jeans and a t-shirt from the pile of clean clothes on top of the dryer, taking them with me into the main bathroom. I'll have to shower in here, because I don't want to wake Bree… but it's a small sacrifice, and it's not like I'm going to be long. I don't want to risk her waking up and finding the place deserted.

I shower quickly, dry myself, and get dressed, then go out into the kitchen, noting that my bedroom door is exactly as I left it, before I put on a pot of coffee, wondering what Bree's gonna want for breakfast… if she's gonna want to stay for breakfast, that is. It's not like I've ever done this before, so I don't know how it works…

"Can I smell coffee?"

I turn at the sound of Bree's voice behind me and almost let out a gasp. Dear God… she looks crazy beautiful this morning. I know she isn't 'just fucked', but she's got that look about her that says she ought to be, and my dick responds in kind as I let my eyes roam. Her hair is disheveled, as is her dress, and she looks all sleepy and mussed up… and more sexy than should be legal.

"Yeah, you can." My voice comes out in a strangled whisper. "Do you want some?"

"I'd love some." I reach up into the cabinet and grab a couple of cups while she comes over and leans against the countertop a few feet away from me. "Did I fall asleep on you last night?"

"Just slightly."

She bites her bottom lip, making my cock ache. "Thanks for letting me use your bed… but… um… just out of interest, where did you sleep?"

I point across the room. "On the couch."

She frowns now and folds her arms across her chest, looking defensive all of a sudden. "Oh… yeah. Of course."

I put down the cups I'm still holding and step in front of her, so we're facing each other. "What does that mean?"

"Nothing."

She's not getting away with that. Something's eating at her, and I want to know what. "You poured your heart out to me last night, Bree." *And I made some serious changes to my life as a result. Not that I'm about to tell you that.* "The least you can do is explain to me what you mean by, 'of course'. Especially when you say it in that tone of voice."

"What tone of voice?"

"I don't know… kinda sneering."

"I didn't mean to sound sneering." She tries to look away, over toward the bank of windows that are currently letting in the morning sunlight, but I clasp her chin in my hand and pull her head back around.

"Well, you did. So tell me… what did you mean?"

She looks up, examining my face. "You don't want me at all, do you?" she blurts out, tears welling in her eyes again, just like last night. "You had the perfect opportunity to sleep with me, and you chose to sleep on the couch." I can hear the crack in her voice, and I close the gap between us, so our bodies are almost touching.

"Yeah. I chose the couch. Because you were upset… and by the time it came down to it, you were also fast asleep. And, believe me, when I spend the night with you, there won't be any sleeping involved." My voice has dropped to an unexpectedly low note, and I know I've just completely revealed my hand with those few words. But I don't give a damn. The look of rejection in her eyes was too much for me.

She stands her ground, although she's breathing hard now, her eyes still fixed on mine. "D—Do you want me then?"

"Like I wanna breathe." I move my hand up a little, so it's now framing her face, and I use the edge of my thumb to caress her soft cheek. "You think I'm immune to you? You think any guy is immune to you… the way you look? Why the fuck do you think those two guys invited you back to their place? Why do you think one of them was touching you like he did? And why do you think that just about every guy you meet comes on to you whenever you go out at night?"

"I don't know."

"Because no-one is immune to you. I'm no different to any other guy." *Except I love you, and I don't want to be disposable… please, Bree.*

Before she can open her mouth to tell me whether I'm different – because I'm so scared I won't be – I lean in and brush my lips over hers. Not only do I not want to hear her opinion, I need to kiss her, like I'll break apart if I don't. She sighs into me, and I run my tongue along the seam of her mouth, eliciting a slight gasp, which gives me access to delve inward, her tongue greeting mine.

I've never really been into kissing. Certainly not for the last nine or ten years. It implies an intimacy that I don't normally feel. But in this instance, I guess I do, because what we're doing is simply incredible. The sensation of our tongues clashing and her breasts heaving into my chest is perfect. But then she moves her hands, letting them rest on my arms, and for a second, I freeze. I'm not used to this…. not without first giving permission, anyway. And that means, I usually know what to expect. I know precisely where the touch is going to come, because I've authorized it. Except… it feels so good to have Bree's hands on me, I don't care. And although I'm still preoccupied with her lips, and her tongue, I let my mind absorb her caresses too, as she gently strokes her way up my arms, before her hands wander across my shoulders and around my neck, and as I feel that soft touch of her fingertips, I deepen the kiss, letting my own fingers twist into her hair, holding her in place. I press my body against hers, allowing her to feel the hardness and the length of my arousal against her hip, and she gasps once more as I break the kiss and lean back, looking into her eyes, breathless with need.

"Is this what you really want?" I ask, struggling for control, because I have to know this isn't another tease. I have to be certain.

She swallows and nods her head. "Yes…" she breathes.

"Are you sure, Bree? Remember what I told you… I'm a storm. I wasn't kidding when I said that. If I take you to bed, I promise you, there's no turning back."

She tilts her head, looking a little confused. "Why are you telling me this?"

"I'm warning you."

"Why? Is it not safe for me to be with you?"

"There's nowhere safer, baby. I promise you."

She smiles now, and moves her hands again, bringing them between us and resting them on my chest. "In that case... I really want this," she says slowly, enunciating each word with care, and I take her hand, stepping back and leading her across the living area and into my bedroom.

I close the door behind us, although I'm not sure why. It's not like anyone's going to interrupt us. And yet, I feel the need to fence us in... to confine what we're about to do and keep it just to ourselves.

Bree must have opened the drapes earlier, before she came out into the living area, because the sunlight is drifting in through the huge window, lighting up the room... and her beautiful face, as I turn to her and pull her over to the bed, leaning down and kissing her once more, our tongues colliding in an instant this time around. My hands roam around to her back, finding the zipper of her dress, and pulling it downwards, until it stops, just above her hips. Her breathing is a little ragged, but I break our kiss and take a half step back, releasing her dress from her shoulders and then kneeling in front of her to ease it over her hips and down to the floor. She's wearing pale pink underwear, made of very fine lace, and if I look up just slightly, I can see her nipples straining against it. Right in front of me though, is the greatest prize of all, and I place my thumbs in the top of her panties and slowly lower them, helping her to step out, before leaning in to kiss the bare skin at the apex of her thighs.

She sighs deeply, moving her feet apart to give me access, which I take full advantage of, running my tongue along her delicate folds and finding her swollen clit. She jumps and gasps at the intimate contact, and then grabs the back of my head, which is too much for me, so I take her hands from behind me and hold them firmly at her sides, clamping them there with my own, while letting my tongue roam freely over her. I tilt my head upwards, and see that she's looking down at me, her eyes on fire, her mouth open, and I can hear her breathing becoming more and more labored as I flick my tongue across her, back and forth. I keep a tight grip on her hands and maintain eye contact with her, right until she lets out a low moan, which builds to a cry, and then a shattering scream, her eyes finally closing, as she throws her head back in ecstasy. Her legs tremble as she grinds her pussy into my face, desperate for more, and when I know she's right at the very peak of pleasure, I stop, releasing her hands, and I get to my feet. She's beside herself, shuddering, shaking in front of me.

"P—Please…" she mutters. "Please."

"I know, baby… just wait."

I lift her into my arms and lay her down on the bed, pushing the covers aside, before yanking my t-shirt over my head and quickly dropping my jeans. I'm not wearing underwear, because there wasn't any in the laundry room, and Bree's eyes widen, although she doesn't seem capable of speech at the moment, and she's still trembling as I crawl up her body, parting her legs with my own and then pushing them higher still, holding them in place with my hands in the crooks of her knees, keeping her where I want her, completely exposed to me, the head of my cock nudging at her entrance.

She cries out as I penetrate her, and I groan loudly, making a lot more noise than I normally allow myself. But that's because she's so tight… and because it's Bree.

I can't hold back. She's too much. And I've waited too long for this… I slam my cock all the way home… and without warning, she comes again, letting out another high-pitched scream and thrashing her head from side to side. I'm not about to let up though, and even as she's writhing beneath me, I start to move, giving her my entire length with every hard thrust.

Eventually, she calms slightly and looks up at me. "Oh my God, Colt," she says, dragging in a breath between each word, her face flushed, her eyes alight. She's so beautiful, lying here beneath me, her perfect soft body yielding to mine as I keep pounding into her, increasing the pace, taking her harder, and then harder still, my eyes fixed on hers the whole time, sweat forming on my back and chest, until she trembles beneath me again.

"I'm… I'm…" she says incoherently, and then she bursts apart once more, riding high on her third orgasm. I'm still not ready yet though, but as she comes back down, I change position slightly, releasing her legs and capturing her hands instead, holding them beside her head and leaning right over her.

"More?" I growl, my lips maybe an inch from hers.

"I—I can't," she stutters, struggling to breathe.

"Yeah, you can."

She shakes her head and I shift forward, leaning down and capturing a distended nipple between my teeth, giving it a gentle bite, which makes her squeal with pleasure. "Oh… oh, yeah…" she mutters and I bite a little harder, swiveling my hips into her, as she arches her back. "What… what are you doing?"

"Making you come." I glance up at her, and as I do, she shatters for a fourth time… and the look in her eyes is too much for me. My body can't take it and, with a last desperate thrust, I let out a howl of pleasure, eleven years in the making, as I finally pour myself into her…

I feel starved of oxygen, gulping in air and trying to breathe, and eventually, I regain sufficient control to roll us over onto our sides, my hand on her ass, pulling her close to me. She's limp in my arms, and yet she's sufficiently able to move her head and rest it against my chest, inhaling deeply, like she wants to breathe me in… which is nice.

"Are you okay?" It's not a question I'm accustomed to asking. But this time, I really need to know.

She nods her head, and I smile, because for myself, I've never felt better – or happier – in my life. And as long as she's okay too, then this is pretty damn perfect. It's so perfect, I'm tempted to tell her right now that I'm in love with her. But I think I'd rather she were a little more conscious when I do that, so I hold her in my arms for a while, stroking her hair, and letting her recover, keeping us firmly joined, my cock still hard inside her.

I've never done this before. Again, like kissing, it suggests an intimacy which is foreign to me. Because, thinking about it, I've never held a woman after sex at all, not even before I got into the control thing. But as odd as it may seem, I'm actually craving that intimacy with Bree. I certainly have no urge to get up, or to be anywhere else, which is what I'd normally be thinking about now. I feel like I belong here. Right here. And that she belongs right here with me.

Bree doesn't take as long to recover as I might have thought, or hoped, given how comfortable this is, and how happy it makes me, and after maybe fifteen or twenty minutes, she raises her head and looks up at me, with a slightly alarming expression on her face. Where I'd hoped to see a smile, or perhaps an embarrassed twinkle in her eye – given that she's just had four very loud and explosive orgasms – I'm getting a kind of frown, like she's a little confused… or maybe cross. I can't tell. I just know, instinctively, that something's not right.

"What's wrong?" I ask her, moving my hand from the back of her head, where I was stroking her hair, around to her cheek, and letting it rest there.

"I think you might have forgotten about something…"

"Forgotten about something?" I echo. What's she talking about?

The corners of her lips twitch upwards and although I'm still bewildered by her, I don't feel so worried. She's clearly trying not to smile, so whatever it is, it can't be all bad.

"Yeah," she says, nodding her head.

"What did I forget?"

She shakes her head, like she can't believe I don't know the answer, and then takes a breath and whispers, "To use a condom?"

I swear to God, my heart actually stops beating in my chest. "Jesus… I'm sorry. I'm so sorry, Bree." I've never done that before. Ever. I'm the most cautious person I know, and I never take risks… I'm not that stupid. Except it seems, I am. "That's never happened to me before." I give words to my thoughts. "The only excuse I can offer is that being inside you felt so good, I temporarily lost my mind."

She giggles, and I have to smile, despite the potential gravity of the situation, because she's also running her fingers down my arm. Which is very distracting.

"It's fine," she whispers. "I haven't been with anyone since Grady… despite my recent behavior."

I nod my head, ignoring the last part of her comment, because I don't really wanna talk about that. I don't wanna talk about Grady either at the moment, but I guess for the purposes of clearing the air, we have to.

"I've always used protection." I explain my own side of things, insofar as she needs to know. "Except with you."

She smiles again. "So it would seem."

"Are… are you on birth control?" I ask, trying not to sound desperate, while keeping the fear out of my voice. It's not that I wouldn't one day like to have kids with Bree. I'd love to. I just don't particularly want that 'day' to be nine months from now. And I don't want our kids to be accidental. I'm not that kind of guy.

"Yes. I get my shots regularly," she replies, her face clouding over slightly. "I used to take the pill, but I kept forgetting it. At the very beginning, I didn't worry too much because I thought I'd quite like to have a child with Grady. But once his jealousy and possessiveness became the key features of our relationship, I went off the idea… and decided I needed a safer method of contraception." She looks up into my eyes and I do my best to smile, to reassure her that I don't mind hearing about her past, even though I do, especially when I'm still buried deep inside her. Although, that said, I am interested in hearing that she wanted to have kids. Back in the day, when I first fell for her, I used to imagine us getting married and starting a family, straight off. I used to picture us sitting together, cradling our newborn child, so in love with each other and the person we'd created, it almost hurt. Of course, that never happened, and over the years, as her marriage to Grady remained childless, I reached the conclusion that she was more interested in her career than in having a family. But now I know the truth of what her marriage was like, I can understand her motives.

She blinks a few times, and then her smile broadens. "Although, to be honest, I was thinking about calling it quits…" she says, and I realize she's still talking about contraception. "I got a message from my gynecologist the other day, reminding me I needed to make an appointment, and I wondered about not bothering… I couldn't see the point when I didn't have a life… let alone a sex life." She leans up and kisses me. "Still, I guess I'd better keep them going now…"

"Sounds like a wise idea." Sounds like a totally fantastic idea, actually. At least for now. Especially as the fact that she's gonna continue with her shots for the time being implies she wants us to keep doing this… and that thought makes my heart flip over in my chest, just as she licks her lips, in a slow, sexy move, which makes my cock twitch, and she gasps.

"Does that mean you want to go again?" she whispers, her eyes widening.

"Yeah… it does." I grind my hips, and she lets out a low moan of satisfaction, her breath catching for a moment.

"Well, if you think you're up to it," she teases, and my body pulses with need for her… except this is a different need. It's a more familiar need, from my perspective, and I lean in closer to her, lowering my voice.

"I've warned you already, about teasing grown men… you need to be careful, Bree. You never know what kind of trouble you could end up in."

She shudders in my arms. "Hmm… that sounds exciting," she breathes, leaning back a little and looking right into my eyes. Hers are sparkling and kind of inquiring, like she's not sure what I'm saying, but she'd quite like to find out.

"Are you serious?" I ask her, cupping her chin with my hand and holding her tight.

"I don't know," she replies. "Are you?"

"I'm always serious."

I pull out of her, and she winces. "Oh…" There's a definite hint of disappointment in that sound, and I kneel up and flip her over onto her front, which makes her squeal.

I straddle her, trapping her body beneath my own, then bend over on top of her, my chest to her back, my mouth beside her ear.

"Do you wanna do this?" I grind out the words, my body on fire.

"Do what?" She turns her head toward mine so she can speak.

"Everything. Anything. Whatever I tell you to do."

"Whatever you tell me to do?" Her voice is barely audible, although she definitely sounds kinda shocked, and I wonder if I've gone too far… if I'm gonna regret letting my need get the better of me. Still, I can't back down now.

"Yeah."

"You… you mean you want me to submit to you?"

I smile, even though she can't see me. "That's exactly what I want."

There's a pause, which is just about long enough for me to start panicking, before she gives a minute nod of her head.

"Is that a 'yes'?" I whisper, the words catching in my throat.

"Yes." I let out a sigh, as she adds, "Sir."

"Don't call me 'sir'. And don't think about calling me 'master' either, in case that thought had crossed your mind."

"Okay," she says softly, although she doesn't ask what she should call me, which is good, because frankly, as long as it's not 'sir', or 'master'… or 'Jack'… I don't care.

"Are you ready?" I ask her, unable to wait any longer.

"Um… I guess so." She's got no idea what's coming, and that thought seriously turns me on.

"Put your arms straight out to your sides." She does as I say, without question, so she's spread before me… sacrificial. "And keep them there," I add. She nods her head, breathing hard, and I move backwards, down the bed, running my fingertip very slowly along the length of her spine. She shudders to my touch, and then moans, when I reach the top of her buttocks… her moan getting louder as I move lower still and let my finger rest for a second over her tightly puckered anus. I'm not gonna loiter there for now. I can come back later… but it's good to know she doesn't seem averse to the idea.

I squeeze her buttocks gently, and then, placing my hands on her hips, I raise them from the mattress and move into position behind her, nudging her legs apart with my own, and placing my dick at her entrance.

I pause, just for a second, giving her time to take a breath, and then I ram my cock into her at the same time as I raise my hand and bring it down hard on her ass cheek.

She screams, a low, throaty, guttural scream… and comes hard, rocking back onto my dick, her whole body shaking. "Yes… yes… yes…" she hisses between her teeth, as I spank her again, and again… her delicate skin pinking already. I lean over her and reach around, rolling her nipples between my thumbs and forefingers, and then giving them a firm pinch, which adds an edge to her climax, and she yells my name at the top of her voice.

I don't relent until her breathing calms, when I straighten, and then pull out of her, shifting back just slightly, so there's no contact between us at all. She groans in disappointment.

"Move your arms down by your sides," I tell her and she does, without question, allowing me to flip her over again, onto her back. Her hair is all over the place, and I lean forward and push it aside, revealing her flushed cheeks and glazed eyes, gazing up at me.

"Please don't stop," she whispers, and bites her bottom lip. And while a tiny part of my brain can't help recalling that I'd have frozen out a sub who spoke to me like that, I'm not worried by Bree's words… because she's not a sub. And because she's Bree.

"I've got no intention of stopping."

I move to the edge of the bed and get up, walking over to the closet in the corner of the room, and opening the left-hand door, I take the black rope down from the hook inside, and turn to face her. She's leaning up on one elbow, looking at me, and when she spots what I'm holding, her eyes widen in surprise.

"Oh, my God," she says. "You're really serious, aren't you?"

I walk back toward her, standing by the side of the bed, untying the rope and playing it between my hands. "Yeah. I told you. I'm always serious." Gazing down at her body, her nipples still erect, her pussy lips swollen and glistening, I already know how much more I can do with her. But I wonder now if she might be having second thoughts about this… whether she's as serious as I am. "Do you remember I said that if I brought you to bed, there would be no turning back?" She nods her head. "Well, I'm gonna give you one last chance…"

"To do what?" she whispers.

"To turn back. If you don't think you can handle this… if it isn't what you want, say so now."

She tips her head to one side, and then turns over onto her front, getting onto all fours, and crawling over to me, looking sexy as hell in the process. She kneels back, and then looks up into my eyes, and before I can stop her, she reaches out and grabs my cock. I can barely control my reaction to being touched so intimately, but I don't have the chance to respond.

"I don't want to turn back, Colt," she murmurs, her eyes holding mine. "I want you to show me everything you can do."

My heart bursts in my chest, because in all my wildest dreams, I don't think I ever imagined a moment quite like this.

"Sure?" I say, because I have to know, and she nods her head. I lean over, my face right in front of hers, our lips almost touching. "Then let go of my dick and put your hands out in front of you."

She sucks in a breath, and does as I say, offering me her hands, like I'm about to handcuff her, which I'm not. Not right now, anyway. Instead, I adjust her position slightly, and then tie her wrists together, binding them tight, but not too tight. I don't want to hurt her, or mark her. When I'm ready, I lift her back over to the middle of the bed, laying her down, her head on the pillows.

"Arms above your head."

She obeys, breathing hard, and I kneel beside her and tie her to the cast iron bedstead. I've never done this before. Not here, in my own bedroom, anyway. And I'm glad now that I chose this style of bed frame. Not only do I like how it looks, but it's eminently practical. At least, it is for me.

Once I'm sure she's secure, I place my hands on her hips and pull her body down the bed slightly, so her back is arched, and then I lean forward and lick her nipples, one at a time. She arches even further into me, desperate for the contact, her body crying out for more, as my fingers work their way down across her taut stomach, seeking out her swollen lips, and I delve inward. She parts her legs wide, and then wider still as I push two fingers inside her, using my thumb to circle her clit, listening to her breathing, and bringing her to the edge of her climax, before I slow my movements, and then stop them altogether, even though she's bucking her hips, raising them into me.

"Please," she whimpers, and I look down at her pleading, beautiful face. "Please, Colt."

"Give it time, baby." I've never called any other woman that before, but this is the third or fourth time I've said that word to Bree, and I like it. It feels right.

"How much time?"

"As long as it takes."

I move my fingers again, keeping a close eye on her, watching for the changes in her movements and breathing, the hardening of her nipples, the goosebumps on her skin, the change in skin tone around her neck… the way her body responds… and I stop again, just as she climbs towards the precipice… right before she falls.

"Colt…" she cries, raising her hips right off the bed in frustration. "Why are you doing this to me?"

"Because I can."

She takes a deep breath, calming herself. "Is… is this some kind of punishment… for what I did the other night, or for what I said to you at the office?"

I pull my fingers from her and straddle her, leaning over so our faces are barely an inch apart.

"No," I say firmly. "I'm not into punishment. Everything I do is about pleasure."

"But you were angry with me, weren't you?" She gazes up into my eyes, her own giving away her confusion, while her need takes a back seat for a moment.

I thought we'd covered this already. "Yes. Very. But I told you last night. I'm not angry anymore. And what I'm doing to you now, has nothing to do with any of that… and it has nothing to do with punishment."

"Then why won't you let me come? Why are you stopping me from…"

"This isn't orgasm denial," I interrupt, although I'm not sure she'll have heard the phrase before.

"Then what is it? Because it sure as hell feels like you're denying me my orgasm."

I smile inwardly. "It's called edging." I'm not used to having to explain myself, or what I'm doing, but actually, it's quite refreshing… or it is with Bree.

"Edging?" She frowns, looking confused again.

"Yeah… as in, keeping you on the edge. You can do it yourself, if you masturbate."

"Why? Why would I want to?"

"Why would you want to masturbate?" I tease.

She smiles, and I feel relieved that at least I haven't scared her off completely. "No, silly," she says. "Why would I want to stay on the edge, rather than just coming?"

I smile myself, not worrying that she can see me doing so, because I love her curiosity, almost as much as I love her. It's stimulating… invigorating.

"Because, when you do come… it'll blow your mind," I whisper, letting my lips brush across hers.

She arches her back and sighs into me. "Will it?" she says.

"Yeah. I guarantee it." She relaxes beneath me, and I shift, kneeling beside her again. "Now… can we get back to where we were?" I ask, accommodating her uncertainty. I wouldn't normally. I wouldn't tolerate it in anyone else. But with Bree, I don't mind.

I don't mind at all.

Chapter Eight

Bree

I never thought it was possible to feel so much.

Every single nerve in my body is crying out with need for him, and all of them at completely different levels... different pitches. He has total control of me, playing me like a musical instrument, and he's a master at what he does... although he told me not to call him 'master', and I've remembered not to, despite the fact that his expertise is unsurpassed, I'm sure. Because I can't imagine there's another man alive, who could make a body sing like he does.

He's been manipulating me, or rather my body, almost non-stop, since yesterday morning, when he first told me he wanted me, like he wanted to breathe, which shocked the hell out of me, being as he'd chosen to sleep on the couch, rather than sharing a bed with me. But then he checked, and he double checked, that going to bed with him was what I really wanted... and it was. Because I was about as turned on by him as I've ever been in my life. Not that I knew what to expect... and even if I had, I wouldn't have done anything different, because the last twenty-four hours have been the most exciting of my life.

When Colt initially suggested I submit to him, right after we'd made love for the first time, I'll admit, I wasn't entirely sure what I was letting myself in for. I've heard of Dominant/submissive relationships, but not in any great detail. Although the overriding thought in my head at the time was the memory of his words, and the look on his face, when he'd said he wanted to put me over his knee and spank me… and how that had made me feel. I felt exactly the same when he said he wanted me to do whatever he told me to do. In a strange way, that felt really liberating. And it has been. For the last twenty-four hours, I've been freed of even having to think. I've just had to *be*… to breathe in and out, to eat when my body needs to, to sleep when I'm tired, and above all, to feel and be pleasured. Repeatedly.

It's been an intense and beautiful experience, and at no time have I felt used by him, because his sole focus during every moment has been to please me. Even yesterday morning, when he was deliberately making me wait – 'edging', as he called it – keeping me right on the verge of an orgasm for nearly an hour, the sensation was intensely satisfying… once I understood what it was all about, anyway. Once I knew he wasn't trying to punish me for my appalling behavior of the previous few days, and that all he wanted was to heighten my enjoyment… I relaxed into his expert touch, stopped trying to fight it, and gave him complete control.

And he was right. When he did finally give me my release, it was so intense, and went on for so long, it was more than I could handle. And when it finally started to subside, I cried… I burst into floods of tears, which I needed, just to free myself of the pent-up emotions. Within seconds, Colt untied the rope that was binding me to the bed, and held me in his arms, close to his chest. He didn't ask me to explain my tears, which is just as well, because I'm not sure I could have done. But when I'd calmed a little, he leaned back and said, "Are you okay, baby?" and I nodded my head, smiling, because I wanted to reassure him, and because I liked the fact that he's started calling me that. It sounds strange coming from the lips of a man who's spent so many years ignoring me, and yet it's oddly comforting at the same time.

I've spent all of my time since yesterday morning in his bedroom, not needing to venture out into the rest of his apartment, which I have to say surprised me with its stylishness. I hadn't realized until I came here that Colt lived in such a beautiful place. And while I know I've been here before, I was drunk then, and not concentrating on my surroundings.

He has a loft apartment, which is enormous, with ceilings that must be twenty feet high in the living area, all of which is in one enormous space. The decor is simple; the walls being white, other than the one which faces you as you enter the apartment, the one which has the vast windows set into it. That's made of red bricks. It gives the space an industrial feeling, but that seems to suit Colt. I didn't really have time to notice his furniture, other than that it featured quite a bit of glass and metal… and that his couch was black leather, and his kitchen was dark gray… a theme which is continued in here, in his bedroom. This is a smaller, more contained room, with pale gray walls, and the same wooden floors as there are throughout the rest of the apartment. All along the wall opposite the window is a series of closets, with black doors, and it's the one on the left-hand side, which seems to house the equipment which Colt uses on me, with spectacular results.

I haven't felt like a prisoner here, though. I simply haven't wanted to leave. We've eaten, not necessarily at regular times, but whenever one or other of us has felt the need; Colt either ordering in, or fixing us something quick, and bringing it into the bedroom for us to share. He's made sure I'm comfortable, and that I have everything I need and want, at all times. In fact, he's surprised me by how attentive he can be, considering how dominant he is… and he really is…

No more so than when we showered together last night.

I'd asked if I could take a shower in his bathroom, not long after we'd finished our Chinese takeout, and he looked down at me and said, "No," firmly.

"Excuse me?" I sat up slightly. I couldn't believe he was going to deny me a shower and was about to argue with him that I'd only ceded control of my body, not my bodily functions.

"*You* can't take a shower," he said, his eyes roaming over my naked body. "But *we* can."

I smiled then, and he got up, pulling me from the bed and onto my feet.

"Wait there," he ordered, and I stood still, wondering what he had in mind, feeling the heat rising in my body again, even though we'd spent the entire afternoon swathed in pleasure.

I watched him stroll across to the closet in the corner. He'd left the door open, having been over there several times – most lately, about an hour or two before dinner, for a very soft leather blindfold, which he fitted around the back of my head, making sure I couldn't see anything. He'd then laid me down on the bed, on my back, my body humming in anticipation, until I'd felt a soft, feathery touch on my skin, directly on my breasts. I asked Colt what it was, and he told me it was a tickler… which seemed appropriate… and while he played it across my nipples, he let his fingers work their magic on my clit, until I came. Really hard.

This time, however, he returned with two leather cuffs in one hand and a chain in the other.

"What are you doing with those?" I asked him.

"You'll see. Hold out your hands."

I did as he said, offering my outstretched hands to him, and he stood in front of me, his eyes boring into mine, knowing I think, that I was placing my trust, as well as my hands, in his care. He took that very seriously too… like everything else, and even as he strapped one cuff to my wrist, he ran a finger around the inside, to check it wasn't too tight.

"Comfortable?" he asked, as he started on the other side.

"Yes."

"Good." He smiled, and finished fastening the other buckle, before taking the chain and hooking the clips at either end into the eyes, which were on the insides of the cuffs. Once he was satisfied they were secure, he stepped back. "Ready?" he asked.

"I guess so." I wasn't sure what I was ready for, but my body was trembling with need, and he took one of my hands and led me into his adjoining bathroom, flicking on the light, and proceeding directly into the shower, which I remembered from the other night… when I'd accosted him in here, and he'd rejected me. I wondered for a minute about the wisdom of this idea… whether it might bring back unhappy memories, but he turned to me.

"Don't think about the past," he said, like he could read my mind. "It doesn't matter anymore."

"Okay." I didn't bother to inquire what he was talking about. We both knew the answer to that… and neither of us wanted to remember that night. He was right. The past didn't matter. It was the present that was important.

He smiled at me again, and then turned, switching on the water and testing the temperature.

"Is that okay?" he asked, and I reached out with my hands.

"It's a little hot for me," I said and he adjusted it.

"Now?" he said, and I tried it again.

"That's fine."

He nodded and then reached up, pulling his facecloth from the hook to the right of the shower head and dropping it to the floor, before he turned and pushed me backwards, until I felt the cold tiles hit my back. He took my hands then, and pulled them up and over my head, drawing them upwards further still, until he'd hitched the chain over the hook. I had a little movement, a little give in my arms, but I was fastened there, nonetheless.

"Okay?" he asked.

"Yes," I breathed, the water cascading over my sensitized skin, my nipples hardening, as he looked down at me, the hunger building in his eyes.

"Good," he said and dropped to his knees, moving my legs and parting my folds with his fingers, before running his tongue across my clit.

"Oh… yes." I bucked against him, and he stopped and looked up at me.

"Hold still."

"Are you serious?"

"Always." He stared and waited.

"I'll be still," I said.

"Good."

He leaned in and let his tongue roam over me again. It was all I could do not to flex my hips, but I did the best I could, while he held onto me, working over me, harder and harder, until… "Oh God… I'm coming…" I screamed as my orgasm peaked without warning. It didn't build or crescendo… it just hit the summit and I crashed, pulling on my restraints, my body crumbling as Colt held me up. "Please… please,"

I whimpered into him, my head tipping forward, and he knew what that meant. I may have just hit another new high, but I needed more.

He stood and lifted me off the ground, relieving me of the weight of my own body, hooking my legs over his arms, and entering me... hard.

I sucked in a huge breath at the feeling of being so stretched, and so deeply penetrated, and he stopped, absolutely still.

"Take me, baby," he breathed. "Take all of me."

I nodded my head, looking up into his eyes. "Yes," I whispered, because I wanted to feel all of him, more than anything, and he started to move, burying himself deep inside me with every thrust of his hips. "Oh, God..." My head rocked forward onto his shoulder. I longed to cling to him, even though I loved being bound and taken.

"Look at me," he said, and I raised my head again, seeing the intensity in those deep dark eyes of his. "I wanna watch you come. I wanna see it in your eyes."

He increased the pace, every muscle in his shoulders, arms and chest tensing and flexing as he moved, the water pouring over his perfect body as he powered into me, until eventually I could take no more and I threw my head back, crying out.

"Look at me!" he roared. So I did. And I saw something fierce, yet beautiful reflected back at me, as he howled out my name and exploded deep inside me, my orgasm still wracking through my body, while we watched each other, locked together in that moment.

It hasn't all been about restraints and orders.

After our shower, we slept for hours. I suppose that's not surprising, considering how much sex we had yesterday, but this morning, he's woken me with breakfast in bed... another surprisingly considerate thing for him to have done, I can't help thinking.

I stretch my arms above my head, looking down at the tray of toast and coffee he's set down beside me.

"Do you always do things like this?" I ask, looking at his magnificent body as he climbs back into bed again, lying on his side, his legs crossed at the ankles. I'm covered by the sheet, but he's exposed… naked… and quite awe-inspiring.

"Like what?" he asks.

"Bring your women breakfast in bed?" I'm teasing… and maybe fishing. Just a little.

"No," he replies simply, a slight frown settling on his face as he picks up the cup of coffee that's closest to him, taking a sip. *God, he's such a closed book.*

"So this isn't normal behavior for you?"

He looks across the top of his cup, his frown deepening.

"No, it's not."

He offers me a slice of toast, making it clear he's not about to elaborate, and I'm not sure how to ask anything more, without it looking obvious that I'm interested in finding out about him. At least, I think I am. Although I'm not sure why that is. I guess I'm just intrigued by him… maybe because he's so private… and possibly also because I feel like I've told him so much about myself, and yet, even though I've known him nearly all my life, I know almost nothing about him, other than the fact that he takes sex to levels I didn't even know existed.

"Are you used to having breakfast in bed?" he asks.

"No… but why is it you're allowed to ask questions, and I'm not?"

He frowns again. "Who said you couldn't ask questions?"

"You did."

"When?" He takes a bite of toast, staring at me.

"Just now… not in as many words, but you wouldn't answer me. You shut me down."

"No, I didn't. I answered you."

"The word 'No' is not an answer, Colt."

I nibble on my own toast, aware he's staring at me. "Okay. So, what do you wanna know?" he says eventually, putting me on the spot.

I can't think what to say now, so I just mumble, "I—I don't know."

"Okay. Well… if you think of anything else you wanna ask me, then just go right ahead and ask."

I nod my head, but decide to leave it for now. I think I've already embarrassed myself enough for one morning, so I take a sip of coffee and eat my toast instead.

Once we're finished, Colt moves the tray to one side and stands up, coming around to my side of the bed, towering over me. "Shower?" he says, holding out his hand.

"Is that an instruction, or a request?" I turn over to face him, the sheet slipping down to reveal my breasts, and I don't bother to cover them again.

He lets his eyes roam downwards, and mutters, "A request."

I throw back the sheet and sit up on the side of the bed. "In that case, I accept."

He smiles. "And if it had been an instruction?"

I stand now and look up at him, grinning. "I'd still have accepted."

He takes my hand and turns me, spinning me around, and slaps his hand across my ass, none too gently. I gasp and sigh, relishing the bite of his touch, as he pulls me into his bathroom and straight into the shower.

I wonder what he's got in store for me this morning, and am surprised when he turns on the water and reaches for the soap, lathering up his hands, before he starts to wash me.

His touch is light, sensuous, and I lean back against the tiled wall for support as he slowly caresses he way down my body, kneeling before me to pay close attention to the area between my legs, his fingers sliding between my folds, intimately.

I'm breathing hard, and within moments, I'm on the brink, but he stops what he's doing and focuses on my thighs and then my shins.

"Are you doing that edging thing again?" I ask, looking down at him.

He raises his face to mine and smiles. "No. I'm washing you." He reaches for the soap again, although he keeps his eyes fixed on mine and says, "Turn around."

I do as he says, using my hands to brace myself against the wall as he works his way back up, pausing at my ass cheeks, squeezing them gently, and letting his soapy fingers delve, and brush over my anus. He did this yesterday morning, and although it was unexpected at the time, I have to say, I liked the sensations it created in my body, which are heightened today, because his fingers are slippery with soap and are sliding over me, circling and insinuating what might be... if only... He

154

moves his hands up again onto my hips and it's only then that I realize how tense I am; how I'm really struggling to breathe, every muscle in my body rigid with anticipation and need. I've never thought about being taken there before… and although Colt is huge, the idea of having him inside me, in that forbidden place, is driving me insane.

As he stands, his hands massaging over my shoulders, I turn around to face him, unable to take anymore.

"I—I…" I stutter.

"I know," he says, and he leans in and kisses me, his lips barely a whisper against my own, before he pulls back and looks down at me. "I'm gonna wash your hair now."

"You are?" *Is that before, or after, you tease me to death?*

"Yeah." He smiles and puts his hands on my arms, moving me directly under the shower, so the soap slides from my body, and he works his fingers through my hair, then reaches for his shampoo.

Standing behind me, he does a truly expert job of lathering up my hair, and then rinsing it, making sure all the suds are completely washed away, before turning me around and taking my hand, pulling me from the cascading water, and grabbing a towel from the shelf, wrapping it around me.

"You've definitely done that before," I say, looking up at him.

"Done what?" he asks, tucking the towel in above my breasts.

"Washed a woman's hair."

He pauses for a moment and then says, "Yeah, I have."

"So you don't bring your women breakfast in bed, but you do shower with them," I muse out loud and he shakes his head.

"I didn't say that, did I?" He frowns.

"Well, no…"

He steps a little closer. "I've never showered with anyone before… but when my mom was sick, I used to wash her hair. It always made her feel better."

Oh, God… "I'm sorry, Colt… I…" I don't know what to say.

"It's okay." He notices my discomfort and smiles. "Go and get dry," he says, nodding toward the bedroom.

"I could stay and wash you, if you like?" I suggest.

"No…"

I turn away, feeling a little rejected, wondering if I've spoiled the moment for him. "Is there a reason for that?" I ask, turning back, because I need to know.

"No." He smiles again. "Well… other than the minor detail that if you wash me, I'm gonna end up fucking you in here again… probably even harder than I did last night." I let out a sigh of relief and hesitate in the doorway while I contemplate taking him up on his offer. But he shakes his head, his eyes dark. "I've got something else in mind," he says firmly. "Give me ten minutes."

I know I've been dismissed, but that dark intensity in his eyes speaks of something promising to come, so I don't mind in the slightest, and I wander back into the bedroom, my body buzzing with anticipation.

I sit on the bed, thinking about Colt's comment about his mom. I was only a child when she died… around nine or ten years old, and I don't really remember it happening. It's not something he's ever talked to me about before… but then he's never really talked to me at all. Until now. And while he still feels kinda closed off, I can't deny we have talked in the last twenty-four hours. Occasionally. In between the sex. I smile, while I pat the towel over my skin, recalling all the things we've done since yesterday morning, and wondering what he's got planned for me next as the heat in my body rises again. I find it hard to believe there are other ways in which he could pleasure me, but I'm willing to find out… to be educated.

As good as his word, Colt appears in the bathroom doorway in less than ten minutes, I'd have said. He's got a towel wrapped low around his hips, droplets of water sliding down his toned hairless chest toward that 'V' that leads down to…

"Kneel on the bed," he says firmly and I know without asking that this time it's not a request, and I do as he says, getting to my feet first and unwrapping the towel, letting it fall to the floor. His eyes graze over me hungrily, before I turn and kneel on the bed, crawling over the mattress a little so I'm facing the pillows, before I settle down, my ass in the air. I hear his slight groan and can't help the smile that touches my lips, even though he can't see me from here. And then I'm aware of him walking away and I look up, twisting my head around to see that he's over by the closet, reaching inside. He turns and looks at me, and I know I'm frowning at him.

"What on earth is that?" I take in the long black pole in his hand, with what appear to be two cuffs at either end, similar to the ones he used on my wrists in the shower last night.

"It's called a spreader bar."

"And what does it spread?"

He comes back over, standing beside the bed, and looking down at me. "You," he whispers, and pulls the towel away from his hips, revealing his enormous erection, standing proud from his body, and I suck in a breath of anticipation, as he puts down the pole and raises his other hand. I hadn't even noticed he was carrying anything else, but he is… and it's a length of rope, which he uses to tie me to the bedstead, my hands bound at the wrists, and then fastened to the metal fixtures. He double checks his knots before clambering off the bed, taking the pole with him, and I feel the weight of him as he shifts onto the mattress behind me.

Placing his hands on my hips, he shifts my position slightly, so my knees are a little closer to the head of the bed and I tingle at the sensation of his skin against mine as he then nudges my legs apart with his own, and I try to edge back into him… to have him where I want him… where I need him. But then he moves away, and I can't feel him anymore, and I let out a sigh of regret, even as I feel him place the pole beneath my feet, before he wraps the cuffs around my ankles, adjusting the position of my legs to get them to fit.

"I'm gonna move your legs apart," he says, once I'm secured in place.

"You are?"

"Yeah. You need to take your weight on your arms." I do as he says, leaning down on my elbows, because the rope by which I'm bound to the bed won't allow me to lean on my hands. I can't see exactly what he's doing, but suddenly, he lifts me up from the bed using the pole as a brace and then, I feel a sharp movement and my already parted feet are shifted even further away from each other, by maybe eighteen inches, so my legs are spread wide, before he deposits me back on the mattress. It feels glorious to be restrained like this, unable to move, and completely open to him, to do with as he pleases… and my body pulses with expectation for whatever Colt has in mind, because it already feels amazing, and I know it's only going to get better.

I'm aware of him getting off of the bed and walking away, but by the time I've turned my head, he's already on his way back from the closet, and I can't see clearly what he's holding. Whatever it is, he puts it down on the bed, and then I feel the mattress dip as he kneels back on it again, behind me once more. I feel him lean over my body, his chest against my back.

"This is gonna be intense, baby," he says, which in itself feels pretty damn intense. "If it gets too much for you, just tell me to stop, and I promise, no matter what, I'll stop. Okay?"

"Okay." I feel a moment of doubt creeping over me, and as he goes to straighten again, I halt him, saying his name.

"What?" he says, leaning forward. "What's wrong?"

"Nothing… I—I just need to be sure of something…"

"What's that?"

"You're not gonna hurt me, are you?" I'm not sure why I suddenly feel the need to ask that, given everything he's already done, and that it's all been about pleasure, and that my body is crying out for his touch. But this feels different. Maybe it's because he felt the need to warn me… I don't know.

He straightens, and then I feel him move around, so he's kneeling beside me and I turn my head, looking up into his dark brown eyes. "I'll never hurt you," he whispers, reaching out and caressing my cheek with the back of his finger. "The intensity I'm talking about will be pleasure… not pain. And I'm only telling you about it in advance because I won't be able to see your face, which makes it harder for me to tell when you're getting near your limits. You're gonna have to communicate with me, if you need me to stop. Okay?"

"Okay." I mean it this time, and he obviously knows that, because he moves away and settles back into position behind me.

I hear what sounds like the opening of a shampoo bottle.

"What's that?" I ask.

"It's lubricant."

"Lubricant?"

"Yeah… don't worry about it."

I remain still, because I don't have any option, and wait until I feel his fingers… two of them, brushing over my exposed anus. They feel cool and slippery, which I guess is what the lubricant is all about, and my body tightens in anticipation again, just as he withdraws his touch.

"Oh…" I can't help the disappointed sigh that escapes my lips.

"Wait," he whispers behind me, and then I feel something cold and hard pressing against me. This definitely isn't his fingers, and as he gently pushes it into my tight opening, I let out a yelp.

"What the hell is that?"

"It's a butt plug." I feel the hard, cold thing being withdrawn from me, not that it was really in me, then Colt moves again, coming around beside me and lying down on his side, our faces only a few inches apart. "Look," he says.

"It's smaller than it feels," I muse, studying the shiny metal object in his hand. It's tapered at both ends, although the one that Colt's holding has a wider kind of handle, into which is set a jewel – like a diamond.

"Please tell me that bit doesn't go inside me?"

"Which bit?" he asks.

"The bit you're holding onto."

He chuckles. "No. That stays on the outside… and it's gonna make your ass looking fucking incredible."

"So… so the rest of it goes inside me?"

"Yes."

"And how many other women have you used this on… before me?" I'm not sure I like the idea of having something inside me… *there*… that's been inside someone else.

"None," he replies without hesitation.

"Really? You expect me to believe you've never done this before?"

"No. Because that's not what I said. I said I'd never used this particular butt plug before. And I haven't. This one is for beginners… I'm used to being with women who are more experienced at this kind of thing, Bree. But you can work your way up to something… more substantial, if you want."

I feel that heat in my body flare, moisture pooling between my legs. "Okay," I whisper. "But if I do… you're buying me new ones."

He chuckles again and leans in, kissing my cheek. "Deal," he says, and gets up again.

I feel him behind me once more and, this time, I'm more prepared for the feeling of the butt plug against my ass, as he pushes it against my tight hole.

"Relax, baby," he murmurs. "Breathe…"

I let out a long breath, and as I do, he pushes a little harder, and I feel a stretch, which kinda hurts a little, but feels too good to worry about, and then the plug just seems to pop inside me.

"Okay?" he asks, stroking his hands over my ass.

"Hmm…" I moan, relishing the divine feeling of fullness. The sensation of his touch is electrifying… but I want more. It seems I always want more… and it seems he knows that too, and before I can say a word, I feel his left hand on my shoulder, at the same time as his erection settles against my entrance, and I suck in another breath, as he flexes his hips, giving me his entire length, at exactly the same moment as he brings his right palm down in a hard slap across my ass cheek.

"Yes!" I scream, and without any warning, I come apart, that tension in my body releasing into the most almighty orgasm, as he pounds into me. The feeling of fullness, between him and the butt plug is almost too much, and my brain kind of switches off, even as the intense pleasure of it all breaks through my body, leaving me breathless and gasping for air.

Even then, Colt doesn't stop. Instead, he gives the butt plug a couple of twists inside me, and although I need to calm, to let my brain re-awaken, to assimilate this latest pleasure, my body just won't obey and I fall, yet again, into another shattering orgasm. I can feel the word, 'stop', on my lips, but I can't say it. Because I never want him to stop. I want this to go on forever… and ever. And yes… I still want more.

"T—Two minutes." I stammer out the words as my mind comes back into focus. "Just give me two minutes."

"No," he says firmly, his right palm coming down hard on my ass cheek a second time. "Again."

"I—I can't."

"Yeah, you can." I feel the sting of yet another spank, his cock pounding even deeper inside me. "Come for me… now!" he bellows, as he tightens his grip on my shoulder, his voice ringing around the room.

I obey… convulsing around him, and I scream, my body shuddering violently, mighty spasms rocking through me, just as I become aware of Colt's own howling voice, echoing in my ears, and the feeling of his release inside me… and I still can't stop the shaking of my limbs, or the contraction of my muscles, or the tingling pleasure that lingers in every fiber of my being. It feels like it really is never gonna end, even though Colt has pulled out of me, gently removing the butt plug at the same time, and has freed my feet, before untying my hands, his fingers working quickly… it still won't stop and I look up into his eyes as he turns me onto my side and pulls me into his arms.

"W—What's…" I falter, my body still twitching as I try to make sense of what's going on.

"It's okay, baby," he whispers, stroking my hair and rubbing my back, which just makes me shudder even more.

"I—It won't stop."

"It will. Try to breathe." I gaze into his eyes and stutter in a breath as he nods his head. "That's it, baby," he says soothingly. "Just relax."

Slowly, my orgasm subsides, and my breathing returns to something approaching normal, although my brain is still struggling with what's just happened to me.

"Why didn't you stop?" I ask him, because that's the only thing I can think of saying.

He frowns, leaning back a little, although he still keeps his eyes fixed on mine. "When?"

"When I asked you to."

"When did you ask me to stop?"

"I asked you to give me two minutes." I'm sure I did. I can't have imagined that.

He sucks in a breath, letting it out slowly. "I know," he says, "but that's not the same as asking me to stop… and besides, pausing then would have spoiled everything."

"Spoiled everything?"

"Yeah. The whole point of this was just to keep you coming… and coming… and coming." He brushes a fingertip down my cheek. "I wasn't sure you'd even be able to do it, until you came straight away the second time, but to stop then would have ruined it. Because I knew the next orgasm would blow your mind."

"It certainly did that." I tilt my head at him. "But I still don't understand… you said you'd stop."

"Yeah… and I would've done, even then… even though I wanted to get you to that third orgasm so much. I still would've stopped… if you'd actually said the word 'stop'. But you didn't. You've gotta remember the instructions, Bree. They're important."

"I'm starting to get that now."

He smiles and moves a little closer, wrapping his leg around me. "Did it feel good?" he asks.

"Good doesn't even begin to cover it. Life changing might be nearer."

His smile widens. "So it was worth not stopping for then?"

"Yes… although it was kinda scary, too. I honestly thought that last one was never gonna end. It felt like it went on for hours."

He chuckles. "Would you be surprised if I told you it was only about a minute and a half… which is pretty impressive in itself, I've gotta say."

"A minute and a half? Really? Is that all?"

"All? Most women are lucky if their orgasms last ten to twenty seconds." He smiles at me. "Although it probably felt like longer than that to you, because you'd gone from one, straight into another… and then another."

"Courtesy of you… yes." I let out a sigh, suddenly overwhelmed with tiredness, and I snuggle down into him as he pulls me closer, and I fall into a deep sleep.

I wake with a start.

"What time is it?" I look at Colt, who's still holding me close against his chest.

"I've got no idea," he says, turning over to check the clock on the nightstand, before looking back at me. "It's three-thirty."

"In the afternoon?"

"Yeah." He smiles. "Why?"

"I've been asleep for hours."

"I know."

"And you stayed here with me, all this time?" I'm surprised.

"Of course. Where else was I gonna go?"

"I don't know… but…"

"But what?" he asks, pulling me back into him again, even as I try to lean back.

"I hadn't realized it was so late. I was planning on going home at lunchtime… but I seem to have slept right through it."

His face falls. "Going home? Do you have to?"

"Yeah. I think I do. I need to get some laundry done before the morning."

He leans back himself now. "Oh… okay."

"Do you mind if I have a quick shower before I go?" I ask him, and he nods his head.

"Sure… I'd offer to come and help you, but it's probably not a good idea…" His voice fades, although his eyes are alight, and I have to ask… I have to tease. I can't help myself.

"Why's that?" I run my fingertip down the center of his chest.

He grabs my hand, holding it tight. "Because I'd be really tempted to tie you up in there, so I could keep you here… and then, once I'd got you restrained, I think I'd wanna see how many different ways I can make you come."

"You mean there are more?" I whisper, and he nods his head, smiling.

I let out a low groan, and he releases my hand, lowering his own and giving me a gentle slap on my ass.

"Now stop teasing and go shower… before I decide to tie you up again, anyway."

I giggle at the thought as I twist away from him and clamber off of the bed, padding my way into his bathroom. I don't need to wash my hair, and make fairly short work of washing my body, using Colt's soap, and trying hard not to recall how it felt when he did this earlier, how turned on I was by his gentle touch, especially now I know what he was planning at the time… and how good it felt.

Stepping out, I wrap myself in a towel, and walk back into his bedroom, where I find him, picking up a length of rope from the floor, and coiling it around his arm.

"We've made quite a mess," I remark, looking at the state of his floor, where we've dropped our clothes and towels, as well as ropes and cuffs, and the bottle of lubricant, which is lying on its side.

"Yeah." He looks over and smiles. "I thought I'd just pack everything away… being as you're leaving." His smile fades slightly and he wanders over to the closet and puts the rope inside, before turning back to me. "Although I'm thinking about getting rid of it all."

I stare at him. "G—Getting rid of it? Why? What did I do?"

He looks up, seemingly surprised by my statement. "You didn't do anything… well, except make that remark about the butt plug."

"What remark?"

"The one earlier… when you asked if I'd used it on anyone else, before you."

"And? Why does that mean you have to get rid of your equipment?"

"Because it made me realize that I'd kinda like to have some new *equipment*, that's just for us."

He emphasizes the word 'equipment' and I wonder if I used the wrong phrase, not that I know what the right phrase would be. And at the moment, I'm not sure I care, because I'm busy focusing on the last three words he said. What does he mean, 'just for us'? That sounds kinda permanent, especially when coupled with the idea of him getting rid of everything in his secret closet… like he sees me as some kind of fresh start. And that all feels a bit too full-on for me. We've had fun. We've had a lot of fun. But I'm not sure where I want this to go. I haven't even had time to think about that yet. He's filled my mind and my body with too many other new experiences for me to even consider what else we might become. So, rather than dealing with that thought, I sit on the edge of the bed and decide to change the subject.

"Are you always like this?"

"Like what?" he asks, coming to sit beside me.

"A control freak."

"I'm not a control freak."

I chuckle. "Really? What would you call yourself then?"

"A man who knows what he likes," he replies.

"And have you ever liked having normal sex? Sex without the equipment, I mean?"

"Yeah… I really liked it, yesterday morning… with you." His voice drops a note or two, and he leans into me. I glance up into his dark eyes and, despite my misgivings that we may not be on the same page here, I can't help thinking about how easy it would be to stay for another hour or two… or three. Or more.

"Do you consider holding me down and bending me in half 'normal'?" I ask, to focus on our conversation, rather than what I know he can do to me… or anything else, for that matter.

"Did it feel good?" he counters.

"Yes."

"Then who cares if it was normal?"

"I suppose my point is, has it always been like this for you?"

He turns away, staring out the window for a moment. "No," he says eventually, and then he looks back at me. "I guess I was what you might consider 'normal', right up until I came out of the military."

"Wow… so what happened? What made you change?"

"It wasn't a 'what', so much as a 'who'," he replies.

"Okay… so who changed you?"

He tilts his head slightly, his eyes fixed on mine. "You did," he says.

"I—I did? But how? I—I don't understand."

He gets up and I wish now that I wasn't sitting here in a towel… and that he had some clothes on. Because this feels like it's about to become a very intense conversation… one that probably shouldn't be had when either party is naked.

"I fell in love with you when you were seventeen years old," he says, looking down at me, and I feel my throat closing over. "Max had been injured, and I came back from that last tour… and came to visit. And there you were, the same Bree Crawford… except you were suddenly all grown up. And I just fell for you."

"Oh… but you didn't say anything."

"No. I still had a few months left to serve, and I decided to let things lie until I'd seen out my time in the army. I thought I'd come back to you, a free man, and then I'd tell you how I felt."

"So why didn't you?" I'm not sure how I'd have reacted if he had, because while I remember him being gorgeous back then, I was ready for adventures, not love. At least that's what I thought, until I met Grady, who seemed to turn love into an adventure… even if only briefly.

"I did. I mean, I came back. But I didn't get to talk to you, because you'd already left for college. Your mom said you'd be home for the holidays, so I thought I'd wait and see you then. It was only a few months, and I figured I'd waited a while already; I could wait a little longer. Only, when Christmas came, you didn't show up. You called instead, announcing that you'd married Grady."

"Oh…"

"Yeah. Oh. I'm not gonna tell you how much that hurt. I'm not sure I even have the words to describe how that felt… but I decided no-one was ever gonna get close enough to hurt me again, and that from then on, I was gonna control my own life. And I have done."

I feel a claw of fear creep up my spine.

"This control thing… h—how far does it go?"

He steps forward, crouching down in front of me. "I'm not Grady," he says firmly. "I'm nothing like him. My need for control – my need for dominance – is purely sexual. And it's entirely about pleasure."

I nod my head, because I know instinctively he's telling the truth. "So you've never let anyone in? Not in all these years?"

"No. I'm not saying I've lived the life of a saint. I think that much is obvious. But I've never had a relationship… and I've never wanted one. Not with anyone but you…" My blood turns icy cold as he kneels. "I've never stopped loving you, Bree… not from that day when I came back and saw you, and you stole my heart. It's been yours ever since. Entirely. You're my world… my life…" His words fade, although I can still hear him talking. I can still see his lips moving, too. But I want to tell him to stop. It's all too much. It's too fast… and I can't take it…

Colt

I've just walked back into my apartment, having taken Bree back to her place, and all I can do is flop down onto the couch. I'm too tired for anything else.

When she first suggested leaving, I'd wanted to ask her to stay for another night, until she said she needed to do her laundry and I realized she didn't have a change of clothes. She only had the dress she'd been wearing on Friday, so she needed to go home, which was a damn shame. And then I realized there was another reason she couldn't stay. She'd arrived here on Friday in a cab, and I can hardly take her to Max's with me in the morning, before driving us all into work together. How would I explain that to Max? I mean, obviously he's gonna have to know about us eventually, but I'd rather spend some time with Bree first, and work my way up to informing her brother that I'm in love with her.

I lean back, closing my eyes, relaxing into the cushions as I let out a slow sigh. The weekend has been amazing. Completely exhausting. But amazing. And I can't help smiling as I think back over all the things we've done together.

Among the most notable, I guess, was not using a condom. Like I told Bree at the time, I've never done that before. And we didn't bother all weekend. It seemed kinda pointless after that first time. And besides, I loved the way she felt too much to put any barriers between us.

That made me think about the past, and the future, though, and on a few occasions over the weekend, while she's been sleeping and I've been watching her, I've contemplated how it might have been, if we'd gotten together all those years ago. I'd have married her in a heartbeat, and I know we wouldn't have made it through a year without having our first child. When she married her loser ex-husband, though, I put all those thoughts behind me, deciding that kids weren't for me… that without Bree, they had no place in my life. But over our weekend together, I'll admit, it's something that's filtered back into my consciousness from time to time, and that image of the two of us sitting together, our infant child between us, bound by our love, has occasionally filled my mind, and made me smile. And given the way I've lived my life over the last nine or ten years, having such domesticated thoughts has surprised me. Although not as much as introducing Bree to my way of doing things…

I knew she was interested – keen, even – just from her reactions. But what I hadn't expected was her willingness to try. And I loved the fact that she was so inquisitive. It's not what I'm used to, I'll admit, but I thought it was fascinating. And it was healthy. And remarkably liberating. She wasn't just submitting to me, blankly, and letting me do whatever I wanted. She had questions. She wanted to know what things were, how they worked, what the point was… how it would feel. That could be a little tricky to describe sometimes, but I've seen too many reactions not to answer her questions.

And speaking of reactions… Jesus… she's incredible.

I wasn't surprised when she cried after that delayed orgasm yesterday morning. I'd deliberately held her on the edge for so long, enjoying her body, soaking up the sight of her, and the fact that she was here… with me, I knew it would all be too much for her.

But that didn't stop her from wanting more… and more… and more.

And I spent the entire afternoon finding novel ways of pleasing her until her body thrummed with pleasure.

I lost count of the number of times she came. I lost count of the number of times *I* came... peaking with our shower last night. Having her suspended, held in my arms, with my cock so deep inside her... there was something about that. It came to me then that, throughout the day, I hadn't been fucking her. I'd been making love to her. And there, in the shower, for the first time in my life, I realized the difference. That's why I had to see her, to watch the pleasure in her eyes, to keep that connection between us... binding us.

Once we'd both calmed, I dried her and then carried her through to the bedroom, lying her down and holding her in my arms until she fell asleep, which didn't take long. And then I simply gazed at her for hours... and hours. I studied her skin, it's pale downy softness, contrasted against the darker tones of my own body, which I'd wrapped around her. I focused on her pouting lips, and her eyes, which flickered every so often... and I wondered if she might be dreaming... maybe of me.

Eventually, sleep claimed me, but when I woke this morning, she was still beside me, and while I was tempted to just lie there again and watch her until she opened her eyes, so that I would be the first thing she saw, I decided to make her breakfast instead, to show I'm not all about demands. Yes, I want to control her body sexually – that's never gonna change – but in every other way, I want us to have a 'normal' relationship. Whatever 'normal' is. I guess it's whatever we decide to make it. Whatever works for us... and if it's going to be anything like this weekend, then it'll be pretty damn perfect.

I put my feet up on the couch, lying out and turning onto my back, staring up at the ceiling, the smile still etched on my face, although I'm not sure that'll ever go. Not now.

I never realized it could feel like this.

I mean, I knew what being in love felt like... but until now, I've always associated it with pain, because my love has been silent, and I've lived a remote existence, keeping my emotions in check the whole time.

Being able to let them out at last… to include my love within my life… it's been a revelation.

Which is why I can't stop smiling.

Or feeling so damn good about myself.

And it's what made it so easy to decide to put my old life behind me. Permanently.

Obviously, I'd already left the agency, but after Bree made that comment about the butt plug, I realized what I had to do. I know she only said it in jest, but it really made me think. The butt plug itself was a brand new one – I wasn't making that up. I'd bought it some time ago when I started out with a new sub, who had left blank all the boxes on her profile that mentioned various degrees of previous anal experience, but had ticked the one that said 'Interested', and who I, therefore, thought might need breaking-in. As it turned out, she'd just neglected to update her details on the agency website, and had already lost her anal cherry to some other Dom, and could easily have ticked every box going. So the butt plug had never been used, until today. But I realized then, that everything else in my closet has… repeatedly. And while I clean everything thoroughly, I want to replace it all, so it's ours, and ours alone. I don't want there to be any connections between my old life and my new one.

Because nothing and no-one compares to Bree.

I still can't forget how she looked when she came apart so spectacularly… three times in a row. That was something else. I hadn't been entirely sure she'd be able to achieve multiple orgasms – and certainly not on quite such a level as that – but I'd given her a way out, just in case. I'd told her we could stop at any time, if she needed to, because I knew how intense it was gonna be for her, if it worked. I'd even thought about giving her a safe word. But I didn't. Because safe words are for subs. And Bree isn't a sub. She's everything I ever dreamed she'd be… and more. And I knew, when I held her, and helped her come down from those spectacular orgasms, that no-one will ever make me feel like she does. But I guess that's because I'm in love with her.

Telling her that felt like the right thing to do in the end. I'd been tempted more than once over the weekend. In the shower, when I was holding her up in my arms, and when she was lying, still shaking, coming down from that intense climax this morning. But in the end, I'm glad I told her the way I did, just kneeling down in front of her, gazing at her beautiful face, her eyes wide and staring into mine. I know I surprised her, because she sat in silence for a long moment after I'd eventually finished pouring out my soul to her, and for a second, I wondered if I'd blown it. But then she kinda snapped out of her trance and just said, "Oh," which I've noticed she has a tendency to do, when she can't think of anything else to say.

I wasn't surprised that she was dumbfounded. Let's face it, she'd come over here on Friday, in a state of some confusion… and had spent most of the evening crying over me. We'd talked some, and then she'd fallen asleep, and then yesterday, I took her to bed… and we've spent the entire weekend there. And I know I've introduced her to a lot of new experiences. She's seen a side of me she never knew existed. The very last thing she probably expected – especially having witnessed that side of me – was for me to throw the 'L' word out there, or to reveal that she's owned my heart for the last eleven years… to the exclusion of everyone else. So, before she felt obliged to say anything, or explain her own feelings – which I imagined were a bit confused – I stood up and told her she should probably get dressed, and that I'd drive her home. She stared at me then, and nodded her head, and while she dressed, I cleared up my room a little more, and then put on some jeans and a t-shirt, before driving her back to her place.

We held hands on the way up to her apartment and parted on her doorstep, with a long, lingering kiss, and no words, because they didn't seem necessary.

Just knowing I love her and that she knows I love her is enough for me.

Fortunately, after I got back from Bree's apartment, and before I went to bed last night, I thought to check Max's schedule.

I normally make a point of doing that every Friday night, so I know exactly what's happening the following week, but my Friday evening was kinda interrupted. In the nicest possible way.

Anyway, when I checked, I discovered Max has a breakfast appointment downtown this morning, and that his entire day is due to be filled with meetings and conferences. It's the last thing I need, because it means I'll spend the day driving, and sitting in other people's reception areas, or in the car… and I won't get to see Bree at all, because she'll be at the office, and I won't.

Still, I guess it can't be helped, and it's just one day.

So, I drive over to Max's for six-thirty, feeling tired still, but happier than I've been in ages.

"Good weekend?" he asks as I hold open the door to his car for him.

"Yes, thanks." I keep my answer noncommittal, although he pauses and looks into my eyes.

"Who was the lucky woman?"

"Who says there was a woman?" I can feel myself blushing, which is unusual. Actually, it's unheard of.

"I do. You look like you've spent the whole weekend in bed."

I raise my eyebrows, letting him know I'm not saying a word. Because I'm not. And he smirks, climbing into the back of the car.

Fortunately, he's got some papers to go over, which keep him occupied on the drive into the city, and once he's gone into his meeting, I'm able to get myself a coffee, before taking a seat in the reception area… where I remain for the next three hours, pretending to read two-year-old magazines, until Max reappears, and we set off to our next destination.

We manage a brief break for lunch, but otherwise our day is filled, and from my point of view, really boring… although to an extent, I'm not complaining. It gives me time to think about Bree… about our weekend together, and about some of the things I could try with her, once I've gotten hold of some new 'equipment', as she called it so cutely, and we can next get together.

Max finishes his last appointment at just before seven o'clock and he looks just as tired as I feel as I hold the door open for him.

"Take me home, Colt," he says wearily. "I've had enough for one day. Especially as it's been such a long fucking day."

"Sure thing."

I close the door behind him, walking around to the driver's side and getting comfortable in my seat.

"It might have been a long day, but was it a good one?" I ask him, to make conversation.

"Productive," he replies as I start the drive back to his house. "But tiring. I hate it when meetings drag on like this. But then I guess you do too."

I smile at him in the rear-view mirror, but don't comment, and for the next ten minutes, we continue in silence.

I'll admit I'm distracted, because I'm wondering whether I could give Bree a call once I've dropped Max at home and picked up my own car. I know I promised myself I wouldn't use my old kit on her, and I haven't had a chance to get rid of it, or buy anything new yet, but that doesn't mean I can't use the butt plug again… and, in any case, I need to see her. It's not like me to need to have sex again so soon, but none of this is like the 'me' that most people would recognize. Because I'm not that man. Not anymore. And yeah, I know Bree's probably gonna think I'm desperate, but that's because I am. And I don't care. Thinking about it… I might suggest she packs a bag, and I could drive by her place on the way home, and pick her up… and she could stay the night. Of course, that would leave me with the problem of getting her and her brother into work tomorrow, bearing in mind that I have to collect Max, and I don't want to tell Dana what's going on yet either. I'm just wondering whether Bree might agree to me staying over at her place instead – because I could easily leave early, before Dana arrives – when my phone rings and I check the display to see it's Dana who's calling.

This feels like déjà vu as I connect the call, except I know it can't be. Not now. Bree's got no reason to go out on her own…

"Hi, Dana."

"Colt." I can tell from the tone of her voice that something's wrong. "What's happened?"

"It's Bree."

I tighten my grip on the steering wheel as my skin prickles.

"What about her?" I try to keep my voice calm, even though I'm frantic.

"I can't find her."

Max leans forward. "What do you mean, you can't find her?"

"I'm sorry, Mr. Crawford, but she told me she had a meeting this evening at the offices of one of the fabric designers."

"Yeah? And?" I can't keep the bark out of my voice, because I wish she'd just get to the point.

"And I took her over there, and I waited outside, like she told me. And then, about an hour later, they started locking up the building. I went to ask where Bree was... only they didn't seem to know what I was talking about. So, I gave them the name of the guy she was meant to be seeing, and they said he's away on vacation, until next weekend."

"For fuck's sake..." I can't hold it in any longer. I turn the car, spinning the wheels, and floor the gas. This time Max seems more prepared. At least he's holding onto the back of my seat and isn't propelled across the car. "Where are you?" I shout at Dana.

"I'm still outside the offices of Conrad Meyer."

"Okay. Get over to Bree's place. Make sure she hasn't gone back there." Not that I think she will have done... not for one minute. "Call me as soon as you know anything."

I hang up, not waiting for an answer.

"What's wrong with her?" Max asks from behind me. "Why's she doing this?"

"I don't know." I'm struggling for control, but I focus on driving us back into the city, my mind in a whirl, because I really don't know why she's doing this. After our conversation on Friday night, I thought I understood her, but now I'm not so sure. Why would she do this? It doesn't make sense... I can't think...

"Where the fuck are you going?" Max yells, when I don't take the turning toward Bree's apartment.

"I'm going to where I think Bree is," I snap over my shoulder.

"And how the hell do you have any idea where she is?"

"Because…" I pause, knowing there won't be any turning back from here, not once I go down this road. "Oh, to hell with it… I know where she is… or at least where she might be, because after she did this the last time, I started following her." I slam on the brakes as the lights turn red, keeping my eyes fixed on them.

"You were following her?" I can hear the surprise in his voice.

"Yeah. In the evenings. And one night, she snuck out of her place and went to this bar… the place I'm driving to now."

"By herself? Without Dana?"

"Yeah… that's what I mean by 'snuck out'."

"And you didn't fucking tell me?"

"No."

The lights turn green, and I floor the gas again. "What was she doing in this bar?" he asks.

"Getting hit on. What else?"

"What did you do?"

"Well, I wasn't gonna sit there and let a stranger feel up your sister, so I dealt with the situation."

"How?" He's calmed down a little now… although I doubt that will last.

"I dragged her out of there and took her home."

"Well, she clearly hasn't learned her lesson."

I suck in a breath… "No. It doesn't look that way, does it?"

My phone rings again. It's Dana and I connect the call. "Well?"

"No sign of her."

"Okay. Wait there. I'm checking out a bar I think she may have gone to, but if I'm wrong, she could come home. If she does, call me."

"Yes, boss."

I hang up, just as I'm parking outside the bar, and Max gets out at the same time as me, not waiting for me to open his door, like he normally does. I get to the wide, smoked glass door ahead of him, though, and enter the bar first, surprised by how busy it is for a Monday evening. It doesn't take me long to spot Bree, sitting in a booth near the rear of the darkened room, with her back to us. There are two suited guys with her, one of them blocking her in, so she's got no way out of there, and I wanna yell at her, just for that. How could she be so stupid?

I turn to Max, but he hasn't seen her yet, his eyes still darting around the room, and I know I'm going to have to come clean.

"She's here," I say.

"Where?"

"Eleven o'clock… booth at the rear."

He looks straight ahead and to his left, focusing in on her. "What the fuck is she doing?"

"I don't know… but I need to find out."

"*You* need to find out?" He tries to dodge past me to get to her, but I put a firm hand on his chest, halting him.

"Max… please."

He stops and looks at me. "What?"

"Can you let me deal with this?"

"Why? She's my sister."

"I know."

"Look, if this is because I handled things badly last time…"

"It's got nothing to do with that," I interrupt and stare at the space between us, letting my hand drop before I raise my face again, making eye contact with him. "She's just spent the weekend at my place, and I—"

"She's what?" He cuts me off, his eyes darkening to black pools of anger as he pushes me back against the pillar beside us, to my right, and I let him… for now.

"She's just spent the weekend at my place," I repeat calmly, even as he puts his forearm across my throat, pressing hard. A few people around us move away and then stand, staring at us.

"What the fuck have you done to her?" Even with his scant knowledge of what I do – what I'm like – I can't blame him for his reaction.

"I haven't done anything she didn't want me to," I say, through my blocked windpipe. "Let me go, Max. We both know I could kill you if I wanted to, without even breaking into a sweat… so let me go."

He hesitates for a second and then releases me, stepping away and breathing hard.

The people around us seem to relax, and Max turns back to me.

"How the hell did she end up at your place all weekend?" he asks, his voice frosty.

"You really wanna know?"

"Yeah." He narrows his eyes.

"Okay… but let's sit down first. We're not exactly being subtle here, and I don't want Bree to notice us and run."

He doesn't reply, but glances around and spots a free table near the front of the room, stalking over to it, without waiting for me. I follow and sit opposite him, and we both glare at each other for a moment before he tips his head to one side, waiting for my explanation.

"If you must know," I say, without holding back, "the fact that she came to my place, is kinda your fault."

"How the fuck do you work that out?"

"Because you made me go to that goddamn function with her last week."

"That was on Thursday night. You're talking about the weekend."

"I know it was on Thursday night… and unfortunately it was then that Bree decided to have way too much to drink."

"Jesus…" He rolls his eyes. "What did she do?"

"She packed away four or five dirty martinis and forgot to pay attention when the guy she was with got a little too familiar."

"She was with a guy?"

"Yeah. In case you haven't noticed your sister is very beautiful."

"I'm aware of that. But it was your job to keep her away from guys…"

"No… it was my job to keep her away from danger. Which is why I stepped in, when the guy looked like he was gonna take advantage of the situation."

"So what did you do?"

"I took her back to my place."

"So you could take advantage instead?"

I glare at him. "No. You know I don't pull shit like that. No matter who the woman is."

He looks down at the table. "Yeah… okay. So what happened? I mean, why did you even take her back to your apartment in the first place. Why not just take her home?"

"To be honest, I started to ask myself that after a while. But at the time I decided my place was closer to the hotel, and she needed to sober up. What I hadn't expected was that she'd come on to me."

"Bree? She came on to you?"

"You don't have to make it sound like a miracle."

"I—I'm not. But…" He doesn't finish his sentence. I'm not sure he knows how.

"It's okay. Like I say, I was just as surprised by it as you are. And I didn't react, even though I wanted to." He raises his eyebrows, but doesn't comment. "I took her home." I add. "And then the next morning, at the office, when I went to see if she was okay, she was… well, really quite offensive about the whole thing, and I told her she was on her own."

"I'm sorry?"

I sigh, deeply. "I told you, on the way here, I'd been watching her, in the evenings, ever since she last went AWOL… but I told her on Friday morning, that I wasn't gonna take being spoken to like the hired help and I wouldn't be coming to her rescue anymore."

"Oh, I see what you mean."

"I guess that must've gotten to her more than I thought, because she turned up at my place on Friday night, in floods of tears. We talked, and then she fell asleep, so I put her to bed, and I slept on the couch."

"So you haven't actually…?" His face clears.

"Let me finish."

He sucks in a breath and nods his head. "Sorry."

I hold up my hands, because the last thing I need right now is an apology from him. "She woke up on Saturday morning, and we talked some more… and then we kissed."

"Oh, Jesus, man…" He shakes his head. "I know where this is going. And I know what you're like."

"I know you do. And so did she. I explained it. She knew what she was getting into, Max." Okay, so it was a learning curve for her, I'll admit. But it was one she was willing to take.

"So, she doesn't mind about the agency, and that you're never exclusive, and that she'll just be one in a long line of subs..." He's struggling not to raise his voice.

"She doesn't even know about any of that."

"But you said you explained it..." He sits forward, his muscles tightening.

"I know what I said. But the thing is, she didn't need to know about the agency, or anything that's gone before. If she ever asks... if she wants to know about my past in that much detail, then I'll tell her. But it's not relevant. Not anymore. Because none of that applies. Bree isn't gonna be one in a long line of subs, because I terminated my agency membership on Friday night... while she was asleep in my bedroom."

He tilts his head, looking confused. "Why? I—I mean, I know she'd come on to you the night before, but she was drunk then. How did you know anything would ever happen between you? How did you know she even meant it?"

"Thanks." I shake my head, running my fingertip along the edge of the table.

"Anytime," he replies. "The point stands. What made you leave the agency?"

"The fact that I didn't want something like that in my life anymore."

"Because you wanted Bree?" he guesses.

"Yes. And I didn't want it to be like it normally is with me." I swallow hard and look right into his eyes. "You may as well know, Max, I've been in love with your sister, since she was seventeen years old."

"What the fuck?" He's shocked, not angry. It's written all over his face. "How the hell didn't I know about this?"

"Because I didn't want you to. But I told her last night. After she'd spent the weekend in my bed... right before I took her home."

"You mean... she knows how you feel about her?"

"Yeah."

"And she's still... here? With two other guys?"

179

"Yeah. And that's why I need to be the one to work this out. I don't expect you to like it, Max, and if it makes you feel better, I'll re-assign myself to another duty, and appoint someone else as your bodyguard."

"You don't need to…"

"I'm not sure what I need to do yet… except talk to Bree."

He nods his head and holds out his hand, palm upwards. "Give me the keys to my car."

"Why?"

"Because I'm quite capable of driving myself home."

"No. I'll get Dana to come and take you."

"It's a half hour drive. I can manage that by myself. And I don't wanna sit around here waiting for Dana, watching you and my sister tearing pieces out of each other. I love you both too much for that."

Jesus… I didn't need that. "I'm not gonna tear pieces out of anyone, Max." I hand him the keys. "Call me, or Dana, if there's any trouble. Okay?"

"Sure."

"And I'll make sure your sister gets home safe… and in one piece."

"No matter what?"

"Yeah… no matter what."

He nods his head and gets up from the table, leaving without another word, and I take a breath, pulling my phone from my pocket. I send a message to Dana, telling her I've found Bree and that she can go home, but to be on standby for the next hour, in case she hears from Max. She sends a quick 'okay' in response, and I put my phone away again.

Then, getting to my feet, I slowly make my way to the back of the bar, my spine tingling as the sound of Bree's laughter reaches my ears, and I have to unclench my fists… not that I was aware I'd clenched them in the first place.

"Excuse me," I say, as I get level with their table, and Bree's head shoots up at the sound of my voice, fear crossing her eyes in an instant. *What the hell is that about? What does she think I'm going to do to her?*

"Can I help?" The blonder of the two guys looks up at me.

"Yeah. I need to talk to Bree."

He smiles. "Well, we're talking to her right now."

He looks across the table at his friend, who grins back at him. "Yeah, maybe come back later," the other guy says, and they both chuckle.

"Hmm… the problem with that is, I'm not a coming back later kind of guy."

They stare up at me, although Bree is looking at her hands clasped in front of her on the table, and I can see the blush creeping up her cheeks.

The blond guy gets to his feet and looks up into my face. "I think you need to remember, there are two of us… and there's only one of you. So maybe you should just fuck off and annoy someone else," he says and I nod my head, which makes him smile, just as I reach forward, my hand clamped tight around his neck, my thumb pressing hard against his windpipe. He starts to choke, to struggle for breath, and his friend stands up too, although I hold him off with my other hand, his arms flailing.

"I could end you, right now," I whisper to the blond guy, as he turns a deep shade of red, bordering on purple. "And I will, unless you and your little friend disappear from my sight in the next five seconds. Understood?"

I release my grip, just enough for him to nod his head, and then I let him go. He slumps, but shifts out of the way, not waiting for his friend as he gulps in a lungful of air and makes his way toward the front of the bar. The other guy follows, muttering to himself, and I glance down at Bree.

"Happy now?" I say to her, but she doesn't respond. So I grab her arm and pull her along the bench seat and onto her feet.

"What are you doing?" she says, glaring at me.

"I'm taking you home."

"What makes you think I wanna go to your place again?" *Wow, that didn't hurt much.*

"Nothing. But then, I didn't say I was taking you to my place. I said I was taking you home."

I pick up her purse from the table and hand it to her, pulling her through the bar, and out onto the street, where I hail a cab, almost throwing her onto the back seat, before climbing in myself.

I give the driver Bree's address and sit in silence, while he makes the brief journey. She sits as far away as possible, her arms folded, staring out the window, and when the cab pulls up, I pay the driver, and get out, waiting for her, as she continues to sit, like a petulant child.

"Don't fuck with me, Bree," I say, bending down and looking at her, while trying not to raise my voice.

She turns and glares, but uncrosses her arms and shimmies across the back seat, before grabbing her purse and climbing out, and then stomping up the steps into her apartment block.

I follow, and reach the elevator door, just as it's opening.

"You don't need to come up," she says, not bothering to look at me.

"Yeah... I do."

"Why?"

"It's my job," I reply flatly.

She turns now and narrows her eyes at me, barely in control, it seems, and then enters the elevator, folding her arms across her chest again. I can feel the tension between us, but I press the button for her floor and stand slightly behind her as we ride up.

The doors swish open and she steps out, unfastening her purse as she gets to her door, trying to find her keys.

"I'm home now," she says, turning to me. "You've done your duty. You can go."

I grab her arms and push her back against the closed door, my body hard against hers, although there's nothing sexual or arousing about this. "Don't you fucking dare dismiss me," I growl at her, my temper flaring, even though I'm doing my best to keep it in check. There's that flash of fear in her eyes again, but she holds it back, defiance winning over.

"I'll do what I like," she says.

"And what is it you like, Bree? Having guys fight over you? Is that what this is about?"

"No... but you don't have to fight anyone on my account. I didn't ask you to. And anyway, I'm not yours to fight over. You don't own me."

I step back slightly, putting a narrow space between us. "I never said I did."

"Then back the fuck off," she yells. "You told me you only wanted sexual control. Remember? So where do you get off trying to dictate the rest of my life to me?"

Her words feel like bullets strafing across my skin, as I think about all the things we've done together, all the things we shared, that I've introduced her to; the secrets I told her about myself, that I've never told anyone else before… and my plans… everything I've been contemplating during our time together and since the last time I stood here, kissing her. A future together. Children. A life. "I'm not trying to dictate anything. How can you say that, when I haven't even spoken to you since last night… when, if you recall, I told you I'm in love with you?" I remind her. "How can you say anyone has control over you, when less than twenty-four hours after I opened my heart to you, I find you're out with two complete strangers? How's that supposed to make me feel, Bree?"

"I wasn't 'out' with them," she says, ignoring my last comment. "I met them at the bar. And they're not complete strangers, they're…" She falls silent, lowering her eyes, and I realize what she's just said, stepping even further back from her, in shock.

"You mean… you mean they were the two guys you were with before? The ones who asked you to have a three-way with them?" She doesn't move or acknowledge my question, so I step forward again and raise my voice. "Answer me, Bree."

"Yes." She almost spits the word at me and I feel a stabbing pain in my chest, which I do my best to ignore, although it's a struggle.

"D—Do you know… do you have any idea what message you were sending them?" I stutter, looking down at her. She doesn't respond, so I continue, "You'd said 'no' once. But you came back. And, rightly or wrongly, in a lot of men's eyes, that's almost the equivalent of saying 'yes', or at least 'I'm thinking about it'. Can't you see that?"

"No," she says, surprising me. "I wasn't sending them any messages. I just went to the bar, and they happened to be there. That's all."

"That's not all. Because you chose to sit with them, knowing what they wanted from you. You made that choice, Bree. And what were you even doing at the bar in the first place? Jeez… you lied to Dana and invented an entire goddamn meeting, just so you could go out tonight. Why would you do that? Why would you put yourself in danger again? After everything we talked about…"

"Because I wanted to!" Her voice rings around the confined space.

I step away from her, rubbing my hand down my face. "You wanted to…" I shake my head. "Do you know what I wanted to do tonight?" I don't let her answer. "I was gonna call you. I was gonna ask if I could come over here, so we could spend the night together, without it causing problems in the morning." I move closer again, although I don't touch her. I can't. "I guess that won't be happening, though, will it? Because you've decided I'm fucking disposable."

Chapter Nine

Bree

I can't answer.

My voice won't work.

I can't even explain to him why I went out tonight. I know why I did it. But I can't explain it to Colt.

I went out because I had no-one to talk to. Again.

And I'd been going crazy all day, ever since last night, when he brought me home and kissed me, reminding me of how good we'd been together… while making me think about the fact that he'd said he loves me. And that's all too much for me right now. I'm not ready for love.

I spent most of the night wondering what to do… his words echoing in my head, mingling with the crazy, intense feelings he provoked in me… and despite all of that, I didn't reach any conclusions.

And then Colt wasn't at work today, because Max had meetings… so I ended up feeling even more alone. Because I think I'd worked out that – yet again – the only person I could talk to about my feelings was Colt. I wanted to try and ask him to slow things down a little, without actually slowing them down. I wanted to ask if he could give me time, without giving me time. And I know that doesn't make sense, but I don't know how else to phrase it. I didn't want to stop seeing him. I didn't want to lose him. And I definitely didn't want to go back to where I was before. But at the same time, the idea of love, commitment, forever…

it all felt too much… too soon. Like the world was crowding in on me. So I guess I needed to ask him if he was capable of being with me, without pressuring me… without loving me. If that was even possible for him.

But by the time it got to four o'clock, I decided he wasn't coming back, and I just needed to escape; to be somewhere else. And my instinct told me where that 'somewhere else' was. It was somewhere I could feel free… and where I wouldn't have to think. Because thinking didn't seem to be getting me very far.

So, I invented a meeting, got Dana to drive me over there at just before six p.m., and once I'd gone inside the building, I snuck straight out the back and called a cab, which took me to the bar. It was insane. I know that. But then I'm starting to wonder about my sanity quite a lot of the time.

I hadn't expected Shawn and Cory to arrive, but I felt kinda relieved when they did – and when they came straight over to me. They were familiar faces, after all. And we took a booth near the back of the bar and talked. That's all we did. We just talked. They made me feel good about myself, without asking for anything in return. No-one made any demands. They didn't make any suggestions this time… and neither did I. And if they had suggested anything, I'd have said a very firm 'no'. I really wasn't interested in anything, other than being somewhere else and pretending my life was my own, with no complications, and nothing to think about… just for one evening.

Colt's staring down at me still, the silence ringing out between us. I've hidden my fear and shame behind anger so far, but his eyes are boring into mine, and as much as I want to ask him all those nonsensical questions that have been swirling around my head all day, I can't. Not now. I've taken things too far tonight, and we both know it.

Eventually, he lets out a long sigh, and shakes his head very slowly from side to side, before he leans into me. I wonder for a fleeting moment, if he's going to kiss me, and I wish he would. I wish he'd give me a way back. But he doesn't. He just whispers, "Take care of yourself, Bree," his voice a low, lifeless monotone, and then he strides off, pressing the button for the elevator, which opens immediately, and he climbs into it, keeping his head bowed as the door closes and he disappears from my sight.

I want to call him back. But I can't. Because I saw the look in his eyes just then, as he turned away from me. It was a look of pain. Pure, unadulterated pain. I've hurt him. Badly. I've done it before – unwittingly – and he told me he'd never let anyone get close enough to hurt him again. He did, though. He let me in… and I've hurt so much more this time.

And I know Colt. I know him better than I did before. And there's no way he's going to make that mistake a second time.

I need sleep.

It's seven a.m. and I've maybe snatched a couple of hours while tossing and turning, and beating myself up.

The memory is still very vivid of the last time I slept properly. It was when I was with Colt… lying in his arms.

But, as he said, that won't be happening again. Because I was too stupid to wait yesterday, so I could talk to him… to explain how scared I was that he was moving things too fast. And he's never going to let me now.

I get up and shower, not bothering with breakfast, and manage to get ready just in time for Dana's arrival. She's quiet this morning… even more so than usual. But I'm not in the mood for talking either, and we ride to the office in silence. I'll admit I'm spending my time on the brief journey trying to work out whether I'll be able to persuade Colt to drop by my office on some pretext. I know he probably won't want to, but I'm hoping he might, if I make it about work. Somehow. And then I can explain what happened, and maybe I can try to ask him those questions I needed to ask him yesterday. If he'll listen. Maybe if I beg… if I…

"Good morning." My head shoots up as I enter my office, and I see Max standing by the window.

"Hi." I walk over to my desk, dumping my purse, and look up at him.

He's staring at me, and he doesn't look too pleased. But then, I guess if Colt's told him about what happened…

"I was there last night," he says, before I have the chance to ask what he wants, his voice low and kinda menacing, and I feel my skin tingle and chill with uncertainty, because I've never seen him quite like this before. "I was with Colt, in the car, when Dana called him. And, before you say anything, I know about you and him as well. He had no choice other than to tell me, because I wanted to be the one to come over to you in the bar and drag you out of there, but he felt he had the right…"

"The right to manhandle me, you mean?" My uncertainty is replaced with anger, just like my embarrassment and fear were last night, when faced with Colt.

"No. I was gonna say the right to come and talk to you… to find out why the hell you're behaving like you are."

"What's going on in here?" We both turn at the sound of Chase's voice. I'd forgotten he was due back today, but he's here, and judging from his appearance, I'd say he's come straight from the airport. He looks tired, and a little disheveled, in jeans and a casual shirt; unlike Max, who's in a dark gray Italian suit, as usual… the two of them looking fairly similar, and yet completely different. Chase stands in the doorway, a puzzled expression on his face, his eyes darting from Max to me. "I can hear your voices from down the hallway."

He steps inside and closes the door, which with hindsight, I should probably have done myself.

Max comes over to my desk, standing on the other side of it.

"Our sister's been behaving like a child," he says, talking to Chase, but narrowing his eyes at me, before he adds, "Again."

"In what way?" Chase sits down, looking relaxed, as though he thinks he can solve all the problems in the world, just with his presence.

"She's been running around town in the evenings, without Dana, getting drunk, letting complete strangers feel her up in public…"

"Excuse me? How did you know about that?" I can't believe Colt told him what Cory did… I can't believe he'd do that to me.

"Because Colt told me he had to rescue you from a guy at that charity function, who'd forgotten how to keep his hands to himself," Max explains, and I feel yet more shame wash over me. Not only did Colt not give away my worst guilty secret, but thinking about it, my behavior in recent weeks has been appalling. It's been worse than that. And Colt's been there, at every turn. And regardless of that, regardless of what I've told him and what he's seen me do, he still wanted me. He still loved me. *Oh, God… what did I do to him?*

"Oh… I see," I mutter, and Max shakes his head.

"And because you don't know when to fucking stop… Colt's left," he yells.

Colt's left?

I flop into my own chair now, in shock.

"What do you mean, 'Colt's left'?" I ask him, and he frowns down at me.

"I mean just that. He's left. He sent me an email late last night, telling me he's allocated a guy called Pierce to be my bodyguard from now on."

"So he's still here at the moment?" I glance toward Max's office, at the end of the hallway, knowing I'm probably clutching at straws.

"No. I told you, he's left. Pierce collected me this morning, and he's sitting in the reception area right now." I recall a tall, blond-haired guy, wearing a black suit, who looked up when I exited the elevator. But I assumed he was here for a meeting. "Colt said he didn't wanna come back here again…" Max continues. "Because of you." He raises his voice again and leans over my desk, just as Chase gets up, putting a hand on his shoulder.

"I don't understand," he says and Max turns to him, his attention diverted. "Why would Bree's behavior bother Colt so much?"

"Because Colt's been in love with her for ages… since she was seventeen years old, evidently."

"And you knew about this?" Chase is as surprised as I was.

"No. Not until last night. Colt's really good at keeping his feelings to himself. He's even better at it than I thought… and I thought I knew everything about him."

"So what happened?" Chase asks, still bemused… but then he doesn't know the whole story… not like I do. Not like Max does. Evidently.

Max lets out a sigh and pushes his fingers back through his hair, turning away from me. "It seems Colt and Bree had gotten kinda close… and she spent the weekend at his place." Chase turns to look at me, but doesn't say a word, as Max continues, "And although Colt told her, before taking her home, that he's in love with her, and has been for years, she did another of her disappearing acts last night, and we found her in a bar, with a couple of strangers."

"Men?" Chase clarifies.

"Yeah, men." Max looks back at him.

"And Colt's really gone?" It's no secret that Chase and Colt don't get along, but even Chase isn't gloating. He sounds concerned.

"Yeah. He's flying out to the West Coast in a couple of days to look after some hot shot movie producer, or something. Pierce was gonna be doing that job, but Colt's swapped places with him. He wants outta here."

Chase turns back to me again. "Would you really have gone with a couple of strangers?"

I feel humiliated… and exposed. And I lash out. "Don't you dare judge me, Chase. You're always picking up strangers. You treat women like they're… disposable." Colt's word springs to mind… but it doesn't help. Because that's exactly how I treated him. Only I didn't mean to… and the shame is almost unbearable.

Chase gets closer, standing right in front of my desk. "Yeah," he says quietly. "Yeah, I do treat women like that. Hell, I've even had the odd three-way myself, in my time. I've never claimed to be a saint, because I'm not. But the difference is, Bree, that I never let anyone fall for me. Ever. That's the whole point of not hanging around. They don't get to know me well enough to even get to like me, let alone love me. But Colt told you he loved you. He told you he was *in love* with you. And you did *that* to him? Seriously… do you think because he's a hard guy, he doesn't have a fucking heart?"

I can't stay here anymore. I can't hear my own shameful actions being played out, over and over.

I grab my purse, and without a word, I run, tears streaming down my face.

Dana's in the main reception area, sitting on one of the three leather couches out here, opposite the man I now know is called Pierce… Colt's replacement.

She gets up when she sees me, stepping forward.

"Bree… are you okay?" She sounds worried, although she's a blur.

"Just take me home. Please?"

"Sure."

She takes my arm and, without another word, leads me toward the elevators.

I know I shouldn't be here.

I've got too much work on at the moment to be sitting at home, on my couch, wallowing in self pity.

But, I know that if I go back to the office, I won't be able to concentrate. And I'd have to face Max and Chase again. And I'm not in the mood for either of them.

Dana was really sweet when she brought me home. She offered to stay, and seemed really reluctant to leave, even though I assured her I'd be fine. I don't think she believed me. Not that I blamed her… I didn't believe myself either. I promised her I wouldn't go out again, though. I've learned my lesson on that one… the hard way.

So, she left, making me promise to call if I needed her. I haven't… called her, that is. I wouldn't go so far as to say I haven't needed her, because I need to talk to someone. Again. However, that 'someone' can't be Dana. Because she works for Colt… and that would be beyond awkward.

At the moment though, as much as I'd love to talk things through with someone – if only so I could try and make sense of it all myself – I need to stop crying, more than anything. I feel as though I've opened the floodgates, and they're showing no signs of closing again anytime soon.

I've gone through nearly half a box of Kleenex and I'm actually starting to feel dehydrated… if only I could be bothered to get up and pour myself a glass of water, or make a cup of…

I jump out of my skin as I hear a key in the lock of my door. Who the hell is that? And what are they doing letting themselves into my apartment? I sit up and then stand... although I don't know what I think that's going to achieve. My hands are shaking and I wish to God Colt was here. He told me to take care of myself. But how can I... without him?

The door opens slowly, and I let out a yelp as Max pokes his head around and peers inside.

"What the hell?" I raise my voice and he looks over toward me as I walk through my living area in the direction of the front door. "Since when have you had a key to my apartment?"

"Since you moved in here. Colt has one too... as does Dana."

Of course... that explains how they got in that night, when Max yelled at me. He's not yelling now, though. He sounds completely matter-of-fact, walking right in, followed by Chase, who closes the door behind them both.

"Just out of interest, why do you have to treat me like a child, Max?" I glare at him, but he holds my gaze.

"I'm not. And before you start arguing with me, you're not being treated any differently to anyone else. Colt has keys to my place, and to Chase's, and Mom's. And Eli has a key to Chase's apartment as well."

"And do you have a key to Chase's apartment?" I ask, even though I already know the answer.

"No."

"Then you are treating me differently." I fold my arms across my chest.

"So sue me for caring." Although he's not yelling at me, there's a harsh edge to his voice, which I've rarely heard before.

"Can we break this up?" Chase says, coming further into the apartment and standing halfway between Max and me, like some kind of referee. He turns to Max. "I thought we came over here to apologize?" he says, tilting his head to one side.

"We did," Max replies, and I get the feeling that Chase has talked him into this, and that in reality, he's still kinda mad with me. I don't blame him. Colt's his friend as well as his bodyguard, and I've messed things up… spectacularly. Again.

"You don't have to apologize," I say, before Max can add anything. "I deserved everything you said to me before. I have been behaving like a child… a spoiled, unruly child, thinking I can say and do whatever I want, and that even if people get hurt, they'll still want to be with me. Except they don't, do they?" I can feel the tears welling again, until there's nothing I can do to stop them from falling, and I cover my face with my hands, too ashamed of myself to even let them see me anymore.

Suddenly, a pair of arms come around me, and I lean into a broad chest, knowing instinctively that this is Max… and not just because I can feel the soft fabric of his suit, but because I know the difference between my brothers. Max is taller and a little broader… much more like Colt, and that thought makes me cry even louder.

"Do you want another chance with him?" Max asks, and I swallow hard, trying to regain a little control as I look up into his face.

"A—Another chance?" I stutter.

"Yeah. Do you have any feelings for him at all? Or was it completely one sided?"

I suck in a breath and take the Kleenex that Chase is holding out to me, using it to dab my eyes as Max pulls me back into the living area and we all sit down on my L-shaped couch, Max and I on the main part, and Chase perched on the smaller end, looking across at me and smiling.

"I spent a weekend with him," I say, through my sniffles, trying to explain. "I hadn't expected to hear that he was in love with me, or that he had been for such a long time. It was so sudden. It came out of nowhere, and I was scared. But I didn't mean to push him away."

"Then what did you mean to do?" Max asks, and I can hear the anger in his voice still.

"I don't know. The whole thing was so confusing. I—I think I needed to talk to Colt. There were things I needed to discuss with him… to ask him. But you were out all day yesterday, so he wasn't around… and I just broke out."

"Rather than waiting?" Chase seems surprised and I turn to him.

"Yeah. You... you've got to understand how it feels... to be me, I mean. Colt helped me work it out, but it's kinda complicated."

"Then try and explain it to us." Max sits forward, listening.

"Well... the way Colt put it was that I went from having Dad controlling my future when we were growing up, to letting Grady control literally everything about me, when I was married to him... and then the moment I found just a little freedom after I left him, you put me in a cage, with a bodyguard at the door."

"But surely you understand why..." His voice fades, his eyes clouding over.

"I'm not blaming you, Max. I'm just trying to tell you how it felt... how it feels. I—I mean, I didn't actually understand it myself. Not until I talked it through with Colt. He's the one who made it make sense. That's why it threw me so much, I guess, when he started talking about us as a couple. I thought he'd understood that I wasn't ready to get tied down again..."

Max stares at me for a moment, and then his lips twitch up at the corners. "Interesting choice of words, Sis," he mutters.

"What the fuck does that mean?" Chase asks, and we both turn to look at him.

"I'm not explaining it." I sit back in the seat and turn to Max, who lets out a sigh.

"Colt's a Dominant," he says in a matter-of-fact way, as though he could have just said, 'Colt's a racing car driver', or 'Colt's a pastry chef', like tying women up, restraining them, and pleasuring them until they're struggling to remember their own name, is perfectly normal behavior.

Chase nods his head. "Okay," he says simply, because nothing seems to faze him, and then he turns to me. "But you just said that Colt was the one who explained your own feelings to you. Right?"

"Yes. I—I think I'd started to work it out for myself... kinda. But I couldn't get it to make sense in my own head. I couldn't understand why I kept behaving the way I did. That wasn't what I wanted... I didn't want to be with a stranger. I didn't want to be running out to bars all the time."

"Then what did you want?" Max asks.

"To be noticed, for me… for myself… and to be loved. Not controlled. Loved."

"So why, when a man tells you he loves you – I man, I might add, who would give his life for you – do you run out and start flirting with other guys?" Max says, sounding exasperated.

"I don't know…" I raise my voice. "Like I said, I was scared. I think I expected to build up to the whole 'I love you' thing, over time… not have it thrown at me right from the start. It was too fast…"

"Why didn't you just tell him that? You could have given him the chance to slow things down," Max reasons.

"I already explained. He wasn't around… and…"

Chase holds up his hand, which I'm kinda pleased about, because I feel like we're going round in circles here, getting nowhere.

"I understand he was going too fast for you, but are you sure it wasn't more than that?" he asks.

"Like what?"

"Like the fact that being a Dominant makes Colt just as controlling as Dad and Grady. Are you sure you weren't rebelling against that? Against his rules?"

"What rules?" I'm confused.

Chase shifts a little closer, resting his elbows on his knees. "Didn't he have a set of rules that went along with being in a relationship with him? Rules that meant you couldn't live your own life and be your own person, even when you weren't in bed with him?"

"Jeez, do we have to talk about this?" Max says, shaking his head.

"Yes. Just give me a minute," Chase replies, and turns back to me. "Well?" he asks.

"No," I mumble. "He didn't mention rules at all. Inside, or outside of the bedroom."

"And he's definitely a Dom?"

"Yes." Max and I both answer at the same time, and Chase smiles and clasps his hands together.

"If you're sure," he says.

"I'm sure." In fact, I'm absolutely positive. I can still feel the sting of his palm on my skin, and the grip of the cuffs on my wrists… and I miss them, nearly as much as I miss Colt.

"Were you worried about him trying to control you, though?" Max asks, but doesn't wait for a reply, before he adds, "Because if you were, you didn't need to be. I don't know as much about Colt's lifestyle as Chase seems to, but I can tell you, Colt's not like that. He wants you to be safe, more than anything… and I doubt he likes the idea of you running around town with other guys… because no man wants the woman he loves to do that. But he's not someone who's gonna hold you back. If you got cold feet because you thought he was gonna extend his lifestyle into your life, then you read him all wrong, Bree."

"I don't know if that's what it was…" I say, finally getting a word in. "Or whether it was just a shock. I just know I needed to talk to him, and he wasn't there…"

"Then I wish you'd waited, instead of running away. You'd have saved us all a lot of trouble."

"I know that now…" I glare at him.

"The thing is," he continues, like I haven't spoken… again, "Colt's a fair guy. If you seriously want another chance with him, then you need to have that conversation. Whatever it was you wanted to say to him yesterday, you need to say it to him now. He'll listen."

I shake my head. "He won't wanna see me now. Not after what I've done. He told me already that, when I married Grady it hurt him so much he closed himself off… and that's when he got into the whole Dominant/submissive scene, so no-one could ever hurt him again. Only, I—I've hurt him even more now. I can't see how he'll forgive me."

Max moves a little closer and leans over, taking my hand in his. "You'd be amazed at what a guy can forgive, when he's in love," he says. "But you fucked up, Bree… and if you wanna make it right, you're gonna have to be the one to say sorry."

"How?"

"You need to see him."

"How?" I repeat. "How can I even get to his place? I can't drag Dana into all of this. She works for him…"

"I know. I'll take you."

Colt

Having collected my car from Max's place, I've spent the rest of my day packing, sorting out my affairs, making sure my bills are all paid and up to date… and refusing to think.

I can do that when I have to. It's a technique I gained in the military. And in this instance, it's necessary. Because I can't afford to think.

Although, I can't help recalling snippets of the conversation I had with Max, when he phoned about two minutes after I emailed him last night, to tell him that Pierce was gonna be taking over from me, starting this morning.

But those are thoughts about Max. He's different.

He was shocked at my decision to leave and tried to persuade me to change my mind. He asked me to go over to his place. I said, "No," even when he reasoned that my car was still there.

"Get a cab and come over," he urged.

"I can't. I'll deal with my car tomorrow."

"When I'm at work, you mean?" He sounded disappointed.

"Yeah."

"Why don't you wanna see me?" he asked.

Because I'm a wreck, and I don't want you to see me like this. I didn't say that out loud. Obviously. "Because you'll try and persuade me to stay. And I can't. She broke my heart," I said instead, surprising myself. It was hard, putting that out there, but it had to be done if he was gonna let it go… and let me go too. He had to understand this wasn't a decision

I'd taken lightly. "I can't be near her, Max... it hurts too fucking much."

"So you're leaving?"

"Yeah. I'm sorry. I wouldn't do this to you if I didn't have to."

I heard him sigh. "You will stay in touch, won't you?"

"Of course. Give me a couple of months to get my head around everything... I'll call you."

"You know our friendship is bigger than any of this, don't you?"

"Yeah." That didn't really need saying, but I was kinda glad he'd said it. It would've been easy for him to take sides. And I wouldn't have blamed him. As it is, I'm still not sure how I'm gonna handle things with him in the long term. But I'll find a way. Somehow.

We didn't talk for much longer. I needed to get in touch with Pierce, and we'd said everything that needed saying. Dwelling on it wasn't gonna help anyone.

I called Pierce after that and told him of the change of plans. If he was surprised, he hid it well, and just accepted my instructions.

He'd been about to fly out to LA in a couple of days, so we're basically gonna switch roles. It was the simplest thing I could think of on the spur of the moment to get myself out of the picture. I'm hoping the change of scene will make this easier, and besides, everything's already set up. Not only is there a job out there to keep me busy, but I've rented a car and an apartment in the company's name, which Pierce was gonna make use of. I can just take his place.

I haven't decided what to do about my own apartment yet. I'm not even sure how long I'll be gone for. The contract in LA is for six months, so that'll be the minimum, but last night, when I couldn't sleep, I started to think about maybe setting up an office out there. We wouldn't be short of clients, and it's not like there's anything left for me here...

Okay, so there's Max.

But he's too close to Bree...

Fuck it... I wasn't gonna think about her.

I sit down and let her drift into my head for a moment.

It's weird, but I'd never realized that a broken heart could hurt as much as a broken bone or a bullet. Except it does. The pain in my chest just doesn't seem to stop… but then she did a good job of breaking me… just like I thought she would.

And if I'm ever gonna make it back from this, I need to leave her behind.

Now.

For good.

Because this is too much. It's way too much.

I startle at the sound of the doorbell, and get up from the couch, wandering over to the door and pulling it open, and that pain in my chest intensifies to fever pitch as I look down at Bree, standing on my doorstep, looking up at me. She's wearing a black fitted dress, which is nothing like that pretty short thing she had on when she last came here on Friday night, when she slept in my bed… and which I peeled her out of the next morning. No, this literally hugs her figure, showing off every single curve, reminding me of what she looks like naked… filling my head with memories of her soft skin, her delicate fragrance, her plaintive cries… like she's taunting me. *Dammit.* It also makes her look kinda washed out, but that's not surprising, because she's clearly been crying and, in spite of everything – including that pain in my chest – my instinct is still to reach out and hold her. Except my anger beats me to it.

"How the hell did you get here?" I yell, raising my voice, and she flinches, taking a half step back. "Haven't you learned anything, for fuck's sake?"

She holds up a hand. "It's okay," she says, in a quiet voice.

"No, it isn't okay. When are you gonna get it into your head? You can't keep going out by yourself. It's not…"

"I'm not by myself," she interrupts. "Max brought me… and Pierce drove us. It's all perfectly safe." I heave out a sigh of relief, which I know she notices, because she adds, "I have learned my lesson, Colt," and the sound of my name on her lips pushes up my pain level yet another notch.

"Okay… so what do you want? Why did you get Max and Pierce to bring you over here?"

She blinks a couple of times, and I wonder if she's gonna cry. I even brace myself against it, my muscles tightening. "I—I wanted to say sorry to you," she whispers, and I struggle to fight the instinct that's burning inside me, to grab hold of her and kiss her. I can't afford to do that though... I know the damage she can do... so damn easily.

"Fine. You've said it."

I step back and push the door closed, but she puts her foot in the way, stopping me, and moves closer, reaching out and putting her hand on my arm. The feeling of her skin on mine is like fire on ice and I look down at the spot where she's melting me, wishing I could let her... *I can't... I can't let her do this.*

"Take your hand off of me," I growl, surprised by the depth of my own voice. "I didn't give you permission to touch me."

"P—Permission?" she flusters, snatching her hand away, but looking up into my eyes. "I didn't realize I needed permission."

"Well, you do."

"But... at the weekend. You let me touch you then."

"Yeah... well, that was the weekend. Things were different then." *I thought we had a future.*

She sighs and I can see her eyes filling with tears. *I need this to stop... now. I can't take much more.* "Colt... I didn't mean to hurt you," she says, her voice cracking, along with the few remaining pieces of my heart, the ones she hasn't already crushed, and I know what I have to do... what I have to say.

"Really?" I shake my head. "That was you trying *not* to hurt me? Jesus, Bree... I'd hate to see what you're capable of when you really mean it." I suck in a quick breath, and then let her have it: "You broke my fucking heart... and whatever you came here for, no-one gets to do that to me twice. Not even you. Now, for both our sakes, will you please just leave."

I know that got to her. I can see it in her eyes, and for a split second, I wish I could take it back. But then she turns and runs away. And I can hear her crying as she goes down the hallway, but I can't go after her. I can't play her games anymore.

She's just too dangerous.

*

I wasn't due to fly out to LA until Friday, but I've caught the Wednesday morning flight instead. After Bree left last night, I decided that hanging around in Boston wasn't gonna help. I didn't feel like another scene with her… or with Max, for that matter. There was no denying I'd been harsh with her, and I couldn't be sure he wouldn't come around to try and defend her. I wouldn't have blamed him if he had… but I wasn't in the mood for any more confrontation. So, I decided to put a few thousand miles between us, in the hope it might help me repair myself. Sometime. Maybe.

The third-floor apartment is actually a lot better than it looked on the realtor's website, although I think the completely open-plan living could take me a while to get used to. I'm accustomed to having a door on my bedroom, and this place only has one door in the whole apartment… and that's to the bathroom. But I suppose I should be grateful for small mercies.

I certainly can't complain about the location of the apartment, which is in the heart of the South Park district of Downtown LA, and is convenient for eating out… if I could be bothered. It's also only a twenty-minute drive from my new client, a Hollywood producer by the name of Brett Baker. He's never had any threats against his person, but one of his associates was recently the victim of a stalker, and it seems to have spooked Mr. Baker into taking action to protect himself. And I'm okay with that. This may be slightly alien territory for me, but he's paying us very well indeed to watch his back.

His PA has sent through his itinerary for the next two weeks, as of Monday, which is when our contract officially starts, and I intend spending the next few days, driving around the city, familiarizing myself with the routes we'll be taking, and any alternates I might need, as well as checking out his employees and the people he meets with on a regular basis. It'll keep me busy… and stop me from thinking too much. Looking at his schedule, Mr. Baker attends a lot of late night functions, so it doesn't seem like I'm gonna be getting to bed much before three a.m., for the foreseeable future. Still, it's not like I've got anything better to do… is it?

I won't be seeing anyone, that's for sure. Not socially. Because, if I can't have Bree, I don't want anyone else. And in any case, I threw away all of my kit before I left Boston. I'd intended to anyway, because of Bree, and wanting a fresh start with her. But once we broke up – although I don't think we were ever 'together', other than in my head – I knew I wouldn't be needing any of it.

And while I can't say I relish the prospect of a life of celibacy, I can't begin to contemplate the idea of being intimate with anyone who isn't Bree. So I'm not going to. I'm not going to think about Bree, or love, or happiness… or children… or any of the things I contemplated when I was with her… when, for a very brief moment, I thought I had it all. And while I've never tried to push my controlling nature quite that far before, I'm sure I'll manage.

Somehow.

Chapter Ten

Bree

Was it arrogant of me to expect forgiveness?

Probably.

Was it presumptuous of me to hope he'd want me back?

Obviously.

Was it stupid of me to think he loved me enough to want to try again?

Yes. It must have been. Because he sent me away.

And that hurts more than I ever thought it would.

Seeing him again, standing in the doorway of his apartment, it was hard not to just throw myself at him. Except I'm not sure he would have caught me. I think he would have let me fall.

He looked more gorgeous than ever, in stonewashed jeans that hugged his thighs, and a white t-shirt that reminded me of his chiseled chest, and how it felt to be held in his arms and rest my head against him. But as I stood there, staring into his eyes, the hurt in them glared back at me, and I realized the enormity of what I'd done. I'd pushed away the only man who's ever really loved me… for me. Which, as I told Max and Chase, is all I've ever wanted. Someone who'll love me, unconditionally, no questions asked, no holds barred. Someone who'll know my faults, no matter how bad they are, and who'll love me, just the same. That's what Colt did. And I hurt him so much, not only would he not have caught me, not only would he have let me fall, but he can't even bear to be in the same state as me… in the same time zone as me.

And I can't stop crying.

Because I miss him so much, it hurts. Deep inside, like a gnawing ache that's slowly eating away at me.

What the hell is wrong with me? Why couldn't I just see when I was well off? Why did I have to throw away the best chance of happiness I've ever had… or am ever likely to have?

And why couldn't I see love… real, bone-deep love, when it was staring me in the face?

It's been three days now since he sent me away, and I feel like I'm never going to function properly again… like I'm never going to breathe properly again… not without him.

"Hey, Sis…" Chase comes straight into my office without knocking. But that's Chase for you, I guess.

I haven't seen much of him since Tuesday afternoon, when Max, Pierce and I left for Colt's place, because Max led me to believe I stood a chance with Colt, if I just said sorry, and explained myself to him. Not that he gave me a chance to explain. He didn't want to know.

Chase went home, rather than coming to witness my humiliation. He said he needed to get some rest… although knowing Chase, that probably meant he went out to get laid.

"Hello." I look up at him as he sits down opposite me. Actually, he does look more refreshed today, so maybe I'm doing him an injustice. Maybe he has been catching up on his sleep, after all. He's gonna need to, if he hasn't already, because he's leaving for St. Thomas again on Monday, to see how things are going, and then I know he's going on to Atlanta to oversee the work we're doing to extend our hotel there.

"Why don't I treat you to lunch?" He sounds like he's making an excuse to talk to me, or to cheer me up… and I'm not in the mood.

I shake my head. "No thanks. I've got a lot of work to get done…"

"Are you okay?" He sounds concerned.

"Yeah. I'm fine. I'm just busy, that's all."

He leans forward. "Wanna run that by me again… and maybe cut the crap this time?"

"Okay. I miss him, alright?" I say, fresh tears welling in my eyes.

"I know you do." His voice is gentler now.

"I got it so wrong, Chase."

He nods his head. "Do you love him?" he asks.

"I—I don't know. But I'd have liked the chance to find out…" I let my voice fade, struggling to control my emotions as I contemplate what I've lost.

"Why are you talking in the past tense? It isn't over yet."

I frown at him. "Max did tell you what happened, didn't he?" I can't imagine he wouldn't have done… I can't imagine he'll have found it easy to forget the sight of me running out of the main entrance to Colt's apartment block, and into his arms, sobbing my heart out… or my garbled explanation of what had happened on Colt's doorstep, or his offer to talk to Colt on my behalf… which I declined. Or our car journey back to my place, which I spent crying on his shoulder. I imagine that's all still fairly fresh in Max's mind. Just like it is in mine.

"Yeah," Chase replies. "He called me on Tuesday night, after he'd taken you home. He told me Colt basically slammed the door in your face."

"He wasn't quite that rude." I defend him instinctively, and Chase smiles.

"The effect was still the same. You ended up on the sidewalk."

"Then why on earth are you saying it's not over?"

"Because it's not. Not unless you give up."

"I can't force him to take me back… I can't make him love me again." I sigh deeply, trying not to cry for the umpteenth time in the last few days. I need to change the subject, because clearly my brother is insane. And I can't do this anymore. "Can I ask you a question?"

"Sure."

"Have you really had three-ways in the past?"

He grins now, instead of just smiling. "I knew you were gonna say that."

"How?"

"Because I knew you didn't wanna talk about Colt at the moment… and I knew you were intrigued. It was written all over your face when I first said it on Tuesday morning."

"And what's the answer?"

"Yes, I have… but only with women. I've never wanted to share a woman with another guy. I'm way too greedy for that." He chuckles.

I study him for a moment, taking in his deep blue eyes, short, dark thick hair, and handsome features, which I'm sure most women would find irresistible. "Why do you do the things you do?" I ask him. "Sleeping around, I mean."

"Because I'm an asshole," he says, simply.

"You're not an asshole."

"Yeah I am, Bree. You've never seen me in action. Colt's never made a secret of the fact that he doesn't like me… or why. And I get that."

"It was Colt who said to me that you treat women like they're disposable," I admit, and he shrugs his shoulders again.

"That's a fairly accurate description. We are who we are, Bree. You're kinda mixed up right now… mainly thanks to Grady, and Dad, and the way they treated you. And I'm not really that different. Dad wanted to rule my life too, and Max's. That's why Max joined the army."

"I know. But what did Dad want from you, apart from your devotion to your education and the family business?" That was a common theme with all three of us.

"Commitment," he replies simply. "And I'm not talking about school, or work. But once Max had settled down with Eden, Dad kept on at me to go the same way… completely ignoring the fact that I was a lot younger, and that I've never wanted that kind of responsibility. I've also never met anyone I wanna spend the rest of my life with. Ever. Don't get me wrong, I understood why Max married Eden, and why he stood by her…"

"Stood by her? What does that mean?" It seems like an odd thing to say. Max and Eden were so in love, they were made for each other. Losing her damn near broke him.

"Nothing… I just phrased that wrong. What I mean is, it's not for me. I couldn't – I still can't – picture ever being tied down to one woman." He smiles and then says, "Sorry, Sis… poor choice of words."

I shake my head at him, although he has at least brought a small smile to my lips.

"Can I say something?" he says, leaning forward and resting his elbows on my desk.

"Yes."

He studies me now. "I'm surprised you're into the whole Dom/sub thing… after the way Grady treated you. I wouldn't have thought you'd wanna be with someone who'd expect to have any kind of control over you. If anything, I would've thought it would be the other way around, with you wanting to be more dominant… more in charge of things. I—I mean, I know we talked about it, and I know you said he's not a typical Dom…"

"What's a typical Dom?" I ask him.

"Like I said the other day, they tend to have rules… things they will and won't do. Things they expect of their subs. But you said Colt's not like that."

"No, he's not."

He nods his head. "Even so, I'm surprised you'd go with a guy like that… with your history."

"I was quite surprised too, when he first explained… about what he wanted to do," I reply. "But he made it very clear that he wasn't looking to take any kind of control outside of the bedroom. And then, when we got into it… that was when I realized it's actually really liberating."

"It is?"

"Yeah. I know that sounds weird… but it's true. I really don't think I'd ever wanna be the one in control… a Dominatrix, is it?" He nods his head. "Yeah. I couldn't do that. I'd feel really uncomfortable. But when I was with Colt, everything just felt right. It was like nothing else mattered. He made me feel so special… like there was no-one else in his world, but me. And I felt the same. It was a strange sensation… being bound and yet completely free at the same time, but that's exactly how it was. Because my brain was just filled with him… and nothing else. And that was just how I wanted it to be."

He nods his head, his lips twitching up into a slight smile. "Can I ask my question again?" he says, sitting back in his chair once more.

"Which question?"

"Are you in love with him?"

"I already said… I don't know yet. I guess I never will now."

"I do." He lets out a sigh. "You're about as in love as anyone I've ever known."

"Don't be ridiculous." That can't be right.

"I'm not. Look, I've had sex with more women than I even wanna think about, Sis… but I've never experienced anything like you're describing. Nothing even close to it. And that's because I've never been in love. Which is why I'm telling you it's not over yet. Because when you love someone as much as you so obviously love Colt, then you don't give up. You never give up. If you screw up, like you have, you do whatever it takes to make it right again. So stop sitting here feeling sorry for yourself and go do whatever it takes… before you really do lose him… for good."

Colt

I haven't had much sleep the last couple of nights.

Maybe that's because I'm not in my own bed. Or because this apartment is new to me. Although I've slept in far worse places before… years ago, I guess. Or maybe it's just because I can't get the thought of Bree out of my head… and it's been driving me quietly insane.

Yeah… that'd be it.

I've been out for most of yesterday and today, grocery shopping, and also driving around town, and up into the Hollywood Hills, getting used to my new surroundings and checking out Brett Baker's regular haunts. I haven't found anything that's rung any alarm bells… not yet, at least.

I made it back here by just after four today, grateful that it's Friday already, and that I'm gonna be starting work after the weekend, which means I'll be kept busy… too busy to think about Bree, anyway. I had a shower and watched some TV, just to unwind, before I ordered in some Chinese food, which I ate while going over Brett's itinerary again, to make sure I hadn't missed anything.

It's nearly nine p.m. now, which to my body feels like midnight, being as I haven't gotten used to the time difference yet… and I'm still not ready for bed.

I'm not ready to lie awake thinking about Bree for another eight hours.

So, I pour myself a large cup of coffee and settle down on the couch, opening my laptop and finding the email I received this afternoon, which contains the preliminary profiles of the people Brett Baker works with.

I don't spend too long studying his PA… a woman called Angela Jackson. She's been with him for nearly five years and seems to be as loyal as they come. She's married, no kids, a couple of dogs… and has 'down-to-earth' written all over her. The next on my list is his personal trainer… Greg Morris. He's only been working with Brett for three months, prior to which he was employed by a gym in San Francisco. There's no indication as to how he came to be employed by Mr. Baker… and that's something I'll need to find out about. I make a note to myself and take a large gulp of coffee, just as the doorbell rings, making me choke.

"Shit…" I mutter, coughing, as I put down my coffee again before I spill it, and set my laptop to one side, getting to my feet. I'm still trying to catch my breath as I walk over to the front door and pull it open. "Shit…" I whisper a second time, my eyes settling on Bree, who's standing right in front of me, looking tired and tearful… and so damn beautiful, it hurts. She's wearing another of her fitted dresses, like she wears to the office most days… a pale blue one this time… and I wonder if she's come here straight from work. I guess she must've done, because she must've caught a flight out here sometime earlier this afternoon. Why, though? Why would she do that? I feel something stir in my chest, something warm and tender, and aimed at her… but I dismiss it. "What are you doing here?" I snap, and she startles slightly. "Did you fly out here by yourself?" If she did, I'm gonna lose it with her… again.

"Yes," she says meekly, looking up at me through her eyelashes. "But before you lose your temper, it's okay." *Oh, is it? That's what she thinks.* "Dana drove me to the airport," she adds quickly, before I can say anything. "And Chase arranged my ticket… and for a car to drive me here. So, please don't be mad at me. I made sure I was safe. But I —I had to come and see you by myself."

"Why?"

"Because I need to say sorry."

That warm, tender feeling in my chest intensifies, and I have to concentrate for a minute, so I'm not overwhelmed by it. I push it down and take a breath.

"You already said sorry… in Boston… at my apartment. Remember?"

"Yes. I know. But I don't think you understood."

I fold my arms across my chest, just so she can't see me clenching my fists. "Yeah, I did. You felt guilty about what you'd done. You wanted to make yourself feel better and saying sorry was meant to achieve that."

Her eyes widen and she pales, which is surprising, because she was already looking washed-out. "You think I feel better? You think any part of this is making me feel better?" Her voice cracks as she speaks, and a sob leaves her mouth, just as her legs give way beneath her.

There's no way I can let her fall. Even now. So I step forward and catch her before she hits the floor, lifting her into my arms and turning back into my apartment as she buries her head in my chest. I kick the door closed, feeling her tears soaking into my t-shirt already, as I carry her through to the living area and set her down in the corner of the couch. And even though a part of me wants to keep hold of her and never let her go, I stand up straight again. Unless it's strictly necessarily, I can't bring myself to touch her, let alone hold her. I'm too scared of what will happen if I let her get near to me again.

So I step back, and sit down in the chair opposite, looking at her, surprised that my already broken heart can be shattering again, at the sight of her crying so hard in front of me. Despite everything, the temptation to go to her is almost overwhelming. But I fight it. I have to. And eventually, her breathing returns to normal, she gulps in more air, and turns to look at me. I hate seeing her like this, but I have to ignore the urge in me to comfort her. It won't get us anywhere.

I hand her the box of Kleenex from the shelf underneath the table and she takes it, putting it beside her on the couch. "Thanks," she murmurs, wiping her eyes. "I—I was so scared," she adds, in a small, stuttering voice, screwing up the Kleenex in her hand and squeezing it tight.

"When?"

"That night. Last Monday night… when I went out. I was feeling scared and lonely, and I needed to talk to someone. I—I thought the someone was probably you… only you weren't there."

"Wait a second… are you saying this is my fault?"

She frowns. "No. Of course not. I'm just trying to explain… in as much as I can. Because I'm not sure I understand it all myself. I just know I was scared."

I shake my head. "You're not that easily scared, Bree."

"You think?" she mutters, dabbing at her eyes with a fresh Kleenex, even though she's got the other one still clenched in her hand.

"Yeah. I mean… what in the world got you so frightened that you thought it was a good idea to dump Dana, catch a cab to that fucking bar and sit in a booth with two guys who'd already suggested a three-way with you, just a few weeks ago?"

"You did," she says, so softly, I can barely hear her.

"*I* did?" *No. I've got that wrong. I must've misheard her.*

"Yes. You scared me, Colt."

I sit forward, filled with fear myself now. "Bree, be truthful with me… how did I scare you? Was… was it the things I did to you, at my apartment last weekend? Was it too much? I have to know… did I push you too far?"

She shakes her head. "No. It wasn't what you did. It was what you *said*."

"Which part?"

"When you said you were in love with me…" Her voice fades, and I feel my broken heart sinking… drowning.

"Well… I was," I mutter, and her head shoots up, like she's surprised.

"Does that mean you're not anymore?" she asks, her tears still threatening to flow.

I can't answer her, because my reply would have to be that I am… and that I always will be. But I'm not about to tell her that. I can't afford to… my heart couldn't take it. We stare at each other for what feels like forever, and eventually she seems to understand that I'm not going to respond, and she lets out a sigh and says, "I wasn't ready to hear that. It was all moving too fast for me."

"Yeah… I think I kinda worked that out for myself. But rather than telling me that, and talking it through, you went back to that bar… to those guys. You knew what they wanted from you, and you went back to them." I struggle to control my temper again as the image of her in that booth comes back into my head.

"I didn't go back to them. I went back to the bar. They arrived after I did."

"And you chose to sit with them, Bree," I reason, making the same argument I did at the time, being as it clearly fell on deaf ears. And then I ask her the question that's been plaguing me, keeping me awake, niggling at the back of my mind ever since she told me who those guys actually were. I didn't dare ask her on Monday night. I was too scared of how I might react, but I need to know. "Did you let them touch you again?" The words fall out of my mouth on a whisper and for a second, I wonder if she's even heard me. She just stares, with her mouth slightly open.

"Of course I didn't," she says, eventually, shaking her head. "All we did was talk, Colt. I promise."

"And if they'd suggested a three-way again?"

"I'd have said 'no'. Again."

"And if they hadn't wanted to take 'no' for an answer the second time around? If they'd thought you were teasing them… leading them on? Can you understand what I meant, when I was trying to explain to you about the messages you were sending out to them?"

She sighs. "I suppose. Although, as I said to you on Monday night, I wasn't aware of sending any messages."

"So does that mean you weren't aware that what you were doing felt like a deliberate attempt to hurt me?"

"I—I wasn't aware of anything," she stutters, and then blinks, allowing another tear to fall.

"How can that be? I'd told you I was in love with you," I carry on, because I need to say this. "I'd opened up to you, like I'd never opened up to anyone in my life… and you snuck out, and met up with two guys, who you knew were interested in you, sexually. You have to have known that would hurt me. You can't have been unaware of that… surely." I cough, because I've gone too far. My emotions are getting the better of me, and I can't allow that to happen. I need to regain control. Now.

"I'm sorry," she whispers. "I shouldn't have done that to you… I shouldn't have done any of it. I shouldn't have put myself in danger, I shouldn't have gone back there and let those guys sit with me, and I shouldn't have shown so little regard for your feelings. You're right. I should have been more considerate… more aware. I should have waited for you and talked through how I felt."

I can't dispute any of that, but I'm not sure what the point of this is, especially as we both agree. "Why are you really here, Bree?" The words leave my lips, and she frowns, like she's confused.

"I told you… to apologize."

"You've done that. Several times."

"I know. But I—I spoke to Chase, and he…"

"You spoke to Chase? You talked to him… about us?"

She nods her head and I can't help feeling disappointed. I guess it must show. "Don't blame me," she says defensively. "It was Max who first told him about us… about you, I mean."

"About me?"

"Yes… that you're a… a Dominant."

Great. That's just what I need. Chase Crawford comparing notes with me.

"What on earth made Max tell him?" It doesn't sound like the kind of thing Max would do. As far as I know, he's never told anyone… until now.

"Max was mad with me – and not being exactly quiet about it – and Chase came into my office."

"Why was Max mad with you?" *Please tell me she hadn't done anything else to put herself in danger…*

"Because I'd made you leave. He was waiting for me when I got into work on Tuesday morning. I don't think I've ever seen him so angry."

I shake my head. "He had no right to be angry… not with you. And you didn't make me leave, Bree. That was my decision."

"Which you took because of what I did."

I can't deny that, so I don't. "That's between the two of us… and it's nothing to do with either of your brothers. So why Max felt he had the right to tell Chase about us – or about me – I don't know."

"Well, he had to explain to Chase why me going to the bar on Monday night would have caused you to leave in the first place… which meant he had to tell him we'd spent the weekend together." That's fair enough, I guess, although I'm still confused about why Max felt the need to tell Chase about my lifestyle. "But then Chase got angry with me, too," Bree adds in a quiet whisper, blinking a few times, like she's remembering something.

"Chase? Why?"

"Because of what I'd done to you. I—I couldn't handle it. I couldn't handle hearing what he said… so I ran."

"Bree… for fuck's sake…" Will she never learn?

"It's okay," she says quickly. "I got Dana to take me home." I let out a slow breath, in the hope she won't notice, which I guess she doesn't because she carries on talking. "Max and Chase both came to see me later on that afternoon, to apologize for the things they'd said. And that's when Max explained… about you."

"Why?"

"Because, when I was trying to explain to them about why I'd gone out on Monday night, rather than waiting and talking to you, I said I wasn't ready to get tied down."

I struggle not to react, realizing the error of her words... but more importantly, their implication, which cuts even deeper than I would have expected. You'd have thought I'd have gotten used to her not loving me. Except it seems I haven't. And I'm not sure I ever will.

"I see," I mumble.

"Max explained about... about the things you're into, and Chase got it. And that's when I tried to explain to them how it felt."

"How what felt?" What the hell has she told them?

"The things you and I talked about on Friday night... about how I'd gone from being controlled by my dad, to being controlled by Grady..."

"To being controlled by me?"

She shakes her head. "No. That was the whole point. That was one of the things we talked about... the fact that you *didn't* want to control me... not outside the bedroom."

"I think I told you that myself, didn't I?" I know damn well I did.

"Yes. But like I said, things moved so fast between us, I didn't really have time to take it all in. I was in too much shock..."

She was in shock, because I'd said I loved her. Oh... that feels just great.

"Did it make more sense... when you talked it over with your brothers?" I ask her.

"I think so."

"And was that why you came to my apartment?"

"I came to your apartment to apologize, just like I said. It wasn't about making myself feel better." She uses my own words, but with no bitterness in her voice, which is kinda admirable in the circumstances.

"What do you want from me, Bree? Other than to apologize... because you've kinda done that now."

She sucks in a breath and lets it out again. "I spoke to Chase again... today. And I told him how it actually felt... being with you."

I sigh myself, wondering what's coming next, and why she can't just get to the point. "And?"

"I told him how liberating it was… how you made me feel free for the first time in years… maybe forever." She stares at me, her eyes locked on mine, but I let my head fall into my hands, her words washing over me, just so I don't have to absorb them… just so I don't have to remember that I felt exactly the same way when I was with her. I can't think like that…

"And what did Chase say?" I ask.

"He told me I should stop feeling sorry for myself and try to make it right again… before I lose you for good."

I look up, studying her beautiful, tear-stained face. I'm still burning with need, longing to hold her…

It would be so easy to take you back, Bree. In less than a second, I could have you in my arms. In less than a minute, I could carry you to my bed. In less than five minutes, you'd be screaming my name…

No! Stop this. I can't. I can't take the risk… I know what she can do.

"I'm sorry," I whisper, my heart aching at the sadness in her eyes when she hears those two simple words. "I'm really sorry, Bree… but you already lost me."

She gasps and gets up from the couch, looking around, like she's floundering, rudderless… like she's lost herself too.

"I—I shouldn't have come," she says, as I stand and move around the table, so I'm beside her.

"Do you understand?" I reach out and hold her shoulders, grounding her for a moment, and she looks up into my eyes, her own welling with more tears. "I can't let you in, Bree. You hurt me so much…"

She swallows hard as I release her, because holding her, even just with my hands on her shoulders, is too much for me. "I—I know. I'm sorry."

"I think you've apologized enough."

She's really struggling and although I'm tempted to pull her into my arms and tell her to ignore everything I've just said… I can't. Because the pain is still too intense.

"I—I should go," she says, looking around again.

"Where to?"

"I don't know…" Her voice fades, and I wonder if she anticipated this working out differently; if she thought she'd be able to stay here with me. God, I wish she could… but it would never work. I can see the hurt and disappointment in her eyes, but we can't go back… not now.

"I'll book you into a hotel for the night. And then I'll take you to the airport in the morning."

"I can get a cab," she says, that familiar defiance rising to the fore again.

"No, you can't."

"Why not? We're not together… what does it matter what I do?"

It matters because I fucking love you!

"My company is still employed by Max. It's my job to look after you." I harden my voice, and she blinks a few times, biting her bottom lip.

"So, I'm part of the job again?" she whispers.

I don't reply, but I grab my laptop, setting it down on the kitchen countertop and finding her a hotel which is fairly close to the airport, about a fifteen minute drive away from here.

I make a reservation in her name, paying for it with my credit card, when I'm given the option to pay in advance, and then I glance over at her. She's still standing where she was a few minutes ago… looking maybe even more lost than she did before.

"Ready?" I say to her and she looks up and slowly nods her head, grabbing her purse from where she must've dropped it, on the couch.

I pick up my keys and phone, and make my way to the front door, and Bree follows.

"I got it so wrong with you," she says slowly as I step aside to let her out, and she looks up into my eyes.

"Yeah… you did."

She walks through and I take a breath. There's nothing more to be said now. We're both sorry.

We're just sorry in different ways… and for very different reasons.

I get up early, having not slept... again.

This time, it's because I've been awake all night, wondering if I did the right thing, wondering if I should have given Bree another chance. I was kinda hard on her; I know that. But I still can't get away from the fact that I'd told her I was in love with her – and I still am, no matter what I let her think last night – and within twenty-four hours, she was out with two other guys. And they were guys she already knew, who'd offered her a three-way, one of whom had touched her, intimately... and while I know she didn't go through with anything, on either occasion, the fact of the matter is, she thought so little of me and of my feelings, she was prepared to hurt me... badly. And not give it a second thought. At least, not until she got caught out. And, if I'm being honest, I'm really struggling to come to terms with that.

When I left her last night at the door to her hotel room, I arranged to pick her up at seven-thirty for the nine-thirty flight, giving her enough time to have breakfast at the airport. So I leave my place at just before seven, because I'm too tired to rush anywhere today, and I take a slow drive over to her hotel.

Parking up, I check my messages, to find there's one from Angela, Brett Baker's PA, timed at 6.23 this morning, which surprises me, considering it's Saturday. She says that Brett has been held up in Europe, meeting some financiers, and he won't be back in LA until the end of next week, so I won't be starting work until Friday. That's really quite annoying, because it gives me even longer to kick my heels and think about Bree. But I fire off a quick reply, thanking her for the update, while wondering to myself if she's always up so early, even at the weekends... and whether she's always so efficient. I hope so. Because as much as her boss seems to be alarmingly flexible, at least if she's organized about it, it's gonna make my life a lot easier.

Inside the hotel, the lobby is empty, and I walk straight up to the reception desk, to be greeted with a warm smile and the fluttering eyelashes of an overly made-up redhead... who really isn't my type. I don't have a 'type' anymore... except for Bree. Obviously.

"Good morning," she gushes, leaning forward to give me a completely unnecessary view of her cleavage. "Can I help?"

I doubt it.

"Yeah… I'm here to collect Miss Crawford. Could you let her know I'm here? She's in room 367."

She nods her head, looking a little deflated, and then turns to pick up the phone before she stops and turns back again.

"Sorry, did you say 'Room 367'?" she asks.

"Yeah. Why?"

"Because the guest in that room checked out in the early hours of the morning."

"What the fuck?"

She ignores my language and taps on the keyboard of her computer before looking up at me again. "Yeah… she checked out at just after midnight, actually… right after I came on duty."

"Only an hour after I dropped her off?"

She shrugs. "I don't know. I wasn't here then. My shift only started at eleven thirty… and I'm due to go home in half an hour." She looks at her watch and then back at me, fluttering her eyelashes again, like I'm supposed to be interested in what time she finishes work. *Oh, please…*

I shake my head, ignoring her. "What the hell is she playing at?"

The woman doesn't reply, but then I don't expect her to, and I pull my phone from my back pocket, making my way toward the doors and going back outside to my car.

Once behind the wheel, I start making calls… to all the airlines I can think of who run flights from here to Boston. I get lucky on my second attempt.

Bree booked herself a ticket on the flight that left at one forty-five this morning. It had a lay-over of just under two hours in Dallas, and is due to land at Logan on time, which the guy on the phone informs me will be at one-forty this afternoon, local time. I check my watch. Allowing for the time difference, that's just over three hours from now… which means I've got another call to make.

I thank the guy and hang up, connecting my third call, which goes to voicemail, not surprisingly. I never really know Max's weekend schedules, but they revolve entirely around Tia, which I guess means he's busy doing something with her... especially as he doesn't have a nanny right now.

"Max, it's me. Call me when you get this."

I know I don't need to say who it is... and I'm not about to go into a long explanation on his voicemail, either. It's too complicated.

I let my head rock back before making my fourth call, which is to Dana. I apologize for interrupting her weekend, but explain the situation and that I need her to collect Bree from the airport.

"I'll text you the flight details," I explain.

"Sure." She sounds kinda miserable.

"Is everything okay?" I ask her, even though I'm sure she's just pissed with me for spoiling her plans... whatever they might have been.

"Yeah."

"Really? Doesn't sound like it to me. I'm sorry for messing up your weekend, Dana, but..."

"It's not that," she interrupts.

"Then what's wrong?"

"I just think it's sad, that's all."

"What is?"

"That you and Bree couldn't work things out."

Hell... I never expected her to say that. I didn't even know she was aware that Bree and I were together. Not that we are anymore, but...

"Yeah, well... sometimes it's not meant to be," I murmur, because I can't think of anything else to say.

She sighs, loud enough for me to hear her. "If you say so, boss."

I don't reply, and we end the call. I text her Bree's flight details, before I start my car and head back to my apartment, where I fix myself some coffee and sit on the couch, trying hard not to remember the sight of Bree sitting here just a few hours ago, or how good it felt to hold her, even briefly, in my arms again.

"Fuck it..." I roar loudly, and let my head fall into my hands, just as my phone rings and I check the screen, feeling kinda relieved to see Max's name there. *Thank God... he'll get it, even if no-one else does. He'll understand.*

"Hi," I say, connecting the call.

"What's up?"

"It's Bree."

I hear him sigh. "What's she done now?"

"Well, I'm gonna guess you knew she'd flown out here?"

"Yeah. Chase told me last night when I got back to the office. I was out all afternoon, but evidently he talked her into coming out there to see you?"

"Yeah, he did."

"So what's happened?"

"We talked…"

"And?"

"And nothing. I booked her into a hotel for the night, with the intention of taking her to the airport this morning… only when I got there, she'd already checked herself out again. She actually only stayed there for an hour, and then she left and presumably got a cab to the airport."

"What the fuck is wrong with her? Why didn't she just stick to your plan?" *I knew he'd get it…*

"I have no idea. But she's booked on the American Airlines flight that gets into Logan at one-forty this afternoon. I thought I'd let you know what's going on. I've arranged for Dana to pick her up, so you don't need to worry… but you might wanna call her, or something. Later on. She was kinda upset."

"Oh… okay, thanks."

"How are you?" It's only been a few days since I left, but I've missed him. I've missed working for him… and although I know Pierce is good at his job, I'd rather be there doing it myself.

"I'm okay." He sounds kinda tense.

"What's wrong?"

"Nothing."

"Cut the crap. What's wrong, Max?"

"I guess I'm just a bit disappointed."

"By what?"

"You."

"Me?" I can't keep the surprise out of my voice. "What the hell did I do?"

"You couldn't even give Bree a chance?" He gives me his answer in the form of a question, which shows he didn't get it after all, and I know I'm gonna have to respond to him, even though I think the reply is obvious.

"No. Why would I? She hurt me. She broke my heart."

"I know. You told me that already. But you love her, don't you?"

"Yeah. I do. But this is so fucking painful, man." It's a struggle to control my voice. "I denied my love for her for eleven years. I buried it, and lived with the pain of knowing she was with that fucking idiot she married, and I thought that was bad enough. But this… this is so much worse than I ever thought it could be."

"And all this pain you're in right now… that gives you the right to hurt her back, does it? You think that's how love works?"

"No… I…" I hesitate, letting his words percolate through my brain. "But, don't you see? Letting her back in… it's too much. What if she does it again? I thought you'd get it…" I let my voice fade, feeling a little disappointed myself now.

"Of course I fucking get it," he shouts. "You think I don't know what you're going through?" The tone of his voice surprises me.

I let out a breath. "Look, man… I get that Eden was killed, that she was taken from you, but…"

"This has nothing to do with her death," he interrupts. "I'm saying that I know how it feels to be hurt… to be betrayed. And to have to decide what you're gonna do about it."

"What the hell are you talking about? Eden never hurt you… not like this. She never betrayed you." I know that's true. He and Eden had the perfect marriage. And he can't be talking about anyone else because there's never been anyone for him but Eden. Ever.

"Yes, she did."

There's a sudden stillness between us, which stretches for a few moments, and several thousand miles, until I whisper, "What are you saying, Max?"

"I—I've never told you this before. I've never told anyone this actually… but Eden had an affair."

"What?" He can't be serious. Eden? Cheating? It's just not possible.

"When she told me about it…"

"She told you about it?" Jesus… it must be true then, and not just a figment of his imagination… or his nightmares.

"Yeah, she confessed the whole thing to me, and when she did, I left her." I can't believe I'm hearing this. "It wasn't just a one-night stand, you see," he says, his voice really quiet and considered. "She didn't get drunk and fall into bed with a stranger, and wake up regretting it the next morning. She had a full-on affair with her boss, that had been going on for over a year when she finally owned up to it."

"When did this happen? Was it when we were overseas, before you two got married?" That happened a lot, even to the guys who'd been married for a while. It was hard being left behind… or at least that was what their wives and girlfriends told them, when they broke them.

"No, it was more recent than that. Much more recent."

"It take it this was before Tia?" It must have been. Surely.

"Yes," he says. "Just."

I wonder at that last remark. "There's no doubt about Tia being yours, is there?" He adores her, but I guess anything's possible.

"No. Tia was conceived after I went back to Eden… after she'd broken it off with *him*." He emphasizes that last word and I can still hear the pain and regret in his voice.

"And you left her? At the time, I mean… when she first told you?"

"Yeah. I did. I packed a bag and walked out… and moved myself into one of our hotels."

"And what happened?"

"I stayed there… for about three nights, quietly falling apart. And then I realized that living without her was so much worse than anything else… even than the thought of her with another man."

"So you got back together?" I know that's what happened, but I'm still stunned.

"Yeah. I'm not gonna say it was easy," he says, sighing deeply. "It wasn't. It was probably the hardest thing I'd ever done… the hardest decision I'd ever had to make. The love was always there, deep down. But the trust was a lot harder to recapture, because of what she'd done. When she was killed, I was still trying to get that back, and she knew that. We were both putting in the work, making the effort, because we knew what we had was worth fighting for. And that's the point I'm trying to make here, Colt… when you really love someone, you give yourself to them… completely. Bree trusted you with her body. I know you say you explained to her what she was getting herself into… but I seriously doubt she fully understood it. And yet she trusted you anyway… not to hurt her, not to push her too far, and not to do anything to her she wasn't ready for."

"Like telling her I'm in love with her, you mean?"

"No," he allows. "You had to tell her that. But you could've given her some time to get on the same page as you."

"I was prepared to do that… I was more than prepared to wait. Except she didn't give us a chance. She went out with two other guys… guys she'd met up with before, who'd she'd already told me about. Guys who'd offered her a three-way…" I don't mention about one of them touching her. I can't do that to her. But I let my voice fade because I can't bring myself to say anything more, and I don't think I need to. In this instance, I'm almost positive Max will get it.

"I didn't know that," he says, sounding grim. "I didn't know she'd been quite that stupid… that hurtful." He proves me right, and then adds, "But stupid or not, even she knows her behavior was appalling. And that's why she came to your apartment the other night, and then flew the best part of three thousand miles… to ask you to forgive her. Only you threw it in her face. Twice. Because you forgot the golden rule of being in love…"

"Which is?"

"That sometimes you have to put your own feelings to one side and try to understand why the person you're in love with is doing the things they're doing. There's almost always a reason. I'm not sure I ever really got to the bottom of it with Eden. I got her version of it, but I always thought there had to be more to it than that. In Bree's case, she told Chase and me it was because things were moving too fast between you guys, and she was lonely and confused… and she needed to talk to you… only you weren't here, because I'd kept you out all day… and she just felt like she had to break out. I don't think she meant anything to come of it with those guys. She was just scared."

"I know. She told me that too."

"Then why can't you give her a chance? Why can't you talk it through and try to work it out with her? You're both fucking miserable right now."

"I can't…"

"Why not? I get that you're hurting. I get that your pride has been more than fucked over… but can't you see? Love isn't always a fifty-fifty thing. Sometimes, one of you is gonna struggle, or screw up. And that's when the other one has to step up and take the strain… because that's how love works."

Chapter Eleven

Bree

Even though it's a Saturday, I suppose I shouldn't have been surprised to see Dana waiting for me at the airport.

I should have known Colt would get to the hotel in LA, find me gone, and then somehow magically arrange all of this.

I can only imagine how angry he was, though… but I'm not going to think about that. I'm not going to think about him at all, if I can help it… at least not once I've spoken to Max, which I'm gonna have to do, now Dana's brought me back to my apartment.

He answers on the second ring, which surprises me, being as I know he'll be doing something with Tia today. She's what his weekends are all about now. His voice is quiet, and he just says, "Hello," although I know he knows it's me.

"Hi. I just thought I'd let you know I'm back from LA."

"Okay," he says.

"And I've decided, I'm not gonna be coming into work for a few days… probably not until Wednesday. I'm…"

"Hey… you don't have to account to me for your time. You own the company too," he interrupts, not acting like the CEO we all know he is, for once in his life.

"I know. But I just thought I'd tell you what I'm doing. I need to take a few days to myself. I need some time." Ideally, I'd like to take more than a few days, but I'm too busy at the moment.

"I do get it," he says, and the sympathy in his voice almost undoes me.

"Can… can I assume you've spoken to Colt?"

"Yeah. He called to let me know you'd checked yourself out of your hotel in the early hours of the morning." He sighs, and I can picture him shaking his head. "You've gotta stop doing shit like that, Bree."

"It's not something I'm planning on doing again, believe me. I—I just couldn't face staying there and seeing him again this morning… knowing he doesn't want me."

"Doesn't he?" I can hear what sounds like surprise in his voice.

"No. I apologized. I tried to explain why I did those things… and how I felt."

"You… you told him you're in love with him?" That's definitely surprise… bordering on shock, I think.

"No. But how did you know?"

"I didn't. I guessed… and anyway, Chase told me about your conversation yesterday, so it was kinda obvious. But why didn't you tell Colt?"

"Because he didn't give me the chance… and I don't think he wanted to hear it. He's made his mind up about me. I hurt him, and he can't forgive me for that." I feel the tears welling in my eyes. "He doesn't love me anymore, Max… so it doesn't matter how I feel, or what I say. We're over."

His sigh is slightly louder this time. "I wish you guys would just talk to each other… or more importantly, listen to each other."

"There's no point anymore. And anyway, I didn't call for a lecture. I called to let you know I've given Dana a few days off, and I'm gonna just stay here and lick my wounds, if it's okay with you."

"Don't be like that, Sis. I'm not lecturing you. I'm trying to help."

The first of many tears falls onto my cheek. "I know," I whisper, hoping he won't hear the crack in my voice. "I just wish I'd done things differently… I wish I could turn the clock back."

"You can never do that, Bree. But the next time you get a chance like this, don't blow it… and call me, if you wanna talk. Okay?"

"Okay." I'm struggling not to sob now, and I hang up, before he hears me, letting out a low whimper as I sit back on the couch, tears streaming down my cheeks.

How can he talk about the 'next time'? I know perfectly well there's never gonna be a next time for me. Not like this… because there's no-one who can compare with Colt.

I just wish I'd worked that out before it was too late.

I'm beyond exhausted, but I'm also in desperate need of a shower, so I drag myself up off of the couch and go through to my bedroom, taking off my dress and underwear, which I've been wearing since yesterday, and throwing them into the laundry basket in the corner of the room, before I walk through to my bathroom, and into the shower, turning on the water and letting it flow over my body.

I wish Colt was here now to hold me, his strong hands on my skin, his fingers caressing me, his lips on mine. I hug my arms around myself, wishing they were his, and let the tears fall, my body wracked with sorrow and anger… at myself… for letting him go. And with longing for the man who'll never know how much I love him.

I don't stop crying, even as I wash myself, and my hair, trying hard not to recall when he did that for me; trying hard not to think at all. And then, stepping out of the shower, I dry my hair and put on my blue and white striped pajama bottoms and a white v-necked t-shirt. It may only be the middle of the afternoon, but I don't care. There's no-one here to see me, and I'm too tired to get dressed again now.

Going back out into the living room, I flop down on the couch, hugging a cushion to my chest, and let myself cry… and cry.

I startle at the sound of the doorbell, ringing loud and long, and I sit up.

I must have fallen asleep, because it's late. And although it's still vaguely light, as I glance out through the window, I can see it's also pouring with rain, the sky a leaden gray, which matches my mood.

The doorbell rings again, even louder it seems to me, and I get to my feet, feeling a little unsteady as I make my way over, only now realizing that I haven't eaten since yesterday… sometime… or was it the day before? I can't remember. Not that it matters, and I pull the door open, standing back in shock.

"You…?"

"What the fuck are you doing?" Colt glares at me, raising his voice. "Why did you just open your door?"

"Because you rang the doorbell."

"Hilarious, Bree." He narrows his eyes. "But you're missing the point. No-one buzzed me up from downstairs, did they?"

"No." I shake my head, although it's still kinda fuzzy, and I have to grab the door to steady myself. "But you know the passcode… and according to Max, you've got a key, haven't you?"

"Yes, I've got a key. But do you honestly think I'd let myself into your apartment, knowing you were here? And you're still missing the point. You just opened your door without checking who was on the other side. What if someone had somehow gotten hold of the passcode and found their way in here? You'd have been alone… with God knows who…" His voice drops and his eyes soften.

"I'm sorry," I whisper. "I've only just woken up… I wasn't thinking. And, in any case, what are you doing here? You're supposed to be in LA."

"I—I came to make sure you got home safely." His eyes lock onto mine, dark and intense, and I feel that familiar heat pooling inside me. I'm also suddenly aware that he's wet, because his t-shirt is glued to his chest, highlighting his toned muscles… and that I'm only wearing my pajamas… and, judging from his expression, I think Colt's noticed that too.

"You flew three thousand miles, in the rain, to make sure I got home safely?" I say, just to make sure I heard him correctly.

"Yeah. Well, no. If we're being precise about it, I didn't fly through the rain. I flew through a storm, and then I rented a car and drove through the rain." He smiles as he's speaking, and it's all I can do not to cry. He's so beautiful. "You ran out on me, Bree."

"Of course I did. You said I'd already lost you, so what was the point in staying? What did you expect me to do, when you'd made it so clear you didn't want me anymore?"

"Yeah... about that," he murmurs and closes the gap between us in two quick steps, his hands reaching out and clasping my face as he bends his head and kisses me, our tongues colliding in an instant, and the sound of his groans filling the space around us. My body craves his and I lean into him, ignoring his wet t-shirt and feeling the heat and strength of his body seeping into mine... except it's not enough and as he deepens the kiss, my legs buckle beneath me. "Whoa..." He moves his hands from my face and catches me in his arms, holding me up. "Are you okay?" He looks down into my eyes and I shake my head.

"I don't feel very well."

"Bree?"

He lifts me, kicking the door closed, and carries me back into my apartment. I let my head rest against his chest, looking up into his face, his jaw firm and chiseled, as he lays me down on the couch, before turning and grabbing the cashmere throw that I keep over the back, putting it across my legs. Then he drops to his knees on the floor beside me, his face a picture of concern mixed with fear.

"What's wrong, baby?" he says, brushing a stray hair away from my face.

"You... you called me 'baby'," I mutter, gazing up at him, unsure why he's here, even though I can still feel his kiss on my lips.

"Yeah. I know... now stop changing the subject and tell me what's wrong."

"I'm hungry."

He smiles. "You're hungry?"

"Yeah. I don't remember when I last ate anything. Certainly not today, I know that much... the food on the flight made me wanna be sick. I didn't eat at all in LA... and I don't remember when I ate yesterday... if I ate at all."

"Jeez..." He lets out a breath and gets to his feet, pulling his phone from his pocket. "Pizza?" he says, looking down at me. "It'll be quicker than anything else, I think."

I nod my head, although the movement makes the room spin, so I stop again. "Yes, please."

He moves away, tapping on the screen of his phone, before he replaces it in his pocket, and goes over to the kitchen, returning a few minutes later, with a glass of water.

"You know you've got no food in your refrigerator, don't you? You don't even have any milk."

"I know… I've not been very good at things like that lately."

He sits down beside me, perched on the edge of the couch, and holds my head up, helping me take a few sips of water. "The pizza will be here in fifteen minutes," he says softly. "Now, do you wanna explain why you haven't been eating?"

"Shouldn't you get out of those wet clothes?" I suggest, and he smirks, raising his eyebrows. "I'm serious, Colt. You're soaking."

"No, I'm not. My jeans are okay, and my t-shirt will dry off quickly enough. You're just trying to avoid answering my question, and we both know it… and even I'm not that easily distracted. So, tell me, why haven't you been eating?"

"It didn't seem important," I admit. *Not compared to losing you.*

"Of course it's important." He shakes his head and puts the glass down on the table, before he glances at my couch, hesitates for a second, and then removes his t-shirt, yanking it over his head and dropping it to the floor. "I guess it is a little damp," he says, smiling as he changes position, lying down next to me and holding me in his arms. Snuggling right into him, I enjoy the feeling of being safe for the first time in ages. "I hurt you, didn't I?" he says.

"Yes," I whisper, feeling his muscles tighten.

"I'm sorry." I want to tell him not to be… this is my fault, not his. But before I can say a word, he continues, "I—I thought it was just me who was hurting, and I let that blind me to what I was doing to you." He leans back a little, brushing his fingertips down my cheek and looking deep into my eyes. "What kind of man am I, putting my pain ahead of yours? Can you…" He falters. "Please… can you forgive me?"

"Stop it. You're not to blame. I am." There. I've said it.

"We both are," he replies, shaking his head. "I'll admit you seem to have a fairly unique capacity for acting on impulse, pulling some crazy-assed stunts, and getting yourself into trouble, but I should've payed more attention. I should have listened to what you were saying… and, more importantly, what you weren't saying. When I told you I was in love with you, you said nothing… absolutely nothing. And I should have known then that something wasn't right. I might never have been in that situation before, and maybe I didn't know what to expect, but I think when a guy tells a girl he's in love with her, he's supposed to hear something more than stoney silence in return."

"I think he's supposed to hear the girl say that she loves him too," I suggest, when he stops talking to catch his breath.

"I guess," he replies, shrugging his shoulders and totally missing my attempt to tell him how I feel. "But only if she feels the same way. And you don't. Or you'd have said so… and what I should have done, when you said nothing, was to tell you it's okay. Because it is." I open my mouth to speak, but he raises his hand between us, placing his fingers gently over my lips. "Let me finish, baby," he says and then pulls his fingers away, kissing me briefly before he adds, "You don't have to feel the same way as me. It's too much to expect. I've had eleven years of loving you. I've had time to get used to it. You'd had a weekend of being with me… a weekend in which I also introduced you to a lot of other new experiences, as well as dropping the bombshell on you that I've been in love with you for more than a decade… and rather than leaving things to chance, or hoping for the best, I should have told you the other thing that was going through my head, which was that I don't need you to love me back. Not if you're not ready. Just having you with me is enough. Just knowing you're here, and that you know how I feel about you… that's all I need." I can hear the desperation in his voice, and it cuts right through me.

"Please, Colt… can you stop talking, just for a few seconds?"

"Sure." He frowns at me.

Now I've got his attention and a room full of silence, I don't know quite what to do with them, but I know I have to tell him the truth. I owe him that much.

"Being without you these last few days has been really hard," I murmur. "And I wish it hadn't had to be that way. I wish you hadn't had to leave town and fly all the way across to the other side of the country for me to work out how I feel about you… and I wish we hadn't had to hurt each other so much for me to be able to tell you I'm in love with you too."

He leans back, staring at me, his eyes studying my face for a full, nerve-wracking thirty seconds before he whispers, "You're in love with me?"

"Yes. I know that sounds improbable, given everything that's gone on, and the way I behaved, but after you'd gone, I realized you're everything I've ever wanted. You're everything I've ever needed. And that's why I came after you… to tell you that."

"But you didn't," he says. "You didn't tell me that at all."

"I know. You didn't give me the chance."

He shakes his head slowly, from side to side. "Y—You're really in love with me?" he says, still sounding incredulous.

"Yes. Why don't you believe me?"

"I do," he says, smiling. "What I'm having trouble believing, is how I got this lucky."

I smile up at him and reach out a hand to touch his face, but pull it back just in time, remembering what he said to me before.

"What's wrong?" His brow furrows in confusion.

"I can't touch you. I don't have permission."

His face clears. "Yeah, you do."

"But you said…"

"Forget what I said. Forget who I was. Please…"

He pulls me closer and kisses me again, slanting his head and deepening the kiss within moments, his tongue finding mine in a slow, gentle caress.

After a few minutes, he leans back. "You didn't answer my question," he whispers, rubbing my bottom lip with the side of his thumb.

"What question?"

"Can you forgive me?"

"I thought we already established… there's nothing to forgive."

"Yeah, there is. I need to know we're okay, Bree."

"I think it should be me asking that question, considering how much I hurt you."

"Don't we seem to be okay?" he asks, the corners of his lips twisting upwards in a wicked smile.

"Yes…" I murmur. "But in that case, why are you asking me?"

His smile fades. "Because the thought of you hurting, and of me having any part in that, is killing me… okay?"

His voice is kinda gruff now, and I caress his cheek with just the tips of my fingers, feeling the prickle of his stubble against my skin. He closes his eyes and lets out a slow sigh. "I'll forgive you, if you forgive me," I whisper, and he opens his eyes again.

"I forgive you," we both say at the same time and he puts a hand on the back of my head, holding me in place while he kisses me again, his deep throaty groan reverberating through my body. I sigh as he places a hand on my ass and pulls me onto him, letting me feel his erection, and then I moan loudly when he grinds his hips into me in an aching, slow, circular movement.

"I need you," I mutter into his mouth.

He pulls back and looks at me. "You need to eat first."

I pout, and he leans forward and bites my bottom lip, with a gentleness I hadn't realized he possessed, before kissing me again, our bodies instantly entwined.

He only stops and releases me when the buzzer sounds, at which point he gets up, going over to the door and pressing the button on the intercom.

"Yeah?" he says.

"There's a pizza delivery guy down here for you." I hear Hank's voice, and my stomach rumbles at the thought of food.

"Okay. Send him up." Colt wanders back to me, picking up his t-shirt from the floor and kissing me again before he puts it back on, pulling it down as far as it'll go, presumably to try and hide the enormous bulge in the front of his jeans. His t-shirt isn't quite long enough, though, and he looks down at me and grins. "Who cares?" he mutters, and I giggle, just as the the doorbell rings and Colt answers it, returning a few moments later with a huge box, which he puts down on the table in front of me.

"Sit up a little," he says, putting his arms beneath mine and helping me into a slightly more upright position, my legs flat out on the couch, as he straightens the throw, which we've kinda messed up and pushed aside in the last ten or fifteen minutes. I look up at him as he sits beside me and opens the pizza box, handing me a slice.

"What did you get?" I ask him, studying the toppings.

"I didn't go crazy. You haven't eaten for a long time, so your stomach doesn't need anything too spicy right now… it's just mushroom, peppers and spinach."

"You went vegetarian?" I smile up at him.

"Just this once, yeah. Now, eat… slowly," he says, watching me, as I take a small bite, savoring the taste of the rich tomato sauce and softly melted cheese.

"That's good," I whisper, nodding my head.

He takes a slice himself and eats more heartily. "Not bad…"

"You sound surprised."

"Well, there's no meat on it… what do you expect?" He grins at me, and our eyes lock as I take another bite.

After we've finished the pizza, Colt clears away.

"We need to get some groceries," he says, coming back from the kitchen and sitting beside me once more.

"Okay."

"And I should probably go back to my apartment…"

"You're leaving again… already? I thought you might wanna stay the night…" I can't hide my disappointment, or that I really want him here with me… for much longer than one night, if I'm being honest.

"Did I say I was leaving?" He leans over me. "I said I was gonna go to my apartment, that's all. But I was thinking of going in the morning, maybe before we go grocery shopping? My car's over at my place still, and I'm not a huge fan of the rental I'm driving around in."

"Oh... I see." I can feel myself blushing. "Are your clothes there too? At your apartment, I mean."

He shakes his head. "No. Most of my clothes are still in LA. Once I'd decided to come back here, I just threw a few things into a bag and raced to the airport. I got on the next flight to Logan... but only because I didn't have any luggage, other than what I was carrying. And I left that on the back passenger seat of my not very comfortable rental car, which is parked across the street."

"You're parked across the street?" I wonder why he didn't park outside, in one of the visitor spaces.

"Yeah," he replies. "You know what this place is like for parking at the weekend."

I suppose he's right. It can get busy... and that explains his wet t-shirt. Not that any of that really matters right now. "So, you have clothes?"

"Yeah... I have clothes."

"And you can stay?" I bite my bottom lip and he smiles, focusing on it, before reverting his gaze to my eyes.

"Try stopping me, baby," he growls and stands, lifting me into his arms. He carries me through to my bedroom, flicking off the lights in the main room and closing the door behind us, before taking me to the bed and dropping me on the soft mattress.

He pulls off his still slightly damp t-shirt and crawls up over my body, slowly and deliberately, his eyes never leaving mine, and then leans down to kiss me. But before he does, I stop him, my hand on his bare chest.

"I—I have a question," I mutter, feeling embarrassed.

He raises himself up above me, looking down, his arms straight, his head tilting slightly to the right. "Okay."

I suck in a breath, letting it out slowly, because I can't go ahead with anything until I know the truth... and yet I'm dreading hearing it at the same time. Even so... I have to know. "Has there been anyone else?" I ask.

"Anyone else?" He sounds confused.

"Yes. Since you left… since we broke up… has there been anyone else? I mean, I don't know much about the Dom/sub scene, but I imagine exclusivity isn't necessarily part of the deal?" I can hear the fear in my voice and then I gasp as he shakes his head, and I try to duck out from under him, even though his hands are either side of me and his body is pinning me to the bed.

"Stop it," he commands, and I still, looking up at him. "Stop it and listen to me. I may still be a Dom, but you are not a sub, and we are not part of that scene. We never have been. I may not have been exclusive before, but I am now. So the answer to your question is no. There could never be anyone else. That's not even possible. I told you, I'm in love with you… you heard me say it. That was the cause of all the trouble in the first place…" It's like he doesn't understand at all.

"I know. But I also heard you put your love in the past tense. And when I asked if you didn't love me anymore, you didn't answer."

"I was still mad at you then… and I was scared."

It's hard to imagine Colt being scared of anything. "Scared of what?"

"Of how much you could hurt me, if I let you in again."

I feel tears sting my eyes. "Oh God, Colt… what did I do to you?"

He lets himself fall to his elbows and kisses me, his lips just briefly touching mine. "Hey… it's okay," he whispers, but I can't talk now, so he does instead. "I was scared," he repeats. "But only because I still love you so much, and I was too proud to tell you that. I was too busy being a guy to express myself. But that doesn't mean I would've fucked someone else, just to try and get you out of my system. I know that's not possible… because I could never get you out of my system before. Not since I fell for you all those years ago." He sighs and runs his fingertips down my cheek. "I've always known that if I ever got to be with you, I'd never want anyone else in my life – or my bed – ever again. And that's exactly how it was." He raises himself up again, and supporting himself on one arm, moves the other down. "You're it for me," he murmurs, his fingers pushing up the soft material of my t-shirt, his skin making contact with mine, and I suck in a breath, looking up at him.

I open my mouth to tell him how good that feels, but he raises his hand from my waist and quickly clamps it across my lips before I can utter a syllable.

"Don't tell me," he says, his voice cracking.

I shake my head, and he moves his hand away again, much more slowly. "Don't tell you what?"

"If… if you've been with someone else, and you wanna confess, then don't. I don't wanna know. I'm not normally jealous, or possessive. But please… just don't tell me. If I don't know about it, I can handle it. I know we weren't together, and you hadn't said you loved me, and that made you a free agent, but I'm not sure I could bear it. Especially knowing it was my fault, because I was too stupid to stay here and work things out with you."

I reach up and touch his cheek. "Colt… there's been no one else. I promise. I've spent all my time missing you. And I don't want anyone else either. I was just gonna tell you how good it was to feel your hands on me again, that's all. I wasn't gonna say anything about anyone else. And I only asked you because I was feeling insecure."

"You have nothing to feel insecure about, Bree. Nothing at all."

"Except that you'd told me you didn't love me anymore."

"I never said that…"

"Yes, you did. In LA."

"No. I just declined to answer your question, because – like I said – I'm stupid. Too stupid to know when I'm well off, anyway."

"Don't call yourself stupid. You were hurting, and that was my fault. I should never have done what I did to you."

"Didn't we go through this once already?"

I manage a slight smile. "Yeah, I think we did."

He nods his head. "And didn't we both forgive each other?"

"Yes."

"Okay… so can we drop it?"

I let out a sigh. "Yes, we can."

He leans down, as though to kiss me, but hesitates, pausing with his lips about an inch from mine. "There's just one thing," he says.

"What's that?"

"I've never begged for anything in my life, but I'm begging you… please, don't ever do that to me again. If you ever feel uncertain, or scared, or unsure of yourself, or of me, or you just need to talk to someone, then find me. I'll never be far away, and I'll make time for you… always. Just please… please don't run from me, don't put yourself in danger, and don't ever look to someone else to fill the gap."

"I won't. I promise." The sight of him like this, the knowledge of what I can do to him, is enough to exact any promise from me. I never want to see him this broken… ever again.

He nods his head. "It's just… I've realized how fragile my heart is, when it comes to you, and it couldn't take being hurt like that again."

Oh, God… "I never wanted to hurt you in the first place," I whisper, gazing up at him. "And I'll never hurt you again. I just wanna be yours, Colt. That's all."

He smiles and his eyes sparkle. "You are mine, baby… all mine," he says, his voice a low growl, and he takes hold of both my hands, moving them above my head and then holding onto them in one of his as he leans down and kisses me, while his other hand roams downward, finding that narrow expanse of skin, where my t-shirt has ridden up, and he pushes it further, until his fingers brush against the underside of my breast, and we both moan at the same time, in perfect harmony. He breaks the kiss and leans up, looking down at me.

"You need to be naked," he says, and before I can reply, he releases me and pulls my t-shirt up over my head, bending down and biting on each of my nipples in turn, which makes me squeal in delight.

He stops what he's doing and kneels back, pulling down my pajama pants, his eyes settling on the apex of my thighs, his head slowly shaking from side to side, a smile settling on his lips, before he stands, undoing his jeans, pushing them to the floor, along with his underwear. He's naked, standing before me, his erection rock hard, and I can't help licking my lips, which makes him smile as he kneels again, the mattress dipping under his weight. Moving closer, he grabs my legs just below the knee, holding them up. "Keep them straight," he orders, and I do as he says, even when he parts them into a wide 'V', exposing me. His eyes gaze down hungrily, but he looks up at me again. "Put your hands under mine."

"My hands?"

"Yes."

I raise my arms up from the mattress, waiting until he shifts his hands slightly so I can slide mine beneath, and then feel his powerful grip come back around me, so my hands are trapped in place at the sides of my knees. He has control of my body now, his muscles tightening as he parts my legs further still and then pulls my ass up off the bed, right before he impales me, giving me his entire length.

"Yes…" I hiss between my teeth, feeling the stretch, as he moves straight away, almost pulling out of me with every stroke, before pushing right back inside me. It's so good to feel him again… to be held by him again… to be dominated by him again. I can see the strain in his arms and shoulders as he supports me, his eyes fixed on mine.

"I love you," he whispers, increasing the pace slightly as my body quivers.

"I—I love you…" That quivering crescendoes and I plunge into oblivion, struggling in his grip as I try to ride out the waves of pleasure, my body straining against him. He holds me firm, every muscle in my body tensed and tingling, until I finally come down to earth, panting for breath, and he releases my hands, bringing my legs up onto his shoulders. And then, without pulling out of me, he bends over, moving his hands around beneath me, and he lifts my whole body off of the bed.

"Hold on to my neck," he orders, as he straightens, and I do what he says, leaning back still, but hanging onto him… completely suspended.

"Oh, that's good… that's really good," I murmur as he moves me up and down the length of his shaft, his right hand on my ass and his left on my hip. I'm completely in his control… again. And I love it. I can already feel my next orgasm building, just as he changes position slightly, taking my weight in his right hand, and bringing his left up behind my head, twisting it into my hair, and pulling just slightly. It's not enough to hurt. But it's enough to let me know he's in control. And with that thought, I'm pushed over the edge into ecstasy, my head rocking back as I scream his name.

I'm breathless… spent… but he pulls me up into his arms, making it clear he's not done yet, as he lifts me off of his straining cock, before he flips me over, keeping one hand on my right arm, while my left gets caught beneath me. He spanks my ass as he enters me, and I cry out with pleasure at the sting of his touch. I've missed that so much, and I want more, even as he bends my right arm up my back and leans over me.

"I've missed your ass so much." His words echo my thoughts and he pounds into me, harder and harder, until he's grunting loudly with every stroke. "Now, Bree…" he groans. "Please…"

"I'm not sure I…"

"Come for me!" His shout echoes around the room, as he brings his hand down onto my ass again, in a biting slap, and my body obeys, tumbling over and over through realm after realm of pleasure, and I hear him howl my name as his whole body stiffens, and he erupts deep inside me.

He flops forward eventually, releasing my arm, his body bent over mine, his chest against my back. "God, I love you," he whispers in my ear.

I turn my head slightly. "I love you too." My breath catches as he pulls us over onto our sides, spooning, his arms tight around me, and we slowly breathe more easily, in unison.

"That was incredible," I murmur, running my hand up and down his arm.

"You were incredible," he replies, kissing my shoulder.

I twist slightly, even though we're connected still, because I need to see his face, and he looks down at me.

"Was that about proving a point?" I ask him, feeling intrigued.

"I don't know," he replies, dragging in a breath. "It might have been… proving you're mine, maybe." He smiles. "Sorry if that's a bit macho."

"I'm not complaining. I like being yours. And it was just what I needed."

"Good. I—I didn't hurt you, did I? That was quite physical."

"No, you didn't hurt me. But I think it was more physical for you than for me."

His smile widens. "It was worth it. Although I guess now would probably be a good time to ask whether you've been to see your gynecologist in my absence?"

"My gynecologist?"

"Yeah. Don't you remember, you said you were supposed to get your shot sometime soon?"

I nod my head. "Oh… yeah. But surely, if you were worried about it, you'd have been better off asking me *before* coming inside me?"

"I'm not worried. And as for coming inside you, that really wasn't optional, baby. But can I assume from your answer that you haven't been to see her?"

"You can. But we're still covered for now, and I'll make the appointment next week."

He chuckles. "Good," he says, kissing me.

"And now we've got that little practicality out of the way… can I ask a question?"

"Sure."

"Do you always have to restrain me?" I ask him, and his face falls.

"Why? Don't you like it?"

"Yes. But I'm just wondering, that's all. I think you've restrained me in some way every time we've made love… even that first time, when you took it kinda easy on me, you still held me down. I'm just asking whether it's something you need. If it's something you have to have."

"No," he replies after a moment's silence, although I can hear something that sounds like doubt in his voice. "I've been a Dom for nearly a decade now. And, to be honest, I can't imagine my life any other way, but if it makes you uncomfortable, I'll change. If you need me to give it up, then I will."

I lean back, feeling alarmed. "Good God, Colt… no. That's not what I meant at all. I don't want you to be anything other than who you are… the man I fell in love with. Please don't change. I love you being dominant. And I like being your submissive."

He frowns. "You're not my submissive, Bree," he says softly, bringing his hand up and brushing his fingertip around my lips in a gentle circular movement. "You're my lover."

"Who happens to like submitting to you?" I look up at him, and he nods his head.

"I hope so… but if you don't…"

"I do. Honestly. I was just intrigued."

"About whether I have a gentler side?" he suggests.

I shake my head. "I already know you do… after the way you opened up to me earlier, I don't think there's any doubt about that. I know you love me."

He pulls out of me, very slowly, and rolls me onto my back, changing position so he's kneeling between my legs, which he parts with his own, raising himself above me.

"I think you… I think you maybe need to see my love," he says softly. "And feel it."

And, without taking his eyes from mine, he enters me slowly, stuttering out a breath as he does.

"Oh… God…" I whisper, taking his length.

He starts to move, but with such tenderness this time, his body melding with mine in perfect synchrony, our breathing harmonized, our sighs and moans merging into one.

"Touch me," he murmurs, but it's an entreaty, not an order, and I raise my hands, letting my fingers drift up his arms, his muscles flexing as I rest them on his biceps, enjoying his strength, and the feeling of being surrounded by him.

He picks up the pace, just fractionally, although his movements are still gentle… still considered. I move my hands around behind him, letting them roam over his back, before settling on his perfect ass, pulling him into me, and I bring my legs up higher, watching as he gasps and his eyes widen.

"Whoa." He seems shocked by his own reaction. "You're gonna make me come." He's shaking his head and shifts downwards just slightly to change the angle, hitting a certain spot inside me now, which makes me tingle and quiver. "Come with me," he urges. "Please, baby. I need this."

I feel my body surrender to him, and as he plunges into me again, I soar upwards, the stars and heavens shattering around me. He groans loudly and I open my eyes for long enough to see a look of pure rapture on his face, and to see him mouth, "I love you," before I'm swept away on a whole new wave of pleasure, my body overwhelmed once more, as he pours himself deep inside me.

I'm aware of him turning us onto our sides, his arms coming around me as I lie against him, my head on his chest.

"Don't change," I mutter into him. "Please don't change. I love what you just did. It was beautiful… and very special. But I need all of you, Colt."

He strokes my hair and I feel him move, just a fraction, his lips beside my ear. "I'm not gonna change, baby," he whispers. "I'm all yours."

I lean back, so I can see him, and look up into his eyes. "You're my Dom."

He smiles. "I'm your man."

Colt

I wake with Bree's head on my chest, her body tucked into mine, all warm and soft, and I smile… because we're back where we belong. Together.

Coming back here was the right thing to do. I just wish I'd never left. Max was right. I shouldn't have put my own pain first. I should have thought about Bree, and what she was going through; and I'm ashamed I didn't. I'm ashamed I needed to be told… to have it explained to me. That's not a mistake I'm gonna be repeating, though. Not that I think we'll ever find ourselves in a situation like that again. Not now… not now I've really opened up to her about how I feel. And she's told me she's in love with me.

That kinda blew me away yesterday. It was the last thing I'd expected. I'd spent most of the flight back here thinking about what Max had said, about how you sometimes have to step up and actually *be* there, instead of just talking about it. And how I hadn't… how I'd failed Bree when she needed me most. Then I'd tried working out how many ways there were for me to say 'sorry' to her. I already knew I was gonna have to put my heart out there and lay it on the line, and I didn't care about any of that. Hell… I'd have put my life on the line, if it meant getting her back. I genuinely just wanted her forgiveness… and another chance. Hearing her say those three magical words to me, knowing that she loves me, like I love her, it was as though all the pieces of my life – the past, the present, and the future – finally slotted into place… making me whole.

She stretches slightly and moans, her hand coming up and resting on my chest, close to her head. She's waking… slowly. And I'm enjoying the process of her body coming to life.

She was spectacular last night. I can't say I'd forgotten how good she felt in the time we've been apart, because I hadn't. Every moment I spend with her is etched permanently in my brain… but I pushed her last night, and I knew it. I needed it, too. Like I said to Bree, when she surprised me by asking outright; I think I was staking a claim. I'm not sure whether I was proving the point to her, or to myself. But that was how it felt.

She surprised me then by asking whether I needed to restrain her. It had never even dawned on me that it might bother her. She's always enjoyed what we've done, so I assumed she was okay with it, but hearing her ask that question made me doubtful… about everything. Which is why I offered to give it up. I would have done too, if that was what she wanted. I'd do anything for her… except she didn't want me to. She made that very clear.

She also made me think, though… and that's why I decided to show her how I feel about her… to make love to her, without holding her down or restraining her. To give her free rein to move and to touch and to do whatever she wanted. The only problem I had with that, was that I found it hard to maintain control. It was strange, not knowing what she was gonna do next, so when she let her hands settle on my ass, pulling me into her, and then raised her legs, it was all I could do not to come. That's never happened to me before, but I kept it together until she got there with me, and it was perfect. Like she said... it was beautiful.

She sighs and moans again, and shifts her body slightly, nestling further into me, her hand drifting further across my chest. I look down to see a smile settling on her lips, even though her eyes are still closed, and I can't help smiling myself. Whatever's going on in her mind, it's making her happy. She groans and rocks her hips a couple of times, and I revise my opinion... whatever's going on in her mind is turning her on, so I gently run my fingertip down her back, in the center of her spine... all the way down to her ass. She shudders against me and opens her eyes, biting her bottom lip as she smiles up at me.

"Good morning," she murmurs, her voice thick with sleep and something else, that I'd say is probably arousal.

"Good morning. Can I do anything for you?"

"Hmm... I was just dreaming about you."

"Were you?" She nods her head, her hand still roaming over my chest. "And was it a pleasant dream?" I ask, teasing her a little.

"It was a sexy dream," she replies, smiling.

"In that case, I'm glad I featured in it."

"Oh... you did a lot more than feature," she murmurs, and I let out a chuckle, rolling her onto her back and settling between her legs, pinning her hands above her head. I hold them both in place with one of my own, and palm my cock, rubbing the head against her soaking clit. "Yes... oh, yes..." she hisses, and her back arches off of the bed as I adjust my position slightly and sink into her, just by an inch or two, bringing my free hand up now and resting it on her breast, taking care not to lean on her, even as I hold completely still inside her. She raises her hips, trying to get more of me, but I pull back, dictating the pace.

"Be still," I whisper, and she narrows her eyes at me, lifting her hips off of the mattress again. I shake my head. "I'll only make you wait even longer."

She huffs out a sigh and I bend, taking her nipple between my teeth and biting down gently, which makes her gasp and sigh, although she does well, keeping her hips still despite my teasing and tempting her.

I bite and lick her distended nipple for a few minutes, driving her insane, if her breathing is anything to go by, and then I lean back up again, keeping my hand on her breast still, as I plunge my cock deep inside her.

"I'm… oh God, I'm…" She comes apart right before my eyes, her body thrashing as she twists and bucks beneath me. I love the way she comes so hard and I hold her firmly in place as I hammer into her, even once she's calming and coming back to earth.

"Keep your hands where they are," I tell her, kneeling up for a moment, and she obeys, watching while I grab her ankles and bring them up over my shoulders, before I lean over again, bending her back on herself, and taking her hands in mine once more. She's completely pinned beneath me, my dick buried deep inside her and I up the pace, my groans matching hers.

I know I can't last much longer like this, but it seems I don't have to, as she starts to tremble, her thighs quivering, and within moments, we're both coming hard, the sounds of each other's names mere whispers on our lips.

"I'm sorry." I turn us over onto our sides and hold her in my arms.

"Why are you sorry?" Bree still hasn't quite got her breath back yet, and looks up at me, confused.

"Because I kinda reverted to type then, didn't I?"

She smiles. "Yes. But I told you, I don't want you to change."

"I know… and that's just as well, because I'm not sure I can. Making love to you last night was a revelation… and you were right, it was beautiful. And we're definitely gonna do that again. But dominating you is something else." She smiles and nestles down into me. "And as for waking up beside you… that's life changing."

"Life changing?" She's surprised and leans back in my arms, looking up into my eyes.

"Yeah. I'd never done it, before last weekend… I…"

She pulls even further back, a frown settling on her beautiful face. "You're kidding me."

"No."

"You seriously expect me to believe you never slept with any of your other subs?"

'Other subs'? What the fuck is that about? "Yes, I do. Because it's the truth. But before we go any further, I told you last night, you're not my submissive, so can you please quit referring to yourself as though you were?"

She blushes. "I think, with you being a Dominant, and us being together, most people are gonna assume I'm your submissive."

I shake my head. "Almost no-one knows I'm a Dom, so they're not gonna assume anything. And besides, it's not about what other people think. It's about what we know. And we know that you're my lover… and I'm yours."

She smiles now, moving closer again. "Did you seriously not sleep with them, though?" she asks.

"No."

"Never?"

"No."

"Was that one of your rules?"

"What rules?" I lean back now, looking down at her. What does she know about my rules?

"Chase… Chase asked me if you had a set of rules that I was supposed to adhere to. I said no – obviously – because you'd never mentioned anything like that… but do you? Are there any rules I should know about?"

I shake my head. "No. Because you're not a sub, Bree."

"So does that mean you did have rules… before?"

"Yes."

She lets out a long sigh and looks up at me again. "Like what?" she asks, in a low whisper.

"Does it matter?" I ask her, because I'm not sure I can see the point of this. "It's in the past. All of that is in the past."

She lowers her head, but doesn't put it back on my chest, letting it rest on the pillow instead, and I know I've screwed up. I remember her reacting kinda like this before, over breakfast in my apartment, when she said I wouldn't answer her questions, and I told her then that I would. Except I've fallen at the first hurdle. And, come to think of it, I also recall saying to Max that I'd tell Bree anything she wanted to know… if she asked me. And she's asked me.

"I'm sorry," I say, placing my finger beneath her chin and raising her face to mine. "I don't want to have secrets from you."

"Then why won't you tell me?"

"I will. Like I say, it's in the past. But if you wanna know, then I'll tell you. I'll tell you anything you want, as long as you understand… none of it matters to me now."

She nods her head slowly, and I lean down and kiss her lips, not deeply, but just allowing my own to brush over hers, back and forth, caressing and stroking, until she's breathing hard, and I pull back again.

"Are you okay?" I say, looking into her eyes. She nods her head. "Am I forgiven?" She nods again. "You wanna know about my rules?"

She pauses and then nods her head, just once.

"Okay… just remember, none of this applies to you… right?" She doesn't nod this time, but just stares at me, blinking occasionally, her eyes wide, expectant, maybe slightly nervous, so I start talking, to put us both out of our misery. "I guess I'd better explain about the agency first, otherwise nothing else is gonna make much sense."

"The agency?" Her eyes widen a little further, and she tips her head to one side.

"Yeah. You can't exactly pick up subs in a bar, or a restaurant… you have to know they're gonna be into the same things as you are, and most of them don't wear labels."

She chuckles and I kiss her forehead. "So there are agencies for this?"

"There are. I guess some Doms might have other methods, but the agency was a good fit for me. It was easy, anonymous, hassle-free."

"How did it work?" she asks, and I'm relieved she put her question in the past tense. At least she remembered that much.

"There was a list of subs… and basically, as a Dom, you'd go through and choose which particular sub you wanted to try out."

"It didn't work the other way around?" she asks, and I smile, because I love her innocence.

"No, babe. That's the whole point. The Dom decides."

She nods. "Based on what?"

"The sub's photograph, and their profile. There was a kind of checklist showing what they would and wouldn't do, which made it easier. It made the process of elimination a lot more straightforward."

"I see… and then what?"

"The Dom would express an interest, and the agency would let the sub know. Then they would be given access to the Dom's profile."

"So your profile was private until you decided to let a sub see it?"

"Yeah. I mean, obviously no-one who wasn't a member could see either of the lists, but all the Doms could see all the subs' profiles."

"But no subs could see the Dom's profile until the Dom had shown an interest?"

"Exactly."

"That seems a bit unfair."

I shrug my shoulders. "It's the way it is, baby. The subs know the regulations when they sign up. And the last time I was on the website, there were over twelve hundred of them to choose from, just on that site."

"Here? In Boston?"

"Yeah. So I don't think they had a problem with it."

"Twelve hundred?" she whispers.

"Yeah."

"How… how many did you…?"

"Not twelve hundred."

"But how many?" she asks again, blinking hard. I suppose I knew this would come up one day, so I'm gonna have to tell her.

"Fourteen."

She tips her head again. "Over how long?"

"A little over nine years, since I actually joined."

"But that doesn't add up. You said you fell in love with me eleven years ago, and I was the one who converted you to this lifestyle." Her confusion is understandable, I guess.

"I did fall for you eleven years ago," I explain. "But then you went and married Grady, and I had to take some time to get over that. Of course, I soon realized that was impossible, and that was when I discovered the dominance thing – or at least my need for it – basically, so I could feel like I had control over something in my life. But it took me a while to work things out… to establish that I actually wanted to pursue that lifestyle, and then to find the agency."

"I—I'm sorry I hurt you," she whispers.

"I'm sorry you married Grady," I reply, and she smiles.

"So am I… in all sorts of ways." She leans up and kisses me and then pulls back, gazing into my eyes. "Was it really only fourteen?" she asks.

"Yes."

"That's… that's not as many as I would have thought."

"I know." I smile at her. "But you have to remember one thing."

"What's that?"

"I was in love with you the whole time. If I was too pre-occupied with you for any reason, I couldn't be with anyone else. It used to mess with my head too much."

"I'm…"

I clamp my fingers over her lips. "Hey… if you're gonna say 'sorry' again, forget it. You've got nothing to be sorry for. And anyway, for me, it was always just a release… a means to an end. Nothing more."

She brings her hands up between us and grabs my wrist, pulling my hand away from her mouth and kissing my fingers, one by one. The sight is mesmeric, and I stare at her as she starts to breathe more heavily, gently licking and sucking on my fingertips.

"Do you want me to stop talking and make love to you?"

She stops, my index finger poised on her lip. It looks like she's in two minds about what to do, but after a moment, she plants a soft kiss on my fingertip and then lowers it.

"No… I want to hear what you have to say," she whispers. "And then I'd like you to make love to me."

I smile. "Oh, would you now?"

"Yes, please."

"Well, being as you've asked so nicely, I'll see what I can do." She nuzzles into me and I kiss the top of her head. "Where was I?"

"You were telling me you'd had fourteen subs, before me."

I lean back, holding her shoulders. "Once again... you are *not* a sub. Okay?"

She sucks in a breath. "Okay. But... fourteen over nine years isn't very many. Did you... did you have relationships with them?"

I pull her close to me again. "No, baby. Not in the way you mean. Like I told you last night, I was never exclusive with any of them. I'd see them once every few weeks, when I needed to, when I wasn't thinking about you too much. I used to alternate them around sometimes, because they liked doing different things and so did I. And we'd carry on like that, until they got annoying, which they usually did."

"Annoying?" she queries, looking up at me.

"Yeah... you know, clingy... demanding."

"Demanding of what?"

"Me. My time. They knew the rules."

"And one of the rules was that they weren't allowed to have any of your time?" she asks, sounding a bit sad, I think.

"Outside of the bedroom, no."

"So, you literally met them for sex, and nothing else? You never went to dinner, or to the movies, or for a walk with them?"

"Hell, no."

She stares at me for a moment. "Would I have known you back then?"

"You did know me. You've known me since you were five years old. But at the time we're talking about, you were married to that loser ex-husband of yours. So I don't think you necessarily noticed me."

She nods her head slowly, like she's trying to work things out in her own mind. "So they weren't allowed to see you socially?" she asks.

"No."

"And what were the other rules?"

"They weren't allowed to touch me, anywhere at all… not without my permission."

"Oh… is that why you said to me I couldn't touch you, when I came to see you at your apartment, before you went to LA?"

"Yeah. I shouldn't have done that." I let out a sigh. "Letting you touch me, at your will, whenever you wanted to, was a revelation. With my subs, it had always been a method of control – of detachment – and it was one that had served me well. With you, I didn't need to take things to that level. And I didn't want to either. I was surprised by how much I enjoyed being touched by you… even when I didn't know what you were gonna do next. But then, having your hand on me when my heart was broken up over you… that was too much for me. It was too hard. Becoming the Dom… instigating my rule with you… it was the only way I could think of protecting myself." Her face crumples, and she buries her head in my chest, her body shaking as she starts to cry. "Hey… baby…" I pull back and raise her face to mine. "Don't cry. Please. I shouldn't have used my rules with you… no matter what."

"But I hurt you so much. Not just now, but back then… in the past… marrying Grady… ignoring you."

"I know… but that's the past. You weren't to know how I felt about you. And as for now, I hurt you, too. We both fucked up." She sniffles a little, and I wipe away her tears with my thumbs. "Wanna stop this for now?" I ask her. "We can carry on later."

She shakes her head. "No. I want to know…"

"Okay." I lean down and kiss her soft lips, and then pull her close to me again, wrapping my legs around her too, which feels good and makes her sigh and shudder, just slightly.

"Apart from not touching, what else couldn't they do?" she says quietly after a few moments of just lying still, enjoying each other.

"They couldn't instigate a sexual act, either by manipulating a situation, or by asking me directly to do something to them."

"Really?"

"Yes. That's the whole point of being a Dominant… the clue is in the title."

"Hmm… I suppose it is." She tilts her head. "And yet I'm allowed to ask. I just asked you to make love you me, when you've finished telling me about your rules… and you said yes."

"I know. As I've already said, the rules don't apply to you."

"But you're still a Dominant?"

She's clearly having trouble with this.

"Yes… just not in the way I used to be. I still want to dominate you… I still need to dominate you. Sexually. But because it's you… and because I'm in love with you, everything else is different. The rules don't matter anymore. Nothing matters, except us. And, like I said last night, if it's too much, and you need me to stop, I'll find a way."

She shakes her head and nestles into me. "I don't want you to stop. I need your dominance, Colt. It makes me feel alive, and free, and wanted."

"You are wanted." I kiss her hard to prove the point, and she writhes in my arms, pressing her body against mine, her hands roaming up and down my back as her breathing changes, becoming more ragged.

"Are you sure you don't wanna finish our conversation later?" I suggest, pulling back from the kiss. She sighs, like she's thinking, although her hands are still stroking my back, very distractingly "You're… you're gonna need to stop that," I tell her.

"Stop what?"

"Y—Your hands… on my back…" I struggle to speak, the contact is so diverting.

"But I thought I was allowed to touch you." She lets her hands fall, confusion and sadness filling her eyes.

"You are, baby. You are. But if you wanna talk, I need to concentrate. And I can't when you're doing that."

A slow smile forms on her lips, and she whispers, "Okay, I'll leave you alone… for now. And you can tell me the rest of your rules."

"There aren't that many more," I murmur. "And that's just as well, because if I don't get inside you again soon, I'm gonna go crazy."

She giggles. "So…" she muses. "What else do you need to tell me?"

"I guess the next most important rule was that subs weren't allowed to kiss me."

"Could you kiss them?" she asks, clearly intrigued.

"Well… it's not that I *couldn't*, but I chose not to."

She looks up at me. "Why not?"

"Kissing is too intimate. It's the same with oral sex. That wasn't allowed either."

"But… but you kissed me. It was the first thing you did… on that Saturday morning. And the first time you made me come, you used your tongue." She sounds shocked and confused now.

"I know." I smile down at her. "But you were never a sub, were you?"

She bites her bottom lip, and then whispers, "Does that mean I could reciprocate sometime?"

My cock twitches against her, just at the thought, and she gasps and then smiles. "Do you want to?" I think I already know the answer to that, but I need to be sure.

"Yes."

"Okay, we can try. But remember… I'm a Dom. I can't guarantee I won't try and fuck your mouth…" She groans, closing her eyes and letting her head rock back a little, her hips grinding into mine, and I move a hand down, resting it on her ass and pulling her tight onto me, so she can feel my hard-on straining between us. "You like the sound of that?" I whisper, surprised by how deep my voice is.

"Hmm… yes, please," she murmurs.

"In that case, we should probably hurry through the rest of these rules… don't you think?"

"Oh, God… yes," she says, and I chuckle. "What's next?" she asks, even more desperate to finish now, it seems.

"Subs couldn't ask personal questions."

"What kind of personal questions?"

"Any kind… you know… where I lived, my occupation, my phone number…"

"They didn't know where you lived?"

"No."

"Then where did you meet them?"

"At a hotel."

She raises her eyebrows. "Was it one of ours?"

"No. I'd never have let my personal life intrude into my friendship with Max."

She nods her head. "Why couldn't you just see them at your place? Or theirs?"

"Again, it was too personal… too intimate."

"So you just used to meet them at a hotel, presumably taking your equipment with you, have sex, and leave?"

"Yes. We'd have sex for quite a long time… usually a few hours. But pretty much, that's exactly how it was. Although, to be precise, they'd mostly leave before me, while I was in the shower. Sometimes they'd still be there when I came out, but they'd be dressed by then, and ready to go." I look her in the eyes. "You've gotta remember, it was very impersonal for me. And I was in charge."

"I see," she whispers and then tilts her head. "But surely, they could have just looked you up and come round to your place, couldn't they? They knew your name."

"No. They knew better than to break my rules, and in any case, I never used my real name."

"So what did they call you?" she asks, clearly shocked.

"Jack."

She frowns. "Why Jack?"

I smile down at her. "Believe it or not, when I was completing the application form for the agency, I was reading a Lee Child novel… you know, one of the Jack Reacher ones. I originally toyed with calling myself 'Lee', but I preferred 'Jack'. It was that simple."

She nods her head, smiling herself now. "Is that it?"

"Apart from the fact that I never spent the night with any of them… which is why waking up with you has been so incredible… and why I said 'no' when you asked me if I'd ever brought anyone breakfast in bed before… yeah, that's about it."

"And do you still belong?" she asks, her voice dropping to an almost inaudible whisper.

"To the agency?" She nods in confirmation. "Of course not." I roll her onto her back and raise myself above her. "I left before anything even happened between us."

"You did?"

"Yeah. I left on that Friday evening, while you were asleep, all by yourself, in my bed."

"But why? I mean, we hadn't made love then. We might never have made love. For all you knew, I might have woken up in the morning and just left."

"I know. But I'd seen a different side to you that night. I'd held you while you slept, for one thing. And you'd opened up to me for the first time. I'd always wanted you to trust me enough to do that, and when you did, there was a vulnerability in you I'd never really known about before. It made me wanna protect you. And I don't mean like a bodyguard. It made me wanna be your friend… and I couldn't do that while having the agency, or any part of it, in my life. It wouldn't have been right."

"But… but what if nothing had ever happened between us? What if we'd just stayed friends?" She sounds almost fearful and I bring a hand up, putting it behind her head, steadying her.

"Then I'd have been satisfied with your friendship."

"And gone without sex forever?"

"If that was the price I had to pay for having you in my life at last, then yes. Don't get me wrong… I'm thrilled it didn't turn out that way, but I value your friendship more than anything. I always will."

She smiles and lets out a soft sigh. "I find it hard to think of you… the man I know, who says things like that, and makes me feel the way you do… being as cold as you were before." Her smile fades. "But then I guess I got a taste of what you could be like, when I followed you to LA."

I shake my head. "Can you stop reminding me how close I came to losing you? Because it was too damn close. I don't wanna think about what might have happened if I hadn't come back."

"Why did you?" she asks. "I know it wasn't really to make sure I got home safely. You could've just called Max or Dana to ask them, if that was what you wanted to know. And when I saw you in LA, you sure as hell didn't wanna let me get close to you again. So what changed your mind?"

"Max," I reply, giving her the simple, truthful answer.

"Max?"

"Yeah. I—I called him from LA, once I realized you'd run out on me again, because I had to let him know you were on your way home. He didn't hold back in telling me he thought I'd been… well, let's say a little insensitive. He made me feel guilty for not seeing you were suffering, just as much as I was, and for not trying hard enough to help you… for not putting you first, and for giving up too easily." I can't tell her about Eden, and what she did to Max, because he told me that in confidence, but… "He made me see that living without the woman you're in love with is a half-life. And I'd lived like that for far too long already. I didn't want to do it anymore. I wanted to start again with you… to work it out and get it right this time around. Because without you, I'm nothing, babe."

"Oh… God, Colt." Tears form in her eyes, but I lean down and kiss her. Hard. She parts her legs wide and I drop to my elbows and hold her head in my hands, loving her like she needs to be loved. And like I need to love her.

She writhes beneath me, her body twisting and bucking against mine.

"You're really shit at staying still… you know that?" I lean up, looking down at her, a smile etched on my lips.

"Then make me," she whispers.

"I don't have any restraints, or cuffs… or rope."

Her face falls. "Oh, no… I guess it's all in LA still…"

"No."

"Did you leave it at your apartment, then?"

"No. I threw it all away before I went out to LA. I'd said I was going to anyway, if you remember? And then, when we broke up… well, like I told you last night, I wasn't interested in being with anyone else, so I didn't see the point in keeping it all."

"So you got rid of it?" I nod my head. "Everything?" She sounds so disappointed, I can't help smiling, and I kneel up, glancing around the room.

"Yeah… but I can improvise."

She looks up at me, and I grin, climbing off of the bed and going over to a gray fabric covered chair in the corner of the room, by the window, over the back of which she's thrown a few scarves. I take my pick, selecting two of the longest ones, before coming back to her and kneeling up again, by her side this time.

I shift her over, just slightly, so she's in the middle of the bed.

"Give me your hands," I tell her and she does, holding them both out. "One at a time," I clarify and she lets one drop, watching with wide eyes while I tie one end of the scarf to her wrist, making sure it's secure. "Now the other one." We go through the same process, and then I take her right hand and bind it to the post of her canopy bed, adjusting the length of the scarf so her arm is stretched tight. I repeat this action on the left side, and then stand at the end of the bed, staring at her. "You look so good like that." She does. She looks perfect, spread out for me, and while I could tie her feet too, there's really no need… she's parted her legs wide, and is gazing at me, her mouth open in anticipation. "You gonna keep still now?" I say as I climb back onto the bed.

"I'll try." Her voice is husky… laced with desire, and I lie between her legs, dipping my head and running my tongue along her soaking, swollen folds, smiling to myself as she raises her hips when I reach her clit. She's really not great at staying still at all. But I don't care, and I flick my tongue over and around her glistening bud before inserting a couple of fingers into her tight entrance. Jeez, she's wet… she's dripping, actually. And it only takes a few minutes before she comes apart, her body arching into me as she screams my name, over and over, and I drink her down.

I don't give her time to calm. Instead, I kneel up and move alongside her.

"Still wanna reciprocate?" I ask, looking down into her upturned face.

She's breathing hard, but licks her lips. "Oh… yes please." She tips her head, glancing at my raging hard-on before she looks up at me, and I see just a hint of doubt in her eyes.

"You don't have to," I whisper, caressing her head.

"No… I want to. I'm just not sure I can."

I smile. "I'm not gonna come… and I'll go gentle with you, I promise." She lets out a breath and nods her head, and I move into position, close beside her. "Tilt your head around this way," I tell her, and she does. "And open your mouth."

I palm my cock, and tap it gently against her lips, and then slowly feed it to her, gasping as she licks around the head, before she starts to suck, shifting her head in her desperation to get more of me.

"Easy, babe…" I pull out and look down at her. "Lie still and let me do this…"

She nods and opens her mouth again, and I slip my dick into her, flexing my hips this time. She groans, low and throaty, and I reach down with my free hand, grabbing a handful of her hair, and holding her head completely still as I move… just an inch or two with each thrust. I'm not trying to choke her… just to give her what I think she needs. She moans even louder and our eyes lock.

"You like that, baby?" I whisper and she nods her head, her eyes alight and shining. "You want any more?"

She shakes her head this time, and I smile, letting her know that's just fine with me, because I'm loving what she's doing. It feels fantastic… almost too fantastic. And after a few minutes, I have to stop and pull out, catching my breath and getting control… because, like I told her, I'm not gonna come. Not yet.

"Was that okay?" she asks, sounding doubtful.

"It was better than okay." I lean down and kiss her, just briefly. "It was fucking amazing. I'm only stopping because I don't wanna come… yet."

She smiles up at me and then glances down at my cock. "Maybe next time I can try taking a bit more…"

"Whatever makes you comfortable, baby."

"You make me comfortable," she whispers, biting her bottom lip.

"That's good to know. But right now… more than anything, I need to be inside you."

She giggles and I move down the bed and nestle between her legs, raising them up by the ankles and holding them wide apart, exposing her, before I lift her up onto my lap, kinda like I did last night… except this is better, because she's tied… powerless… and I'm gonna make her come so damn hard.

"Ready?" She nods her head and I enter her, giving her my whole length, right up to the hilt.

"Yes!" She yells and her body comes apart there and then, thrashing wildly, her arms pulling against the scarf restraints, as she writhes and bucks, letting out a breathless scream, while I pound into her relentlessly, harder and harder.

As she calms, I slow the pace, taking in the sight of her, bound beneath me, and how fine she looks like this. She's desperate for more, though. It's written all over her face and her body, and I pull her ankles up, resting them on my shoulders as I lean over her, balancing on one arm, reaching down between us with the other, and rubbing my thumb over her clit.

"Oh my God… oh my God…" She stares up into my eyes, and then throws her head back, screaming through yet another orgasm, her body convulsing in fierce spasms. And I join her, a savage howl leaving my lips as she milks me dry.

I release her legs, lowering them to the mattress and fall to my elbows, looking down at her, and brushing a damp hair from her cheek. "Better?" I whisper.

"Yes," she breathes. "But what are we gonna do?"

"What about?"

"Well," she says softly, "it seems I like being restrained… and I like the things you do to me when I'm restrained… only you got rid of all your equipment."

"Yeah… but that doesn't mean we can't buy some more."

She grins. "Can we?"

I have to chuckle. Her enthusiasm is so cute. "Yeah." I pull out of her, being gentle about it because my dick is still hard and throbbing. And then I get up and find my jeans, reaching into the back pocket for my phone.

"What are you doing?" she asks, and I look up and laugh, realizing that I've left her tied to the bed.

"I'm finding my favorite website… but I guess I'd better untie you, if you're gonna take a look at it."

"You mean you'll let me choose?" I laugh again. She's so fucking adorable.

"Of course." I put my phone down and climb over her, undoing the scarves. "Do your shoulders hurt?" I ask her, rubbing them gently.

"No. They're fine."

I nod my head. "Okay… but you have to tell me if anything we do makes you feel sore or uncomfortable. Okay?"

"Okay."

She sits up and nestles back into the pillows, and I hand her my phone. "I'm just going to the bathroom for a minute… the site's already loaded. You look and see what you feel like buying. I'm paying, by the way, but don't let that hold you back. Just let your imagination run riot."

She smiles and bites her bottom lip at the same time, and I shake my head, although I'm smiling too, because this is so damn perfect… and I genuinely can't believe I got this lucky, when I came so close to blowing it.

In the bathroom, I take a minute to mull over the last couple of hours, partly to think about the fact that I've just woken up next to Bree, when I thought that would never happen again, not after LA. I've also just told her about my past, and my rules, and although I made of point of telling her that none of it applied to her, I was kinda scared she might be frightened off by what I was telling her. I thought she might find some aspects of my former life kinda scary. Except she didn't. None of it seems to have fazed her at all. Of course, I've also made love to her… spectacularly. And it seems she wants more, because she's currently outside, browsing through my favorite website… the place where I buy all my kit. That thought makes me smile even more. And with that in mind, I'd better get back to her… to see what she's doing.

I wash up and open the door, walking back into the bedroom to find Bree curled up on the bed, studying my phone, a serious expression on her face.

"You look confused," I murmur, settling down beside her.

"I am."

"Why?"

She turns the phone toward me. "Because there are so many things on here I don't understand."

"Such as?" I'm intrigued.

"Such as this spreader bar. It looks kinda like your old one… the one you used on me before. Except it's got four cuffs on it, and I don't get why."

I smile and take the phone, looking down at the image she's been staring at, so I'm sure we're both talking about the same thing.

"It's so your feet and wrists can be secured at the same time," I explain.

"And would my wrists go on the outside, or the inside?" she asks.

"Inside, baby. You bend over, with your wrists bound between your legs."

She looks up, her eyes on fire. "That sounds exciting."

"It is."

"You mean you had one?"

"Yes."

"And you didn't use it on me?" She's faking a sulk now.

"Yes, I did. I just didn't use the wrist cuffs."

"Why not?" She sounds kinda disappointed, which makes me smile.

"Because I was breaking you in gently." I lean in and kiss her as she chuckles.

"If that was your idea of gentle, we need to have a serious talk."

"Are you complaining?"

"No." She looks up at me before glancing back at the phone. "So… can we get one?"

"Of course. But we'll get one more like my old one… where the wrist restraints are detachable…" I flick back through the product list and find what I'm looking for, showing it to Bree. "You see? It's got hooks in the middle."

"Yeah?" She shimmies closer, resting against me.

"Well, you can either use it purely as a spreader bar, the way I used it on you, or you can attach the wrist cuffs that come with it… or you can use a chain, which links through the cuffs and the hooks, and gives you a little more flexibility. Not much... but a little."

"Oh... I definitely I think we should get one of those... and the chain thing too." She smiles up at me, and I add one to the cart, noticing there are already six items in there.

"What have you been buying?" I ask, glancing down at her. She looks up through her eyelashes, and I tap on the cart and can't help smiling. "Thigh, wrist, and ankle restraints, huh?"

"I thought they looked interesting."

I lean over and kiss her forehead, my dick straining at the thought of her being bound and helpless. "They'll be more than interesting by the time I've finished with them." She chuckles, and I scroll down. "A rabbit vibrator?"

"The reviews made it sound... um... stimulating."

I laugh, and look back at the phone, smiling when I see she's added a feather tickler, and I recall using my old one on her... and...

"Wait a second..." I turn and look at her.

"What?"

"A ball-gag?"

She shakes her head. "I wasn't sure about that," she says.

"Good. But if you weren't sure, why did you add it to the cart?"

"Because I wanted to ask you about it, and I didn't want to have to find it again."

I look down at the picture... the leather strap, with gold fastenings, attached to a large silicone ball. She's chosen a stylish one, I'll give her that.

"You want to know what it's for?" I ask her, and she nods her head.

"Obviously, I get that it's a gag... because of the name, and I even understand that the ball goes into your mouth, because there was a picture which showed that. But what I don't understand is why?"

"Why someone would want to use one?" I ask, just to make sure.

"Yes."

I hesitate for a moment, choosing my words carefully. "They're used for all kinds of reasons. For some Doms, it's about the ultimate control... it's about the submissive not being able to communicate, and the Dom having to read her… to understand her limits, just by watching her. For Doms who are into pain, or punishment, in whatever form, the same thing can apply… it's still about control. But in those situations, a ball-gag can be useful for giving the sub something to bite down on. For me, it was just because silence helped to keep things more impersonal."

She looks up at me, tilting her head. "You… you mean, you've used one?"

"Yes."

"D—Do you want to use one on me?" Her earlier excitement evaporates, and I drop the phone by my side, pulling her into my arms.

"No. I don't. The very last thing I want to do, is to gag you. That's why I said, 'Good,' when you said you weren't sure about it. I love hearing your voice when we're making love. And I especially love hearing you say my name… so there's no way I wanna stop you from speaking."

"Sure?" she asks.

"Positive. What we're doing… it's something I want us to enjoy together. I thought you did too."

"I do," she says. "I really do. It's just that some of this is a bit more full-on than I'd expected."

"Yeah…. on second thoughts, I probably should've stayed with you while you checked out the website. I guess elements of it can be kinda shocking, if you're not used to it."

"Hmm… Did you know, there's an entire section just for collars?" she says, like she's telling me a secret.

"Yes, I know."

She pulls away slightly. "Oh… does that mean you've used a collar before, too?"

"Yes."

"But… but from what I could see of the pictures, they have leads attached to them. Does that mean you like leading your subs around?"

"No, it doesn't. First, because I don't have subs anymore, do I? I have you, baby… and, once again, you're not a sub. And second, I never used a lead. Just a collar. Mine used to have attachments… like wrist restraints, or nipple clamps."

She sucks in a breath and bites her bottom lip. "Nipple clamps?" she whispers.

"Yes."

"Attached to a collar?"

"Yes." I smile down at her. "Do you like the sound of that?"

She nods her head. "I think I do."

"Okay. We'll get one then."

I kiss her, letting my tongue clash with hers for a moment, in a heated exchange, before I pull back and grab the phone again, adding the full set of a thick leather collar, with detachable nipple clamps and wrist restraints to the cart.

"Let's see what else you've got in here, shall we?" I say and she nestles back into me, letting her hand rest low down on my stomach, just an inch or so above the base of my erection. "A leather hogtie?" I smile down at her.

"There was a picture. It looked very… sexy."

"I'm sure it did. But you know I can achieve the same effect with a rope, don't you?"

"You can?" Her eyes widen, and she runs her tongue over her bottom lip.

"Yeah. But I don't see any reason not to get this. It'll be quicker."

"Can you get the rope, too?" she says in a hushed whisper. "I—I like the idea of something that's quick, but the anticipation of what you're going to do to me can be just as arousing, and it's kinda fun to prolong that…" Her voice fades and I kiss the top of her head, because even though this is all new to her, I love that she's getting into it so much, and that she's trying to understand it too.

"Of course I can get some rope. I was going to anyway." I keep scrolling through the cart and suck in a breath. "Um…"

"What's wrong?" she says.

"This butt plug, baby."

"What about it?"

"It's way too big."

"Is it? I thought it looked okay… and it's very pretty."

"It'll look even prettier in your ass." It's got a jewel in the base, which I know is gonna look amazing. Except this is way too large for her. "But we need to start you off smaller… and build up to this."

"Oh…" She sounds disappointed. "That's a shame. I was hoping to try something… much bigger…" She lets her voice fade and her eyes roam downward to my dick, which is straining just at the thought of what I'm gonna be able to do with her.

I follow the line of her gaze and put the phone down on my chest for a moment. "Are you saying you want me to take your ass?" She blushes slightly, but doesn't answer, and I turn over, facing her, the phone falling between us. "Bree, if that's what you want, then you've gotta tell me. There's a lot of trust involved in all this, for both of us… so at the very least, you've gotta be able to talk to me about it."

"Yes," she says simply. "Yes, I'd like you to take me… *there*. I'd like to try, anyway."

I grab her behind the neck and pull her close, kissing her hard, her soft moans echoing through my body as I groan into her. My dick is hurting now, knowing what she wants… but we can't rush at this. It's gonna take time.

"Do you want that too?" she asks, when we finally break the kiss.

"Oh, God… yeah."

"Have… have you done it before?" Her voice is filled with uncertainty, and I wonder whether my answer might make her change her mind.

"Would it surprise you, if I said 'no'?"

Her face gives her away, before she says, "Yes, it would."

I smile at her. "As you might have already guessed, I like anal play. I know the pleasure it gives and I like the control it can offer, as a result. But I've never actually gone that far before. I've never wanted to."

"But you want to… with me?"

"As long as it's what you want, yes, I do."

She smiles. "It's what I want."

I kiss her again, just briefly, and pick up the phone. "In that case, we're gonna need to get some smaller butt plugs."

"Why?" She looks confused.

"Because I'll have to train your ass. We'll work our way up to where we want to be."

She moans softly and closes her eyes, like she's imagining what's to come.

"Is there anything else we need?" she asks, her voice a little strangled.

"Other than the rope... just a couple of blindfolds... some extra cuffs, and maybe some anal beads..."

"Anal beads?" See looks up at me. "What on earth are anal beads?"

I smile down at her. "You'll find out. But I think you're gonna like them."

"Is that it?" she asks, almost panting with anticipation now.

"No... I think we'll get you a wand too."

"A wand?"

"Yeah... it's a magical one," I whisper and she stutters out a breath.

I complete our purchases, adding some lubricant, and selecting express delivery... because there's no way I wanna wait any longer than is strictly necessary, and then make the payment, before dropping my phone on the bed and pulling Bree into my arms.

"It'll be here tomorrow..."

"Even though today is Sunday?"

"Yeah... I figured it was worth paying the extra." She giggles and I lean down and kiss her, pulling back eventually. "Wanna shower with me?"

She nods with disarming enthusiasm, and I get up, holding out my hand and pulling her to her feet.

"And when we've showered, I'm gonna take you grocery shopping."

"Somehow that doesn't sound quite as exciting as coming back to bed."

"We can do that after we've been shopping. But I need to make sure you're fed first. I'm back now. It's my job to look after you you... to keep you safe... to make you happy. In every way imaginable. I'm not gonna neglect you again. And I'm not gonna let you go again either. I love you too much to lose you, Bree," I whisper, gazing down at her.

And then I lean down and kiss her, and as she moans softly into my mouth, I walk her backwards into the shower.

I wake early, because my body is trained to do that on work days… even when I'm not working. Which I'm not… not yet.

Bree is still sleeping though, and I can't bring myself to get up, or risk waking her, so I lie still and stare at her beautiful face, feeling her body close to mine, her head on my chest, and I bring my arms around her.

We had a fabulous day yesterday. Even grocery shopping was fun… well, it was with Bree, and when we got back, I cooked us some lunch, and afterwards, she fell asleep on me, on the couch, and I just lay there and enjoyed holding her, until she woke, and I made love to her, without restraining her, taking hours over pleasuring every part of her body.

We cooked together in the evening, keeping it simple, and then we came to bed.

I know that, one day, we'll probably come to bed and go straight to sleep, even if only out of sheer exhaustion. But we haven't gotten to that day yet. Thank God.

She stirs beside me, and I look down to see she's gazing up into my eyes.

"Good morning, beautiful."

"Hello."

I let out a sigh. "It's nearly six-thirty," I whisper, leaning down and kissing her gently. "What time is Dana due to come over?"

"She's not." Bree stretches in my arms. "I decided to take a couple of days off work."

"You did?"

"Yeah. I—I spoke to Max when I got back here on Saturday and told him I needed some time… to try and come to terms with losing you."

I feel a stabbing at my heart, knowing how much I must've hurt her. But I ignore it. We've gone over that so many times now, neither of us needs to say anything more. We both know we're sorry for what we've done.

"So, when were you planning on going back into the office?" I ask her.

"Wednesday."

I nod my head. "Okay... I—I should probably go in there today, I'm afraid."

She leans up on one elbow, looking down at me. "Why?"

"Because I've gotta see Pierce... and talk to your brother. I need to tell him I'm back and check whether he's okay with me working for him again."

"I seriously doubt he's gonna have a problem with that," Bree says, smiling.

"I hope not. But I also need to let Pierce know what's going on. He's gonna have to fly out to LA to take over the job I was doing... which was originally his job in the first place."

She frowns and seems to deflate slightly. "Does that mean you're gonna have to start working for Max again straight away?"

"No... the guy in LA is stuck in Europe until Friday, so as long as Pierce gets out there by Wednesday, it should be fine. I've done all the groundwork already..."

"S—So you could spend the next two days here... with me?"

"Of course... once I've been to see Max."

"You mean 'we', I think."

"You wanna come with me?"

"Naturally."

I chuckle and roll her onto her back. "I'm so glad you said that, baby..."

I drive us into the office, in my car, feeling relieved that we picked it up yesterday before we went shopping, because the rental car was gonna drive me crazy before much longer.

"What will we do if the parcel is delivered while we're out?" Bree asks suddenly, turning to me.

"Parcel?"

"Yes… you know… the equipment…" She says the last word in a kind of hushed whisper, and I have to smile.

"Your doorman will take it in, like he usually does with parcels, and we'll collect it when we get back."

"But, surely… he'll see where it's come from." I don't have to look at her to know she's blushing already and I reach across and rest my hand on her bare knee, grateful that she's wearing one of her less formal, shorter dresses today. She's not working after all, and I like being able to touch her.

"The packaging is very discreet, baby. He won't know a thing."

"Oh… okay." She settles back into the seat, and I complete the short drive, parking up in the garage beneath the office building, using Bree's space, which Dana normally parks in, because Pierce is using Max's one, where I'd usually be parked… if I were working.

I climb down and go around, helping Bree from the car and then hold her hand as we walk across to the elevator, which takes us straight up to the eighth floor. As the doors swish open into the lobby, where there are a few couches and a coffee machine for visitors who have to wait to see members of the management team who reside on this floor, Bree goes to pull her hand from mine.

"People will see," she whispers under her breath as I maintain my grip on her.

"I know. I want them to."

She raises her eyebrows as I pull her from the elevator and turn around to face her, walking backwards and pulling her with me. "Really?" She's surprised.

"Yeah. You're mine. I'm yours. I want the whole fucking world to know."

She grins and I spin around again, glancing across at the two familiar sales guys who are sitting on one of the couches, both of their mouths hanging open as they watch us pass through without a word.

"I dread to think what Valerie's gonna say," I mumble under my breath, and Bree snorts out a laugh.

We continue down the corridor, past her deserted office and then through the double doors at the end, into Max's sanctuary, where

Valerie glances up from her desk, over the top of her glasses. She looks from Bree, to me, and then down to our joined hands.

"Is he in?" I ask, nodding to Max's door.

"Yes," she replies, standing up.

"Don't bother," I say, stepping forward. "I think he knows us both well enough to skip the formal introductions, don't you?"

She glares at me, but doesn't argue – because she never does with me – and I pull Bree toward Max's door, pushing it open and letting Bree enter ahead of me.

"I didn't think you were coming in…" I hear him say, and then I walk in behind her and his expression changes from one of confusion, to one of understanding, as he sees our joined hands and a slow smile settles on his face.

"She's not," I tell him, smiling back. "But I thought I ought to put in an appearance and let you know I'm back."

"So I see." He comes around his desk and stands in front of us. "Is this a flying visit, or are you back for good?"

"For good," Bree says, before I can answer, and I let go of her hand and pull her into a hug.

"I take it this means you guys worked things out?"

"If you mean did I see sense, fly back here and beg your sister to forgive me and let me have another chance… then yeah… we worked things out."

"I'm glad to hear it," he says, grinning now.

"So, the question is, can I have my old job back?"

"You need to ask?"

"Always. I kinda let you down. I'm not making any assumptions about coming back."

He shakes his head. "There's nothing wrong with Pierce," he says, shrugging his shoulders. "But he and I don't have the same history. I need you here, man."

I smile at him and turn around to see the couch is empty. "Speaking of Pierce, where is he?"

"He doesn't sit in here with me, like you did. We're not on those kinda terms. He's just gone down to the coffee shop, I think. But normally, he sits in the reception area, like Dana does during the day."

I nod my head. "Okay. Well, I'm gonna have to wait for him to get back, so I can fill him in on what he's gotta do."

"Which is?" Max leans back on his desk, folding his arms across his chest.

"Fly out to LA and take over from me."

"As of when?"

"As of Tuesday night, or maybe Wednesday morning, depending on the flights. He's not due to start working out there until Friday, so he'll have plenty of time. And when he gets out there, he can have all my things shipped back here. I left in a hurry and didn't have time to bring much with me."

Max smiles. "You left in a hurry, did you?"

"Yeah. I had something I needed to do."

Bree looks up at me. "What was that?" she asks, teasing.

"Make it right with you again." She smiles and leans into me and I turn back to Max. "Just so you know, I'm gonna be moving into Bree's place."

She pulls away from me again, and I look back down at her. "You are?"

"Yeah. Your apartment's bigger for one thing. But more importantly, it has better security than mine. And sometimes your brother has me working late. I need to know you're safe, baby."

"But… living together?"

"Yeah. Do you actually think I'm gonna let you go, now I've got you back?"

She sucks in a breath and shakes her head. "And I thought you were only a Dominant in the bedroom," she mutters, and Max chokes.

"Then you thought wrong," I reply, ignoring him. "And anyway, this isn't about dominance… or submission. It's about loving you." I lean down and kiss her on the lips. "Why? Is that a problem?" I ask. "Am I going too fast again?"

"Yes, you are. But I don't mind," she says as she shakes her head, smiling a little indulgently, and I have to smile back.

Max clears his throat. "Are you two finished yet?"

"Never," I reply, and he smiles himself now.

"So, when are you coming back to work?" he asks.

"Wednesday. Pierce can finish up tomorrow… and Bree tells me she's got a couple of days off, so we're gonna spend some time together. We've got a lot of catching up to do."

Max pulls a face. "That's my sister you're talking about," he growls.

"I know, but if you didn't want me to talk about her like that, you shouldn't have encouraged me to come back here, should you?"

"Yeah, I should," Max says, looking down at Bree. "You were both so fucking miserable, like I told you. And, between you, you were making everyone else miserable too."

Bree shrugs herself out of my grip, and I let her go as she walks over to Max and puts her arms around his waist. He pulls her into a hug and she looks up at him and says, "Thank you."

"You're worth it," he whispers, and she pulls back again, turning toward me. I hold out my hand and she takes it, coming back to me. Back where she belongs. And I hold her tight. "You two look good together," Max says, like he's thinking out loud. "If… if you'd rather work with Bree," he continues, looking directly at me, "I won't mind. You can switch out with Dana, if you want."

"Are you saying you don't want me back now?" I ask.

"No. But I'll understand if you'd rather spend your time with Bree."

Shaking my head, I tighten my grip on her. "I can't do that," I explain. "I can't be Bree's bodyguard."

"Why not?" She looks up at me.

"Because it wouldn't be very professional, baby. I'm supposed to watch out for the people I'm guarding, not just watch them. Being with you all day would be too damn distracting." She smiles, and I turn back to Max. "Thanks for the offer, but we'll leave things the way they are. I'll come back to work for you, and we'll leave Dana with Bree during the day… and then I can take over from her in the evenings."

"Does Bree still need watching in the evenings?" Max says, tilting his head to one side, like he's confused. "I thought she'd have learned her lesson by now. She's not gonna go rushing off to bars anymore, is she?"

"No, I'm not," Bree replies. "I've got better things to do now."

"Yeah, she has," I say. "But I'm gonna be watching her anyway… just because I can."

Epilogue

Bree

Can it really be two months already?

It doesn't feel like it. And while I'd like to say I haven't noticed the time passing because we've been having so much fun, I think it's more likely because I've been so damn busy.

And so damn tired.

It wasn't like that to start with. At the beginning, for those first couple of days, we just got on with enjoying ourselves, and making the most of our time together.

The new 'equipment' had arrived by the time we got back from the office, on that Monday morning, giving us the rest of that day, and the day after, to enjoy it. And Colt made sure I enjoyed it. The first thing he did, once he'd stripped me out of my clothes, was to take me out onto the terrace and make me kneel on the daybed that nestles in a completely secluded position in the corner. It was beautifully warm, with just a light breeze, which played across my skin, and I watched him over my shoulder as he bound my ankles to my thighs with the new restraints, before cuffing my wrists, and clipping them on to the thigh restraints, too. I was powerless then, which he demonstrated when he pushed me over onto my back, and I was left lying there, with my legs bent up, unable to right myself, or even move… completely exposed to him. He stared down at me for a while, before he undressed, slowly and deliberately, telling me he'd thought of nothing but having me like this, ever since he'd seen the items I'd decided to buy from the website. I was shivering with anticipation, especially when he covered my eyes with a silky black blindfold, while I panted hard, almost begging him to let me come… and he hadn't even touched me yet. Then he moved away for a moment, before he returned, and I felt something bulbous and cool directly against my clit, which made me jump.

"What's that?" I asked him.

"This is a little bit of magic," he replied, enigmatically. "And I'm gonna use it to make you come, over, and over… as many times as you can take. But if it gets too much, don't go putting time limits on it… don't ask me for two minutes, or thirty seconds… just say 'stop'… okay?"

"Okay." His words had me on fire, and stopping was the last thing on my mind. I just wanted him to start, and was on the verge of asking him to, when the thing he was holding against me began to vibrate… at an alarming speed, and I came… hard… tugging against the restraints, grateful they were padded, so I didn't damage myself, in my wild thrashing.

As I calmed, he removed the vibrator, only to replace it moments later… and I came yet again. And again. And again. I lost count of how many times he urged me to newer, greater heights, telling me I could get there, even when I thought I couldn't; ordering my body to obey him, knowing it would. Eventually, unable to take any more, the word, "Stop" left my lips, and he did. Just like he'd said he would. He didn't release me, though. Instead, he bent over and kissed me, before he pulled away the blindfold, letting me see the burning need in his eyes, the loving smile on his lips. And then he flipped me over onto my knees, still restrained, my ass in the air, and with a hard slap, he entered me.

He was relentless that morning.

And I loved him for it.

Because it was just what I needed.

I've needed him ever since. But unfortunately, life has had a habit of getting in the way, to the extent that it's occasionally felt like a conspiracy. The last two months may have been the happiest of my life – thanks to Colt – but they've also been the busiest. Thanks to Max, mainly. The list of hotels he wanted me to look at has grown slightly shorter, but the hours I've had to put in have been stupid. I've been getting home from the office really late and literally falling into Colt's arms. He's cooked, held me, and then carried me to bed, fast asleep. Every. Single. Night. It probably wasn't quite what either of us had in mind when he suggested moving in here, but at least we've had the weekends. Because I've refused to work then, regardless of how busy I am. That said, I've slept through most of them. Not that he's complained. Not once.

We haven't had time to do much, other than work, eat and sleep, although Colt has mentioned us buying some new furniture, and even had me looking at things online. I'm not sure I can see the point in it myself. After all, my furniture isn't that old, being as I only bought most of it when I got divorced from Grady. But I guess he just wants us to have some things that are 'ours'. The apartment is more 'mine' than 'his', and sometimes I wonder if he feels that. Not that I've had a chance to talk to him about it. I will make some time, though. Soon.

Eva's been back from Houston for a few weeks. She did so well in Chicago, I had her oversee the work in Houston too, but she's off to St. Thomas on Monday, so we've spent most of the last few days going through the plans for the new hotel. This is the biggest job she's taken on yet, and while I have every faith in her, I know she's nervous about it. Our meeting today didn't finish until four-thirty, which meant I had a lot of catching up to do once she'd left the office, as a result of which Dana's only just dropped me back at the apartment. I'm exhausted, I'm fed up, and the only thing that makes it all worthwhile is that it's Friday, and I'm gonna get to spend the entire weekend with Colt. He's been a little distracted, too, this week, but when I asked him about it on Wednesday, he just said Max was keeping him busy, and he hated the fact that he wasn't getting to spend much time with me. I couldn't disagree with that, even if I didn't have the energy to anything about it. All I want to do now, though, is to lie in his arms, preferably naked, maybe order some takeout, and go to bed. I smile as I let myself into the apartment, thinking about how relaxing that sounds.

"I'm home… at last," I call out, to be greeted by a stoney silence, which doesn't make sense, because I know Max left the office at five – over two hours ago. He stuck his head round my door and told me he'd had enough today and wanted to get home to Tia. The agency he uses found him a new nanny, and she's been with Tia for over a month now, but Max is still doubtful about her… at least that's what Colt says. I'm not sure what Max's doubts are, but it was clear from the look on his face earlier that he just wanted to get home. Colt had already gone down to the car, evidently, but he didn't leave any message to say he'd be delayed, or late home. "Colt?" I raise my voice, walking further into the apartment, and putting my purse down on the dining room table, but still there's no reply. He's not here.

I pull my phone out of my jacket pocket and check my messages. Except there are none.

So, at the risk of seeming paranoid, I connect a call to him and wait. It rings five times until his voicemail kicks in, and I hear him telling me, quite stiffly, to leave a message.

"Hi. It's me. I'm just wondering where you are." I can't think what else to say, so I hang up and put my phone down on the table, standing still for a while, as I gaze around the apartment, wondering where on earth he can be.

I pace back and forth, uncertain what I should do, just as my phone rings and I snatch it up.

"Colt?"

"Yeah… what's wrong, baby?"

He can clearly tell that something is, even though I've only said his name.

"Where are you? You left the office ages ago."

"I'm on my way back now," he replies. "Has something happened?"

"No… but I just got home, and you weren't here."

"Yeah. Sorry about that. I had a couple of errands to run, and there was someone I had to see."

"Oh? Who was that?"

"No-one you need to worry about." His answer is evasive and his voice is kinda distant.

"Colt? What's going on?"

"Nothing's going on."

"Then why won't you tell me who you've been with?" My blood chills. "H—Have you been with another woman?" I ask, thinking about our almost non-existent sex life over the last few weeks, and the way he's been so preoccupied of late.

"No." Again, he sounds remote, and my chilled blood starts to freeze. Inspired by some kind of sixth sense, I wander into the master bedroom, going over to the closet where Colt keeps all his equipment – well, our equipment, I suppose, since we bought it together – my breath catching in my throat when I open the door to find the closet is completely empty.

"C—Colt?" His name escapes my lips, in a cracked whisper, as the first tear hits my cheek. "Don't lie to me."

"I haven't lied to you. Are you crying?"

"Yes… and you have lied to me."

"No, I haven't."

Although my tears are falling fast now, my anger is building, too. "In that case, why is the closet in the bedroom empty? If you haven't been with someone else, why did you need to take all the equipment with you?"

"Fuck it," he whispers, and then, in a louder voice, adds, "It's not what it seems."

"Oh… really?"

"Yeah. Really."

I suck in a breath. "Don't bother coming back here, Colt."

"What?" I can hear his astonishment.

"I said…"

"I heard what you said. I'm less than a minute away. Just let me…"

"I don't care how far away you are. I don't want you here. You've still got an apartment of your own. I suggest you go back there."

"Bree, don't do this," he pleads, as I wander aimlessly back into the living room again. "Don't ruin…"

"I'm not the one who's ruining everything. You are."

"Let me… let me explain," he says.

"No."

"I—I thought you loved me."

"I do."

"Then why don't you trust me?"

I don't have an answer to that, so I hang up instead and drop to my knees by the couch, feeling like my heart's been ripped from my chest as I let out a howl, my body wracked with pain. I release my phone, letting it fall to the floor and clutch my arms around my middle, trying to hold myself together, because I feel like I'm gonna break as I picture Colt with another woman… another sub. *Oh, God…* "How could you, Colt? How could you do this to me?"

"Do what?" His voice makes me jump and I look up to see him standing by the front door, his keys in his hand, breathing hard, like he's been running.

"Get out."

He shakes his head and closes the door behind him, dropping his keys into his jacket pocket as he walks over, his eyes fixed on mine.

"What is it you think I've done?" He stands over me, his eyes dark, his expression unreadable.

I bite back my tears, and rather than let him see how much I'm hurting, I go on the offensive. "You're only supposed to be a Dominant in bed, so…"

"Fine…" He grabs my arm and pulls me up to my feet, dragging me into the bedroom.

"Let me go!" I try to break free.

"No. If geography matters so much to you, we'll talk in here." He throws me down on the bed, straddles me and leans over, holding my hands on either side of my head, his body raised above mine.

"How could you?" I hurl the words at him, refusing to feel intimidated. *I will not submit to him.*

"How could I what?"

"How could you do that… with another sub…?"

He closes his eyes and lets his head drop, before he raises it again and looks at me, letting out a sigh. "I haven't done anything with anyone... but, once and for all, will you stop referring to yourself as though you were a sub? You're not. You never have been."

"No. Because I'm nothing. I don't mean a damned thing to you. Evidently."

He sighs again, even more deeply, and stares down into my eyes. "You wanna know what you mean to me?"

"Yeah... I think I do. I think I'd like you to show me what nothing looks like."

He narrows his eyes. "Okay... come with me. I'll show you *exactly* what you mean to me."

He climbs off of the bed, although he keeps hold of one of my hands and pulls me with him and, without letting go, he marches us through the apartment, picking up my phone from the floor and grabbing my purse as we pass, thrusting them both at me.

"Where are we going? And why do I need my purse?" I say, looking up at him.

"You'll find out."

He opens the front door, guiding me through it and I glance back at him, and seeing the darkness in his eyes, I feel a shiver run through me because this feels horribly like he's become the storm again... and as much as I'm confused, and angry, and hurting... that thought is too scary for words.

Because I can remember how it feels to be in the storm. It feels like I'm on the outside... and I'm losing him.

Colt

This has gone about as badly as it could have done.

It's taken me weeks of planning; of sneaking out of work when Max didn't need me, and when I was certain Bree was too busy to notice whether I was there. Weeks of clandestine phone calls and emails. Weeks of worrying and wondering if I'm doing the right thing… and I've kept all of it a secret too. Not even Max knows what I've been doing. I couldn't risk Bree finding out… and spoiling the surprise. The surprise which is now falling apart around me. Like my future seems to be.

"Where are we going?" Bree asks, turning to face me as I drive us out of the city, heading north.

I glance over at her, notice the suspicious look on her face, and feel a return of the fear which I've been trying to keep under control since we left her apartment. "Do you trust me?" That feels like the sixty-four thousand dollar question right now, considering her reaction to finding that the closet in the bedroom was empty. Not that I'd expected her to go looking in there tonight… not that I'd expected to be quite as late getting home as I was. Things just took a little longer to set up than I'd hoped they would. Although I can't explain that to Bree… being as that's part of the surprise.

She hesitates before she answers. "I—I don't know."

Well, I guess at least that's honest. Not what I wanted to hear. But honest. "Okay. Until tonight, when you thought you'd caught me in a lie, have I done anything to earn your distrust?"

"No." Her reply is immediate.

"In which case, can you give me the benefit of the doubt for the next thirty minutes or so?" She hesitates again, and feeling desperate, I add the word, "Please?"

"Okay," she allows, folding her arms across her chest as she looks out through the windshield again, and I heave out a sigh of relief.

Maybe the whole thing isn't blown, after all.

We continue in silence for another ten minutes, my mind playing over my plan, hoping she'll at least give me a chance to see it through, before she turns to me again.

"Why are you taking me to Max's place?"

"I'm not."

"But this is Lexington… Max lives in Lexington."

"Yeah. I know. But we're not going to Max's."

I turn off of the main road, proving my point, being as Max lives a little further along, by about five minutes, and then once I've driven a couple of hundred yards, I pull up outside the substantial Colonial property which is familiar to me, but not to Bree, and she looks over, yet again.

"What are you doing?" she asks, confused, as I tap a six-digit code into the device on the gatepost and wait for the cast iron gates to swing inwards before I continue slowly up the driveway and park outside the main house, ignoring the double garages off to one side.

"Showing you what you mean to me," I explain, while telling her absolutely nothing, as I exit the car, walking around to her side and opening her door. She hesitates when I offer her my hand, but eventually takes it and lets me help her down, while she looks up at the pale gray painted façade of the wooden clad house.

"Why are we here?" she whispers, like she's worried she'll be overheard. "Do you know the people who live here?"

"Kinda… yeah." I gaze down at her and, keeping a firm grip on her hand, I pull her up the steps toward the front door. She hesitates, waiting for me to ring the doorbell, but I surprise her by putting the key into the lock and turning it.

"Colt… what on earth…?"

I turn and look down at her. "I figured it was high time we got a place of our own," I say, moving a little closer to her, because despite her accusations, she's still a magnet for me. She always will be. And I can't blame her for misunderstanding.

She raises her eyebrows. "Is that where you've been today?" she asks. "Arranging for us to come and see this place?"

"Something like that, yeah."

She frowns at me and I half expect her to ask why that meant I needed to empty the closet in her bedroom back at the apartment… but she doesn't. Instead, she takes a step forward into the house, and I smile when I hear her gasp.

"Oh… it's beautiful," she says, looking around at the huge lobby area, with its double-height ceiling and galleried landing above. The walls are white and the floor is laid with stripped oak boards, and Bree looks down at that, before removing her shoes and kicking them to one side, while I close the door.

"This way." I indicate to our right, and let her lead the way into the first of two sitting rooms, which is quite small and has bookcases along one wall, and a fireplace opposite, with a large sheepskin rug set in front. It's furnished simply, with a cream-colored couch, over the back of which is a teal throw. It's intimate in here, perfect for the two of us, and she looks around, taking everything in.

"Whoever owns this place has excellent taste," she whispers. "I love that couch… and as for the colors…"

I struggle not to smile, because she hasn't recognized the furniture, even though it's only two weeks since she admired it on the Internet with me.

"Come and see the kitchen…" I direct her into the next room, which is enormous by comparison, and she lets out a long sigh.

"Oh, my God," she breathes, wandering around and taking in the white handmade doors, the gray granite countertops and central island, and the sliding doors which lead directly onto the decking beyond. "This is incredible," she says, turning to face me.

"You like it?"

"Of course. What's not to like?"

"Well, there's another, much bigger, living room, and a formal dining space around the other side." I point to the archway on the far side of the kitchen. "And there's an office too." She nods her head as I pull her back into the lobby to the bottom of the stairs. "But I want to show you something else… up here…" I start to climb, and she follows, her hand drifting up the hardwood banister railing, as she looks back over her shoulder to the lobby area below.

"It—It's a beautiful house, Colt," she says, sounding kinda wistful. "Actually, it feels like home to me. But…"

"But what?" I stop halfway up the stairs, trying so hard not to smile, and turn to her.

"We need to talk."

"I know… but will you humor me, just for a few more minutes?"

She takes a deep breath, letting it out slowly, and shrugs her shoulders, which I take as a 'yes', when she starts walking up the stairs with me again.

At the top, we have the option to go around to the left, where all the guest rooms are, or to the right, where there's just one door… which leads to the master suite. And that's where I'm taking her.

Outside, I feel truly nervous for the first time. What I'm about to do is something I'd consigned to the realms of my dreams. And while this evening's events haven't helped, I still can't help hoping that my dreams are going to come true… that I'm going to finally get the one thing I've always wanted. More than anything.

I push the door open, and Bree gasps again, even more loudly this time, before she turns to look at me and I smile down at her.

"W—What's going on?" she says, her eyes wide.

"I told you… I'm showing you what you mean to me."

I give her hand a tug and she follows me into the room, her eyes roaming around, over the oak floors, the white walls, the soft gray drapes… and my enormous cast iron bed, which is made up with brand new, crisp white bed linen, with a quilted throw folded across the foot of the mattress. There's a single chair over by the window and the room is lit by two lamps on tables either side of the bed, and on the chest at the end, is an ice bucket, containing a bottle of champagne, with two glasses standing beside it.

She turns and looks up at me. "Colt? I—I don't understand."

"Answer me a question… do you like the house?"

"Yes. I do."

"Would you like to live here?"

"That's two questions, and like I said, we need to talk."

"We don't, Bree. Not in the way you mean. I know you're scared and angry, and confused, but you don't need to be."

"But…" I raise my hand, putting my fingers across her lips to silence her.

"I get it, babe. I really do. You think, because the closet in your bedroom was empty, that means I must've spent my evening… or at least part of it… using the contents of the closet, with a sub. Is that right?" She nods her head, I drop my hand, and even in the dim lighting, I can see tears welling in her eyes. "Okay… come with me."

"Where to now?" she asks, sounding a little exasperated.

"Just through here."

I lead her into the dressing room, flicking on the lights to reveal that it's lined with floor-to-ceiling closets, finished in dark wood. I open the double doors on the left, unveiling a series of drawers.

"Open them," I tell her and she does, one at a time, tears pouring down her cheeks as each drawer offers up its secret contents… namely the ropes, restraints, cuffs, and other 'equipment' she assumed I'd been using on someone else.

"I don't understand," she repeats, turning to me, tears pouring down her cheeks. "What's it all doing here?"

"It lives here now… just like we do."

"We… we…" She can't talk.

"I've bought this house, baby. It's ours. I haven't spent my evening with someone else. I've spent it here, getting this place ready for us… after I met the realtor to collect the keys. That was the person I had to see." I turn to her, clasping her face in my hands and wiping her tears away with my thumbs. "Please, don't cry."

"But I'm so confused."

I smile. "I know."

I take her hand and lead her back into the bedroom, sitting her down on the edge of the mattress, where I join her. Then, turning to face her, I reach up to brush a few stray strands of hair from her face. "Please understand that I would never betray you. Ever. I don't really know how you could think that of me, and the fact that you could tells me I've still got some work to do with you, and your self-confidence… and that's gonna start off with me explaining to you that the thought of being with someone else ever again is abhorrent to me. I can't imagine putting myself in that position. It wouldn't even cross my mind. I'm yours, Bree. I—I thought you understood that."

She blinks rapidly, and a lone tear falls down her left cheek. "I'm sorry. It's just that I saw everything was missing, and couldn't work it out."

I let out a sigh. "I get that… well, kinda. But you've gotta trust me, baby. I could never hurt you. Not after the last time. Not after I came so close to losing you."

She nods her head and leans into me as I put my arm around her, pulling her close and kissing the top of her head. "I'm sorry," she murmurs. "Are you still mad at me?"

"Do I look like I'm mad at you?"

She leans back and gazes up at me. "Not now, no. But at my apartment…"

"At your apartment, I was scared, not mad. It might not have looked like that, but you'd told me not to come home to you. I thought you were leaving me… or making me leave you, anyway. In situations like that, I tend to…"

"Revert to type?" she suggests.

"Yeah… something like that."

"I know." She sucks in a breath. "You looked…"

"I looked what?"

"You looked like you did before… before we got together. When you rejected me in your shower. Do you remember? You called yourself a storm."

I smile down at her. "Yeah, I did say that, didn't I? But you don't need to worry. I'm not that guy anymore. You tamed him a long time ago."

"It didn't feel like it tonight."

"Then I'm sorry if I scared you."

"You didn't. Not in the way you mean. I'm never scared when I'm with you. But for a moment, I thought I might have lost you."

"Never, baby. You'll never lose me. And besides, you were right when you said there isn't a storm in the world that can hurt you when I'm with you. There isn't. Because I'll never let anything hurt you." I pull her closer, holding her tight. "You still don't really get it, do you?"

"Get what?"

"How this works. You think because I'm a Dominant, I'm the one in control…"

"Well, you are," she interrupts.

"No. You're the one with all the power."

She shakes her head. "How do you work that out?"

I take a breath. "Because you're the only woman – the only person – who could break me."

She gasps. "I won't. I'll never break you. And I'm sorry if I hurt you – again – by not believing in you."

"Don't be sorry… just learn to have a little more faith. Please?"

"I know. I should have trusted you," she whimpers, and I lean right back, looking down at her.

"I meant you should have more faith in yourself. Do you actually think I would do anything to jeopardize what we have?"

She looks up at me and takes a moment before she shakes her head.

"Damn straight I wouldn't," I say, leaning down and kissing her lips before pulling back again and cupping her face in my hands. "I'm sorry if I've been kinda distracted lately. I suppose, that's why you reacted the way you did, when you found the closet empty. Because I know I've been behaving a little out of character over the last week or so. It was just that, once I got the buyer for my apartment, I…"

"You've sold your apartment?" She's shocked.

"Yeah. I'm not poor, baby, but if I was gonna buy somewhere like this, I was always gonna have to sell my old place first… and before you tell me you could've helped out, I appreciate that. But I wanted to do this by myself. I had a plan, and I had to be the one to carry it out."

"A plan?" she queries, looking confused.

"Yeah. It's something I've been thinking about for a long time. So, I put my apartment up for sale about six weeks ago. The realtor found me a buyer within a couple of days, which was great. The only drawback was that he wanted to move in by today. It all happened a lot quicker than I'd expected, to be honest… and that meant I had to find us somewhere else to live."

"Why?" she asks. "We've got my place. You've been living there anyway."

"Yeah. I know. But it was all part of the plan, you see. I spent hours on the Internet at work, when Max thought I was working… and I eventually found three houses that I thought were right for us. But when I looked around them, only this one actually felt right. It was weird… I walked in here, and it was just like coming home." I smile down at her, recalling her comment on the stairs. I think she must be remembering that too, because her eyes are locked on mine and her lips have parted, just a fraction, and for a moment, neither of us moves, or even seems to breathe.

"So you bought it?" she says, eventually.

"Yeah. The previous owners had already moved out, and they wanted a quick sale, so then it was just a question of waiting for everything to happen… and getting hold of some new furniture."

"Why? We both have furniture."

"I know. But the guy I was selling my apartment to was an overseas buyer, and he wanted to take my place furnished… and was willing to pay top dollar for that. So, other than my bed – which we're currently sitting on, in case you haven't noticed – I let him have everything. And I could hardly start moving your furniture into here, could I? I think you might have noticed that… and it would have spoiled the surprise."

She narrows her eyes. "So is that why you've been asking me about couches and dining tables?" she asks.

I nod my head. "Didn't you notice the couch downstairs? It's the same one you picked out from that website I showed you a couple of weeks ago… when I asked which one you'd have if you could take your choice."

"But I—I thought you were talking about us maybe buying some new things for the apartment."

"Well, I had to invent a reason for bringing up the idea of new furniture in the first place, and that seemed like as good an excuse as any. But I haven't furnished all the rooms," I admit, holding up my hands. "I just got the essentials for now, and I figured we could do the rest together. Later. I just wanted us to have this weekend… here… together… with enough furniture to survive, and without letting you know about it."

"The weekend?" she says.

"Yeah. The weekend."

"And what are we going to do about food?" she says, the corners of her lips twitching upwards.

"The refrigerator's already stocked."

"It is?"

"Yeah. Why do you think I rushed you through the kitchen and brought you up here?"

"Because this is where the bed is?" Her lips make it into a full-on smile, and I have to return it.

"Okay… so that had a huge part to play. But it was also because I couldn't afford to risk you checking out the refrigerator and finding that I'd already filled it."

"So we can just stay here? All weekend?"

"We can."

"But what about clothes?" she says, tipping her head to one side.

"We won't be needing any." I lower my voice, and she grins up at me.

"That's all well and good," she says, after a moment, her smile fading, "and I appreciate that there's probably a laundry room here, but what will happen on Monday morning, when we both go into work, wearing the same clothes we've had on all day today? Don't you think someone might notice?"

I shrug my shoulders. "I'm not sure I care if they do. But you're not spending the weekend doing laundry… and neither am I. So I'll confess now, that I snuck out at lunchtime, and went back to the apartment… and I packed us a bag, which is in the trunk of my car."

"So we have clothes?" she says, her smile returning.

"Yeah… but not very many. Because, like I say, we're not gonna be needing them."

She giggles and, probably for the first time since I got her message on my phone over an hour ago now, I actually start to relax.

"Tell me the house is okay." I look down at her, wanting her seal of approval for all my craziness.

"The house is perfect."

I smile at her. "We can explore it properly tomorrow and you can decide how you want to furnish it, and we can move in properly during the week, or next weekend, or whenever we have the time… but for now…" I pull her jacket from her shoulders and drop it to the floor by my feet, before I reach around behind her and pull down the zipper on her dress, and she shudders against me. "Easy, baby," I whisper. "We've got all night."

"All weekend…" she murmurs, and I smile.

"We sure have."

I pull down her dress, just a little way, and my smile widens when I see that she's wearing black lace underwear. I left home early this morning, before she'd finished drying her hair, so I wasn't aware she'd put this on… but this is one of my favorite sets. She looks perfect in it. Completely perfect.

"Stand up," I instruct her, and she obeys, getting to her feet and standing before me, while I lower her dress, to reveal her beautiful breasts, encased in gossamer lace. My cock is rock hard before I've pulled it down as far as her hips… but as I go lower, her garter belt comes into view… and then her panties… and finally the tops of her black stockings. She's been wearing stockings for the last couple of weeks, since the weather has turned cooler, and I for one am not complaining. Not that I've had the opportunity to do much about what she's wearing, or not wearing for that matter… but I'm still not complaining. Because she looks good enough to eat… and I intend to.

But only when I'm through telling her – and showing her – what she is to me.

Leaving her in her underwear, I stand, wander over to the window and shrug off my jacket, throwing it onto the chair, pulling off my tie, and undoing the top two buttons of my shirt, before turning back to her, my eyes raking over her sexy body.

"Before we take this any further, shall I open the champagne?"

"Okay," she whispers, letting her own eyes roam downwards, stopping when they reach the bulge in the front of my pants, before she raises them again, and I notice they're on fire.

I make my way back and pick up the champagne bottle, which is nicely chilled, removing the foil before twisting it and letting it pop gently. I pour the champagne, then replace the opened bottle in the ice bucket and bring the glasses to Bree, who's standing waiting for me.

I hand one to her and she takes it.

"I love you," I say, clinking my flute against hers.

"I love you," she replies, looking into my eyes. She pauses, the glass halfway to her lips.

"Drink." I lower my voice, forming a slightly deeper instruction, which makes her body shudder just as she bites her bottom lip.

"I'd rather just…" She breathes deeply, her breasts heaving, and I know exactly what she'd rather do.

"Drink." I turn my instruction into a very definite order, becoming the Dom, and her eyes widen, even as her breathing deepens still further, and she raises the glass to her lips, my cock twitching as I watch her. At the last second, she lets her eyes drop from my face to the glass, just as she tips it up, and then they widen further as she straightens it again. She glances at me, blinks, and looks back at the glass, where there's a white gold solitaire diamond ring, resting at the bottom, champagne bubbles floating around it.

"Colt?" she whispers.

"You wanted to know what you mean to me? Well… this is it, baby. I told you earlier I'd been thinking about this plan for a long time, and that's the truth. But the house was only a small part of that. This is the part that really matters." Her eyes glisten in the dim light as she stares up at me. "Drink the champagne, Bree," I tell her, and she sucks in a breath, raising the glass to her lips, and swallowing down a long sip, before lowering it again.

Without taking my eyes from hers, I remove the glass from her hand, putting mine down, so I can tip hers and pluck the ring from beneath the last inch of champagne, a few drips falling from my fingers to the wooden floor, onto which I drop, on one bended knee.

Bree sucks in a breath as I take her left hand in mine.

"I need you, Bree. I need you to let me be your rock, so you'll always feel safe and grounded. I need you to let me be your light, so you'll always have someone to turn to, even if everything seems dark. I need you to let me be your best friend, so you'll never feel alone again. I need you to let me be your love, because my heart is yours and would break without you. And I need you to let me be your husband... because I want nothing more than to walk through life with you beside me..."

Bree drops to her knees in front of me and nods her head.

"Are you saying 'yes' to marrying me?" I ask, just to be sure.

"Yes," she whispers, as her tears start to fall, and I raise her left hand and place the ring on her finger before licking off the champagne, then sucking her finger into my mouth, my tongue playing over it. "Oh... God..." she breathes, watching me, her eyes alight, as I let her finger pop from my lips, kissing the tip. She takes a breath and puts her arms around my neck.

"Is this really okay?" I ask, looking into her eyes. "I'm not moving too fast for you again? Because, if I am, you only have to say. We don't have to get married straight away. If you need some time... we can wait. Not too long... but we can wait."

She smiles. "It's not too fast," she whispers, and then lowers her head. I place my finger beneath her chin and raise it again, seeing the uncertainty in her eyes, my heart sinking, despite her words.

"What's wrong?"

"Nothing. It's just that I married you-know-who in the winter... and I really don't wanna go there again. So would... would it be okay... would you mind waiting until the summer?"

I smile myself now. "Of course not. I've waited eleven years for you. Another few months won't hurt."

"You're sure?" She seems doubtful. "You won't get bored and wanna give up, waiting for me?"

"Bored? Not a chance, babe... and I'll never give up on you. You know that."

She leans into me, holding on tight, and I let her, putting my arms around her waist and pulling her closer. "D—Did you really plan all of this?" she says softly, like she can't quite believe it, although I don't know why. I love her, after all.

"Of course. Although I seriously thought the whole thing was gonna go up in smoke after you got back to the apartment and found I wasn't there…"

"Thank God it didn't," she whispers, and she pulls back a little and then leans up, as though to kiss me. I bring my hand around, putting it over her lips, stopping her, and she frowns, clearly confused by my actions.

"I think you're forgetting something…"

Her frown deepens, and I lower my hand so she can say, "Am I?"

"Yeah."

"What's that?"

I grab hold of her and stand, turning around and dropping her down on the bed, kneeling up and leaning over her. "I'll give you anything you want… anything at all. But I'm still the Dom… okay?"

"Yes," she whimpers, parting her legs and I smile down at her, before standing again, and pulling my shirt from my pants, slowly undoing the buttons, while she leans up on her elbows, admiring the show. I stand still, my shirt undone, and stare down at her. "What's the matter?" she asks.

"Nothing. I'm just trying to decide what to do with you." She lies back down again, her head on the mattress, although she's still staring at me as she lowers her hands to her thighs and strokes them up over her soft skin, pausing when she gets to her lace panties and caressing herself intimately through the fine material for a few enthralling moments. I'm spellbound, watching, as she grinds her hips, moaning and sighing, pleasuring herself, before she stops, sighs, and moves her hands upwards, letting her fingertips wander over her flat stomach to her gossamer-covered breasts, which she cups. She moans, hissing out a sigh between her teeth as she tweaks her nipples, my ring sparkling on her finger, and I suck in a breath, my cock straining against my zipper. "Are you trying to tease me?"

"Yes." She grins.

"You're a bad girl."

"Does that mean you're gonna have to punish me?" she says, letting her hands fall back to her sides as she licks her lips, biting the bottom one.

I lean over her again, my face just an inch from hers. "You know very well I don't believe in punishments…" As I'm talking, I reach down between us, letting my hand delve inside her lace panties. She's soaking, and I slide my fingers through her folds and gently caress her clit as she bucks her hips off of the bed. "Stay still," I growl, halting my movements, and she stares up at me. She knows I'm waiting for her response, and eventually she nods her head. "You're gonna be still?" I say, just to be sure.

"Yes," she whimpers.

"Why?" It's my turn to tease now.

"Because I want you to make me come," she says, and I struggle not to smile as I slowly circle my fingertips around her drenched clit again. She parts her legs wider still. "More," she urges, so I stop again, and she groans. "You are punishing me."

"No."

"Are you edging me?" she asks, and this time I have to smile. I can't help it. Those words, on her lips, sound so damn cute. At least, they do to me.

"No," I reply again.

"Then what are you doing?"

"Proving a point."

Without another word, and using just the tip of my middle finger, I rub her clit really hard. She screams, slapping her hands down onto the mattress and grabbing handfuls of bedding as her body trembles beneath my own.

"I'm… Oh, God… I'm…" she wails, and then her words become garbled and her voice becomes an even louder, piercing scream, as she thrashes violently, all thoughts of stillness forgotten… by both of us. Her orgasm is intense, and she takes a while to calm, and to focus on me again.

"Okay?" I whisper once I know she's paying attention.

"Hmm… yes, thank you."

"You don't have to thank me for doing that. Ever." I lean down and kiss her.

She looks up at me. "What was the point you were proving?" she asks.

I lean down and kiss her. "You need to ask?"

She tilts her head. "That you're still the Dom?"

"You've got it."

She smiles and reaches up, putting her hands on my biceps. "I don't think that was ever in any doubt… do you?"

"Maybe not. But it was fun proving it."

She giggles. "Yes, it was. I'm sorry if I deafened you. I didn't mean to make so much noise."

"Hey, don't worry about it. It's not like we've got neighbors here… and one of the things I liked most about this house, is the layout."

"The layout?" she queries, looking confused.

"Yeah. This bedroom is on its own; kinda isolated. All the others are separate, over the other side… so at least we know the kids won't hear us."

She blinks and stills, and her eyes widen. "W—What kids?"

"Ours. I—I know you said you went off the idea when you were with that loser you used to be married to… but…"

"You wanna have kids?" she interrupts.

"Yeah. As long as I'm having them with you. Why? Don't you?" Don't tell me I've read this wrong.

She sucks in a breath, and then the most perfect smile forms on her lips. "Yes… yes, I do."

"You're sure?"

"Yes. I—I mean, I kinda dismissed the idea from my life, because I never thought motherhood would be something that would happen to me. And I wasn't sure that having children was something you'd want."

"Then maybe you need to reconsider that…" I take a breath. "We don't have to rush into it, but there's nothing I want more than for you to be pregnant with my child."

"You're really serious, aren't you?"

"Absolutely. I told you. I'm always serious." She throws her arms around my neck, holding on fast and I let her for a while, relishing the feel of her body against mine, and then she slowly releases me and lies back down, looking up at me with the most tempting expression on her face.

"You're teasing me again," I whisper, and she struggles not to smile. And with that, without giving her any warning, I kneel up and flip her over onto her front. She squeals as I lean over her again, my mouth beside her ear. "So… future wife… future mother of my children… what shall I do with you?"

"Everything," she breathes. "Just everything…"

The End

Thank you for reading *Taming the Storm*. I hope you enjoyed it, and if you did I hope you'll take the time to leave a short review.

And if you want to find out more about me and my books, including forthcoming releases, please visit my website at www.suziepeters.com, where you can also sign up to become a member of Suzie's Circle, giving you access to **exclusive free stories**.

In the meantime, if you want to find out what happens next in this series, keep reading for an excerpt from book two…
Chasing the Dream.

Chasing the Dream

Never Give Up: Book Two

by

Suzie Peters

Chapter One

Eva

"Is this your first time in St. Thomas?" The flight attendant looks down at me with a friendly smile on her face as she gathers up plastic beakers and stray wrappers, reminding passengers to put their trays back into place before we land.

"It's my first time in the Caribbean," I reply, and her smile widens.

"Well, I'm sure you'll have a lovely vacation."

She moves on, making platitudes with the next passenger, not giving me time to point out that I'm not on vacation. I'm not even on holiday. My trip is for business, through and through. And I'm dreading it.

Even so, looking out of the window at the lush greenery of the island below, I can't help but feel relieved that at least my journey is almost over. I've been travelling since before six this morning, and it's nearly three in the afternoon now. Which could explain why I'm exhausted.

I can't wait to get to the hotel complex, have a shower, something to eat, and fall into bed. Because I know the next four weeks are going to be ludicrously busy, and incredibly stressful, and I want to make the most of this one evening by myself, before it all goes downhill.

I look down the aircraft at the backs of other people's heads… most of them going on holiday, I guess… not travelling on business, like me. That makes sense, really, considering the island of St. Thomas in the Caribbean is a popular holiday destination. And that's why the company I work for is building a brand new hotel down there. They have one already – the one I'm going to be staying at, which is in a place called Point Knoll – but the new one is going to be something else. It's going to be very sophisticated, featuring everything the discerning holidaymaker could wish for. And that's not the Crawford Hotels sales brochure talking. That's me. Because I helped to design it. Well… I helped to design the interior, anyway. Actually, I'm probably doing myself an injustice. I *did* design the interior. It was the first job I took on when Bree Crawford – who owns the company, together with her two brothers, Max and Chase – first brought me out to the States last June… just four short months ago. She 'discovered' me, for want of a better word, last autumn. That was during a competition I'd been persuaded to take part in, by my brother Ronan, which was being organised by a charity in conjunction with the university where I was studying interior design. Being naturally quite shy and unsure of myself, I'd been reluctant to put my work forward. But Ronan convinced me I had nothing to lose… and he was right. Because, as it turned out, Bree Crawford was one of the judges, and she liked my designs so much she offered me a job. There and then. On the spot.

I can still remember standing, staring at her, with my mouth open, and the smile that formed on her incredibly beautiful face, while she waited for me to come back to my senses and reply.

"I'm still at university," I said eventually, my voice quiet, as usual.

"I know." She nodded her head, her dark curls bouncing. "But I'm willing to wait for you."

That shocked me even more than her job offer, I think.

"I—I won't finish my course until next summer. You do realise that, don't you?"

"Yes."

"And you want me to come and work for you? In America?"

"Yes. Our head office is in Boston, and don't worry about any of the red tape… you know, the employment regulations?" I hadn't realised there was any red tape, and I knew nothing about employment regulations, but I nodded my head, pretending I understood exactly what she was talking about. "I'll take care of it all," she said.

"Where will I live?" I asked her. Back then, I was living in a rented flat close to the university campus, in south-west London. But Ronan had arranged that for me. I had no idea how to go about finding a property… especially not in America.

"Don't worry about that either," she said, brushing away my concern with a wave of her hand. "It'll be easier if I just find you an apartment and make it part of your package."

"You… you mean I won't have to pay rent?"

She grinned. "No. You won't have to pay rent."

I felt like I'd be a fool to turn down such an opportunity, so I said, "Yes." And then I spent the next eight months wondering if I'd imagined the whole thing. Obviously I knew I hadn't, because Bree kept in touch, via e-mail. She sent me through my contract of employment, and then details of the apartment she'd found for me, which made my jaw drop, in terms of its luxury. It was certainly a lot more palatial than the little studio flat I'd been living in for the last couple of years. And when I arrived in Boston in June, having graduated with a First in my course, I found the apartment – and Boston itself – to be even nicer than I'd expected.

My flat is in a red-brick building about a ten-minute walk from the Crawford Hotels offices, and it has a large foyer downstairs, with a gym in the basement. Not that I've ever used that. I'm afraid I'm too shy to venture down there. My flat itself is absolutely beautiful, though. The colour palette is neutral, with each room having a feature wall. In the living area, it's a deep grey, while the furniture is paler, with bright purple accents. My bedroom is a kind of duck-egg blue, although everything else in there, even down to the curtains, is white. And the guest room is navy. The kitchen, which is slotted into one corner of the living space, is incredibly modern, although it is a little on the small side. But Bree explained that a lot of people eat out over here, which I guess makes sense of not needing much space to cook. I haven't eaten out myself. I haven't wanted to. It's not that I'm worried about eating on my own. It's just that I wouldn't know where to go… and the kitchen is more than big enough for me.

I love the fact that I can walk to work, even if everyone at the office thinks I'm crazy for doing so, especially Bree's bodyguard, Dana. But why would I want to do anything else? Like I say, it's only ten minutes away, so it hardly seems worth catching a bus or taking a taxi. And I enjoy the fresh air. Plus the walk gives me some exercise… being as I'm too shy – or is it too scared – to go to the gym.

I glance out of the window again as we come in to land, the tarmac runway coming up to meet us, and then the wheels bumping slightly as the plane touches down. There seems to be a collective sigh of relief, which I don't really understand. It's as though the passengers in the plane were holding their breath, and now they've let it out. Still, I smile to myself, because I think I probably did the same thing on my first flight… which was only when I came over to America to start work.

Since then, in the ensuing four months, I've travelled a fair amount, I suppose. At least I have compared to the previous twenty-one years of my life, when I remained firmly settled in England… either at home in Oxford, or at university in London.

But since June, I've been to both Chicago and Houston. I didn't see very much of either city though, because I had to spend my time at the Crawford hotels in each place, working on refurbishing the bedrooms and main public spaces.

That was a task which had been given to Bree – and, therefore, to me – by her brother, Max, who kind of runs the company. Bree and her other brother Chase definitely have an equal share, but Max is the one they defer to. Not that I blame them. He's quite a commanding character. At least, he's very tall, if that counts as commanding. He's friendly enough, though… and has always been very pleasant to me, so I'm not complaining. Although other people had been… not about Max, but about the decor in some of the Crawford hotels, which was why he'd asked Bree to upgrade them. A lot of them. The list was extensive, and when he first gave it to her, I could tell she was a little overwhelmed. We were already really busy, and given her kindness to me, it felt like the least I could do to help out. So, I made us a schedule, working out which hotels were most in need of attention, and then we got on with it. And I think that, because I was so organised – or at least

I came across that way – Bree asked me to oversee the first of the refits, in Chicago, back in August.

And I hated it.

I hated every moment of it.

Bree must've been pleased with my work, though, because she sent me to Houston to do the same job there. But that doesn't mean I enjoyed the process, in either case.

I was given a team of people to work with, and they were obviously used to each other's company… and to working with Bree. She has the family name, and a lot more personality than me. And it didn't seem to matter to them that I'd been tasked with taking charge of the refits. They rode roughshod over everything I said. They undermined me at every turn, until I wondered if I should just jump on the next flight home… to London, that is. And by the end of each project, I felt so out of my depth, it seemed as though I was drowning.

I haven't told Bree any of that, because I don't want to appear weak, or incompetent. I know that handling the refits themselves is part of my job, and I'm not much use to her if I can't do it. And maybe one day I'll grow a backbone and it'll get better.

The thing is, though, if I'm going to do that, I need to do it soon. Because most of the people I worked with in Chicago and Houston are going to be joining me here in St. Thomas… which could explain why I'm so nervous. And why I'm looking forward to spending tonight by myself, before I have to face them all again.

As I exit the airport building, I'm hit by an oppressive wall of heat and humidity. I pull my sunglasses down from on top of my head, just as a taxi driver leaps from his car and comes over to me.

"Here, let me help you with that, miss," he says, taking my suitcase and grinning broadly.

I have to smile back, because he's like a ray of sunshine in his bright green t-shirt and red baseball cap.

"Thank you." I watch while he loads my case into the boot of his saloon car, and then opens the rear passenger door, waiting while I climb in. I nod my head in thanks and he smiles again before getting back behind the wheel.

"Where to, miss?" he says, turning around to look at me.

"The Crawford Hotel, Point Knoll," I tell him, and he nods his head.

"Ahh… you're on vacation," he says, selecting 'drive' and pulling out of the taxi rank. "From England, I'm guessing. In which case, you'll like the fact that we drive on the left over here. It'll make you feel at home."

Somehow I doubt that, but I give him a smile, anyway. "I'm not on vacation, I'm afraid. Although I am originally from England. I'm here on business to oversee the interior design work on the new Crawford hotel at the Mermaid's Chair?" I give my answer as a question, because I'm still not entirely sure about the place names.

He nods his head, pulling the car out of the airport complex. "I know it," he says. "My brother is one of the electricians working up there. He tells me they've been having a few problems… getting hold of supplies, I think."

"Oh… I don't know anything about that." I'm lying. I know exactly what he's talking about. Bree told me earlier in the autumn, when we first started planning this trip, that her brother Chase had informed her of some issues with the construction. She reassured me at the time that everything had been smoothed out. But then, just before I left, Bree said there were still some delays, and that Chase had flown down here a couple of weeks ago to iron them out. It's not ideal, but these things happen. And the least said about it, the better. I'm sure no-one at Crawford Hotels wants any adverse publicity when we're so close to having the new site completed.

The driver doesn't respond for a few minutes as he drives us through Charlotte Amalie. It looks lovely, and just how I'd imagined a Caribbean town would be, with little red-roofed buildings meandering down leafy lanes and up green covered hills.

"That's where the main part of the town is," the driver says, pointing to a turning, as we whizz on past. "That's where you'll find the market and all the restaurants and cafés… and obviously Fort Christian."

Obviously. I nod my head, taking a look down the road, even though I can't see anything. Not that it matters. I won't be visiting the local sights, anyway.

Within minutes, we've left the town behind and are on a winding single-lane road, with just the odd cluster of cottages, and the occasional sea view to break up the greenery. I settle back in my seat and wind the window down, letting the breeze play through my long blonde hair, smiling to myself as I think about how different my life is to anything I'd ever imagined.

I certainly never expected to be working in America, or taking on big design projects, single-handed in the Caribbean, that's for certain. It's so far out of my comfort zone that anyone who knows me would probably wonder at my sanity. I often do myself, actually.

But that's because my childhood was so sheltered and quiet. Which probably explains why I'm the same... unobtrusive to the point of going unnoticed. That's what most people say about me... "Oh, I'd forgotten you were here," or words to that effect. And I don't mind that in the slightest. I've never wanted to be the centre of attention. Not once.

I suppose that stems from my very early childhood, that abiding feeling of never really belonging. It was nobody's fault I felt like that. It was just the way things turned out.

My parents died before I was even aware of their existence, in a car accident, when I was eighteen months old. As a result, my brother Ronan and I were taken in by our paternal grandmother, who was the only parent I've ever known. She was a lovely lady, but she was quite old when our parents died. So, she sent us both off to boarding school at the first opportunity, partly because it was easier for her, and partly because it was traditional in her family. Our father had gone, and that meant we were going too. And in Ronan's case, because he's eight years older than me, he was snatched from me just a few short weeks after our parents' deaths, at the start of the next term.

Because of his absence, I spent a lot of my early youth by myself, and I think that's why I'm so shy. I just got used to living in a silent world, being quite content with my own company.

It's also the reason I found it hard to mix with other children when I finally went off to school. I didn't form any friendships, and I relished the school holidays, when I could go home and see Ronan. That is, until our grandmother died. I was twelve at the time, and he moved me into his flat in Oxford because I had nowhere else to go. I saw my chance then, and I asked him if I could go to the local school, rather than having to spend so much time away from him. He agreed. No questions asked. And life became a lot better.

It might seem odd that I'm as attached as I am to a brother who's so much older than me, but he's always been there for me. The only constant. My best friend and my only confidant. I suppose you could say he's been like a guardian angel. He remains that to this day, even though he's now back at work in Oxford, his summer having been spent on an archeological dig in Greece.

I smile to myself as a gust of wind catches my hair, because I can still remember how surprised he was when I telephoned him last autumn and told him I'd accepted a job in America. I told him it was his fault, too, because he'd persuaded me to enter the competition in the first place. He laughed and congratulated me. Then he came down to London to see me the following weekend and helped me through the process of applying for a passport, because I didn't even possess one. I was in a bit of a panic about it, even though I had months to go until I was due to start working in the States. But, as ever, Ronan was there for me. And while we worked everything out, he told me he'd come and see me in Boston... and we even set the date, there and then. We decided November would be a good time. It would give me some time to settle in, and Ronan was scheduled to undertake a dig in South America, and he thought he might be able to squeeze in a brief visit before it started. And now his visit is only a few weeks away, I can't wait to see him again.

The driver pulls up outside the canopied entrance to the hotel complex and I look up at the bright blue and white painted building. It's not quite what I expected, having been to two other Crawford hotels, and found them to be modern, quite sterile places – at least before we'd completed the make-overs we'd been tasked with. But then, we are in the Caribbean. And this isn't really a hotel. It's an apartment building, with a few beach-side cabins, and lots of on-site facilities, such as two restaurants, a bar, a café, a pool, and a gym, as well as a beauty salon, I believe. And, in any case, the Crawfords didn't build this place. According to Bree, this is one of Max's acquisitions, which he made a couple of years ago as a first step into the Caribbean. From what I can gather, he always meant to build further hotels down here, but it's taken him a long time to find the right plot of land, and then to get all the permissions in place… and then for Chase to design it, of course.

I check the meter and then climb out of the taxi, as the driver fetches my suitcase, and I take it from him. I make sure to tip him generously, because he's been welcoming and informative, and then I stand back as a porter, dressed in a quite unprepossessing uniform of beige trousers and shirt, bustles in to remove my case from my hand.

"Welcome to the Crawford Point Knoll," he says, with a wide-toothed grin, giving the driver a bit of a glare at the same time, which I regard as something of a facial accomplishment.

"Thank you," I reply, although I'm not really sure which one of them I'm addressing, and the driver gives me a kind of half salute before he climbs back into his cab and pulls away.

"This way, miss," the porter says, and I follow him through the wide double doors, into the reception area, which is wonderfully cool. Everything in here is very tropical, from the brightly coloured sofas, to the potted palms and ferns that are dotted around. And I have to say, the overall impression is a bit over-the-top.

The porter leads me to a desk on the far side of the room, where the receptionist, who's wearing a bright red blouse, turns her pearly white smile on me.

"Welcome to the Crawford Point Knoll," she says, repeating the porter's greeting, with an astounding lack of originality.

"Thank you. I'm booked into one of the cabins," I explain. "My name is Eva Schofield."

"Ah, yes... Miss Schofield." The receptionist smiles even more broadly. "We've been expecting you."

That doesn't surprise me in the slightest, and neither does the warmth of the greeting. I worked out during my previous two stays at Crawford hotels, in Chicago and Houston, that a visit from someone at head office warrants special attention. And while I don't feel worthy of such notice, I'd rather be greeted with smiles than misery.

She opens a drawer and selects a card – like a credit card, but with nothing printed on it, other than a bar code – which she hands to the porter, rather than to me.

"Gregory will show you to your cabin," she says, with a nod of her head.

"Thank you." I nod in reply, and turn to the porter, who waves his arm, indicating a door at the rear of the reception, which leads out onto the pool area.

"This way, miss," he says, repeating himself, while opening the door, and I pass through, waiting for him on the other side, as I don't know which way to go. The pool is quite large, and is surrounded by loungers, about half of which are currently occupied. A few of the sunbathers look up, some of them bothering to lower their sunglasses and assess me, I presume, as we pass by, around the side of a low hedge that encloses the pool to either side. Their gaze follows us and I'm happy to admit I'm quite relieved once we're beyond their view.

In front of me now is a wide expanse of beach, with white sand, and deep blue water... and a row of maybe ten log cabins, stretching off around the shoreline.

The porter takes off at a pace, and I struggle to keep up, eventually stopping to remove my shoes. They're only making it harder to walk through the sand... and I wonder why there's no path, maybe behind the cabins, to make this journey easier. It would certainly be more sensible. And it might be worthy of suggesting...

"Which one am I in?" I ask the porter, when I catch up to him.

"The last one," he replies, pointing to the final cabin in the row. I want to roll my eyes, because I'm not looking forward to making this trek every day... twice a day. Perhaps if you're here on holiday, and can take this walk at a slower pace, wandering along the sand, hand in hand with someone you love, then it wouldn't be such a trial. But when you're here to work, it's a nuisance.

"There should be a car ordered for me, for tomorrow morning?" I say to the porter, as he swipes the card against a reader beside the door, and the light at the top flashes green.

"There is a car, miss… yes."

I nod my head, relieved that my transport to the new hotel site is organised. Me not driving hasn't been an issue since my arrival in America, because – as I said – I can walk to work, and when I went to Houston and Chicago, I was staying on site. But here, I knew it would be a problem, and I asked Bree what I should do. She told me to have a car pick me up and bring me back here each morning and evening. Of course, being me, and not having a clue, I had to ask exactly how I would go about organising that… but Bree was as kind and helpful as ever, and said she'd do it for me. And, thank goodness, it seems she has.

The porter waits for me to enter the cabin, and I step inside, letting him follow, and take in my surroundings.

The room before me is larger than I would have expected, especially as the cabin didn't look that big on the outside. Directly to my left is a small kitchen, with a breakfast bar which separates it from the main living area, where there are two long sofas, either side of a low coffee table, and beyond those, a rectangular dining table, with six chairs surrounding it. The whole of the left-hand wall, on the other side of the kitchen, is made of glass, bi-folding doors, leading out onto an area of decking, furnished with a corner sofa and table, and what appears to be a patio heater, although why you'd need one of those here, I've got no idea. The colour scheme is, essentially, yellow. But it's not the kind of yellow that makes your eyes bleed, and is actually quite cheering.

I can live with this, I muse to myself, admiring the neatly arranged flowers on the breakfast bar as I turn and see that the porter has made his way towards one of the three doors on the right. I let my handbag drop from my shoulder onto the floor by the sofa and walk over to him.

"This is the bedroom," he says, opening the first door, and I follow him inside, where he puts my suitcase on the end of the bed, and I smile to myself. The bed is simply enormous. It's made up with white bed linen, but otherwise, there's no furniture in here, although there's a large window, which overlooks the sea, to the front of the property.

Waking up to that view every day for the next month isn't going to hurt, and I tip the porter, taking the key card from him and returning his smile as he leaves. And then I hear the front door close and know that I'm alone, and I feel the relief wash over me, as I flop down onto the mattress and lie back, looking up at the still ceiling fan above my head.

"Gosh, this is nice," I say aloud to myself, and get up again, finding the switch for the fan, which is near the door, given away by the small 'fan' symbol printed on it, in red. I watch, kind of mesmerised, as it starts to spin. I'm not sure how to adjust it though, so I make do with the rather gentle speed with which it's rotating, and open my suitcase, looking around the room, and wondering where on earth I'm supposed to put my clothes, being as there is literally no furniture in here.

"How bizarre."

There's a door in the corner of the room, and I open it... and all becomes clear, as I discover a tiny dressing area, made out of a corridor really, which contains some hanging space behind a sliding mirrored door, and a narrow chest of drawers, set into an alcove, leading on to a small shower room beyond. It may not be the most roomy of wardrobes... if it even qualifies as a wardrobe, but I can make do with it. And I don't mind. It means the bedroom is completely clutter-free. And I like that. It feels very calming.

I set about unpacking, and make quick work of it, being as I've mainly brought shorts, t-shirts, sleeveless blouses, and the odd vest top, because those are going to be the most practical for working. And I've packed a few sundresses too, to wear in the evenings. I won't be going anywhere, of course, but I do like to shower and change my clothes when I've finished work.

I find some space in the dressing area for my suitcase, storing it on end in the bottom of the wardrobe. Then I go into the shower room to unpack my toiletries, putting them where I need them, before I get undressed, leaving my clothes on the floor, and step straight into the walk-in-shower.

The water is beautifully cool, and I tip my head back, relishing the feeling of it cascading over my body. The hotel has provided some body-wash, but I use my own for now. It's citrus scented, and I wash off the grime of the journey, feeling invigorated, as I step out and wrap a towel around me, fastening it under my arms.

I pad back through to the bedroom, my feet leaving prints on the tiled floor, and I stop dead…

"There's no getting away from it. I'm gonna have to speak to Trent… again." The male voice rings out loud.

"Yeah, looks like you are."

Oh, God… there are two of them. Two men. Both American. And they're here… in my cabin.

They continue to talk, although their voices have become mere background noise as I look around the room in a state of panic. There's no telephone in here… mainly because there's nowhere to put one. And my mobile is in my handbag, out in the living room, where I left it.

What shall I do?

I can't stay in here and do nothing, especially not as the bedroom door is ajar and one or both of them could walk in here at any moment… so I think it's best if I take the bull by the horns, and go out there. Because this is my cabin after all, and whatever it is they think they're doing, they can just go and do it somewhere else…

Chase

I open my eyes to searing bright sunlight and promptly snap them closed again.

Hell… I must've forgotten to close the drapes last night. But that's not surprising. I don't really remember very much at all about last night… except that I drank far too much. I was probably letting my hair down – metaphorically – because I'm finally finished here in Atlanta. At least I am for the time being, and having been here for what feels like forever, I'm keen to move on. There's nothing wrong with Atlanta, and I kinda like this hotel, but I could really do with going home. I won't be doing that, of course… because I've gotta head down to St. Thomas again, which is probably the other reason I got drunk last night… to try and forget that I've got yet more trouble-shooting to do. And, if there's one thing I hate, more than all this damn traveling around, it's clearing up other people's shit.

This job in St. Thomas has been nothing but trouble from beginning to end. First there was the land, which cost a damn fortune, thanks to the greed of the original owner. Then there were all the permissions we needed to build our hotel there, which my brother Max dealt with, thank God, because I don't have the patience for all that crap. And once that was all signed and sealed, and I stepped in and designed the hotel building, it's just been one thing after another… mainly revolving around supplies, and getting them onto the island in the right order, at the right time. I suppose I should've guessed that constructing our first hotel in the Caribbean wouldn't run as smoothly as building one in the States, but I never expected this level of crazy.

Which is why I really need to get my eyes open, regardless of the bright sunlight that seems to want to burn them to smithereens. Then I need to get showered and packed, and get to the airport… because the sooner I do that, the sooner I can wrap things up down there, then move on to our hotel in Denver… and then – finally – get home for a few weeks' well earned R&R. And I mean well earned. I've been traveling around the country for months now, and I could do with a break. But first I need to deal with whatever the hell it is that's gone wrong in St. Thomas. And I know something's gone wrong, because I've had our site manager, Trent Anderson, on the phone, telling me we're never gonna open in time. And that's not something I'm willing to accept.

Apart from anything else, I promised Max I'd get this job done… and my little sister Bree has arranged for her new assistant, Eva something-or-other, to bring her team down to St. Thomas in just a couple of weeks' time to start on the interiors… so we kinda need some interiors for her to work on. Or it's all gonna be a colossal waste of time. And money. And I'm gonna be the one who gets it in the neck, because it's my team working down there, so it's my responsibility.

I let out a sigh and pluck up my courage, opening my eyes again, more gingerly this time. Then I turn over to my left, away from the two large windows that fill the wall, a smile spreading across my lips as I come up against the soft female form lying beside me. Her copper colored hair is spread out across the pillow, and her slender body exposed, where she's pushed the sheet down, letting it twist around her ankles. She's got her back to me, but her ass is so shapely, my body responds quite naturally to the sight of her.

I have to say, this isn't an unusual state of affairs. I often wake up beside one woman or another, and it's a fairly common occurrence – as in this instance – that I have absolutely no recollection of who she might be. If I ever knew in the first place. But for now, I don't care about any of that. I'm simply giving thanks that all our hotels come with emperor sized beds, so I've been able to sleep in peace. And clearly so has she. Neither of us aware of the other's presence.

Even so, that doesn't mean I can't take advantage now that I am aware, and I shift across from my place in the center of the bed, getting closer to her, and slipping my right hand between her slightly parted legs. She moans in her sleep and I smile as she instinctively parts them wider, allowing me access to her smooth, shaved pussy, letting me slide my fingers between her wet folds, to give her clit a gentle rub with my middle finger. She grinds her hips, even though I'm damn sure she's still asleep, and I slip my finger inside her, gathering up her juices before returning my attentions to her hardened nub, which makes her sigh gently and part her legs again.

I palm my cock with my other hand, stroking it while I play with her and trying desperately to remember what I might have done with her last night… not that anything is coming to mind right now.

"Do you want any help with that?" I jump out of my skin, my hand dropping from my dick, as the whispered voice behind me interrupts the moment, and I turn my head to see a cute brunette with baby blue eyes smiling at me from the other side of the bed.

Well, well, well... How the hell could I have forgotten this?

I give her a smile, but before she can do anything, I turn onto my back and switch hands, using my left on Red's now dripping pussy, while my right goes to work on Blue Eyes. I kinda wish I could remember their names, or that I'd maybe written them in marker pen across their foreheads, or something, because I feel slightly disadvantaged at this moment. But then, I'm not sure these two will remember who I am, either... and it doesn't really matter. We won't be seeing each other again. Not after today.

Blue Eyes moans loudly as I dip a couple of fingers inside her, and I can sense that Red is close to coming, just from the way she's now grinding her hips into the mattress. And I've gotta say, bringing off two women at the same time is kinda gratifying, especially when one of them still seems to be asleep. They start to sigh and groan, almost in unison, while I try desperately to focus my mind on last night... on how this rather fantastic state of affairs came about in the first place... and whether their names might be somewhere in the depths of my memory.

I recall being at the bar, with a couple of women... presumably these two. I can even vaguely remember coming back here to my room, with one of them on each arm. Eli – my bodyguard – was walking behind, with a tiny blonde beside him, and he gave me a wink as he went into his room, which is opposite mine. But the rest of the evening is a blur. I've got no names, that's for sure... and no matter how hard I try, all I'm getting is a hazy fog of writhing bodies.

"Oh... yeah. Right there... right there..." Blue Eyes starts to shake beside me, her body bucking off the bed, and then she lets out a loud howl, her orgasm claiming her, as my fingers work their magic over her clit.

Red startles, presumably at the noise, and she comes hard, thrashing against me and screaming something incoherent.

I smile to myself as they slowly regain their breath and Red turns to face me, the two of them leaning over, and I raise my hands, crossing them over and holding my fingers up.

"Taste," I whisper, and their eyes widen as they both grab at my hands and lick my fingers of each other's juices… and my cock almost explodes, just watching them. *Fuck, that's hot.*

Once they're satisfied, they look at each other with a kind of deep hunger and lean closer, their tongues meeting before their lips do, in the most erotic of French kisses, right before my eyes. I lie back and watch them until they break apart, and slowly move down the bed, coming face-to-face with my straining cock, and I suck in a breath as they join together in an ecstasy of lips and tongues, to my sole benefit.

I close my eyes, relishing the sensation of their diligent attention, the crazy feeling of being sucked by one pair of generous lips, while having the base of my cock, and my balls kissed and licked, all at the same time. It's kinda mind blowing, in the best possible way. But just as I'm getting used to it, they stop, and I open my eyes in time to see Red kneeling up and crawling across the bed, reaching over to the nightstand for a condom. She brings it back, tearing into the foil packet with her teeth, before she unrolls it over my cock and straddles me, lowering herself down. Her head rocks back, she lets out a low moan of pleasure, and I smile as Blue Eyes, who's kneeling beside me, leans in, circling her fingertips over and around Red's clit.

"Oh, yeah… Dani, yeah… make me come," Red moans, leaning forward and kissing her friend.

Dani? Okay… so I've got one name. Blue Eyes must be called Dani. Or Danielle. Or Daniela. Who cares. Dani works for me, especially when she's doing such a good job of bringing the woman who's riding my cock to orgasm. Red grinds down onto me, circling her hips, and then reaches up, pulling at her nipples with the forefingers and thumbs of each hand as she tips over the edge, the word, "Yes," leaving her lips over and over, until she slumps forward, completely spent.

Dani raises her friend's face and they kiss, very tenderly, their tongues touching and dancing without their lips even making contact… and a memory flits into my head. It's hazy, but it's there, nonetheless. I recall lying on the bed last night, propped up on the pillows and feeling kinda worn out. I'm not sure what we'd been doing, but whatever it was, it had obviously taken its toll and I clearly needed some recovery time. The girls didn't, though. They needed more, and they weren't willing to wait for me… so they'd gotten on with things themselves, and while I took my time and watched the show, they got into each other, fondling, caressing, kissing and licking… And once they'd brought each other off, very loudly, I was sufficiently recovered to join in again… I think. Well, I can't imagine I wouldn't have been, because just the thought of that is enough to make me wanna come…

Dani breaks the kiss with Red and looks down at me with a hungry expression on her face. And while I'd love to lie here and let her take me, I'm in the mood for something more… pro-active. So, as Red climbs off of me and lies back on the bed, exhausted, I kneel up and lift Dani into my arms before I lower her onto my cock. She lets out a sigh, wrapping her legs around me and using her arms around my shoulders as leverage to ride me hard.

"You have an amazing cock," she whispers, grinding her hips into me. "Has anyone ever told you that?"

"Once or twice, yeah." I can't lie. And why would I?

"He's good, isn't he?" Red's voice rings out and I glance over Dani's shoulder, realizing that Red's clearly not as tired as I'd thought she was, because she's parted her legs and is gently rubbing her clit, while she watches us, her eyes fixed on the point where our bodies are joined. And I have to admit, I'm kinda mesmerized by what she's doing. I want a closer look. Much closer. And with that in mind, I lower Dani down onto the bed, taking care to lie her directly between Red's parted legs, her head resting at the very top of Red's thighs.

Red surprises me then by moving her hand away, and slowly licking her own fingers while she avidly watches me fuck her friend.

I'm disappointed that Red has stopped the show, but then I love the whole concept of making two women come at the same time, and although I've already done it once today, once is never enough for me. So, balancing on one arm for a moment, I move Dani's hair out of the way with my free hand and then lean down, running my tongue along the length of Red's exposed pussy, from her soaking entrance, to her swollen clit. She gasps and parts her legs even further before she brings her hand down on the back of my head.

She's dripping… literally. And I lap up her juices, swallowing them down as I let my tongue flick over her.

Beneath me, Dani's writhing and bucking as I up the pace and pound into her pussy, while I suck and lick Red's clit. And between the two of them, their moans and sighs fill the room.

"Fuck her harder. Make her come." Red's voice is breathless, urgent, and I oblige, sensing that Red is close to coming herself… as am I. Dani's head is right beside mine in the valley of Red's thighs, and I'm aware of a building crescendo of noise coming from her, which matches the one that's coming from Red. Dani tightens around my dick at the same time as Red's hand forces my face even further into her pussy… and they both come in unison. And that's all it takes for me to explode… deep and long, and hard.

We all kinda slump at the same time, and I pull out of Dani and roll to one side, catching my breath, a smile settling on lips…

Wow… what a way to start the day.

By the time I've showered, dressed and have poured myself a coffee, the two of them are on their way. They smile contentedly and give me a cute wave as they leave… and that's exactly how I like my women. Happy, satisfied and preferably closing the door behind them after a good night's fucking.

We said our goodbyes with smiles, not kisses. We didn't exchange numbers and I've still got no idea what Red's real name is. And I don't care. We all had a good time. And that's all any of us wanted.

I'm not into anything else. I'm certainly not into commitment, or ties. And I'm definitely not interested in settling down. I know people do it all the time. Hell, my little sister has just got together with my brother Max's bodyguard. And although they're happy, they went through hell to get there. I know they'd say it was worth it, and maybe it was. For them. But that's not the life I want. It never has been.

I guess that might have something to do with our dad. He was something of a tyrant when we were growing up, and if that sounds a little melodramatic, all I can say is, you had to be there.

He planned out our lives, including what we'd study at college and where we'd work, before we were even old enough to understand what we might want for ourselves. For Bree, it was laid down that she'd study interior design and go straight onto the board of the company who did all the work on our hotels. For me, he decreed I should study construction engineering, and be employed by the firm who undertook all the design and construction of our new hotels. And as for Max, he got the top prize. He was to become CEO of Crawford Hotels itself, and sit at Dad's right hand. We all knew our places, although Max kinda spoiled Dad's rigorous planning by enlisting in the military straight out of high school. Dad got his way in the end though, and after Max was injured in the line of duty, he left the army and joined the family firm – just as Dad had always intended – and that was when Max married his high school sweetheart, Eden.

I can remember standing at their wedding, watching them together, and wondering why anyone would want to do that. Everyone there said they were the happiest couple they'd ever seen, and although I still didn't really understand the concept, I guess I couldn't argue with that. It was like they were meant to be together. They both wanted the same things, were both serious about their careers. And they were so in love it was sickening.

They'd been that way ever since they'd first met, when they were both seventeen years old, after Eden's family had moved to Boston from Portland. Max was absolutely besotted with her, right from day one. He was like a dog with his tongue hanging out, following her around, like he had nothing better to do with his life. And she was the same, from what I could see. I thought it was kinda pathetic, but then I was only a kid at the time and hadn't really worked out what girls were for. Even when I did work it out, though, I still couldn't see the point in limiting myself to only one of them at a time. That just felt like a waste to me. It still does.

But it wasn't that way for Max and Eden. So, when he joined the military, they waited for each other. And when he came home again, after he'd been injured really badly and had nearly died, she sat by his bedside, weeping and willing him to get better. He did. Obviously. And then he proposed to her, only waiting until he was able to get down on one knee without breaking something.

And she accepted. Naturally.

I can still hear Dad's voice even now, as we waved them off on their honeymoon…

"So, Chase… when are you gonna find yourself a good woman and settle down?"

I was still at college at the time, and was having a blast. Settling down – with any kind of woman, good or otherwise – wasn't part of my plan. I told my dad that and he just huffed at me and walked away.

And then a few days later, he dropped another hint… and another… and another, until in the end I snapped, and yelled at him…

"I'll work my ass off for you, Dad. In case you haven't noticed, I already have. And I'll continue to do so. I'll study hard and I'll learn whatever has to be learned. But I won't sacrifice my entire life for you. And I'm sure as hell not gonna settle down. Ever. I'm not your puppet, and you don't own me…"

I kinda ran out of puff at that point and he glared at me and then said, in a very quiet whisper, "You were always destined to be a disappointment. I knew it the moment you were born."

That cut deeper than I would ever let him see.

I'd already sacrificed a lot at the altar of his ambitions. And yet, it wasn't enough. I wasn't enough. And even though Max had defied him and gone into the military, against Dad's wishes, he was still being held up as the golden boy.

And that was how it continued. Even once I'd graduated and gone to work for the company Dad had selected, he still kept telling me how Max was so great at this, and so fabulous at that… and how happy he and Eden were.

Of course, Bree had taken a little of the heat off of me, when she'd gone to college herself, a couple of years behind me, and promptly married the first guy she met. He turned out to be a complete loser by the name of Grady Sharp. At the time, of course, Bree didn't know how miserable he was gonna make her and she seemed happy enough. Dad wasn't, and he threatened to write her out of his will altogether. It was an idle threat that he never saw through, although he gave her a really hard time. And even though I thought she'd been hasty, and probably a bit dumb in marrying the guy – as did Max – I was grateful to her, because at least I wasn't the only disappointment in the family anymore.

She had the good fortune to be living away from home, and as for myself, I did my best to ignore our father, and not to take his rejection too personally, especially where my relationship with Max was concerned. After all, it wasn't Max's fault, any more than it was mine. But Dad continued to drive the wedge between us, forcing us to compete for everything… most especially his time and attention.

That all came to an end when our father died. I was on the west coast when Max called to say Dad had suffered a massive heart attack, and I only just made it back to Boston in time. I did though, and we stood around his bed, a family united at last, and watched him pass. What Max and Bree were thinking at the time is anyone's guess. I don't know, because I've never asked them. I know the only thought that was going through my head was that it was such a waste. He had three children who'd have given anything for a few minutes of his time, and an ounce of his love. And yet he couldn't even give us that. And I vowed then that I'd never have children of my own. I mean, it's not a viable prospect anyway, given the way I live my life. But the thought of my own children looking down at me on my deathbed and feeling nothing was enough for me to make the decision. In a heartbeat.

After Dad died, of course, we inherited a fortune each, and our share of the company. Then Max brought Bree and myself into the family firm, allowing us to set up our own departments and run things how we wanted. I finally felt like I had the freedom in my professional life to match the freedom I'd always maintained in my personal one. Things were working out.

Of course, working with Max gave me constant reminders of how I'd 'disappointed' our father by not settling down myself. But I solved that problem by avoiding the office as much as possible. Instead, I traveled around the country, getting laid at every opportunity, and only returning home when either work or exhaustion got the better of me. In the meantime, he and Eden continued to be blissfully happy... or at least that was what it felt like... until that afternoon a few years ago, when I was driving through the center of town and saw Eden getting out of a cab in the company of another man. That wasn't anything to write home about. But as I pulled up at the lights and waved out the window to attract her attention, my hand froze in mid-air... because the guy she was with leaned in and kissed her. And I'm not talking about an innocent peck on the cheek. I'm talking about a full-on kiss, in which I had little doubt there would have been tongues involved. She dropped her briefcase on the ground and returned the kiss, letting her hands wander up his arms and onto his shoulders, making it clear to anyone who happened to be watching – like her brother-in-law – that there was something going on between the two of them.

I drove away, in a state of confusion, my initial instinct being to go straight back to our offices – even though I'd only just left them – to tell Max what was going on. I didn't want to gloat. I didn't want to crow that his marriage wasn't what he, or anyone else, thought it was. I just felt he had a right to know. But what if I'd been mistaken? How much trouble would I be causing if I'd misunderstood the situation? I didn't really see how that was possible, given what I'd witnessed, but even so, I decided in the end that the best course of action was to confront Eden instead. Doing nothing wasn't an option. I couldn't just pretend it hadn't happened. Max was my brother and although we still weren't that close, I didn't like the idea of him being played.

So I went around to Eden's office the next morning. She was surprised to see me there, and completely floored when I told her what I'd seen. She didn't deny it, though. In fact, she admitted she'd been having an affair with the guy – who, it transpired, was her boss – for a little over a year. That shocked the hell out of me, and I couldn't stop myself from asking her why.

"You and Max have always seemed so happy," I reasoned, when she didn't answer me straight away. "He loves you."

"I know," she replied, staring at her desk and not at me. "But I've never been with anyone else, Chase." She sounded truly pathetic. "I guess curiosity got the better of me."

"Curiosity?" I shook my head at her. "That's bullshit, Eden. Curiosity is a one-night stand, to find out what it's like to fuck another guy. It's not having an affair for over a year. There's a big difference between the two things."

She looked up and narrowed her eyes at me then. "What the hell would you know? You've never done anything except have one-night stands."

"I know. But we're not talking about me." I stood up then and leaned over her desk. I'm not as tall as Max, but at six foot two I'm still quite intimidating, and it showed on her face. "You know Max has never been with anyone else either, don't you? You were his first, and he's been faithful to you... all the way through."

"I know," she whispered, looking down at her hands.

"Then how would you feel if it was the other way around?" I raised my voice. "How would you feel if he cheated on you?"

She paled then, and I straightened up, feeling angry and disappointed in her.

"Are... are you gonna tell him?" she said, fear written all over her face.

"No." Her relief was obvious and sickening. She sat back then, looking just a little smug, until I added, "You are."

Her mouth dropped open. "I—I can't. He'll leave me."

I shook my head. "That's a chance you're gonna have to take. I won't keep your secret, Eden. He deserves better than this. He deserves better than you." She blinked a few times then, and I wondered if she was gonna cry. She didn't. Not that I'd have cared either way. "I'll give you twenty-four hours to tell him... or I will."

I left her sitting there at her desk, staring at me, like she didn't believe I'd actually go through with it. I would have done... but in the end, I didn't need to. Because Eden came clean. She must've gone home from work that evening and told him. I know that because Max moved out of their house in Lexington, and into one of our hotels later that day. I felt guilty and responsible, even though I wasn't the one who'd been cheating, and I tried to call him, but he'd turned his phone off, making it clear he wasn't in the mood for talking, and I know Max well enough to know when to leave him alone.

A few days later, though, he moved back into the house. I half expected to hear that Eden had moved out, but that never happened, and instead Max took some time out of work. Unfortunately, I had to go away just a couple of days later, so I didn't get to ask him what was going on. I was gone for a few months, visiting different locations… and when I came back, I was surprised to find out that Eden was pregnant. Tia was born around five months later.

He's never talked to me about what happened, and I've never raised the subject with him either. It seemed to me like they'd got their lives back on track, and although Eden would occasionally shoot me a glance, I kept my mouth shut and made out like nothing had happened. I figured that, if Max could forgive her, then it had nothing to do with me. But I knew then that, in his shoes, I'd never be able to do the same thing. I'd never be able to forgive that kind of deception or betrayal. Not that anyone ever gets close enough… but there's no way I'd give anyone that kind of chance. Not ever.

Of course, what no-one saw coming was that, just a couple of months after Tia was born, Eden would become the target of a kidnapper, who picked her up outside the gym she'd just joined, and held her hostage… or that the police would screw up so badly, resulting in her death.

Max was there when it happened, and he watched her die. And because I've never known love, I can't imagine what that felt like. And I never want to. He fell apart. Not that he shared any of it with me, or with Bree. He turned to Colt, his old army buddy. And I tried hard not to take that personally. It was another situation where the rift between us was too great to bridge, and I guess he felt closer to Colt than to either of us. I wish it hadn't been that way. But it was.

And even now, although he never talks about it, the pain is visible in his face…

And that's why, every time I look at my brother, I'm reminded of why it doesn't pay to get involved…

Because love hurts.

Besides, why would I want to go through any of that when I'm having so much fun? Obviously, I don't get to wake up quite like this all the time. It's happened twice before… once after a party in Boston, when I was approached by a couple of women. And once when I was at one of our hotels on the West Coast. I can't deny the pleasure I get from having two women at the same time… and if they're willing, my attitude is, why not?

In this instance, although my memories are still a bit of a blur, even after a shower and two cups of coffee, I do recall talking to them at the bar, sharing a few drinks – or maybe more than a few – and thinking to myself at the time that I'd have trouble choosing between them. They both had attributes I enjoy. Dani – as I now know her to be called – was stacked. And I mean seriously stacked. And Red… well, she had an ass to die for. As it turned out, of course, I didn't need to choose, because they were willing to share. And there's more than enough of me to go around…

There's a single tap on my door and then it opens and Eli comes in, pocketing his own copy of my key card. He smiles across at me.

"Good night?" he asks.

I smile back. "Not bad. What about you?"

"About the same. I take it they've gone?"

"Yeah."

He nods his head and then checks his watch. "Do you want me to order up some breakfast? We've got time before the flight."

"Sounds good."

He picks up the phone, while I pack my clothes, ready for our departure.

It would be easy to resent the intrusion of having a bodyguard, but I don't. And that's entirely down to Eli, and the way he manages things between us. The need for a bodyguard only arose after Eden's death, when Max became paranoid about the rest of us, and our safety. I don't blame him for that, even though I was kinda shocked when he first told me his plan to have his old army buddy Colt Nelson provide guards for himself, Tia, our sister Bree and our mom… and me. I didn't baulk at the idea in itself, but I do often wonder what Max and Colt would say if they knew that, while Eli does his job perfectly well, he's also partaking of whatever is on offer… just like me.

Eli and I are two of a kind, really. But then maybe Colt knew that, and that's why he assigned Eli to guard me in the first place. Because on the face of it, Eli and I shouldn't get along, simply because he's ex-military, just like Colt and Max. Except that's where the similarities end, because he's nowhere near as uptight as they are. He gives me all the latitude I need to have a good time, while letting me know he's there when I need him.

"They'll bring it up in fifteen minutes," Eli says, hanging up the phone and turning around to face me. "That should just about give you time to clear up this mess."

"It's not a mess. I know where everything is," I reason. "Vaguely."

He chuckles and walks over to the window, sitting down on the couch. "How long are we gonna be down in St. Thomas?" he asks. This trip has been kinda thrown in at the last minute, so all the arrangements are a little disorganized compared to normal.

"Two weeks," I tell him. "I've gotta be in Denver by then."

"And we're gonna need the whole two weeks, are we?"

"I've got no idea, until I get down there and see how bad things are. Why? Have you got somewhere else you need to be?"

He smiles. "No. But I'm thinking about sub-letting my apartment. I'm never there anymore."

I shake my head. "I know the feeling. Still, the sooner we get there, the sooner we can leave again… speaking of which, if you wanna help me pack…"

He laughs and sits back on the couch, getting comfortable. "I'm your bodyguard, not your maid…"

"Yeah, but you'd look great in the outfit."

He picks up a cushion from behind him and throws it at me. I catch it and throw it back, and get on with my packing… because unfortunately it's gotta be done.

***

Our time in St. Thomas has been nothing short of hell.

We've been here for two weeks already and we ought to have been on our way to Denver today. That's not gonna happen, though, and I've had to call ahead and delay my arrival there by a week. I can't leave it any longer than that, because if I don't make it there by then, that project is gonna fall too far behind… and then Max will be really mad with me.

As it is, I've kept him in the dark about the problems down here, but whether I can continue to do that now, I'm not so sure. Because it looks to me like the problems begin and end with Trent Anderson.

And that's unfortunate.

Trent was one of the first people Max employed when he became CEO of Crawford Hotels, after our father died. He was a good choice. Trent's background in the construction business helped Max to pave the way for the new direction he wanted to take the company. We stopped just running hotels, buying up new ones and modernizing them… and started to construct our own. I'd been involved in the modernization side of things too, but only from a distance. And I didn't work exclusively for Crawfords, unlike Bree, who did, when she started working for Taylor & Sutton on the interior designs.

Even though Max brought us both in-house, I think he was concerned about my lack of experience in the hotel construction field, and Trent was a good fit for helping me out. I'm not going to deny that. And for the most part, things have worked out okay. It's my name on the door, and it's my department. But there have been times over the last few years when I've had to remind Trent of those two minor facts. There have also been times when Trent has made a point of reminding me he's got nearly twenty years of experience… and that I'm a mere novice by comparison. And that's true. He's been around a lot longer than I have, and he understands the business better than I do.

Except this time around, Trent isn't firing on all cylinders. That much is obvious. We're short of supplies, just when we need them most.

328

There are problems with the labor force that he should have, and could have, resolved without my intervention. And he's letting the schedules run away with him. As for the budgets… I'm not gonna think about them right now.

I've tried talking to him before now, because it's been clear to me for a while that things aren't right down here, and every time, he's found someone else to blame. But now I'm here again, and can see how he's running the site first-hand, it's obvious he's making excuses. I'm just not sure why. And whenever I raise the subject, he finds some way to dodge the issue… or to 'pull rank' and remind me he knows better than I do.

I'm getting kinda sick of being spoken to like an errant schoolboy, especially by someone who actually works for me. And although I know some of this is probably down to me, for letting things slide for too long – and because man management has never been my strongest suit – I'm damned if I'm gonna let this project fail. That said, I'm not sure quite what I am gonna do. Calling Max is out of the question, because although I know he'd help me out, he'd also ball me out for not telling him about the problem sooner.

"You're looking kinda frayed around the edges," Eli says to me as we walk along the beach to our cabin.

"I'm feeling frayed around the fucking edges." I don't look up at him, but shake my head. "To be honest, I'm sick of yelling at people. It's not who I am."

He lets out a sigh. "Try and forget about it for tonight. We'll grab a shower and head out to the restaurant, shall we? Who knows, we might get lucky…" He lets his voice fade and I try hard not to think about the fact that I haven't gotten lucky since that night – and the following morning – back in Atlanta with Red and the other girl, whose name has escaped me. Again. God, that was good… but it feels like a dim and distant memory now.

"Yeah, maybe you're right." I turn and look at him now. He's grinning, and I smile back. "But don't let me drink too much."

"Why the hell not?" He frowns.

"Because that assistant of Bree's is arriving today… sometime… and my sister sent me a message earlier saying, as we're still here, could we give this Eva Whatever-her-name-is a ride to work in the morning. I agreed, obviously, but the last thing I'm gonna need is a hangover, while I try to explain to her that half the hotel is still a construction site."

He chuckles and says, "Okay… I'll track her down later and make the arrangements for the morning. And I'll make sure you're sober."

"And I really need to deal with things at the site," I remind him, before we both get carried away with the idea of an evening of relaxation… and sex.

He opens the cabin door, using the key card. "I know," he says, his voice quietly resigned, as I walk inside ahead of him.

"There's no getting away from it. I'm gonna have to speak to Trent… again."

"Yeah, looks like you are."

He closes the door, throwing the key card into the bowl on the breakfast bar.

"Do you want a beer?" I ask him, going over to the refrigerator in the small kitchen area.

"Yeah… why not?"

I open the door and pull out a bottle, taking off the top and handing it to him, before grabbing another for myself as he makes his way over to the couch.

"We'll drink these and then shower and head on out, shall we?" I suggest and he gives me a knowing smile, raising the bottle to his lips, just as the first door on the right of the living room opens, and we both stand there, our mouths dropping open at the sight before us.

… to be continued

Printed in Great Britain
by Amazon

45857538R10188